The report of a gun rang out, the sound of the
attack pressed thin and nonthreatening by the radio.

A new voice came.

"*Connaught*? You there?"

"Still here," Michio said. "To whom am I speaking, please?"

"Name's Sergio Plant," the voice said. "Acting captain of
the *Hornblower*. I'm offering up our surrender. Just no one gets
hurt, okay?"

Evans grinned their triumph and relief.

"Besse to hear from you, Captain Plant," Michio said. "I accept
your terms. Please prepare for boarding."

She killed the connection.

By James S. A. Corey

THE EXPANSE
Leviathan Wakes
Caliban's War
Abaddon's Gate
Cibola Burn
Nemesis Games
Babylon's Ashes
Persepolis Rising

THE EXPANSE SHORT FICTION
The Butcher of Anderson Station
Gods of Risk
The Churn
Drive
The Vital Abyss
Strange Dogs

BABYLON'S ASHES

BOOK SIX OF THE EXPANSE

JAMES S. A. COREY

orbit

www.orbitbooks.net

Copyright © 2016 by Daniel Abraham and Ty Franck
Excerpt from *New York 2140* copyright © 2017 by Kim Stanley Robinson
Excerpt from *Provenance* copyright © 2017 by Ann Leckie

Cover design by Kirk Benshoff
Cover illustration by Daniel Dociu
Cover copyright © 2016 by Hachette Book Group, Inc.

Orbit
Hachette Book Group
1290 Avenue of the Americas
New York, NY 10104
orbitbooks.net

Originally published in hardcover and ebook by Orbit in December 2016.

First Trade Paperback Edition: October 2017

Orbit is an imprint of Hachette Book Group.
The Orbit name and logo are trademarks of Little, Brown Book Group Limited.

The publisher is not responsible for websites (or their content) that are not owned by the publisher.

The Hachette Speakers Bureau provides a wide range of authors for speaking events. To find out more, go to www.hachettespeakersbureau.com or call (866) 376-6591.

Library of Congress Cataloging-in-Publication Data

Names: Corey, James S. A., author.
Title: Babylon's ashes / James S. A. Corey.
Description: First Edition. | New York : Orbit, 2016. | Series: The expanse ; book 6
Identifiers: LCCN 2016037890| ISBN 9780316334747 (hardback) | ISBN 9780316217644 (trade paperback) | ISBN 9780316546430 (hardcover (special edition)) | ISBN 9781478965374 (audio book CD) | ISBN 9781478909521 (Audio book downloadable) | ISBN 9780316217637 (ebook (open))
Subjects: | BISAC: FICTION / Science Fiction / Space Opera. | FICTION / Science Fiction / Adventure. | GSAFD: Science fiction.
Classification: LCC PS3601.B677 B33 2016 | DDC 813/.6—dc23 LC record available at https://lccn.loc.gov/2016037890

ISBNs: 978-0-316-21764-4 (paperback), 978-0-316-33474-7 (hardcover); 978-0-316-21763-7 (ebook)

Printed in the United States of America

LSC-C

10 9 8 7 6 5 4 3 2 1

To Matt, Hallie, and Kenn,
who get none of the credit and make everything possible

Prologue: Namono

The rocks had fallen three months ago, and Namono could see some blue in the sky again. The impact at Laghouat—first of the three strikes that had broken the world—had thrown so much of the Sahara into the air that she hadn't seen the moon or stars for weeks. Even the ruddy disk of the sun struggled to penetrate the filthy clouds. Ash and grit rained down on Greater Abuja until it piled up in drifts, changing her city to the same yellow-gray as the sky. Even as she'd helped the volunteer teams to clear the rubble and care for the injured, she'd understood that her wracking cough and the black phlegm she spat out came from breathing in the dead.

Three and a half thousand kilometers stretched between the crater where Laghouat had been and Abuja. The shock wave still had blown out windows and collapsed buildings. Two hundred dead in the city, the newsfeeds said, four thousand wounded. The medical clinics were swamped. If you were not in immediate distress, please stay home.

The power grid degraded quickly. There was no sun to drive the solar panels, and the gritty air fouled the wind farms faster than the teams could clean them. By the time a fusion reactor was trucked north from the yards at Kinshasa, half of the city had spent fifteen days in the dark. With the hydroponic houses and hospitals and government buildings taking precedence, there were still brownouts more days than not. Network access through their hand terminals was spotty and unreliable. Sometimes they were cut off from the world for days at a time. It was to be expected, she told herself, as if any of this could have been foreseen.

And still, three months in, there came a break in the vast, blindfolded sky. As the reddened sun slid toward the west, the city lights of the moon appeared in the east, gems on a field of blue. Yes, it was tainted, dirty, incomplete, but it was blue. Nono took comfort in it as she walked.

The international district was recent, historically speaking. Few of the buildings were over a hundred years old. A previous generation's fondness for wide thoroughfares between thin, mazy streets and curved, quasi-organic architectural forms marked the neighborhoods. Zuma Rock stood above it all, a permanent landmark. The ash and dust might streak the stone, but they could not change it. This was Nono's hometown. The place she'd grown up, and the place she'd brought her little family back to at the end of her adventures. The home of her gentle retirement.

She coughed out a bitter laugh, and then she just coughed.

The relief center was a van parked at the edge of a public park. It had a leafy trefoil icon on its side, the logo of the hydroponic farm. Not the UN, not even basic administration. The layers of bureaucracy had been pressed thin by the urgency of the situation. She knew she should have been grateful. Some places, vans didn't come at all.

The pack of dust and ash had made a crust over the gently sloping hills where the grass had been. Here and there, jagged cracks and furrows like vast snake tracks showed where children had tried to play anyway, but no one was sliding down it now. There was only the forming queue. She took her place in it. The others that waited with her had the same empty stare. Shock and exhaustion and hunger. And thirst. The international district had large Norwegian and Vietnamese enclaves, but no matter the shade of their skin or the texture of their hair, ash and misery had made a single tribe of them all.

The side of the van slid open, and the queue shifted in anticipation. Another week's rations, however thin they might be. Nono felt a little stab of shame as her turn came near. She'd lived her whole life without ever needing basic. She was one of those who provided for others, not one who needed support. Except that she needed support now.

She reached the front. She'd seen the man handing out the packs before. He had a wide face, brown speckled with black freckles. He asked her address, and she gave it. A moment's fumbling later, he held out a white plastic pack to her with the practiced efficiency of an automaton, and she took it. It felt terribly light. He only made eye contact with her when she failed to move away.

"I have a wife," Namono said. "A daughter."

A flash of raw anger rose in his eyes, hard as a slap. "If they can make the oats grow faster or conjure rice out of thin air, then do send them to us. Else, you're holding us up."

She felt tears welling up in her eyes, stinging them.

"One to a household," the man snapped. "Move on."

"But—"

"Go on!" he shouted, snapping his fingers at her. "There's people behind you."

She stepped away and heard him mutter something obscene at her as she left. Her tears weren't thick. Hardly enough to wipe away. It was only that they stung so much.

She tucked her relief pack under her arm and, as soon as her eyes had recovered enough to see, put down her head and started home again. She couldn't linger. There were others more desperate or less principled than herself who were waiting at the corners and in the doorways for the chance to steal water filters and food from the unwary. If she didn't walk with purpose, they might mistake her for a victim. For a few blocks, her starved and exhausted mind entertained itself with fantasies of fighting off thieves. As if the catharsis of violence might somehow bring her to peace.

When she'd left their rooms, she'd promised Anna that she'd stop by Old Gino's on the way home and make sure the elderly man was getting to the relief van. But when she reached the turn, she kept going straight. Weariness was already sucking at her marrow, and the prospect of propping the old man up and going back through the queue with him was more than she could face. She'd say she forgot. It would almost be true.

At the curve that led from the wide avenue into the residential cul-de-sac that was home, she found the violent fantasies in her mind had shifted. The men she imagined herself beating until they apologized and begged her forgiveness weren't thieves, but the freckled relief man. *If they can make the oats grow faster.* What was that supposed to mean, anyway? Had he been joking about using their bodies as fertilizer? Had he dared to make a threat against her family? Who in hell did he think he was?

No, a voice said in her mind, as clearly as if Anna had been there to speak the words. *No, he was angry because he wanted to help more, and he couldn't. Knowing that all you can give isn't enough is its own burden. That was all. Forgive him.*

Namono knew that she should, but she didn't.

Their house was small. A half dozen rooms pressed together like a child squeezing a handful of damp sand. Nothing quite lined up; no corner was perfectly square. It gave the space the feel of something natural—a cave or a grotto—more than something built. She paused before she opened the door, trying to clear her mind. The setting sun had fallen behind Zuma Rock, and the grit and smoke in the air showed where the wide beams of light streamed past it. It looked like the stone had a halo. And in the darkening sky, a pinpoint of light. Venus. Tonight, there might be stars. She latched onto the thought like a lifeboat in the sea. There might be stars.

Inside, the house was clean. The rugs had been shaken out, the brick floors swept. The air smelled of lilac thanks to the little sachet-and-candle that one of Anna's parishioners had brought them. Namono wiped away the last of her tears. She could pretend the redness in her eyes was only the outside air. Even if they didn't believe her, they could pretend to.

"Hello?" she called. "Is anyone home?"

Nami squeaked from the back bedroom, her bare feet slapping on the brick as she barreled toward the door. Her little girl wasn't so little anymore. She came up to Nono's armpit now. Or Anna's shoulder. The gentle pudge of childhood was gone, and the awkward coltish beauty of adolescence was clearing its throat. Her skin was barely lighter than Nono's and her hair was as rich and kinky, but the girl had a Russian smile.

"You're back!"

"Of course I am," Nono said.

"What did we get?"

Namono took the white relief package and pressed it into her daughter's hands. With a smile that was like complicity, she leaned close. "Why don't you go find out, and then come tell me?"

Nami grinned back and loped off to the kitchen as if the water recyclers and fast-grown oats were a brilliant present. The girl's enthusiasm was vast and partly sincere. The other part was to show her mothers that she was all right, that they didn't need to worry for her. So much of their strength—all their strengths—grew from trying to protect each other. She didn't know if that made it better or worse.

In the bedroom, Anna lay on her cushions. A thick volume of Tolstoy rested beside her, its spine bent by being reread. *War and Peace.* Her complexion was grayish and drawn. Nono sat beside her carefully, putting her hand on the exposed skin of her wife's right thigh just above where her knee had been crushed. The skin didn't feel hot anymore, and it wasn't stretched drum-tight. Those had to be good signs.

"The sky was blue today," Nono said. "There may be stars out tonight."

Anna smiled her Russian smile, the one her wife's genes had also given Nami. "That's good, then. Improvement."

"God knows there's room for it," Namono said, regretting the discouragement in her voice even as she spoke. She tried to soften it by taking Anna's hand. "You're looking better too."

"No fever today," Anna said.

"None?"

"Well, only a little."

"Many guests?" she asked, trying to keep her tone light. After Anna's injury, her parishioners had made such a fuss, bringing by tokens and offers of support until it was impossible for Anna to rest. Namono had put her foot down and sent them away. Anna had allowed it mostly, she thought, because it also kept her flock from giving away the supplies they couldn't afford to do without.

"Amiri came by," Anna said.

"Did he? And what did my cousin want?"

"We're having a prayer circle tomorrow. Only about a dozen people. Nami helped clean the front room for it. I know I should have asked you first, but…"

Anna nodded at her distended, swollen leg as if her inability to stand at the pulpit was the worst thing that had happened to her. And maybe it was.

"If you're strong enough," Namono said.

"I'm sorry."

"I forgive you. Again. Always."

"You're good to me, Nono." Then, softly so that Nami couldn't hear them, "There was an alert while you were out."

Namono's heart went cold. "Where's it going to hit."

"It won't. They got it. But…"

The silence carried it. But there had been another one. Another rock thrown down the gravity well toward the fragile remnants of the Earth.

"I didn't tell Nami," Anna said, as if protecting their child from the fear was another sin that required forgiveness.

"It's all right," Namono said. "I will if we need to."

"How is Gino?"

I forgot floated at the back of Namono's throat, but she couldn't speak the lie. To herself, maybe, but Anna's clear eyes forbade it. "I'm going there next."

"It's important," Anna said.

"I know. It's just that I'm so tired—"

"That's why it's important," Anna said. "When the crisis comes, we all pull together naturally. It's easy then. It's when things drag on too long that we have to make the effort. We need to make sure everyone sees we're all in this together."

Unless another rock came and the Navy didn't catch it in time. Unless the hydroponics collapsed under the strain and they all went hungry. Unless the water recyclers failed. Unless a thousand different things happened, any one of which meant death.

But even that wouldn't be failure for Anna. Not as long as they were all good and kind to each other. If they helped carry each other gently into the grave, Anna would feel she was following her calling. Perhaps she was right.

"Of course," Namono said. "I just wanted to bring the supplies back to you first."

Nami rushed in a moment later, a water recycler in either hand. "Look! Another glorious week of drinking cleaned-up piss and filthy rainwater!" she said with a grin, and it struck Namono for the millionth time what a perfect distillation of her mothers their daughter could be.

The rest of the package was oatmeal pucks ready to be cooked, packets of something that claimed in Chinese and Hindi to be chicken stroganoff, and a handful of pills. Vitamins for all of them. Painkillers for Anna. So that was something.

Namono sat with her wife, holding her hand until Anna's

eyelids began to droop and her cheeks took on the softness that spoke of coming sleep. Through the window, the last of the twilight glowed red, fading to gray. Anna's body relaxed a degree. The tightness in her shoulders released. The furrows in her brow smoothed. Anna didn't complain, but the pain of her injury and the stress of being suddenly crippled had mixed with the fear they all shared. It was a pleasure to watch it all fall away, if only for a moment. Anna was always a handsome woman, but when she slept, she was beautiful.

Nono waited until her wife's breath was deep and regular before she rose from the bedside. She was almost to the door when Anna spoke, her voice rusty with sleep.

"Don't forget Gino."

"Going there now," Nono said softly, and Anna's breath went back to its deep sleep-slow tide.

"Can I come too?" Nami asked as Nono went back to their street door. "The terminals are down again, and there's nothing to do here."

Nono considered *It's too dangerous out there* and *Your mother might need you*, but her daughter's eyes were so hopeful. "Yes, but put your shoes on."

The walk back to Gino's was a dance in shadows. Enough sunlight had struck the emergency lights' solar panels that half the houses they passed were glowing a little from within. Not much more than a candle's brightness, but more than there had been. The city itself was still black. No streetlights, no glow in the skyscrapers, and only a few bright points along the sinuous length of the arcology to the south.

Namono had the sudden, powerful memory of being younger than her own daughter was now and going up to Luna for the first time. The utter brilliance of the stars and the starkly beautiful Milky Way. Even with the dust grit still in the high air above them, there were more stars out now than when the light pollution of the city had drowned them. The moon shone: a crescent of silver cupping a webwork of gold. She took her daughter's hand.

The girl's fingers seemed so thick, so solid compared to what they had once been. She was growing up. Not their little baby anymore. There had been so many plans for her university and traveling together. All of them gone now. The world they'd thought they were raising her in had vanished. She felt a twinge of guilt about that, as if there were something that she could have done to stop all this from happening. As if it were somehow her fault.

In the deepening darkness, there were voices, though not so many as there had been. Before, there had been some nightlife in the quarter. Pubs and street performers and the hard, rattling music recently come into fashion that clattered out into the street like someone spilling bricks. Now people slept when the darkness came and rose with the light. She caught the smell of something cooking. Strange how even boiled oats could come to mean comfort. She hoped that Old Gino had gone to the van, or that one of Anna's parishioners had gone for him. Otherwise Anna would insist that he take part of their supplies, and Namono would let her.

But it hadn't happened yet. No need to call for trouble before it came. There was enough on the road already. When they reached the turn to Old Gino's street, the last of the sunlight was gone. The only sign that Zuma Rock was even there was a deeper darkness rising up thousands of meters above the city. The land itself raising a defiant fist to the sky.

"Oh," Nami said. Not even a word so much as the intake of breath. "Did you see it?"

"See what?" Namono asked.

"Shooting star. There's another one. Look!"

And yes, there among the fixed if flickering stars, a brief streak of light. And then another. While they stood there, hand in hand, a half dozen more. It was all she could do not to turn back, not to push her daughter into the shelter of a doorway and try to cover her. There had been an alert, but the remnants of the UN Navy had caught this one. These smears of fire across the upper atmosphere might not even be the debris from it. Or they might.

Either way, shooting stars had been something beautiful once. Something innocent. They would not be again. Not for her. Not for anyone on Earth. Every bright smear was a whisper of death. The hiss of a bullet. A reminder as clear as a voice. *All of this can end, and you cannot stop it.*

Another streak, bright as a torch, that bloomed out into a silent fireball as wide as her thumbnail.

"That was a big one," Nami said.

No, Namono thought. *No it wasn't.*

Chapter One: Pa

Y ou have no fucking right to this!" the owner of the *Horn-blower* shouted, not for the first time. "We worked for what we have. It's *ours*."

"We've been over this, sir," Michio Pa, captain of the *Connaught*, said. "Your ship and its cargo are under conscript order of the Free Navy."

"Your relief effort bullshit? Belters need supplies, let them buy some. Mine is mine."

"It's needed. If you'd cooperated with the order—"

"You shot us! You broke our drive cone!"

"You tried to evade us. Your passengers and crew—"

"Free Navy, my fucking ass! You're thieves. You're *pirates*."

At her left, Evans—her XO and the most recent addition to her family—grunted like he'd been hit. Michio glanced at him, and his blue eyes were there to meet her. He grinned: white teeth and a too-handsome face. He was pretty, and he knew it. Michio muted her microphone, letting the stream of invective pour from the *Hornblower* without her, and nodded him on. *What is it?*

Evans pointed a thumb toward the console. "So angry," he said. "Like to hurt a poor coyo's feelings, he goes on like that."

"Be serious," Michio said, but through a smile.

"Am serious. Fragé bist."

"Fragile. You?"

"In my heart," Evans said, pressing a palm to his sculpted chest. "Little boy, me."

On the speaker, the owner of the *Hornblower* had worked himself into a deeper froth. To hear him tell it, Pa was a thief and a whore and the kind of person who didn't care whose babies died so long as she got her payday. If he was her father, he'd kill her instead of letting her dishonor her family. Evans snickered.

Despite herself, Michio laughed too. "Did you know your accent gets thicker when you flirt?"

"Yeah," Evans said. "I'm just a complex tissue of affectation and vice. Took your mind off him, though. You were starting to lose your temper."

"Not done losing it yet," she said, and turned the mic back to live. "Sir. *Sir!* Can we at least agree that I'm the pirate who's offering to lock you in your cabin for the trip to Callisto instead of throwing you into space? Would that be all right?"

There was a moment of stunned silence on the radio, then a roar of incoherent rage that resolved into phrases like *drink your fucking Belter blood* and *kill you if you try.* Michio lifted three fingers. Across the command deck, Oksana Busch waved her own hand in acknowledgment and tapped the weapons controls.

The *Connaught* wasn't a Belter ship. Not originally. She'd been built by the Martian Congressional Republic Navy, and she'd come equipped with a wide variety of military and technical expert systems. They'd been on it for the better part of a year now, training in secret at first. And then when the day came, leading her into the fray. Now Michio watched her own monitor as the *Con-*

naught identified and targeted six places on the floating cargo ship where a stream of PDC fire or a well-placed missile would peel open the hull. The targeting lasers came on, painting the *Hornblower*. Michio waited. Evans' smile was a little less certain than it had been. Slaughtering civilians wasn't his first choice. In fairness, it wasn't what Michio would have picked either, but the *Hornblower* wasn't going to make its journey through the gates and out to whatever alien planet they'd thought to colonize. The negotiation now was only what the terms of that failure would be.

"Want to fire, bossmang?" Busch asked.

"Not yet," Michio said. "Watch that drive. If they try to burn out of here? Then."

"They try to burn on that busted cone, we can save the ammunition," Busch said, derision in her voice.

"There's people counting on that cargo."

"Savvy me," Busch said. Then, a moment later, "They're still cold."

The radio clicked, spat. On the other ship, someone was shouting, but not at her. Then there was another voice, then several, each trying to cut above the others. The report of a gun rang out, the sound of the attack pressed thin and nonthreatening by the radio.

A new voice came.

"*Connaught*? You there?"

"Still here," Michio said. "To whom am I speaking, please?"

"Name's Sergio Plant," the voice said. "Acting captain of the *Hornblower*. I'm offering up our surrender. Just no one gets hurt, okay?"

Evans grinned their triumph and relief.

"Besse to hear from you, Captain Plant," Michio said. "I accept your terms. Please prepare for boarding."

She killed the connection.

History, Michio believed, was a long series of surprises that seemed inevitable in retrospect. And what was true of nations and planets and vast corporate-state complexes also applied to the smaller fates of men and women. As above, so below. As the OPA and Earth and the Martian Congressional Republic, so with Oksana Busch and Evans Garner-Choi and Michio Pa. For that matter, so with all the other souls who lived and worked on the *Connaught* and her sister ships. It was only because she sat where she did, commanded as she did, and carried the weight of keeping the men and women of her crew safe and well and on the right side of history that the smaller personal histories of the *Connaught*'s crew seemed to have more significance.

For her, the first surprise in the many that had brought her here was becoming part of the military arm of the Belt at all. As a young woman, she'd expected to be a systems engineer or an administrator on one of the big stations. If she'd loved mathematics more than she did, it might have happened. She'd put herself through upper university because she thought she was supposed to, and failed because it had been a horrible fit. When the counselors sent her the message that she was being disenrolled, it had been a shock. Looking back, it was obvious. The clarifying lens of history.

She'd fit better with the OPA, or at least the arm of it she'd joined. Within the first month, it became clear that the Outer Planets Alliance was less the unified bureaucracy of the revolution than a kind of franchise title adopted by the people of the Belt who thought that something like it should exist. The Voltaire Collective considered itself OPA, but so did Fred Johnson's group based on Tycho Station. Anderson Dawes acted as governor of Ceres under the split circle, and Zig Ochoa opposed him under the same symbol.

For years, Michio had styled herself as a woman with a military career, but with an awareness in the back of her mind that her chain of command was a fragile thing. There was a time it had made her reflexively protective of authority—her authority over her subordinates and the authority of her superiors over her. It was what put her in the XO's chair of the *Behemoth*. What put her in the slow zone when humanity first passed through the gate and into the hub of the thirteen-hundred-world empire to which they were heir. It was what had gotten her lover, Sam Rosenberg, killed. After that, her faith in command structures had become a little less absolute.

Once again obvious in retrospect.

As to the second surprise, she couldn't have said exactly what it was. Falling into a collective marriage or her recruitment by Marco Inaros or taking possession of her new ship and its revolutionary mission with the Free Navy. Lives had more turning points than seams of ore, and not every change was obvious, even looking back.

"Boarding team's ready," Carmondy said, his voice flattened by the suit mic. "You want us to breach?"

As the leader of the assault team, Carmondy was technically in a different branch of command than Michio, but he'd deferred to her as soon as he and his soldiers had come aboard. He'd lived on Mars for a few years, wasn't part of the plural marriage that formed the core of the *Connaught*'s crew, and was professional enough to accept his status as an outsider. She liked him for that, if little else.

"Let's let them be nice," Michio said. "If they start shooting at us, do what needs doing."

"Savvy," Carmondy said, and then switched channels.

Both ships were on the float now, so she couldn't lean back in her crash couch. If she'd been able to, she would have.

When the news had come out that the Free Navy was taking control of the system and that the ring gate was closed to through traffic, the fleet of colony ships on the burn for the new worlds beyond faced a choice. Stand down and give their supplies over for redistribution to the stations and ships most in need, and they would be allowed to keep their ships. Run, and they wouldn't.

The *Hornblower*—like who knew how many others—had done the calculation and decided the risk was worth the reward.

They'd killed their transponders, spun their ship, and burned like hell, but briefly. Then spun again, burned again, spun again, burned. Hotaru, they called it. The strategy of going bright only for a moment, and then going dark in hopes that the vastness of space would conceal them until the political situation changed. The ships had enough food and supplies to last the would-be colonists for years. The volume of the system was so massive that if they avoided detection at the front, finding them later could be the work of lifetimes.

The *Hornblower*'s drive plume had been detected by Free Navy arrays on Ganymede and Titan both. The thing she hated most was that the chase had led them up out of the plane of the ecliptic. The vast majority of the sun's heliosphere extended above and below the thin disk where the planets and the asteroid belt spun in their orbits. Michio had a superstitious dislike of those reaches, the huge emptiness that, in her mind, loomed above and below human civilization.

The ring gate and the unreal space beyond it might be stranger— *were* stranger—but her unease about traveling outside the ecliptic had been with her since childhood. It was part of her personal mythology, and a herald of bad luck.

She set her monitor to show the boarding team's suit cameras and play soft music. The *Hornblower*, as seen through twenty different perspectives while harps and finger drums tried to soothe her. A dark-skinned Earther was in the airlock, his arms spread wide. Half a dozen of the cameras were locked on him, barrels of their weapons visible. The others shifted, watching for movement on the periphery or coming from outside the ship. The man reached up and used a handhold to flip himself around, putting his arms behind him for the zip-tie restraint. It had a sense of practice that left Michio thinking that Captain Plant—if that's who this was—had been forcibly detained before.

The boarding team moved into the ship, its eyes and attention shifting down the corridors in teams. Movement on one screen mapped to a figure seen in another. When they reached the galley, the crew of the *Hornblower* floated in ranks, arms out, ready to accept whatever fate the *Connaught* had in store for them. Even at the very small size the individual panes had taken to fit her monitor, she could see the clinging sheen of tears creeping over the captives' faces. Grief masks formed of saline and surface tension.

"They're going to be fine," Evans said. "Esá? It's our job, yeah?"

"I know," Michio said, her gaze fixed on the screen.

The boarding team moved through the decks, locking down control. Their coordination made them feel like a single organism with twenty eyes. The group consciousness of professionalism and drills. The command deck looked ill kept. A hand terminal and a drinking bulb on the float had been sucked against an air intake. Without thrust gravity to coordinate them, the crash couches lay at a variety of angles. It reminded her of old videos she'd seen of shipwrecks back on Earth. The colony ship was drowning in the endless vacuum.

She knew that Carmondy would be calling her before he did it, and drew the music gently down. The request came through with a polite chime.

"We've taken control of the ship, Captain," he said. Two of his men were watching him say it, so she saw his lips and his jaw making the words from two angles even as she heard them. "No resistance. No trouble."

"Officer Busch?" Michio said.

"Their firewalls are already down," Oksana said. "Toda y alles."

Michio nodded, more to herself than to Carmondy. "The *Connaught* has control of the enemy ship's systems."

"We're setting a perimeter and securing the prisoners. Automatic check-in set."

"Understood," Michio said. Then, to Evans, "Let's pull back far enough to be outside the blast range if it turns out they're hiding nukes in the grain silo."

"On it," Evans said.

The maneuvering thrusters shifted her against her restraints, not even a tenth of a g, for the burn's scant handful of seconds. Taking the things that other people thought they deserved to keep was dangerous work. The *Connaught* would watch over the boarding team of course, the ship's gentle fingers on all their pulses. And in addition, Carmondy would ping every half hour using a onetime pad protocol. If he failed to check in, Michio would turn the *Hornblower* into a diffuse cloud of hot gas as a warning to the next ship. And a few thousand people on Callisto, Io, and Europa would have to hope the other Free Navy conscription missions came through.

The Belt had finally shrugged off the yoke of the inner planets. They had Medina Station at the heart of the ring gates, they had the only functioning navy in the solar system, and they had the gratitude of millions of Belters. In the long term, it was the greatest statement of independence and freedom the human race had ever made. In the short term, it was her job to see the victory didn't starve them all to death.

For the next two days, Carmondy and his men would see that the would-be colonists were sealed on secured decks, where they could ride out the transit to a stable orbit around Jupiter. Then make a complete inventory of what had been gained by the taking of the *Hornblower*. Once they were done, it would still be a week before the salvage drives were in place. In that time, the *Connaught* would stand as guard and captor, and little enough for Michio to do but scan the darkness for other refugees.

She wasn't looking forward to it, and she was sure the others in her marriage group weren't either. Still, there was more than that in Oksana's voice when she spoke.

"Bossmang. We got confirmation from Ceres."

"Good," Michio said, but with an uptick in her inflection that meant she'd heard whatever Oksana wasn't saying. Oksana Busch had been her wife almost as long as the group had been together. They knew each other's moods well.

"Got something else too. Message from himself."

"What does Dawes want?" Michio asked.

"Not Dawes. *Big* himself."

"Inaros?" Michio said. "Play it."

"Under captain-only encrypt," Oksana said. "I can pipe it to your cabin or your terminal if—"

"Play it, Oksana."

Marco Inaros appeared on the monitor. From the drape of his hair, he was either on Ceres or under burn. There wasn't enough visible background behind him to say if he was on a ship or in an office. His smile was charming and reached his warm, dark eyes. Michio felt her pulse step up a little, and told herself it was dread and not an attraction. For the most part, that was truth. He was a charismatic bastard, though.

"Captain Pa," Marco said. "I'm glad to hear you took the *Hornblower* cleanly. It's another testament to your ability. We were right to have you in command of the conscription. Things have gone well enough, we're ready to move on to the next stages of our plan."

Michio glanced over at Evans and Oksana. He was plucking at his beard, and she was trying not to look at Michio.

"We'll want to route the *Hornblower* directly to Ceres," Marco said. "And before that, I'm calling a meeting. Strictly inner-circle. You, me, Dawes, Rosenfeld, Sanjrani. At Ceres Station." His grin widened. "Now that we're running the system, there are some changes we should make, eh? The *Pella* says you can make it there in two weeks. It'll be good to see you in person."

He made a sharp Free Navy salute. The one he'd come up with. The screen went blank. The mix of confusion and distress and relief that flooded Michio's gut wasn't easy to make sense of. Having her mission change like that, so quickly and with so little explanation, left her on the wrong foot. And going into a meeting of the inner circle still had a little of the sense of danger that it had before the Free Navy had announced itself. Years of moving in shadows left habits of thought and feeling that were hard to step out of, even if they'd won. But at least they'd be back in the plane of the ecliptic, and not high up in the black, where ominous things happened. Bad things.

Things, a small, still voice in her head said, *like being called to an unexpected meeting.*

"Two weeks?" Michio asked.

"Possible," Busch answered almost before the question was out. She'd already run the plan. "But it'll mean burning hard. And no waiting for the *Hornblower.*"

"Carmondy won't like that," Pa said.

"What's he going to say?" Oksana said. "It's himself giving the order."

"It is," Michio agreed.

Evans cleared his throat. "So we're going?"

Michio held up a fist. *Yes.* "It's Inaros," she said, ending the coming argument by invoking his name.

"Well. Bien," Evans said, but the tone of his voice said something different.

"Something?" Pa asked.

"Just isn't the first time plans changed," Evans said, his face wrinkled with worry. He wasn't as pretty that way, but he was her newest husband, so she didn't point it out. Pretty men could be so fragile.

"Continue," she said instead.

"Well, there was the money thing with Sanjrani. And the Martian prime minister wound up making it safe to Luna when half the Free Navy was trying to take him out. And I hear we tried to kill Fred Johnson and James Holden both, and both still breathing and walking free. Leaves me wondering."

"Like maybe Marco isn't as infallible as he plays?" Michio asked.

For a moment, he didn't answer. She thought he might not. "Something like," Evans finally said. "But even thinking like that feels like it might get sticky, no?"

"Something like," Michio agreed.

Chapter Two: Filip

There was no one he hated more than James Holden. Holden, the peacemaker who'd never made peace. Holden, the champion of justice who'd never sacrificed anything for justice. James Holden, who crewed up with Martians and Belters—with *one* Belter—and moved through the system as if it made him better than everyone else. Neutral and above the fray while the inner planets shoved humanity's resources out to the thirteen hundred–odd new planets and left the Belters to die. Who, against all odds, hadn't died with the *Chetzemoka*.

Fred Johnson, the Earther who'd gone native and started speaking for the Belt, was a close second. The Butcher of Anderson Station, who'd made his career by slaughtering innocent Belters and continued it by patronizing them all into an arc that led toward their cultural and individual deaths. For that he deserved hatred and disdain. But Filip's mother hadn't died directly because of Johnson, and so Holden—James *pinché* Holden—owned first prize.

It was months since Filip had beaten his hands against the inner door of the airlock while his mother, her mind twisted by too much time in Holden's cultlike presence, had spaced herself and Cyn along with her. Stupid deaths. Needless. That, he told himself, was why it hurt so much. That she hadn't needed to die, and she'd chosen it anyway. He'd broken his hand trying to get her to stop, but it hadn't helped anything. Naomi Nagata had picked a bad death in the void over a life with her true people. It was proof of how much power Holden had had over her. How deeply she'd been brainwashed, and how weak her mind had been from the start.

He didn't tell anyone on the *Pella* that he still dreamed about it every night: the closed door, the certainty that something precious—something *important*—was on the other side of it, and the sense of vicious loss that he couldn't make the door open. If they knew how much it haunted him, he'd seem weak, and his father didn't have room for men who couldn't do their part. Not even his own son. Filip took his place as a Belter and a man of the Free Navy or he found a place on a station and stayed there as a boy. He was nearly seventeen now; he'd helped to destroy the oppressors on Earth. His childhood belonged in his past.

Pallas Station was one of the oldest in the Belt. The first mines had been there, and following them, the first refineries. The newer facilities had followed, because this was where the industrial base was. And because it was easier to use the older, unretired crushers and spin separators as overflow capacity. And from habit. Pallas had never been spun up. The gravity it had was the naturally occurring microgravity of its mass—two percent of Earth's full g. Hardly more than a persistent direction of drift. The station swooped above and below the plane of the ecliptic, like it was trying to elbow its way out of the solar system. Ceres and Vesta were

larger and more populous, but the metal for ship plating and reactors, for station decks and shipping containers, for the guns that
studded the Free Navy's liberated warships and the rounds that
they fired all came from here. If Ganymede was the breadbasket
of the Belt, Pallas was its forge.

It only made sense that the Free Navy should pass through
there in its constant voyage through the liberated system, and that
it should make sure to leave no resources behind.

"S'yahaminda, que?" the harbormaster said, floating in the
meeting room's wider end. It was a Belter room. No tables, no
chairs. Little reference to up or down in its architecture. After so
long in a ship built with thrust gravity in mind, Filip thought it felt
like home. Authentic in a way that the Martian-designed spaces
never could.

The harbormaster himself was the same. His body was longer than someone who'd spent their childhood with even low,
intermittent gravity. His head was larger compared to his body
than Filip's or Marco's or Karal's. The harbormaster's left eye
was milky and blind where even the pharmaceutical cocktail that
made human life in freefall possible had been insufficient to keep
the capillaries from dying. He was the kind of man who would
never be able to tolerate living on a planetary surface, even for a
short period of time. The most extreme end of the Belter physi-
ological spectrum. He was exactly who the Free Navy had risen
up to protect and represent.

Which was likely why he seemed so confused and betrayed now.

"Is it a problem?" Marco said, shrugging with his hands. The
way he said it made emptying the warehouses into the void seem
like an everyday thing to ask. Filip hoisted his own eyebrows to
echo his father's disbelief. Karal only glowered and kept one fist
on his sidearm.

"Per es esá mindan hoy," he said.

"I know it's everything," Marco said. "That's the point. So long as
it's all here, Pallas will be a target for the inners. Put what you have
in containers, fire them off, and only we will know their vectors.

We'll track where they are and salvage what we need when we need it. It's not just keeping it out of their hands, it's showing that the station warehouses are empty before they even reach for them, yeah?"

"Per mindan …" the harbormaster said, blinking in distress.

"You'll be paid for it all," Filip said. "Good Free Navy scrip."

"Good, yeah," the harbormaster said. "Aber …"

His blinking redoubled and he looked away from Marco as if the admiral of the Belters' first real armed force was floating half a meter left of where he was. He licked his lips.

"Aber?" Marco prompted, matching his accent.

"Spin classifiers v'reist neue ganga, yeah?"

"If you need new parts, then buy new parts," Marco said, his voice taking on a dangerous buzz.

"Aber…" The harbormaster swallowed.

"But you used to buy from Earth," Marco said. "And our money doesn't spend there."

The harbormaster lifted a fist in acknowledgment.

Marco's smile was gentle and open. Sympathetic. "No one's money spends there. Not anymore. You buy from the Belt now. Just the Belt."

"Belt don't make good parts," the harbormaster whined.

"We make the best parts there are," Marco said. "History's moved on, my friend. Try to keep up. And package everything there is for push-out, sa sa?"

The harbormaster met Marco's gaze and lifted his fist again in assent. It wasn't as if he had a choice. The advantage of being in command of all the guns was that no matter how nicely you asked for something, it was still an order. Marco pushed off, the thin gravity of Pallas bending the path of his body. He stopped his motion by grabbing handholds at the harbormaster's side, and then embraced him. The harbormaster didn't hug him back. He looked like a man holding his breath and hoping something dangerous wouldn't notice him as it passed by.

The corridors and passageways leading from the harbormaster's office to the docks were a patchwork of ancient ceramic plating and newer carbon-silicate lace. The lace plating—one of the first new materials put into manufacture after the proto-molecule's appearance threw physical chemistry ahead by a few generations—had an eerie rainbow sheen as they floated past it. Like oil on the surface of water. It was supposed to be more resilient than ceramic and titanium, harder and more flexible. No one knew how it would age, though if reports from the other worlds were to be trusted, it would likely outlast the people who'd fashioned it by at least an order of magnitude. Assuming they were making it right. Hard to know.

The Pallas shuttle was waiting when they reached it, Bastien strapped into the pilot's couch.

"Bist bien?" he asked as Marco cycled the airlock closed behind them.

"As well as could be hoped," Marco said, glancing around the small craft. Six couches, not counting Bastien's pilot's station. Karal was strapping into one, Filip into another. But Marco drifted slowly to the shuttle's floor, his hair settling at his shoulders. He lifted his chin as a question.

"Rosenfeld went already," Bastien said. "Been on the *Pella* for three hours."

"Has he now," Marco said, and his voice had an edge that maybe only Filip could hear. He slid into his couch and cinched down the straps. "That's good. Let's join up."

Bastien cleared with the dock control system, more from habit than need. Marco was captain of the *Pella*, admiral of the Free Navy, and his shuttle would take precedence over any other traffic. But Bastien checked anyway, then went through the seals and environment controls again, for what was likely the tenth time. For anyone raised in the Belt, checking the air and the water and the seals on ships and suits was like breathing. Not something you even thought about, just something that happened. People who didn't live that way tended to leave the gene pool early.

They grew a degree heavier as the shuttle launched, then the gimbals in the couches all hissed at once as Bastien fired the maneuvering thrusters. It wasn't even a quarter-g burn, and still they reached the *Pella* in minutes. They cycled through the lock—the same one Naomi had chosen to die in—then floated out into the familiar air of the *Pella*.

Rosenfeld Guoliang was waiting for them.

All through Filip's life, from his very first memories, the Belt had meant the Outer Planets Alliance, and the OPA had meant the people who mattered most. His people. It was only as he'd grown up and started being allowed to listen when his father spoke with other adults that his understanding of the OPA became deeper, more nuanced, and the word that redefined his people was *alliance*. Not *republic*, not *unity government*, not *nation*. Alliance. The OPA was a numberless wash of different groups that formed and fell apart and formed again, all of them tacitly agreeing that, whatever their disagreements might be, they were united against the oppression of the inner planets. There were a few large standard bearers under the OPA's flag—Tycho Station under Fred Johnson, and Ceres Station under Anderson Dawes, each with their militias; the ideological provocateurs of the Voltaire Collective; the openly criminal Golden Bough; the nonviolent near-collaborationist Maruttuva Kulu. For each of those, there were dozens—hundreds, maybe—of smaller organizations and associations, cabals and mutual interest societies. What brought them together was the constant economic and military oppression of Earth and Mars.

The Free Navy was not the OPA, and it was not meant to be. The Free Navy was the strongest of the old order, forged together into a force that didn't need an enemy to define it. It was a promise of a future in which the yoke of the past was not only shrugged off but broken.

That didn't mean it was *free* from the past.

Rosenfeld was a thin man who managed to slouch even on the float. His skin was dark and weirdly pebbled, his eyes sunk deep in their sockets. He had tattoos of the OPA's split circle and the knifelike V of the Voltaire Collective, a bright and ready smile, and a sense of barely contained violence. And he was the reason Filip's father had come to Pallas.

"Marco Inaros," Rosenfeld said, spreading his arms. "Look what you've done, coyo mis!"

Marco launched himself forward into the man's embrace, spinning with him as they held close and slowing when they pulled back. Any distrust Marco held toward Rosenfeld was gone. Or no, not gone, but shifted away for Filip and Karal to feel so that his own pleasure at the reunion could be pure.

"You look good, old friend," Marco said.

"I don't," Rosenfeld said, "but I appreciate the lie."

"Do we need to transfer your men over?"

"Already done," Rosenfeld said, and Filip glanced to Karal, catching the little scowl at the corner of the older man's mouth. Rosenfeld was a friend, an ally, one of the inner circle of the Free Navy, but he shouldn't have been able to bring his private guard on the ship when Marco wasn't there. The *Pella* was the flagship of the Free Navy, after all, and temptation was temptation. Marco and Rosenfeld reached out together, slowed their two-body rotation with a handhold jutting off the lockers, and still arm in arm, pushed out to the corridor and into the ship. Filip and Karal followed after.

"Going to be a hard burn getting to Ceres in time for the meeting," Marco said.

"Your fault. I could have taken my own ship."

"You don't have a gunship."

"I've lived my whole life in rock hoppers—"

Even with only the back of his father's head to see, Filip could hear the smile in Marco's voice. "That was your whole life until now. We've changed the game. Can't have the high command moving unprotected. Even out here, not everyone's with us. Not yet."

They reached the lift that ran the length of the ship, shifted around it, and swam headfirst through the air, down toward the crew decks. Karal looked behind, toward the operations and flight decks, as if to be sure none of Rosenfeld's guard were at their six.

"Why I waited," Rosenfeld said. "The good little soldier, mé. Too bad about Johnson and Smith making it safe to Luna. Only took down one out of three?"

"Earth was the one that mattered," Marco said. Ahead of them, Sárta appeared, floating up past them toward ops. She nodded her greeting as they passed. "Earth was always the prime target."

"Well, Secretary-General Gao's with her gods now, and I hope she died screaming"—Rosenfeld mimed spitting to the side after he said it—"but this Avasarala who's taken her place—"

"A bureaucrat," Marco said as they hauled themselves around the corner and into the mess. The tables and benches bolted to the floor, the smell of Martian military food, the colors that had until recently been the banner of the enemy. They all stood in contrast to the men and women in the space. Belters all, and still Filip could pick out the Free Navy he served with from Rosenfeld's guard. Self from not-self. They could pretend the division wasn't there, but they all knew better. A dozen people, all told, like it was the change of shift. One of the *Pella*'s crew for each of Rosenfeld's, so Karal wasn't the only one to think a little vigilance between friends was a good thing.

One of the guards tossed Rosenfeld a bulb. Coffee, tea, whiskey, or water, there was no way to know. Rosenfeld caught it without missing a beat in the conversation. "Seems like a bureaucrat with a hate on. You think you can handle her? Nothing personal, coyo, but you've got a blind spot underestimating women."

Marco went still. Even as Filip saw it, his mouth flooded with a coppery taste. Karal grunted softly, and when Filip looked to him, his jaw had slid forward and his hands were fists at his sides.

Rosenfeld took a place against a wall, his expression a mask of empathy and apology. "But maybe this isn't the place to say it. Sorry for the sore spot."

"Nothing hurt," Marco said. "We'll chew it all through on Ceres."

"Gathering of the tribes," Rosenfeld said. "Looking forward to it. Next phase should be interesting."

"Will be," Marco said. "Karal can put you and yours in the right cabins. Should plan to keep there. It's going to be a hard burn."

"Will do, Admiral."

Marco pulled himself out of the room, floating down toward the machine shop and engineering without so much as meeting Filip's eye.

Filip waited for a moment, uncertain whether to follow or stay here, whether he'd been dismissed from duty or was still at his post. Rosenfeld smiled and winked a bumpy eyelid at him before turning to his men. Something had happened there; he could feel it in the air and in the way Karal held himself. Something important. And from the way his father acted, he had to think it was something to do with him.

He put his hand on Karal's wrist. "What is it?"

"Nothing," Karal said, lying badly. "Nothing to worry over."

"Karal?"

The older man pressed his lips together, stretched his neck. He didn't look at Filip.

"Karal. Something I should ask *them*?"

Slowly, Karal shook his head. He shouldn't ask. Karal licked his lips nervously, shook his head again, sighed, and spoke low and calm. "Was a report back a while. Observation data from the... ah... from the *Chetzemoka*. About how the ships with Johnson and Smith didn't die?"

"And?"

"And," Karal said, the word as dense as lead.

Then he went on, which was how Filip Inaros, in front of Rosenfeld and his half dozen smirking guards, learned that his mother was still alive. And that everyone on the *Pella* knew it but him.

Under burn, he dreamed.

He was standing at the same door as before. Even though it would change what it looked like, it was always the same door. He was screaming, beating his hands against it, trying to get in.

Before, there had been the sense of fear, the oceanic sorrow of impending loss, the dread. Now there was only humiliation. Rage lit him like a fire, and he pushed to get through the door, into whatever chamber lay beyond it, not to save something precious but to end it.

And shouting, he woke. The weight of a full g pressed him into the gel. The *Pella* murmured around him, the vibration of the drive and the hushing of the air recyclers like a voice whispering something just too softly to make out. It was an effort to wipe away the tears. They weren't tears of sorrow. For that he'd have to be sad. He was only certain.

There was someone he hated more than James Holden.

Chapter Three: Holden

There was something to be said for living a life that didn't involve lengthy interrogations. By that standard, at least, Holden had not lived his well. When he and the rest of the *Rocinante*'s crew had agreed to be debriefed, he'd guessed that it would be more than just the events surrounding the attack on Earth by the Free Navy. There was more than enough to talk about, after all. The chief engineer on Tycho Station who'd been exposed as a mole for Marco Inaros, the abduction and rescue of Monica Stuart, the loss of the proto-molecule sample, the attack that had nearly killed Fred Johnson. And that was just for him. Naomi and Alex and even Amos would have whole volumes of their own to contribute.

He hadn't expected that the questioning would spread out from there like a gas to fill all available space. For weeks now, his days had been filled with twelve to sixteen hours of talking through anything and everything in his life. The names and histories of all eight of his parents. His school records. His abortive naval career. What he knew about Naomi, about Alex, about Fred Johnson. His relationship with the OPA, with Dmitri Havelock, with Detective Miller. Even after hours of review, he wasn't sure about that last one. Sitting in the small room across from the UN interrogators, Holden had done his best to take apart his life until that point and lay it open before them.

The process chafed him. The questions cycled back and jumped around, as if they were trying to catch him out in a lie. They went into strange little cul-de-sacs—What were the names of the people he'd served with in the Navy? What did he know about each of them?—and stayed there far longer than seemed justified. His two primary questioners were a tall, light-skinned woman with a long, serious face named Markov and a short, pudgy man called Glenndining with hair and skin the same color of brown. They took turns pushing him and building rapport, subtly cutting him down to see if he'd get angry and what he'd say when he did, and then being almost uncomfortably affectionate with him.

They brought him limp, greasy sandwiches to eat or fresh pastries with some of the best coffee he'd ever had. They turned the lights down almost to darkness or brightened them until they were nearly blinding. They strolled in the hopping lunar shuffle down through the hallways from the docks or they stayed in a cramped steel box of a room. Holden felt as though his personal history was being scraped down to dry pulp like a lime at a really cheap bar. If there was a drop more of juice in him, they'd press it out somehow. It was easy to forget that these were his allies, that he'd agreed to this. More than once, he'd been curled up in his bunk after a long day, hovering on the edge of sleep, and found his mind half-dreaming plans to break the ship out of prison and escape.

It didn't help that, in the dark sky above them, Earth was dying by centimeters. The newsfeeds that remained had mostly relocated to the Lagrange stations and Luna, but a few were still functioning down on the planetary surface. Between the interrogation sessions and sleep, Holden didn't have much time to watch them, but the snippets he heard were enough. Overstrained infrastructure, ecosystem trauma, chemical changes in the ocean and atmosphere. There had been thirty billion people on the overcrowded Earth, dependent on a vast network of machinery to keep them fed and hydrated and not drowning in their own waste. A third of those, by the more pessimistic estimates, had already died. Holden had seen a few seconds of a report discussing how the death count in Western Europe was being done by assaying atmospheric changes. How much methane and cadaverine were in the air let them guess how many people were rotting in the ruined streets and cities. That was the scale of the disaster.

He'd felt guilty turning the feed off. The least he could do was watch. Be there as the ecosphere that bore him and his family and everyone else not very many generations back collapsed. Earth deserved witnesses. He was tired though, and frightened. Even after he'd killed the feed, he hadn't been able to sleep.

Not all the news was bad. Mother Elise got a message through to him that the farm in Montana, while badly damaged, had proven self-sufficient enough to keep his parents alive. There was even enough surplus that they'd been able to help with some of the relief efforts in Bozeman. And as the muddy clouds of grit and ash settled down to poison the oceans, more and more relief flights had been able to dive down the gravity well and come back up filled with refugees.

The physical capabilities of Luna Base were beginning to be stressed, though. The air recyclers were being pushed to their limits so that every breath Holden took in the halls and corridors of the station felt like it had just come out of someone else's mouth. Cots and privacy tents filled the food courts and public spaces. The crew of the *Rocinante* had given up their quarters in the station and moved back onto the ship to make more space. And also to live in their own bubble of clean air and well-filtered water. It was a little disingenuous to pretend the move was altruistic. The ship was quiet and empty and familiar. The only things that kept

Holden from feeling perfectly comfortable were the silence that came from the powered-down reactor and the ghostlike presence of Clarissa Mao.

"Why does she bother you so much?" Naomi asked. They were in their shared cabin, held to the bunk by the moon's fractional gravity and their own exhaustion.

"She killed a bunch of people," Holden said, his sleepiness robbing him of the ability to think clearly. "Is that not enough? It seems like it should be enough."

The cabin was at low light. The crash couch cradled their paired bodies. He felt Naomi's breath against his side, familiar and warm and grounding. Her voice had the same slushy softness as his. They were both almost too tired to sleep. "That was a different her."

"Everyone else seems certain of that. Not sure how we got there."

"Well, I think Alex is still not sure about her."

"But Amos is. And you are."

She made a thick sound in the back of her throat. Her eyes were closed. Even in the dimness, he could see the deeper darkness of her lids. He thought for a moment she'd managed to fall asleep, but then she spoke. "I have to believe she can change. That people can."

"You weren't like her," Holden said. "Even when...even when people died, you weren't like her. You're not a cold-blooded killer."

"Amos is."

"True. But Amos is Amos. It's different in my head."

"Because?"

"Because he's Amos. He's like a pit bull. You know he could tear your throat out, but he's loyal to a fault and you just want to hug him." She smiled slowly. She could do that. A drawing up of a muscle in her face, and Holden filled with hope and warmth and even a kind of grim optimism that said the universe couldn't all be shit if it had a woman like this in it. He rested his hand on her hip. "You didn't fall in love with me for my ethical consistency, did you?"

"Despite it," she chuckled. Then a moment later, "You had a cute butt."

"Had? Past tense?"

"I need to get back on the system," she said, changing the subject. "Don't let me fall asleep until I've checked for updates."

"The missing ships?" he asked, and she nodded.

As hard as his own inquisition had been, Naomi's was worse. She'd always been quiet about her past, about how she'd become the woman she was. Now she had traded that privacy away for a blanket amnesty for the crew, and for herself. Her versions of Markov and Glenndining weren't just asking about a failed naval career and contract work for Fred Johnson. She was their window straight into Marco Inaros. She'd been his lover. The mother of his child, a fact Holden was still trying to wrap his head around. She'd been held captive on his flagship before and after the hammer fell on Earth. He knew the toll the marathon debriefing was taking on him. It had to be a thousand times harder for her.

Which, he assumed, was why she threw herself into the mystery of the missing ships. She'd been the first among them to notice that the set of vessels that had vanished in their transits through the ring gates and the stolen Martian warships that became the Free Navy didn't overlap. Some ships were stolen by Marco and his crew, and some just vanished without a trace. There were two things going on, and he couldn't begrudge her wanting to spend her off time focused on the other one.

But she had to sleep. If for no other reason than his belief that if she finally slept, he would too.

"I promise nothing," he said.

"Okay," she said. "Then wake me up early so I'll have time to check before the next session."

"Promise."

He lay beside her in the gloom until her breath stuttered, deepened, became the regular, powerful pulse of sleep. When he was still awake after five minutes of listening to her, he knew his own rest wasn't coming. He stood, and for a moment, she went silent, moving up toward wakefulness before the deep breath returned. Holden let himself out.

The halls of the *Rocinante* were also dim, set for a night cycle. Holden made his way to the lift. Voices filtered to him from the galley: Amos' affable rumble and the thinner, reedy sound of Clarissa's voice. He paused, listened, then hauled himself up the ladder to the ops deck. The lunar gravity was light enough that using the lift seemed silly, so he just pulled himself up, hand over hand, until he got there. The cabin lights were out, so Alex was only lit by the backsplash from the screen.

"Hey there," Alex drawled as Holden settled himself into a couch. "Can't sleep?"

"Apparently not," Holden sighed. "You?"

"I hate the gravity here. It feels like we're moving too slow. I keep wanting to gun the engines. But there aren't any engines and we aren't going anywhere. It should be a drive holdin' me down, but it's just a big hunk of rock." Alex gestured toward the newsfeed playing silently on his screen. A woman in a bright red hijab was speaking earnestly into the camera. Holden recognized her as a well-respected Martian journalist, but he couldn't remember her name. "It just keeps coming. They're calling it a mutiny. Keep talking about dereliction of duty and abandoning their post and black market sales of equipment."

"That doesn't sound good."

"Sounds better than what it was," Alex said. "It was a coup. It was a civil war, only instead of fighting, a fifth of the military just packed themselves off through the ring gates with all our stuff. Well, all our stuff they didn't trade to these Free Navy assholes."

"Any word where they were going?"

"Nope," Alex said. "At least none they're reporting."

The woman in the hijab—Fatim Wilson, *that* was the name—vanished, but the feed spooled on with images of empty docks on Mars and then a group of protesters milling around and shouting at the camera. Holden couldn't tell what they were for or against. The way things were now, he wasn't sure they'd have been able to tell him either.

"If they ever come back, they'll all be tried for treason," Alex said. "Makes me think they weren't planning to get back home anytime soon."

"So," Holden said. "Martian coup. Free Navy killing the shit out of Earth. Pirates stripping down all the colony ships that were heading out. Medina Station's gone dark. And we-don't-know-what eating some of the ships that go through the gates."

Alex opened his mouth to reply, but his screen flicked and chimed. A high-priority connection request.

"One damned thing after another," Alex said, accepting the connection, "when it ain't a whole bunch of damned things at once."

Chrisjen Avasarala appeared on the screen. Her hair was perfectly in place, her sari a gemlike shimmering green. Only her eyes and the set of her mouth showed the fatigue.

"Captain Holden," she said. "I need to meet with you and your crew. At once."

"Naomi's asleep," Holden said without pausing to think. Avasarala smiled. It wasn't a pleasant expression. "So I'll go wake her up. And we'll be right over."

"Thank you, Captain," the acting ruler of Earth said and signed off.

Silence filled the deck. "You notice how she didn't say anything obscene or offensive?" Holden said.

"Did notice that."

Holden took a deep breath. "That can't be good."

The meeting room was near the moon's surface, and it was built like a classroom or a church: a podium at the front and rows of chairs before it, but the podium was empty and a dozen of the chairs had been pushed into a rough circle. Avasarala sat with

Fred Johnson—the head of Tycho Station and once a spokesman of the OPA—and Martian Prime Minister Smith to her left and Bobbie Draper to her right. Both Smith and Johnson were in their shirtsleeves, and all of them looked tired. Holden, Naomi, Alex, and Amos sat together in a group across from them, a couple of chairs marking the border on either side. Holden didn't realize until they'd all sat down that Clarissa hadn't come. He hadn't even considered bringing her. This was a meeting of the *Rocinante*'s crew, after all, and she was ...

Avasarala tapped her hand terminal. A schematic popped into place in the space in the center of the circle. Earth, Luna, the Lagrange stations were all glowing gold. The naval ships that formed the blockade that intercepted and destroyed the Free Navy's follow-up attacks were in green. A separate model showed the inner system—Sol, Mercury, Venus, Earth, Mars, and the major Belt stations like Ceres and Pallas—with a scattering of red dots like the lesions of a rash.

"The red's Free Navy," Avasarala said. In person, her voice sounded raspy, like she'd been coughing. Holden couldn't tell if she'd only been talking too much or if she'd been breathing in Lunar fines: dust too small to be stopped even by the best filters and that still made the station air stink of gunpowder. "We've been tracking their movements. There's an anomaly. This one."

She prodded her hand terminal, and the two displays merged, one expanding, the other shrinking, until they showed the same stretch of space. The red dot stood off apart from the stations and planets, floating in a vast emptiness where the orbital mechanics left it mostly alone. Naomi leaned forward, fighting to keep her eyes focused. She was too tired for this.

"What's that doing out there?" Naomi asked, and her voice was clear enough.

"Spotting," Fred said. "Its transponder's off, but it appears to be a prospecting ship. The *Azure Dragon* out of Ceres. It's crewed by radical OPA."

"Meaning now maybe with the Free Navy. The rocks they've been throwing?" Holden said.

"Coordinated by that little fucker there," Avasarala said. And then, with an exhausted shrug, "We think. What we know is this: As long as those pigfuckers can keep throwing rocks at us, we're pinned. Our ships don't dare move, and Marco Inaros can claim whatever the hell he wants in the outer planets."

Smith leaned forward, speaking with his calm, almost apologetic tone. "If Chrisjen's intelligence service is right and this ship is guiding the attacks, this is a critical target against the Free Navy. You know that Colonel Johnson, Secretary-General Avasarala, and I have been forming a joint task force? This will be their first field operation. Capture or destroy the *Azure Dragon* and reduce the ability of the enemy to launch assaults against Earth. Give some damn breathing room to the combined fleet." It was the first time Holden had heard the term *combined fleet*, and he liked the way it sounded.

He wasn't the only one.

"Shit," Amos said. "And here I was enjoying being so absolutely thumb-up-the-ass useless."

"You want a little ass-play, that's your business," Avasarala said. "Only you can do it in a crash couch. The *Rocinante* isn't part of the fleet, so losing it won't leave a hole in our defenses. And I understand you've got a few after-market add-ons—"

"Keel-mounted rail gun," Alex said with a grin.

"—that scream of overcompensating for tiny, tiny penises, but might prove useful. The mission commander has requested you and your ship, and honestly none of you are worth a wet slap at this point except Miss Nagata anyway, so—"

"Wait," Holden said. "The *mission commander*? No."

Avasarala met his gaze, and her expression was hard as granite. "No?"

Holden didn't flinch. "The *Rocinante* doesn't go under anyone's command but ours. I understand that this is a big joint task force and we're all in everything together. But the *Roci* isn't just a ship, it's our home. If you want to hire us, fine. We'll take the job, and we'll get it done. If you want to put a commander in place and expect us to follow their orders, then the answer's no."

"Captain Holden—" Avasarala began.

"This isn't a negotiation. This is just how it's going to be," Holden said.

Three of the most powerful people in the solar system, the heads of the central factions that had struggled against each other for generations, looked at each other. Smith's eyebrows rode high on his forehead and he looked anxiously around the room. Fred leaned forward, staring at Holden like he was disappointed in him. Only Avasarala had a glint of amusement in her eyes. Holden glanced at his crew. Naomi's arms were crossed. Alex's head was lifted, his chin pushed forward. Amos was smiling exactly the way he always did. A unified front.

Bobbie cleared her throat. "It's me."

"What now?" Holden said.

"It's me," Bobbie repeated. "I'm the mission commander. But if you really don't—"

"Oh," Holden said. "No. No, that's different."

Alex said, "Yeah," and Naomi uncrossed her arms. Bobbie relaxed.

"Should have said so in the first place, Chrissy," Amos said.

"Go fuck yourself, Burton. I was getting to it."

"So, Bobbie," Holden said. "How do you want to do this?"

Chapter Four: Salis

Wait wait wait!" Salis shouted into his suit radio. The base of the rail gun was ten meters across, built in a rough hexagon, and massing more than a small ship. At his words, a half dozen construction thrusters along the great beast's side fired off, jetting ejection mass into the void. The calibration meter on Salis' mech cycled down to zero; the hairbreadth movement of the great beast stopped. They floated together—inhumanly large weapon, softly glowing alien station, and Salis in his spiderlike safety-yellow construction mech.

"A que, coyo?" Jakulski, their tech supervisor, asked in his ear.

"Reading drift," Salis said, playing his ranging lasers over the rail gun and the socket mount it was meant to lock into. It had been hard work, fitting the alien station with the three wide belts of ceramic, carbon-silicate lace, and steel. Now it looked like a vast blue ball with rubber bands around it, each at right angles to the other two. And where the lines crossed, rail gun turrets squatted. It had turned out it was impossible to drill into the alien station. Welding didn't work, because the surface wouldn't melt. Wrapping the whole damn thing up had been the only viable alternative for attaching things to it.

"Que mas que?" Jakulski asked.

"Shift one minute ten seconds relative z, minus eight seconds relative y."

"Savvy," Jakulski said. The construction thrusters along the length of the rail gun stuttered, impulse and counterimpulse. All around them, the gates dotted the sky with only a little over thirteen hundred bright spots, barren and empty and threateningly regular. Medina Station itself was the only other object, and it was far enough away that Salis could have covered the whole structure—drum, drive, and command—with his outstretched thumb. The slow zone, they still called it. Even though the weird limit on speed had been lifted, the name was the name, and it carried a sense of strangeness and doom with it. Most of his work was inside Medina. Heading out into the vacuum was a rare thing, and now he was here he didn't like it much. He kept turning away from the job to look out into the black. It had been almost the end of his first week on the job before he realized he was looking for the Milky Way, and that he kept looking because it wasn't there.

"Bist bien?" Jakulski asked.

"Moment," Salis said, checking the ranging lasers again. He glanced up the length of the great barrel while the mech struggled again to get a fix on the thing's skin and the socket. The few rail guns he'd seen before had been made from titanium and ceramic. These new materials Duarte was sending through the Laconia gate were bleeding-edge, though. It wasn't only the iridescence of the carbon-silicate lace plating. The power cores that ran the guns and the frictionless ammunition feeds that supplied them were... strange.

The designs were elegant, sure. But they were just magnetic rails powered by fusion cores same as any ship's. And they did what they needed to do, but there was something off about the way they came together, a sense of being not manufactured so much as tested for. A kind of awkwardness and beauty that made Salis think of plants more than machines. It wasn't only the new materials that went into them. Ever since the ring gate lifted itself off Venus, there had been bits of new one thing and another. It was the scale of it. And maybe something else.

The ranging lasers reported back.

"Bien," Salis said. "Bring the bastard home."

Jakulski didn't reply, but the thrusters fired. Salis kept painting socket and rail gun alike, making manual reading after manual reading. It was the sort of thing he usually left to the mech's system, but the new materials sometimes caused the laser to throw false errors. And it was better to be certain. The station had been still as stone in the years since the gates had opened. Didn't mean ramming a great damned machine into it wouldn't provoke a response.

It took the better part of a shift to bring the massive thing in, but eventually it locked into place. The turret settled, absorbed what little momentum was left in it. The socket closed around it, leaving Salis with the uncomfortable image of gigantic lips closing very slowly around a huge straw.

"Pulling back," Salis said.

"Clar à test, you?"

"Moment," Salis said, pushing off from the station. He floated out into the emptiness to where Roberts and Vandercaust waited, strapped into their own mechs. The mech's attitude thruster brought him to a relative stop at their side and turned him back to look at their work. On the group channel, Roberts grunted.

"Víse ca bácter," she said. It was true enough. With the guns strapped at the top and bottom of all three axes, the station *did* look a little like something seen through a microscope. A macrovirus, maybe. Or a minimalist streptococcus.

"In place," Salis said. "Clar à test."

"Three," Jakulski said, "two, *one*."

The rail gun beneath them shifted in its socket like something waking from sleep. For a moment, it seemed to drift like a reed caught in a current of aether. Then it snapped into place, jittering from one position to the next too quickly for Salis' eyes to see the motion between, faster than the twitch of an insect's leg. It cycled through, taking aim on each of the gates in its field of vision. With the layout they had, at least two of the guns would be able to sight every gate, and most gates fell in the arc of three. Salis had seen pictures of old fortifications overlooking the sea back on Earth. They'd never made sense to him before—too flat to apply to his own experience—but this was the same thing. The high guns that would protect Medina Station from invading ships forever. He felt some emotion stirring in his chest, and it could have been pride or dread.

"Bien," Jakulski said. He sounded almost surprised. Like he'd expected the gun to rip itself loose and spin out into the nothing sky. "Pull back for live fire."

"Pulling back, us," Vandercaust said. "Don't put a round through us, sa sa?"

"I do, and you let me know, eh?" Jakulski laughed. Easy for him. Not like he was out here. And then, not like the guns couldn't turn Medina to chaff too. Salis and the others pulled back fifty klicks, flipped, and decelerated for another fifty. The darkness was unnerving. Back on the other side of the gate, it was never this dark. There was always the sun and the stars.

"Stopped and stable," Roberts said. "Hast du dui painted friendly?"

"Do. It shoots you, that'll mean something's wrong. Setting target," Jakulski said, and Salis upped the magnification on his mech. There, in false-color readout, was the alien station. This far out, he could see three of the six guns. "Sensor arrays bist bien. Firing in three, two, one ..."

A puff of vapor spat out the tip of the gun—charged gas making a brief extension to the barrel and putting a little more speed into the round. Salis' mech shuddered, the magnetic spill from the rails affecting his systems even this far out. He didn't see the rounds the rail gun fired. In the time it took for the harsh feed-back tick to go from his radio to his ear, the tungsten slug was already through the target gate. Or out into the weird non-space between them. In the false-color display, a ripple passed through the alien station like what he'd see in a sphere of floating water when one part of it got touched. The ripple died out before it even circled the station once.

"La que vist?" Jakulski asked.

"Nothing," Salis said. "It looks fine. Tu?"

"Station glow only thing," Jakulski said. In all of their tests, the only reaction the station ever had to being pushed by the rail gun shots was a shower of photons.

"Nothing else?"

"Nope."

"Drift?"

"No drift."

It was what they wanted to see. The rail guns were big enough, powerful enough, that even keel-mounted on a ship, firing them would have been difficult. Mounted on turrets like they were, they should have been as much thruster as weapon, driving them-selves away from whatever they were shooting at fast enough that they'd be hard to catch.

Except the station.

Whatever the aliens did to shrug off equal and opposite reac-tions, it only generated enough energy to throw a little light, and it didn't seem to bring any kind of countermeasures against them. Still, Salis wasn't exactly looking forward to heading back and checking the sockets and bases.

"You hear Casil talk?" Vandercaust said. "About why it don't move when we push it?"

"No," said Roberts.

"Said it does, but the ring space moves with it, so we can't see it happening."

"Casil's crazy."

"Sí ai."

"Sending us back in?" Salis asked into his radio.

"Moment," Jakulski said, and then, "Bien. Cleared, you. Keep tus augen wide, anything not right."

Not right meaning cracks in the housings, meaning leakage of the fluid tanks, meaning failures in the reactors or the ammunition feeds.

Meaning the eyes of an ancient god looking at them. Or something worse.

"Savvy," Salis said, checking his thrusters. "Going in."

The three mech drivers shifted and launched themselves back toward the station. Medina floated to his right: the still drive cone, the turning drum. Salis looked out past it like he was searching for a familiar face, but the stars still weren't there.

The internal drum section of Medina Station had a straight-line sun that burned at the center of rotation from the command center all the way down to the engineering decks. The full-spectrum light from it came down on the curved farmland and the wide, bent lake that had once been meant to carry a city of Mormon faithful to the stars. Salis sat in an open-air bar with Vandercaust and Roberts, drinking beer and eating white kibble that tasted of cheese powder and mushroom. Behind and before him, the landscape curved up to lose itself in the sun's bright line. To his left and right, the full length of the drum spinning at about the g of Luna. The gentle breeze that breathed against the back of his neck came from spinward, same as it ever did.

When he'd been a boy, Salis had seen the Big Room caverns on Iapetus. He'd walked under the false skies on Ceres. The drum at Medina was the nearest thing he could imagine to sitting on Earth as it had been before the rocks came down: unregulated atmosphere above him and the thin crust and mantle holding him above the core of molten stone. No matter how many times he came here, it felt exotic.

"Flyers up again," Roberts said, squinting up into the light.

Salis looked up. There, almost silhouetted by the brightness, five bodies floated in the air, arms and legs outstretched. They seemed to be flying from behind Salis, curving up ahead like the fields of soybean and maize, but the truth was they were the bodies at rest. About five months before, some adolescent idiot had figured out how to lay down a temporary track that could accelerate people anti-spinward to match the drum's rotation and let them launch themselves up, weightless in the air. So long as no one got too near the artificial sun or failed to match the drum's acceleration before they came back down, it was supposed to be good fun.

Two streaks of vapor reached out from the engineering decks toward them, and Salis pointed toward them. "Security got them, yeah."

Vandercaust shook his shaggy gray head. "Ton muertas."

"Young and stupid. But it's what the Roman said: Fihi m'fihi," Roberts said. Her voice had more sympathy, but she was also nearer the age of the illegal flyers. "You born stone and sober, que?"

"Born with respect," Vandercaust said. "*My* shit only kills *me*."

Roberts' shrug was a surrender. On ships—real ships—back on the right side of the gates, keeping the environment safe was always the first thing. Double-check what had already been double-checked, clean what was already cleaned. Playing fast and loose was a quick way to die, and your family and crew along with you. There was something about the big stations—Ceres, Hygeia, Ganymede, and now Medina—that gave kids license to be dumb. Reckless.

Stability, Salis thought. Having a room as massive as the drum did something to people's heads. He felt it too; it seemed too big to break. Didn't matter that nothing was really that big. Anything could get broken. *Earth* got broken. Acting like risks weren't risks put all of them in danger.

Even so, there was part of him that was sorry to see the security crew lock down the flyers. Kids being kids. There should be a place for that somewhere. Martians had that. Earthers had that. It was only the Belters who'd spent too many generations dying for their first fuckup to let their kids play sometimes.

He squinted into the brightness. The security and the flyers were heading down to the surface now, foggy trails of their suit thrusters making wide, slow spirals centered on the bright line of sun as they came down.

"Too bad," he said. Vandercaust grunted.

"You hear about the gang showers in F-section?" Roberts said. "Blocked up *again*."

"Alles designed con full g," Vandercaust said. "Same thing with the farms. Fields aren't draining like they should. Spin the drum up the way los Mormons meant, it'd work."

Roberts laughed. "It would, we wouldn't. All smashed flat, us."

"Better to change it," Vandercaust said around a bite of kibble.

"We do enough, it'll work," Salis said. "Ship with this much redundancy? If we can't make it right, we don't deserve it."

He drank the last of his beer and stood, lifting a hand to ask if either of his crewmates wanted another. Vandercaust did. Roberts didn't. Salis stepped across the dirt to the bar. That was part of it, he decided. The plants and the false sun and the breeze that smelled of leaves and rot and fresh growth. Medina's drum was the only place he'd ever lived where he could walk on soil. Not just dirt and dust—those were everywhere—but *soil*. Salis didn't know why that was different, but it was.

The man at the bar swapped out Salis' bulb for a fresh, and a second besides for Vandercaust. When he got back to their table, the conversation had moved on from the flyers to the colonies. Wasn't that big a shift. From people taking stupid risks to people taking stupid risks.

"Aldo says there was another bunch of threats coming out of the Jerusalem gate," Roberts said. "We send their reactor core, or they come get it."

"Surprise them if they do," Vandercaust said, taking the fresh bulb from Salis. "Guns up, and it's past time for alles la."

"Maybe," Roberts said, then coughed. "Maybe we should give it to them, yeah?"

Vandercaust scowled. "For for?"

"They need and we have is all," Roberts said.

Vandercaust made a dismissive wave of his hand. *Who gives a shit what they need?* But something in Roberts' voice caught Salis' attention. Like she'd said more than she'd said. He met her dark eyes and lifted his chin as a question. The words she was trying to say pushed her head forward like a nod.

"Can help if we want. Might as well, sí no? No reason no, since we're not what we were anymore, us," she said. Vandercaust scowled, but Roberts went on. "We did it. Us. Today."

"Que done que, us?" Vandercaust said. His voice was rough, but if Roberts heard it, she didn't stop. Her eyes glittered like she was about to cry. When she spoke, it was like water coming out a snapped pipe. Her voice gushed and pulsed and gushed again.

"Always, it's been when we find place. Ceres o Pallas o the big Lagranges never got built. Mi tía talked about making a station for all Belters alles. Capitol city à te void. It's this. Belters built it. Belters live in it. Belters gave it power. Y because of guns *we* put in, it's ours forever. We made this place home today. Not just our home, ours. *All* of ours. Esá es *homeland* now. Because of us three."

Tears dripped down her cheeks, slow in the sixth g. Joy lit her from inside like a fire, and it left Salis embarrassed. Seeing Roberts like this was like walking in on someone pissing—intimate and wrong. But when he looked away, the drum spread out around them. The plants, the soil, the land above him squinting down at him like a sky.

He'd been on Medina for fifteen months. Longer than he'd ever been on a station in his life. He'd come because Marco Inaros and the Free Navy needed people here. He hadn't thought about what it meant, except he'd known in his gut he was more OPA than the OPA, and that was what Free Navy meant. Now, maybe, he caught a glimpse of what it was behind that. Not a war forever. A place.

"Homeland," he said, speaking carefully. Like the word was made from glass, and could cut him if he said it too hard. "Because the rail guns."

"Because something's ours," Roberts said. "And because now they can't take it away."

Salis felt something in his chest, and he let his mind poke at it. Pride, he decided. It was pride. He tried a smile and turned it to Roberts, who was grinning back. She was right. This was the place. Their place. Whatever else happened, they'd have Medina.

Vandercaust shrugged, took a long pull from his bulb, and belched. "Besse for us," he said. "But here's for that? They ever do take it away, we sure as *shit* never get it back again."

Chapter Five: Pa

I don't trust anything about this," Michio Pa said.

Josep yawned and propped himself up on one elbow, looking down at her. He was a beautiful man in a slightly ruined way. He wore his hair longer than a crew cut, shorter than his shoulders. The gray in it still only a highlight in the black. Decades had roughened his skin, and the ink there told the story of his life: the neck tattoo of the OPA's split circle that had been covered over later to make the upraised fist of a radical collective long since collapsed. The elaborate cross on his shoulder, inscribed in a moment of faith and kept after that faith had crumbled. Phrases written along his wrists and down his side—*No more water, the fire next time* and *To love someone is to see them as God intended them* and *Ölüm y chuma pas pas fóvos*—spoke of the various men he had been in his life. His incarnations. That was part of why Pa felt so close to him. She was younger than him by almost a decade, but she'd been through incarnations too.

"Which 'this'?" he asked. "There's so many things not to trust."

"Inaros calling in the clans," she said, rolling over and gathering a blanket with her as she did. It wasn't that she was uncomfortable naked, only now that their coupling was done, she was ready to go back to their more formal roles. Or something closer to them. Josep noted it and without comment went from being one of her husbands to her chief engineer. He crossed his arms and leaned against the wall.

"Is it the meeting or the man?" he asked.

"Any of it," she said. "Something's not right."

"You say it, and I believe."

"I know. This is the part where I always do this. The coyo in charge changes the plan and I start looking for them to be the next Ashford. The next Fred fucking Johnson. It's my pattern."

"Is. Doesn't mean your pattern doesn't match. What's in your head?"

Pa leaned forward, chewing her lip. She could feel the thoughts bumping around like blind fish, searching for the words that would give them form. Josep waited.

By the terms of their ketubah, the marriage group was seven people: her and Josep, Nadia, Bertold, Laura, Evans, and Oksana. They had all kept their own surnames, and they made the *Connaught*'s permanent crew. The others who served under her came and went, respected that she was captain, that her orders were fair, and that she didn't show any overt favoritism to her spouses, but there was the understanding always that the core of the ship was her family, and no threat to it would be tolerated. The idea of separating family from crew was an inner-planets thing, one example of the unconscious prejudice that made Earthers and Martians treat life aboard ships as somehow different from real life.

For them, the rules changed when the airlock closed, even if they didn't know themselves well enough to see it. For Belters, there was no division. The Doctrine of the One Ship, she'd heard it called. That there was only one ship, and it had countless parts as a single body had countless cells. The *Connaught* was one part, as were all the ragtag ships under her command: *Panshin*, *Solano*, *Witch of Endor*, *Serrio Mal*, and a dozen more. And her fleet was only part of the Free Navy: a vast organism that passed information between its cells with tightbeam and radio, that consumed food and fuel, that worked its own slow destiny among the planets like a massive fish in the greater sea of the sky.

By some interpretations, even the Earther and Martian ships were part of the same one-ship, but for her, that always ran into conversations about cancers and autoimmune disorders, and the metaphor failed.

Still, there was a reason she was thinking of it now.

"We aren't coordinated," she said, trying out the words as she said them. "When you push off with a foot, you reach out with a hand. One movement. We aren't like that. Inaros and military. Sanjrani and the finances. Rosenfeld and his production and design. Us. We're not the same thing yet."

"We're new at this," Josep said. The words could have been a refutation, a way to explain away her unease. From him, it was an offering. Something to react to that would help her mind come clearer.

"Maybe," she said. "Hard to say. May be we're supposed to be puppets and the strings all run to the *Pella*. Himself changes his mind, and we all jump."

Josep shrugged, his warm eyes narrow. "He's delivered. Ships, fuel, ammunition, drives. Freedom. He's done what he said he'd do." She could feel the gentle provocation in his words, and it was what she needed.

"He's done what he says he said. His real record's not so good. Johnson's alive. Smith's alive. Ganymede's only gone neutral. We're still throwing rocks at Earth and no surrender's coming from them anytime soon. Go back and look at everything he promised, and it's not what's on the plate."

"Politicians since immer and always, that. Still more than anyone else has done for the Belt. Inners are on their heels now. And with the *Hornblower* and ships like her, we'll have stockpiles to last years. That's our part. Keep everyone with food and air and supplies. Give us a chance to make the Belt without a boot on our necks."

Pa sighed and scratched her knee—her nails against her skin with sound as soft and dry as sand. The air recycler clicked and hummed. The drive that pressed them both down toward the deck throbbed.

"Yeah," she said.

"But?"

"But," she said, and left it at that. Her unease didn't find any further words that fit. Maybe they'd come in time or maybe she'd come to peace without having to speak them.

Josep shifted his weight and nodded toward the crash couch. "You want me to stay?"

Pa considered. It might have been a kindness to say yes, but the truth was whoever she shared her body with, she slept better alone. Josep's smile meant he'd heard her answer anyway. It was part of what she loved about him. He stepped forward, kissed her on the forehead where her hairline met the skin, and started pulling on his jumpsuit. "Tea, maybe?"

"I don't think so," she said.

"You should," Josep said. It was more than he usually did.

"All right." She shrugged off the blanket, cleaned up, and put her own clothes on too. When they stepped out into the Martian gunship's galley, she leaned against him. None of the other crew were there, after all. Just Oksana and Laura finishing bowls of mushroom and sauce. Just family. Josep angled toward a different bench, and she let him set them a little apart from their wives. Oksana laughed at something. Laura said something acid and cutting, but she said it without any heat. Pa didn't catch the words.

Josep pulled bulbs of tea for them both and then sat in companionable silence. She sipped, and the astringent bite of the tea mixed with the aftermath of sex to settle her without her even knowing she'd been unsettled. When she sighed, Josep raised his eyebrows.

"Yes," Pa said. "You're very smart. This is what I wanted."

He sketched a bow, and then sobered. "Thinking about what you said? About coordinated?"

"Don't worry," she said, but he went on.

"You've been betrayed by men who were supposed to be your leaders. Johnson when we were OPA. Ashford on the *Behemoth*. Okulski with the union. We went independent *because*, yeah? Only now we're not independent. Now we're Free Navy, because Inaros convinced us to. Not just you. *Us*."

"You're right," Pa said. "I'm probably just pushing back on what already happened. I should let go of it."

"Shouldn't let go of being educated," he said. "Universe spent a lot of time telling you something. Now you're second-guessing it. Maybe all those other things were getting you ready for this."

Something in Pa's chest slipped a little tighter. "You don't trust him either."

"Me? You don't want to judge anything by me. I don't even trust God."

"You are absolutely the worst mystic ever," Pa said, but she said it laughing.

"I know," Josep said, shaking his head. "Sad failure of a prophet, me. But"—he lifted a finger—"I know you. And I know you're the kind that likes to pretend she doesn't know things she knows so that there won't be friction. So if you're thinking maybe you're wrong so things are okay, you better check again, make sure things are okay. The universe needs a knife, then it makes a knife. And no one sharper, you."

"And if it turns out the universe is just a bunch of chemicals and energy bashing against each other until the light runs out?"

"Then pattern-matching's still a good way to not get bashed," he said. "You tell me if Himself matches the pattern. You've seen more than I have."

"Doubt that," she said, but she took his hand. He held hers. After a moment, Laura came over to sit with them, and then Oksana. The talk turned to less dangerous subjects—all the ways

Martian design was worse than Belter, the latest news from *Witch of Endor*'s capture of yet another colony ship, Carmondy's report from the overhaul of the *Hornblower*. The business of running the *Connaught*. But the little knot sat just under her ribs, reminding her that something was wrong.

When she went back to her cabin, she went alone. She fell into the crash couch, pulled the blanket over her head, and dreamed of a huge, fragile creature swimming through the currents of the deep ocean, only the sea was made of stars, and the animal was built from ships, and one of them was hers.

Nothing as big as a revolution can survive with only one account of it. The rise of Ceres Station—or its fall, according to the inners—was the precursor to Marco Inaros and the Free Navy. Looking back, the death of a water hauler seemed a pathetically small thing to have set Earth and Mars against each other, even for just a little time, but it had been enough. With the traditional oppressors of the Belt pointing guns at each other for a change, the OPA had stepped in, taken control of the port city of the asteroid belt.

No one back then had expected it to last. Sooner or later, Mars and Earth would get their feet back under them, and then Ceres would fall. Anderson Dawes, the de facto governor of the station, would lose the power he'd grabbed and either move on to some new scheme or live on in spirit, a martyr to the cause. Every autonomous space was temporary.

Only the fall never came.

The collapse of Ganymede and the exposure of the Mao-Kwikowski protomolecule program captured the attention of the powers that be. Then Venus hatched out the great and mysterious structures that made the first gate. By the time the *Behemoth* accompanied the combined forces of Earth and Mars to explore the gate and consider its vast and complex implications, Anderson Dawes had woven a web of relationships. Corporations on Luna and Mars, the Lagrange stations, the Belt, the Jovian moons—none of them could allow trade to stop for the years it might take to reconquer the port. In the way of humankind since before the first contract was pressed into Sumerian clay, the temporary accommodations lasted long enough to become invisible.

And when the gates *beyond* the gate opened and the flood of humanity lurched out toward the new planets and suns, there were powers and money with interests in keeping Ceres as it was. And Anderson Dawes had known which palms to grease and when to compromise in order to keep the port's traffic flowing uninterrupted.

Through long, careful management the great negotiator had outlasted his status as a rebel and become instead a politician. Dawes became respectable, and Ceres Station became first city of the Belters just in time for it not to matter.

And then the Free Navy had come and kicked the whole carefully built sandcastle into the waves. And Dawes, like any politician, had considered the players and the powers, the chances and the certainties. The story of the rise of Ceres Station, instead of a triumph of opportunism and political deftness, became the precursor of the Free Navy. Dawes embraced this new version of himself and his station. He'd chosen his side, just the same as she'd done.

He stood in the dock now, waiting for her to cross over from the *Connaught*. The spin gravity of the station locked her ship in its clamps. Even if the power failed, momentum would keep the ships from dropping out into the black. Pa still didn't like leaving her ship behind. It felt like an unnecessary risk.

"Michio," Dawes said, taking her by the hand and beaming. "It's good to see you in the flesh."

"You too," she said. It wasn't true. Dawes had spent too many years allied too closely with Fred Johnson to ever have the stink entirely washed away. But he was a necessary evil, and on good days probably did more to help the Belt than to compromise it. He gestured toward an electric cart with two police guards in light armor.

"Am I under arrest?" Pa asked, keeping her voice light and amused.

Dawes chuckled as they walked. "Ever since the rocks fell, the security's been tighter," he said. His acne-scarred cheeks tightened and a darkness came into his expression. "There are millions of people living on Ceres. Not all of them are comfortable with all that's happened."

"Have there been problems?" Pa asked as they reached the cart.

"There are always problems," Dawes said, then after a brief hesitation, "but there have been more of them."

The cart lurched, turned toward a wide ramp leading up into the station. The mildly adhesive wheels made a sound between a hiss and crackling as they rolled away from the docks. Pa looked back toward the *Connaught*'s berth. Maybe she should have brought guards of her own with her. Carmondy's men were still all back on the *Hornblower*, but Bertold and Nadia were both combat trained. Too late now.

The administration levels were out nearest the skin of the station where the Coriolis was least pronounced. The old tunnels and corridors had been redone since the OPA claimed the station, but there was still a sense of age. Dawes made small, inane conversation intended to put her at ease, and his skill was such that it worked. If they were really talking about which restaurants made the best sausage and black sauce and what had happened when a religious convocation was booked in the same halls as a raï music festival, the situation couldn't be that dangerous. She knew it was an illusion, but she appreciated it all the same. Neither of them mentioned the reason they were there. Inaros' name didn't come up.

The meeting itself was in a garden in the administrative level. A wide, arching ceiling glowed with full-spectrum light. Devil's ivy draped columns and walls, and wide ferns spread massive fronds like herons about to take flight. The air smelled of hydroponic plant food and wine. She heard Sanjrani's high, reedy voice before she turned the corner. *Without a solid inventory of the fer-*

tilizer base on every station, a nitrogen-based currency is going to be swamped by illegal inputs. Another variation on his constant theme. It was almost good to hear it again. Dawes touched her elbow, gestured down a path between a small fountain and a spiral fern, and then they were there. The five leaders of the Free Navy. Nico Sanjrani, looking more like a middle-aged shopkeeper than the chief economist of a budding empire. Rosenfeld Guoliang, with his dark, pebbled skin and his too-ready smile, general of the second fleet and industrial czar. And sitting in a chair of woven cane, Marco Inaros, the man behind it all.

Victory suited him. His hair flowed down to his shoulders, and he held his body with an animal ease. When he rose to greet her and Dawes, she felt an echo of his pleasure in her own heart. Whatever else the man was, he had a charm that could coax the venom out of snakes. It was, she presumed, the gift that had put him in position to trade with the Martians for their ships, their munitions, all the material that allowed them to stage their revolution. The only other person there was Inaros' skinny, crazy-eyed son, Filip. Pa made a point of not looking too closely at the boy. There was something about him that bothered her, and it was easier to stay aloof than to engage.

"The brilliant Michio Pa!" Marco said. "Excellent! We're all here now. The founders of our nation."

"Do you have stats on the new acquisitions?" Sanjrani asked, either unaware that he was stepping on Marco's moment or at least unconcerned. "I need to get a complete accounting."

"Carmondy's working on that," Pa said.

"Soon, though."

"Nico, my boy," Rosenfeld said. "Don't be an ass. Say hello to Captain Pa first."

Sanjrani scowled at Rosenfeld and then at Inaros, and finally turned back toward her and nodded curtly. "Hello."

"Now that the inner circle's all here," Dawes said, "perhaps we could hear what's brought us all together? Not that being in one room isn't a pleasure in itself, but…"

Marco smiled as his son, behind him, fidgeted with the holster of his pistol. "We've broken Earth and beaten Mars. Johnson's OPA is shown up as the collaborationist sham that it was. Everything we set out to do, we've done. It's time to begin the third phase."

Everything we set out to do except kill Smith and Fred Johnson, Pa thought but didn't say. The silence from the others wasn't about that, though.

When Dawes spoke, his voice was carefully light and conversational. "I didn't know you had a third phase in mind."

Marco's grin could have been anger or pleasure, rage or satisfaction. "Now you do," he said.

Chapter Six: Holden

I feel like we should be whispering," Holden said. "Going around on tiptoes."

"We're on the float," Naomi said.

"Metaphorical tiptoes."

The ops deck was dark apart from the backsplash glow of their monitors. Alex was sleeping in his cabin, leaving the monitoring to Holden and Naomi. Last he'd seen them, Bobbie and Amos were touring the ship, testing everything but the comms—PDCs, thrusters, the keel-mounted rail gun, the environmental systems. Ever since the mission had begun, Bobbie had been careful not to make Holden feel like she was taking over the ship, but her deference didn't extend so far that she wouldn't refamiliarize herself with every centimeter of the *Roci* before the fighting started. Even if it was just running through how Amos had rerouted the water feeds to the galley, watching the two of them always felt like listening to a conversation about weapons. The serious, professional talk between people who understood that they were working with equipment that could get people killed. It left him feeling like he'd been a little too casual about the ship up to now.

Clarissa…he didn't know where Clarissa was. Ever since the last hard burn, he'd only caught fleeting glimpses of her, like she was a spirit they'd picked up that couldn't bear being seen straight on. Most of what he heard about her—that she was building up her strength, that her black market implants were making her less nauseated, that she'd tracked down the bad coupler that was making the machine shop lights dim—he heard from the others in the crew. He didn't like it, but at least he didn't have to talk to her.

The plan was simple. The *Azure Dragon* wasn't a gunship, but a geological surveyor. The protection she had was that space was vast, the ship was small, and her orbit kept her far enough away from Earth and Luna that she could burn hard back out to the Belt or the Jovian moons if anyone started coming for her. All of her active systems—transponder, radar, ladar, radio—were shut down to keep her from announcing herself. She couldn't stop the light from bouncing off her hull, and she couldn't hide her waste heat, but she could run as quietly as possible. It limited her to passive sensors and tightbeam. Enough for her to do the work of coordinating the stones thrown at Earth, but still half-blind.

And that was what Bobbie was counting on.

They'd laid in a course that would put them close to the *Azure Dragon*, then arranged for a shifting of the combined fleet that would hide the flare of their burn. It was a balance of getting to the enemy quickly but not being able to make the classic halfway-point flip-and-burn. They only built up enough velocity that they could shed it when they got close, and then the *Roci* went dark and drifted. With no active sensors, the *Azure Dragon* would have to see them visually—a tiny point in the vastness— and identify them as a threat without radar or ladar.

And they would, eventually. But by then, if it all went the way Bobbie intended, it wouldn't make a difference.

It was a slower approach than Holden remembered making to anything in all the time they'd had the *Roci*, and it left him antsy and impatient.

The voices came from the lift: Bobbie serious, sharp, and professional; Amos cheerful and amiable. They floated up into the deck, first Bobbie and then Amos. Bobbie grabbed a handhold and pulled herself to a stop. Amos tapped the deck with his ankle as he passed it and killed his own momentum by planting his feet on the ceiling and absorbing it with his knees. He floated upside down. The *Roci* usually ran at less than full g to conserve reaction mass and for Naomi's benefit, but they almost always had a consistent down. Going totally on the float was weird.

"How's it going?" Bobbie asked.

Holden gestured at his screen. "Nothing new. It doesn't look like they've noticed us yet."

"Their reactors are still down?"

"The heat signature's just sitting there."

Bobbie pressed her lips together and nodded. "That's not going to last much longer."

"We could shoot 'em," Amos said. "It ain't my call, but in my experience the guy that throws the first punch usually wins."

"Show me the estimated range," Bobbie said. Holden pulled up the passive sensor array. At roughly five million klicks out, the *Azure Dragon* was about ten times as far from them as Luna was from Earth. It probably wouldn't crew more than a dozen people. In the infinite star field, it would have been invisible to the naked eye. Even if the enemy had been on a full burn, the exhaust plume would have only been one point of light among billions. "How accurate is that?"

"I'm not sure," Holden said. "Normally we'd be using ladar."

"Give it ten percent either way," Naomi said. "At this range and scale, passive sampling errors expand pretty fast."

"But with the ladar?" Bobbie asked.

"Within a meter," Naomi said.

"You ever think about how much ammo's flying around out

there?" Amos said, reaching up to brush the floor with outstretched fingers. The contact started him drifting almost imperceptibly toward the ceiling and at the same time rotating back toward consensus upright. "Figure all those PDC rounds that didn't actually hit something; most of the rail-gun rounds, whether they went through a ship or not. All out there someplace going at the same speed as when they left the barrel."

"If we shoot them, they'll still look for who did it," Naomi said.

"Might not," Amos said.

Naomi looked at Bobbie. "We're going to have to start a braking burn soon or we'll skin right past them."

"How long?" Bobbie asked.

"Three hours," Naomi said. "Anything more than that, and we'll need to go on the juice or risk the deceleration g popping a bunch of blood vessels we'd rather keep whole."

Bobbie tapped the tips of her right middle finger and thumb together in a rapid stutter. When she nodded, it was more to herself than to them. "Screw this. I'm tired of waiting. I'll go wake Alex up. Let's get it over with."

"All right, boys and girls," Alex drawled. "Everybody strapped in and ready?"

"Check," Holden said on the open channel, and then listened as the others reported in. Including Clarissa Mao. It was an illusion built from anticipation, but Holden felt like the lights were a little brighter, as if after weeks in dock, the *Roci* was excited to be doing something important too.

"Reactor's good," Amos reported from the machine deck.

Alex cleared his throat. "All right. We're good to go in ten... nine..."

"She's seen us," Naomi said. "I've got action from her maneuvering thrusters."

"Fine, then. Three-two-one," Alex said, and Holden fell back into his crash couch hard. The gel pressed in around him, and the ship rumbled the deep bass of the drive as it spilled off speed. To the *Azure Dragon*, it would be like a bright new star had appeared. A supernova light-years away. Or something less dangerous but much, much closer.

"Ladar's up," Naomi said. "And...I've got lock."

"Is their reactor up?" Holden asked, at the same time that Bobbie said, "Give me fire control."

Naomi answered both. "Their drive's cycling up. We probably have half a minute. You have control, Bobbie."

"Holden," Bobbie snapped, "please ring the doorbell. Alex, surrender maneuvering to fire control."

"Done," Alex said.

Holden switched on the tightbeam. The *Roci* found a lock at once. "*Azure Dragon*, this is the *Rocinante*. You may have heard of us. We are on approach. Surrender—"

Thrust gravity cut out and their crash couches hissed as the ship spun on two axes.

"Surrender at once and prepare for boarding."

Naomi's voice was calm and focused. "Enemy reactor is coming up."

The ship seemed to trip, throwing Holden and Naomi up against their straps. The keel-mounted rail gun pushed the whole ship backward in a solid mathematical relationship to the mass of the two-kilo tungsten round moving at a measurable fraction of c. Newton's third law expressed as violence. Holden's gut knotted and he tried to lean forward. The long seconds dragged.

Naomi made a small, satisfied sound in the back of her throat. "Okay, their reactor's shutting down. They're dumping core. We're not seeing nitrogen in the plume. I don't think they've lost air."

"Nice shooting," Amos said on the open channel.

"God damn," Bobbie said as the *Roci* shifted back. "I have missed the hell out of this."

Thrust gravity returned, pushing Holden back as they slowed toward the drifting science ship. It was harder now—a solid two g he could feel in his jaw and the base of his skull.

"Please respond, *Azure Dragon*, or we'll shoot you some more," he said.

"This doesn't feel right," Naomi said.

"They started it," Alex said from above them in the pilot's deck. "Every rock that dropped, they had a part in."

Holden wasn't sure that was what she'd meant, but Naomi didn't press it, so maybe it had been. "Not getting any response, Bobbie," he said. "How do you want to play it?"

In answer, the former Martian marine climbed down from the gunner's station, hand over hand in the high gravity. The muscles in her arms were like cords of wire, and her grimace said both that the sheer effort hurt and that she kind of liked it. "Let them know that if they open up on us, they won't get crash couches on the way to jail," she said, passing down toward the airlock. "I'm just going to slip into something more comfortable."

The crash couches shifted a little as Alex bent their trajectory so they wouldn't melt the *Azure Dragon* to slag in their drive plume. Bobbie grunted and took a new grip on the handholds.

"You know there's a lift, right?" Holden said.

"Where's the fun in that?" Bobbie said as she sank out of sight.

Naomi shifted against the high gravity so that he could see her face. Her smile was complex—discomfort and pleasure and something that looked like foreboding. "So that's what she looks like when she takes herself off the leash."

Shedding the last of their velocity and matching orbit wasn't fast. Holden listened with half an ear while Alex, Amos, and Naomi coordinated with the *Roci*'s systems to bring them alongside. Bobbie chimed in now and again when she wasn't putting her powered armor together and running through its system checks. The greater part of his attention stayed on the enemy. The *Azure Dragon* floated in silence. An expanding cloud of radioactive gas that had been its fusion core slowly dissipated behind it until it was hardly denser than the surrounding vacuum. No emergency beacon. No announcement of defiance or surrender. No response to his pings and queries. The silence was creepy.

"I don't think we killed them," Holden said. "We probably didn't kill them, did we?"

"Doesn't seem likely," Naomi said, "but I suppose we'll find out. Worst case, we did, and it still makes it easier to keep the rocks from dropping on Earth."

Something in the tone of her voice caught him. Her eyes were on her monitor, but she didn't seem focused. Her mind a million kilometers away.

"Are you all right?"

Naomi blinked, shook her head like she was trying to clear it, and put on a smile that was only a little bit forced. "It's just strange being out here again. And I can't help wondering whether I know anyone on that ship. It's not something I thought about much before."

"Things have changed," Holden said.

"Yeah, you used to be the one with the high profile," she said, and her smile became a degree less forced. "Now I'm the one all the best interrogators want to sit down with."

Alex announced that he had positive lock on the *Azure Dragon*'s airlock. Override was coming. Bobbie acknowledged it, said she was prepped for boarding action. She'd be back when the enemy was cleared. It all sounded very military, very Martian. There was an excitement in their voices. Some of it was their fear dressing up in party clothes, but some of it wasn't. For the first time that he could remember, Holden found himself imagining how it would sound in Naomi's ears. Her friends preparing themselves to attack and possibly kill people who'd grown up the way she had. The way that no one else on the *Rocinante* would ever totally understand.

They'd worked on all sides of the confused mess that humanity had made of the Belt and the scattering of colonies beyond it. They'd fought pirates for the OPA. Taken contracts with Earth and Mars and private concerns with their own agendas. Thinking of Naomi now, not only as herself but also as the product of the life she'd lived—the life she was still bringing herself to reveal to him—changed how he saw everything. Even himself.

"We had to stop them," he said.

She turned to him, confusion in her eyes. "Who? These assholes? Of course we did." A deep clanking sound ran through the ship as the airlocks connected. An alert popped up on Holden's screen, but he ignored it. Naomi tilted her head as if Holden was a puzzle she hadn't quite figured out. "Did you think I felt bad for *them*?"

"No," Holden said. "Or yes, but not exactly. Everyone on that ship thinks they're doing the right thing too. When they're throwing rocks at Earth, it's to . . . to protect kids on ships that had to run with too little air or bad filters. Or people who lost their ships because the UN changed the tariff laws."

"Or because they think it's fun to kill people," Naomi said. "Don't romanticize them just because *some* of the justifications they use are—"

A second clank came, deeper than the first. Naomi's eyes widened at the same moment Holden felt his gut tighten. It wasn't a good sound.

"Alex? What was that?"

"I think we got us a little problem, folks."

"I'm all right," Bobbie said, and the way she said it made it clear that it was a live issue.

Naomi turned to her monitor, lips pressed thin and tight. "What've we got, Alex?"

"Booby trap," Alex said. "Looks like some kind of magnetic lock from their end. Froze up the works. And Bobbie—"

"I'm stuck between their outer lock and ours," Bobbie said. "I'm fine. I'm just going to bust my way through and—"

"No," Naomi said as Holden's attention flicked to the alert still flashing on his own monitor. "If it's really bound, you could break both locks. Just sit tight, and let me see what we can do to get you unstuck."

"Hey," Holden said. "Anyone know why we just lost a sensor array?" Another alert popped up on his screen. Raw alarm started sounding in his head. "Or that PDC?"

The others were silent for a moment, and then for what felt like hours and was probably five or six seconds, there was only the tap of fingertips on control panels and the chirp of the *Rocinante* reporting back to queries. Even before he had confirmation, he was sure of the answer. The external camera swept the *Roci*'s skin. The *Azure Dragon*, hugged against her, felt like a parasite more than a prisoner. And then a flicker of sparks and a flash of safety yellow. Holden shifted the camera. Three spiderlike construction mechs squatted midway down the *Roci*'s side, welding torches lit and clawing at the hull.

"They're stripping us," Holden said.

When Alex spoke, his false politeness didn't cover his rage. "I can put on a little burn if you want. Drop them into our drive plume and be done—"

"You'll fold the airlocks together," Holden said, cutting him off. "It'll crush Bobbie to death."

"Yeah," Alex said. "All right. So that's a bad idea."

Holden took control of a PDC and tried to shift its arc far enough down to catch one of the mechs, but they were too close in. A fresh alert popped up. A hardened power conduit was throwing off errors. They were digging deeper into the hull. It wouldn't be long before they could do some real damage. And if they managed to burrow their way between the hulls...

"What happens if Bobbie breaks the docking tube?" Holden snapped.

"Best case, we can't use it until we get it repaired," Naomi said. "Worst, they rigged their coupling with a secondary trap that kills Bobbie and spills out our air."

"It's all right," Bobbie said. "I can take the risk. Just give me a second to position—"

"No," Holden said. "No, wait. We can find a way out. No one dies. We've got time."

But they didn't have much. A welding torch flared again. When Amos spoke, his voice sounded wrong. Too small, too close. "You know, Cap, we've got another airlock. Cargo bay's right down here by the machine shop."

The penny dropped. Amos sounded different because he was already wearing a vac suit. He was talking through a helmet mic.

"What are you thinking, Amos?"

"Nothing real subtle. Figure we hop outside, kill a few assholes that need killing, patch stuff up when we're done with the first part."

Naomi caught his eye and nodded once. Years together and an uncountable list of crises weathered made a kind of telepathy between them. Naomi would stay and get Bobbie safely out of the trap. Holden would go out with Amos and keep the enemy at bay.

"All right," Holden said, reaching for his restraints. "Prep a suit. I'm on my way down."

"I'll leave you one," Amos said, "but I think we'll get a head start without you."

"Wait," Holden said. "We?"

"We're cycling out now," Clarissa Mao said. "Wish us luck."

Chapter Seven: Clarissa

Her second year in prison, Clarissa had agreed to participate in a poetry course that the prison chaplain had put together. She hadn't had much hope for anything to come out of it, but it was half an hour every week she could sit in a gray-green room with steel chairs bolted to the floor and half a dozen of her fellow inmates and do something that wasn't watching censored entertainment feeds or sleeping.

It had been a disaster from the start.

Of the men and women who came there each week, only she and the chaplain had been to university. Two of the women were so dosed with antipsychotics that they were barely present at all. One of the men—a serial rapist who'd killed his stepdaughters by torturing them with a chemical stun spray until they stopped breathing—was so taken with a section of Pope's *Essay on Man* that he'd compose hour-long epics in rhyming couplets that didn't quite scan. His favorite subjects were the injustice of a legal system that didn't allow enough for character and his own sexual prowess. And there was a round-faced boy who seemed too young to have done anything deserving a life in the hole who wrote sonnets about gardens and sunlight that were more painful than any of the rest, though for different reasons.

Clarissa's own contributions had been minimal at first. She'd tried some free verse about the possibility of redemption, but she'd read Carlos Pinnani and Anneke Swinehart and HD at her literature tutor's insistence, so she knew her work wasn't good. Worse, she knew why it wasn't good: She didn't really believe her thesis. On the few occasions she considered shifting to a different subject—fathers, regret, grief—it seemed less like catharsis and more like strict reportage. Her life had been squandered, and whether she said it in pentameter or not didn't seem to matter much.

She quit because of the nightmares. She didn't talk about those to anyone, but the medics knew. She might be able to keep the exact content of the dreams to herself, but the medical monitor logged her heartbeats and the activity in the various parts of her brain. The poetry made them come more often and more vividly. Usually, they were of her digging through something repulsive— shit or rotting meat or something—trying to reach someone buried in it before they ran out of air. When she stopped attending, they faded back. Once a week, say, instead of nightly.

Which wasn't to say that the course hadn't borne fruit. Three weeks after she'd told the chaplain that she didn't want to be part of his little study anymore, she'd woken up in the middle of the night fully rested and alert and calm with a sentence in her head as clear as if she'd just heard it spoken. *I have killed, but I am not a killer because a killer is a monster, and monsters aren't afraid.* She'd never spoken the words aloud. Never written them down. They'd become her words of power, a private prayer too sacred to give form. She went back to them when she needed them.

I have killed, but I am not a killer...

"We're cycling out now," she said, her mouth dry and sticky, her heart fluttering in her chest.

...because a killer is a monster...

"Wish us luck."

...and monsters aren't afraid. She cut the transmission, hoisted the recoilless rifle, and nodded to Amos. His grin, half hidden by the curve of his helmet, was boyish and calm. The outer door of the airlock slid soundlessly open on an abyss filled with starlight. Amos took the edge of the airlock, hauling himself forward and then ducking back in case someone was there waiting to shoot. When no one did, he grabbed a handhold and swung himself out, spinning so that the suit's mag boots would land on the ship's skin. She followed less gracefully. And less certain of herself.

The body of the *Rocinante* under her feet, she looked back at the drive cone. The hull of the ship was smooth and hard, studded here and there with blocky PDC mounts, the clustered mouths of thrusters, the black and deep-sighted eyes of sensor arrays. She held her rifle at the ready, finger near the trigger, but not on it the way that the Martian marine had shown her. Trigger discipline, she'd called it. Clarissa wished that she was the one trapped in the airlock and Bobbie Draper could be here instead.

"Moving forward, Peaches. You watch our six."

"Understood," she said, and started walking slowly backward, her boots grabbing to the ship and then letting go only to grab hold again. It felt like the ship itself was trying to keep her from spinning away into the stars. No enemies popped up as they moved around the curve of the ship, but to her right, the body of the *Azure Dragon* appeared like a whale rising up from the deep. It was so close to the *Roci*, she could have turned off her boots and jumped to it. The light of the sun streaming up from below threw harsh shadows across a hull scarred and flaking in places where too many years of hard radiation had scoured the coatings into a white, fragile glaze. It made the *Roci* seem solid and new

by comparison. Something flickered behind her, throwing her
shadow and Amos' out before her. She took a slow, stuttering
breath. Nothing had attacked them yet.

They were the attackers.

"Well, shit," Amos said, and at once, Naomi's voice was on the
common channel.

"What are you seeing, Amos?"

A small window appeared in the corner of Clarissa's helmet,
the HUD showing the stretch of hull behind her. The three bright
yellow spiders stood in a cloud of sparks. Two were braced against
the hull, ready to haul back a section of ceramic and steel, while
the third cut it free.

"All right," Naomi said. "They're going to get between the
hulls."

"Not if me and Peaches have anything to say about it. Right,
Peaches?"

"Right," Clarissa said, and turned to see the enemy with her
own eyes. The brightness of the welding torch forced her helmet
to dim, protecting her eyes. It was like the three mechs stayed the
same, and the stars all around them winked out. There was nothing left but the people who wanted to hurt her and Amos and the
darkness.

"You ready?" Amos asked.

"Does it matter?"

"Not a lot. Let's see what we can do before they notice."

Clarissa crouched close to the hull, lifted her rifle, sighted
down it. With the magnification on, she could see the human form
cradled in the mech—arms, legs, head encased in a suit not so different from her own. She dropped the bright red dot of the sight
on the helmet, put her finger on the trigger, and squeezed. The
helmet jerked back, like it was startled, and the remaining two
mechs turned and pointed yellow steel legs at them.

"Get moving!" Amos shouted as he jumped into the black sky.
Clarissa turned off her mag boots and leaped after him, almost
too late. A white line appeared on the hull where she'd been, the

bullet gone off behind them before her suit could even warn her it was coming. The suit thrusters kicked on, driving her out and shifting her unpredictably as it avoided the string of bullets she couldn't see except as lines in her HUD.

"Keep 'em busy, Peaches," Amos said. "I'll be right back."

He shot off, angling forward and around the body of the *Azure Dragon*. Clarissa turned, letting the suit push her in the opposite direction, putting the horizon of the *Rocinante* between her and the mechs. Her heart sounded like a ticking in her ears; her body shook. The red dot found the welding mech, and she pulled the trigger, missing with the first round. The second struck, and the mech rocked a little under the unexpected thrust of escaping volatile gas. Her suit threw up an alert, and she thought it was malfunctioning until she looked at her leg and saw the blood there. She'd been shot. It was like a point of intellectual interest.

"Report!" Naomi was shouting. Clarissa meant to say something, but the mechs were scuttling across the *Roci* toward her, and it took all her attention to retreat and return fire.

"I got a boarding party back here, waiting to go," Amos said.

"How many?" Naomi barked.

"Five," Amos said. And then, "Four now. Now three."

The stars were coming back, but they didn't seem as bright as before. The hull was glowing under the light of the sun, now almost directly overhead. The mechs crawled toward her faster, like something out of a nightmare. One scuttled past the barrel of a PDC and vanished.

"Got one," Alex said, and Clarissa laughed. But her attention slipped. She'd pulled out too far from the hull. She had to get back into cover. She dove toward the *Roci*, but too fast. She hit with her feet, trying to roll with the impact the way she'd learned as a girl in her self-defense classes. Her sense of up and down swam, and for a moment she was falling into the stars.

"How you doing, Peaches?" Amos asked, but she was moving. Rushing backward away from the remaining mech. Their friend's unexpected death by PDC had slowed them, made them more cautious. She went farther around the *Roci*, paused to line up a shot, and waited for the enemy to walk into it. It was hard. The sun was in her eyes now, and the helmet struggled to keep it from blinding her. Her leg ached, but it didn't *hurt*. She wondered if that was normal. The mech lurched into view, and she fired, driving it back. How many rounds had she used? It was on the HUD someplace, but she couldn't remember where. She fired again, and saw a small green six become a five. So. Five rounds left. She waited, a hunter in her blind. She could do this. The red dot jittered and shifted. She tried to bring it back in line. She could do this ...

"Peaches!" Amos shouted. "Your six!"

Clarissa spun. The *Azure Dragon* loomed behind her, the sun high above. She'd run back so far, she'd looped. And arcing up over the enemy ship, two bright, moving shapes. The crew of the *Azure Dragon* wouldn't be able to force their way onto the *Rocinante*, but they could have some small vengeance here. There was no place for her to take cover. She could only stand here and face the remnants of the boarding party descending toward her or charge into the guns of the remaining mech.

"Amos?" she said.

"Go to the airlock! Get back inside!"

She raised her gun, aimed at one of the incoming figures. When she fired, they shifted out of the bullet's path. Her HUD reported fast-movers. It was time to go. She turned toward the drive cone. It seemed farther away than she expected. The suit thrusters kicked in, and she skimmed along, a meter above the hull like a bird flying just above the surface of a lake. Something exploded in her arm, spinning her. Her HUD told her what she already knew. Another wound. The suit was already squeezing at her shoulder to hold as much blood in as it could. To her left, a flash of yellow. The mech, riding plumes of its own thrusters, and coming closer. She dropped her rifle, and it fell away behind her. With one arm, she couldn't aim it anyway, and a little less mass meant a little more speed.

This was it. This was how she died. The idea was weirdly consoling. She'd end here, under billions of stars. In the unending, unshielded light of the sun, fighting for her friends. It felt bright, like a hero's death. Not the cold fading away on a hard, gray cot in the prison infirmary she'd expected. How strange that this should feel like victory. Time seemed to slow, and she wondered if maybe she'd triggered her implants by mistake. That would be silly. Amping up her nervous system would do her exactly no good when all her speed came from the thruster's nozzle. But no. It was only fear and the certainty that she was rushing to her death.

Naomi and Alex were shouting in her ears. Amos too. She couldn't make sense of any of it. It occurred to her like a conclusion she was watching someone else make that Amos might feel bad when she was gone. She should have told him how grateful she was for every day he'd given her outside the hole. Her helmet alerted. She had to start braking or she'd overshoot the ship. She killed the thrusters and flipped, more from a sense of obligation than from any real hope of living. One of two boarders was spinning away sunward, arms and legs flailing and out of control. The other was above her with their back turned, facing a fast-moving body that had to be Amos. The mech flickered, drawing closer. When she started braking, it seemed to surge toward her, an illusion of relative velocity, but with enough truth to end her.

And then, inexplicably, the mech driver slumped against his harness. The mech arms waved, suddenly uncontrolled. One reached down, gouging the hull and sending the great yellow machine spinning away from the *Rocinante* and toward the stars. She watched, uncomprehending, until a hand grabbed her uninjured shoulder and an arm looped across her back. In the bright sunlight, the other suit's helmet was opaque. She didn't understand what had happened until she heard the voice over her radio.

"It's all right," Holden said. "I've got you."

Amos woke her. His wide face and bald head seemed like a dream. But that was likely just the drugs playing with her perceptions.

The regrowth cocktail did strange things to her mind, even if the painkillers didn't. Given the choice of feeling numb and stupid or alert and in pain, she chose pain. Wide elastic restraints held her to the bed of the medical bay. The autodoc fed her body what it needed, and only occasionally threw out errors, confused by the leakage from her after-market endocrine system. Her humerus was shattered, but growing back together. The first bullet had carved a groove ten centimeters long through the muscles of her thigh and shocked the bone, but didn't break it.

"You okay, Peaches? I brought you some food, and I was just going to leave it for you, but you were… You looked …" He waved a hand.

"I'm fine," she said. "I mean all shot up, but I'm fine."

He sat on the side of her bed, and she realized they were under thrust. The smell of artificial peach cobbler was inviting and nauseating at the same time. She undid her restraints and sat up on her good elbow.

"Did we win?" she asked.

"Oh hell yeah. Two prisoners. Data core off the *Azure Dragon*. They tried to scrub it, but between Naomi and the *Roci*, we'll put it back together. Bobbie's straight-up pissed that she missed the action."

"Maybe next time," she said, and Holden came into the room.

He and Amos nodded to each other. The big man left.

"We should probably have had this talk before," Holden said.

The *Roci*'s captain stood at the bedside, looking like he wasn't sure whether to sit. She couldn't say whether it was the trauma or the drugs, but she was surprised to notice that he didn't look like her mental image of him. In her mind, his cheeks were higher, his jaw wider. The blue of his eyes more icy. This man looked—not older. Only different. His hair was messy. There were lines forming around his eyes and the corners of his mouth. Not there yet, but coming. His temples were touched with gray. That wasn't what made him look different, though. The James Holden who was king of her personal mythology was sure of himself, and this man was profoundly ill at ease.

"Okay," she said, not certain what else to say.

Holden crossed his arms. "I…um. Yeah, I didn't really expect you to come on this ship. I'm not comfortable with it."

"I know," she said. "I'm sorry."

He waved the comment away. "It's made me skip this part, and I shouldn't have. That's on me, okay? I know you and Amos trekked across a big part of North America after the rocks came down, and I know that you handled yourself just fine then. And you have experience on ships."

Experience as a terrorist and murderer, he didn't say.

"The thing is," he went on, "you aren't trained for this kind of action. Going out on the float with a gun in your hand is different from being on the ground. Or being a technician inside a ship. You've got those implants, but using them out there, you'd have wound up crashing out and choking to death on your own vomit, right?"

"Probably," she said.

"So going out again like that's not something you should do. Amos took you because…because he wants you to know you belong here."

"But I don't," she said. "That's what you're saying."

"Not everyplace Amos goes, no," Holden said. He met her gaze for the first time. He looked almost sad. She couldn't understand why. "But as long as you're on my ship, you're crew. And it's my job to protect you. I screwed that up. You don't go into battle in a vac suit anymore. At least not until I think you're trained. That's an order. Understood?"

"Understood," she said. And then, trying the word out to see how it felt in her mouth, "Understood, sir."

He had been her sworn enemy. He had been the symbol of her failure. He'd even become a symbol, somehow, of the life she could have had if she'd made different choices. He was only a man in his early middle age that she barely knew, though they had some friends in common. He tried a smile, and she returned it. It was so little. It was something.

She finished her cobbler after he left, then closed her eyes to rest them and didn't know she'd fallen asleep until the dream came.

She was digging through slick, black mud-sticky shit, trying to get down to where someone was buried. She had to hurry, because they were running out of air. In the dream, she could feel the wet cold against her fingers, the disgust welling up at the back of her throat. And the fear. And the heartbreaking loss that came from knowing she wouldn't make it in time.

Chapter Eight: Dawes

The first session of Marco's impromptu summit began when Michio Pa arrived, looking pleasant and implacable in equal measures. Her ship had docked halfway through a day cycle, so Marco only kept them for a few hours. The following three days were more punishing, the meetings lasting over thirteen hours each day without even so much as a break for meals. They'd eaten at the meeting tables while Marco laid out his vision for a grand, system-spanning network of Belter civilization.

Free spin stations, automated factories and farms, power stations hunkered close to the sun and beaming energy to the human habitations, the large-scale stripping of biological resources from the corpse of the Earth. It was a grand and beautiful vision with a scope and depth that dwarfed even the Martian terraforming project. And Marco Inaros presented it all with a ruthlessness and intensity that made the objections the rest of them brought up seem small and petty.

Sanjrani wanted to know how the labor force needed to create Marco's massive snowflake-complex void cities would be trained. Marco waved the problem away. Belters were already trained to live and build in space. That knowledge was their birthright. Bred into their brittle bones. Pa brought up the problem of keeping food and medical supplies flowing to all the stations and ships already feeling the pinch from the loss of supply lines from Earth. Marco agreed that there would be lean times, but assured Pa that her fears were greater than the actual problem. No objection any of them raised swayed his commitment. His eyes were bright, his voice rich as a viol, his energy was boundless. After the meetings were done, Dawes went back to his quarters, weary to the bone. Marco went to the bars and pubs and union halls and spoke directly to the citizens of Ceres. If he slept, Dawes didn't know when.

On the fifth day, they took a break, and it felt like collapsing at the end of a long run.

Rosenfeld's interpretation did little to help.

"Coyo is manic. He'll come back down."

"And then what?" Dawes asked.

The pebble-skinned man shrugged. His smile had very little to do with pleasure. "Then we'll see where we are. Inaros is a great man. For our purposes, he's *the* great man. It isn't a role that's fit for a wholly sane person."

They sat in the gardens of the governor's palace. The smell of plants and soil mixed with the textured protein and grilled peppers that Rosenfeld preferred for breakfast. Dawes leaned back from the table and sipped from his bulb of hot, milky tea. He'd known Rosenfeld Guoliang for almost three decades, and he trusted him as much as he trusted anyone. But not completely.

"If you're saying he's gone mad," Dawes said, "that's a problem."

"It's not a problem, it's a job requirement," Rosenfeld said, waving the concern away like it was a gnat. "He's slaughtered billions of people and remade the shape of human civilization. No one can do something on that scale and see themselves as fully human anymore. He may be a god or he may be a devil, but he can't stomach the idea of being just an unreasonably pretty man who stumbled into the right combination of charisma and opportunity. This particular fever will pass. He'll stop sounding like we're making the first weld next week and start saying that our grandchildren's grandchildren will finish it. Never been anyone as good at changing the song without missing a beat as our man Marco. Don't you worry."

"Hard not to."

"Well. Only worry a little." Rosenfeld took a thick bite of the protein and pepper, his rough eyelids lowering until he looked almost half-asleep. "We're all here because he needed us. Apart from Fred Johnson, I had the only fighting force large enough to cause him trouble. Sanjrani's a prat, but he ran Europa's artificial economy well enough that everyone thinks he's a genius. And who knows? Maybe he is. You control the port city of the Belt. Pa's the poster child of dissenting from the OPA for moral reasons, and so she makes a fine Father Christmas for redistributing wealth to the groundlings and bringing the old loyalists over to us. No one in these meetings is here by chance. He put this team together. As long as we keep a unified front, we can keep him from floating away on his own grandiosity."

"I hope you're right."

Rosenfeld chewed and grinned at the same time. "So do I."

Anderson Dawes had been part of the OPA since before he was born. Trying to curry favor with their corporate overlords, his parents had named him after a mining company. Later, Fred Johnson's butchery turned that same name into one of Earth's greatest crimes against the Belt. He'd been raised to see the Belt as his home and the people living there—however different, however divided—as his kin. His father had been an organizer, his mother a union lawyer. He'd learned that all humanity was a negotiation even before he'd learned how to read. Everything in his life since then was an elaboration of the same simple theme: push hard enough that he never lost ground and never let an opportunity pass.

Always, his intention had been to put the Belt in its right place and end the casual exploitation of its people and wealth. How exactly that happened, he'd let the universe decide. He'd worked with the Persian Gulf Shared Interest Zone in rebuilding the station at L-4 and made contacts in the expatriate community there. He'd become a voice within the OPA on Ceres by showing up early at every meeting, listening carefully before he spoke, and making certain the right people knew his name.

Violence had always been a part of the environment. When he'd had to kill people, those people had died. When he found a promising young tech, he knew how to recruit them. Or an old enemy ripe to be turned. He'd brought Fred Johnson, the Butcher of Anderson Station, into the fold when everyone called him crazy, and then accepted their accolades when he'd bloodied the nose of the United Nations by doing it. Later, when it became clear that Johnson was unwilling to cooperate with the new regime, he'd agreed to cut him out. If watching his namesake go from a moderately successful Belter mining station to the rallying cry of Belter revolution had taught him anything, it was this: Situations change and clinging too tightly to what came before kills you.

And so when Marco Inaros struck his deal with the blackest black market on Mars to create a successor to the Outer Planets Alliance, Dawes had seen only two choices: Embrace the new reality or die with the past. He'd picked the way he always had, and because of it, he was at the table. Sometimes for thirteen hours while Inaros ranted his utopian dream-logic, but at the table nonetheless.

Still, there was part of him that wished this Winston Duarte had chosen to raise someone else up with his Mephisthophelean arms deal.

He took another bite of his breakfast, but the peppers had gone cold and limp, and the protein had begun to harden. He dropped his fork.

"Any word from Medina?" he asked.

Rosenfeld shrugged. "Do you mean the station, or past it?"

"Anything, really."

"Station's well," Rosenfeld said. "The defenses are in place, so that's as it should be. Past that…well, no one knows, sa sa? Duarte's keeping up his end, sending shipments of arms and equipment back from Laconia. The other colonies   "

"Problems," Dawes said. He didn't make it a question.

Rosenfeld scowled at his plate, avoiding eye contact for the first time since their unofficial meeting began. "Frontiers are dangerous places. Things happen there that wouldn't if it were more civilized. Wakefield went silent. Some people are saying they woke something up there, but no one's sent a ship out to look. Who has time, yeah? Got a war here to finish. Then we can look back out."

"And the *Barkeith*?"

Rosenfeld's gaze stayed fixed on the peppers. "Duarte's people say they're looking into it. Not to worry. Not blaming us."

Everything in the other man's body told Dawes not to press further, and he was almost ready to let it go. He could change the angle of attack, at least. "How is it all the other colonies are fighting to grow enough food, not have their hydroponics collapse like on Welker, but Laconia's already got a manufacturing base?"

"Just means it's better planned. Better funded. The thing you don't understand about this pinché Martian Duarte is—"

Dawes' hand terminal blatted out an alert. High-priority connection request. The channel he used for station emergencies. Captain Shaddid. He held up a finger, asking Rosenfeld's patience, and accepted the connection.

"What's the matter?" he said instead of hello.

Shaddid was at her desk. He recognized the wall behind her. "I need you down here. One of my men is in the hospital. Medic says he may not make it. I have the shooter in custody."

"Good that you caught him."

"His name's Filip Inaros."

Dawes felt a weight drop into his gut. "I'll be right there."

Shaddid had given the boy his own cell. She'd been wise to do so. From the moment he walked into the security station, Dawes had felt the shock and rage like a charge in the atmosphere. Shooting a security officer on Ceres was a short way to an airlock. Or it would have been for most people.

"I put an automated monitor on him," Shaddid said. "Slaved it to my system. No one else turns it on or off."

"Because?" Dawes said. He was sitting at her desk. She might be the head of security, but he was the governor of Ceres.

"They'd turn it off," Shaddid said. "And you wouldn't ever see that little piece of shit alive again. And just between us, you'd be doing the universe a favor."

On the screen, Filip Inaros sat against the cell wall, his head tilted back and his eyes closed. He was a young man. Or an old child. As Dawes watched, the boy stretched, wrapped his arms around himself, and settled back without looking around once. He couldn't tell if it was the movement of someone certain that they were untouchable or frightened that they might not be. Dawes could see the resemblance to Marco, but where the father seemed to radiate charm and confidence, the son was all rage and a vulnerability that made Dawes think of abrasions and raw wounds. Under other circumstances, he might have felt sorry for the prisoner.

"How did it happen?" Dawes asked.

Shaddid tapped on her hand terminal and threw the data to the screen. A corridor outside a nightclub up nearer the center of spin. A door swung open and three people came out, all Belters. A man and woman, their hands caressing each other like they were already in private, and a second young man. A moment later, the door opened again, and Filip Inaros stepped out. There was no sound, so Dawes didn't know what Filip had shouted at the retreating figures, only that he had. The single young man turned back, and the couple paused to watch. Filip's head was back, his chest out. For generations, humanity had been free of the gravity well of the inner planets, but the posturing of young men spoiling for a fight never changed.

A new figure stepped into the frame. A man in a security uniform, hands lifted in command. Filip turned toward him, shouting. The security man shouted back, pointed to the wall, ordering Filip against it. The couple turned away and pretended not to know anything about it. The young man who'd been coming back to the fight slowly stepped back, not turning away, but willing to let his enemies spend themselves against each other. Filip went terribly still. Dawes had to force himself not to look away.

The security man reached for his weapon, and a gun appeared in Filip's hand, the kind of magic flicker that comes of hundreds of hours of practicing a fast draw. And then, as part of the same motion, the muzzle flash.

"God dammit," Dawes said.

"It's not subtle," Shaddid said. "He was given a security order. He refused and fired on the agent. If he was anyone else, he'd be feeding mushrooms right now."

Dawes pressed his palm to his mouth, rubbing until his lips felt bruised. There had to be something. Some way to walk this back. "How's your man?"

There was a pause before Shaddid answered. She knew what he was really asking. "Stabilized."

"Not going to die?"

"Not out of the woods yet either," she said. And then, "I can't do my job if people get away with shooting security. I understand there's diplomacy involved, but with respect, that's your job. Mine is to keep six million people from killing too many of each other on any given day."

My job's not so different, he thought. This wasn't the time to say it. "Contact Marco Inaros. He'll be on the *Pella* in dock 65-C," Dawes said. "Tell him to meet me here."

At the end of particularly bad days, Dawes would sometimes pour himself a glass of whiskey and sit for a time with his prized possession: a printed volume of Marcus Aurelius that had belonged to his grandmother. The *Meditations* were the private thoughts of a person with terrible power—an emperor who could order to death anyone he chose, create the law by speaking it, command any woman to his bed. Or any man, if the mood took him. The thin pages were filled with Aurelius' private struggle to be a good man despite the frustrations of the world. It left Dawes feeling not comforted but consoled. All through human history, being a moral person and not being pulled into the dramatics and misbehavior of others had caused intelligent people grief.

Dawes had spent decades with that beneath all his personal philosophy. There were bad people everywhere, stupidity and avarice and hubris and pride. And he had to navigate it if there was ever to be hope of a better place for Belters. It wasn't that things were worse now than they'd been before. Only that they weren't better.

Tonight, he suspected, would be a good one for rereading his Aurelius.

Marco swept into the security station like he owned it. Smiles and laughter, and a sheer animal presence that filled the space. The security agents unconsciously moved to the edges of the room and didn't meet his gaze. Dawes went out to lead him back to Shaddid's office and found himself shaking the man's hand there in front of everyone. He hadn't meant to do that.

"This is embarrassing," Marco said as if he was agreeing with something that had already been said. "I will see that it doesn't happen again."

"Your son could have killed one of my people," Dawes said.

Marco sat back in his chair and opened his arms, an expansive gesture that seemed intended to diminish what anyone else could say. "There was a scuffle, and it got out of hand. Dawes, tell me you've never had something like it."

"I've never had something like it," Dawes said. His voice was cool and hard, and for the first time, Marco's jovial expression shifted.

"You aren't going to make this a problem, are you?" Marco said, his voice sinking low. "We have a lot of work to do. Real work. Word's come that Earth took out the *Azure Dragon*. We have to reassess our strategy down sunward."

It was the first Dawes had heard of it, and he had the sense that Marco had kept the information private, ready to play it when he wanted a subject changed. Well, he'd find Dawes harder to throw off than that.

"And we will. But that's not why I called you here."

Shaddid coughed, and Marco turned to scowl at her. When he looked back at Dawes, his expression had changed. His smile was as wide, his expression as open and merry, but something in his eyes made Dawes' stomach clench.

"All right," Marco said. "Bien, coyo mis. Why did you call me here?"

"Your son can't be on my station," Dawes said. "If he stays, I have to put him through a trial. Have to protect him from anyone who might get impatient waiting." He paused. "Have to follow through the sentence, if there is one."

Marco went still, a copy of his son on the assault footage. Dawes made an effort not to swallow.

"That sounds like a threat, Anderson."

"It's an explanation. It's why you need to take your boy off my station, and never bring him back to it. I'm doing this as a favor. Anyone else, and things would just take their course."

Marco drew in a long, slow breath and let it out between his teeth. "I see."

"He shot a security agent. He may have killed him."

"We've killed a world," Marco said, waving the words away.

But then he seemed to remember something, nodding as much to himself as to Dawes or Shaddid. "But I appreciate your bending the rules for me. And for him. I won't let this go by. He and I will have a serious conversation."

"All right," Dawes said. "Captain Shaddid will release him to you. If you want to bring some of your people down before she does—"

"That won't be necessary," Marco said. No bodyguards were called for. None of the security force would dare face down Marco Inaros of the Free Navy. And what was worse, Dawes believed Marco was right. "We'll have a meeting tomorrow. About the *Azure Dragon* and Earth. Next steps."

"Next steps," Dawes agreed, and stood. "You know this isn't temporary. Filip can never set foot on Ceres again."

Marco's smile was unexpected and deep. His dark eyes flashed. "Don't worry, old friend. If you don't want him here, he won't be here. That's a promise."

Chapter Nine: Holden

The sound reached all the way to the galley: a deep thud, then a pause, then another thud. Each time it came, Holden felt himself flinch a little. Naomi and Alex sat with him, trying to ignore it, but whatever they started a conversation about—the state of the ship, the success of their mission, the question of whether to give in to fate and convert a section of the crew quarters into a brig—it died out under the slow, unending beat.

"Maybe I should talk to her," Holden said. "I think I should."

"Don't know why you think that," Alex said.

Naomi shrugged, abstaining. Holden took one last bite of his fake lamb, wiped his mouth with the napkin, and dropped everything into the recycler. Part of him hoped that one of them would stop him. They didn't.

The *Rocinante*'s gym showed its age. No two resistance bands were quite the same color, the green-gray mats had white lines where the fabric had worn thin, and the smell of old sweat soft-ened the air. Bobbie had strung a heavy bag on a tight line between the ceiling and the deck. Her exercise outfit was tight and gray and soaked with sweat. Her hair was tied back, and her eyes were locked on the bag as she shifted on the balls of her feet. As Holden stepped into the room, she turned to the left, putting her weight into a roundhouse kick. This close, the thud sounded like some-thing heavy being dropped. The system reported a little under ninety-five kilograms per square centimeter. Bobbie danced back, her focus locked on the bag. She shifted to the right, and kicked with her other leg. The thud was a little softer, but the reading went up by three kilos. She danced back, reset. Her shins were red and raw-looking.

"Hey," she said, not looking at him. Thud. Reset.

"Hey," Holden said. "How're you doing?"

"Fine." Thud. Reset.

"Anything you want to talk about?"

Thud. Reset. "Nope."

"Okay. Well. If you ah"—Thud. Reset.—"change your mind."

"I'll track you down." Thud. Reset. Thud.

"Great," Holden said, and stepped back out of the room. Bob-bie hadn't looked at him once.

In the galley, Naomi had a bulb of coffee waiting for him. He sat across from her while Alex dropped the last of his food into the recycler. Holden drank. The *Roci*'s processors were calibrated once a week, and they'd stocked up before leaving Luna, so it was almost certainly his imagination that made the coffee more bitter than usual. He put a pinch of salt in it anyway, swirling the bulb to stir it.

"You knew that wasn't going to work," he said.

"I expected it wasn't," Naomi said. "I didn't know."

"Just suspected."

"Strongly suspected," she said. It was almost an apology. "I could have been surprised."

"You got to give Bobbie her room, Cap," Alex said. "She'll come out the other side of it."

"I just...I wish I understood what's bothering her so much."

Alex blinked. "She's been spoiling to take the fight to some bad guys ever since Io. Now she got one, and she was stuck in a box while the rest of us did the shooting."

"But we won."

"We did," Naomi said. "And she watched us do it while we tried to figure out how to get her out of a trap. By the time she was free, it was over."

Holden sipped at the coffee. It was a little better. That didn't help. "Okay, so what I meant was I wish I understood what was bothering her in hopes that then there'd be something I could do about it."

"We know," Naomi said. "The difficulty isn't lost on us."

Amos' voice came over the ship's comm. "Anybody there? I've been paging ops for the last ten minutes."

Alex thumbed the system on. "On my way up now."

"Okay. I think I tracked down the last leak. Let me know what it looks like from your end."

"Will do," Alex said, nodded to the two of them, and headed up toward ops and the ongoing repair effort. The *Azure Dragon*'s crew hadn't had all that long, but they hadn't been trying for clean either. It was easier to cut through a lot of hull quickly when you didn't care what broke while you did it. Knowing that the ship wasn't right yet was like an itch he couldn't quite reach. Part of that came from knowing how strapped the shipyards on Luna were going to be. The days of sloping into Tycho and having Fred Johnson's teams patch the ship up were probably gone, and Luna had Earth's navy to take precedence over Holden and his crew.

It wasn't just that, though. It was also the same thing he'd felt driving him to talk to Bobbie. And to Clarissa Mao before that. He wanted things to be all right, and he had the growing feeling that they weren't. That they weren't going to be.

"What about you?" Naomi said, looking at him from under a spill of dark, gently curled hair. "Want to talk?"

He chuckled. "I do, but I don't know what to say. Here we are, the conquering heroes with prisoners and a salvaged data core, and it doesn't feel like enough."

"It isn't."

"Always so comforting."

"I mean you're not wrong. You aren't uneasy and disturbed by all this because there's something wrong with you. This is all uneasing and disturbing. You aren't fucked up. The situation is."

"That doesn't... You know, that actually does make me feel a little better."

"Good," she said. "Because I need to know this isn't about Marco and Filip. That...all that isn't making it hard for you to have me around."

"No," Holden said. "We covered that."

"And we'll cover it again after this, I'm sure. But if you'd just keep saying it?"

"I would put everyone else that exists headfirst out an airlock just to keep you around. It isn't that. The only concern I have about you and Marco Inaros is that he'll try to hurt you again."

"That's nice to know."

"I still love you. I will always love you."

He was answering the question he thought she was asking, but her gaze cut away. Her smile was rueful, but it was also real. "Always is a long time."

"I'm captain of this ship. Technically, I could marry us right now."

Now she laughed. "Would you want to?"

"I'm easy. It seems a little redundant. Husband and wife seems like a less interesting and committed relationship than Holden and Naomi," he said. "He can't win, you know."

"Of course he can. Marco's the one who decides when he wins."

"No, I've been thinking about it. The Free Navy...is untenable. They did a lot of damage. They killed a lot of people. But all of this is really about the gates. If it wasn't for all the people rushing out to try to found a new colony, Mars wouldn't be collapsing. The Belters wouldn't be worried that they'll get marginalized out of existence. None of the things that gave Marco a toehold would have happened. But the gates aren't going away. So all the pressures he's fighting against? They'll outlast him. People are still going to want to get out to the new systems, and they're going to find ways to do it. And the colonies that are already out there are going to want to keep in contact and trade with us. At least until they're really on their feet, and that could take generations."

"You think he's on the wrong side of history."

"He is," Holden said.

"Then what does that say about people like me? I grew up in the Belt. I wouldn't want to live down a gravity well. The gates aren't going away, but neither are the Belters. Unless they are."

"What do you mean?"

She shrugged. "Human history has seen plenty of genocides. If you're right, then the long term is either the gates or the Belters. And Belters…We're human. We're fragile. We die. The gates? Even if we could destroy them, we wouldn't. There's too much real estate involved."

Holden looked down. "All right. That was my turn."

Naomi lifted a questioning eyebrow.

"That was less comforting than I meant it to be," he said. "Sorry."

"It's all right. Anyway, that's not what I meant when I said Marco decides when he wins. You don't understand how slippery he can be. Whatever happens, he'll shift so it was his plan all along. If he were the last person alive, he'd say we needed the apocalypse and declare victory. It's what he is."

Even though they were the agents of Chrisjen Avasarala's will, it took seventeen hours for the *Rocinante* and the *Azure Dragon* to get berths on Luna. When they finally did, they were at a military yard outside Patsaev complex, where the civilian relief ships were landing. The docks were crowded with people in bunches and lines, some of them staring blankly ahead like victims of a fever, some weeping with relief or exhaustion or both. The air stank of sweat and felt stale, even where the intakes made the greatest breeze.

The Luna Station complex—shipyards and convention centers, hotels and residence centers, schools and office complexes and warehouses—was big enough to fit a hundred million bodies, but the environmental infrastructure would overload at something like half that, even with the advantage of the moon's mass and conduction to soak up waste heat. The Lagrange stations had less margin. Holden tried to do the math in his head as they forged their path through the crowd. The estimates said that one-half of Earth was dead already. Fifteen billion gone or going so fast there was no way to save them. Of those still alive, two-thirds were living in what the newsfeeds were calling "distressed situations." Ten billion people who needed food or water or shelter. And up the well, there were places for maybe as many as a quarter million. Two-and-a-half-hundred-thousandths of a percent of the people in need. He couldn't believe that was right, and tried to figure it again. He came to the same number.

And a thousand worlds out there, just on the other side of the gates. Hostile worlds, most of them, but not more hostile than Earth. Not now. If there were a way to teleport them from Boston and Lisbon and Bangkok, maybe they'd be saved. Maybe they'd go on to raise something new and beautiful out of the ruins of Earth, and if one system didn't, there'd be a thousand other chances.

Except that there wouldn't be, because the transportation was too hard. So they'd die where they stood because there was no way to get them all someplace better fast enough for it to matter.

"You okay, Cap?" Amos asked.

"Fine. Why?"

"Looks like you're getting ready to hit someone."

"No," Holden said. "Wouldn't help."

"Over here," Bobbie said.

The guards outside the administrative offices carried small automatic weapons and wore body armor. They stood aside and let Bobbie shuffle through the wide gray door, and all of the others behind her in a line like ducklings. The offices could have been a different world. Full-spectrum lights glowed like Holden's memory of a summer afternoon. Ferns and ivy bobbed in the gentle breeze from the air recyclers. The hallways were half a meter wider than the corridors of the *Rocinante*, and felt luxurious. Only the faint gunpowder stink of moondust and the one-tenth g spoke of Luna. Everything else would have looked at home in the UN offices at The Hague.

Bobbie led them like she knew where she was going, down one hall, past another pair of armed guards, and through a set of frosted glass doors. The room was built like a lounge—chairs and divans around low tables. Eight or ten people were scattered around in pairs and small groups, and for a few seconds, Holden didn't understand who they were.

At some point, everything had been either black or white, but use had left splashes of color. The brown ring of a coffee stain on a cushion, the greenish scrape along the side of a chair. Avasarala stood at the far side of the room, her orange sari blazing like a torch while she talked to a white-haired woman with dark skin and narrow hips. When Avasarala looked up to smile at him, the woman turned. Holden stumbled.

"Momma Sophie?" he said, and then, like a lens coming into focus, he saw all the others for who they were. The years had changed them all, and seeing them through cameras and screens wasn't the same. Father Tom had gained weight, and Father Cesar had lost it, but they were there, hand in hand, walking toward him. Father Anton had gone bald, and Mother Elise seemed older, and frailer in person than she had on the screen. And shorter. Everyone seemed shorter, because the system at the farmhouse had been on a desk. He'd been looking up at all of them from that desktop for years and hadn't realized it until just now.

All eight of his parents crowded around him, their bodies pressing gently against his, their arms around each other, the way they had when he'd been a child. Holden found himself weeping, swept away by the memory of being a little boy surrounded and protected by the loving bodies of eight strong adults. He stood among them now, the strongest of the lot, shaken by the love and the joy and the terrible understanding that both the boy he'd been and the men and women they were then were gone and would never come back. They were all crying too. Father Dimitri, Mother Tamara, Father Joseph. And his new family too.

Naomi pressed her hand to her lips, like she was trying to hold words or emotions in. Alex was grinning as widely as any of Holden's family, his eyes shining. Avasarala and Bobbie seemed pleased, like people who'd pulled off a good surprise party. Weirdly, Clarissa Mao, standing alone with a pressure cast on her wounded arm, was shaking with barely controlled sobs. Amos looked at all of them like he'd walked in on the last line of a joke, then shrugged and let them get on with whatever the hell this was. Holden felt a rush of affection for the man.

"Wait," he said. "Wait. Everyone, I need you to meet…everyone else. I guess. This is Naomi, everyone."

His parents all turned toward her. Naomi's eyes widened a degree. The little, panicked flare of her nostrils was probably something only he could see. There was a pause he hadn't expected, a stuttering moment when he saw her through their eyes: Here is the Belter girl their son was sleeping with. Here is the ex-lover of the man who killed the world, the representative of everything that had happened. One of *them*. It lasted a heartbeat, then another. It was vast as the space between worlds.

"I've heard so much about you, dear," Mother Elise said, moving to Naomi and taking her in a wide embrace. The others followed, queuing up to welcome her to the family. But it wasn't an illusion. The moment had been there. Even when his two families diffused into each other—Father Dimitri and Father Anton and Alex talking about the ship, Mother Tamara and Amos looking at each other with a kind of amused bewilderment—Holden felt the hesitation. They would love her if he said so, but she wasn't one of their kind.

He barely noticed Bobbie at his side until she spoke. "This is how she does it. She finds a way to pay you."

She nodded toward the back of the room. Avasarala stood alone, watching with a smile that didn't quite reach her eyes. Holden went to her.

"They told me they were all right," he said. "When I talked to them, they said they weren't in danger."

"It was true, as far as it went," Avasarala said. "The reactors hadn't failed there yet. And they had more food stored than most. They might have lasted another…month? How should I know? Canning. Who the fuck does their own canning anymore?"

"But you evacuated them."

"Another week, another month. Not another year. They wouldn't have been safe forever, and once they realized they were fucked, all the slots would have been filled. I flagged them as priority evacuees. I get to do that kind of shit. I'm the boss."

"Where …"

She shrugged. "They'll have quarters here or on L-4. Not as big as they had in Montana, but together. I can do that much. Maybe they'll even go back to their farm someday when all this is done. Stranger things have happened."

Holden took her hand. It was cool and hard and stronger than he'd expected. She turned to look him in the eye for the first time since he'd come into the room. The smile edged into the corners of her eyes.

"Thank you," he said. "I owe you one."

Her smile shifted, losing the formality and coolness and distance it had carried beneath the surface. She chuckled deep in her throat.

"I know," she said.

Chapter Ten: Avasarala

She didn't sleep anymore, or at least it didn't help when she did. The bed in her suite was spongy, but she didn't sink into it the way that a lifetime at normal gravity made her body expect, so it felt too soft and too hard at the same time. And sleep was supposed to mean rest. There was no rest anymore. She closed her eyes and her mind stumbled on like it was falling down stairs. Mortality rates and supply windows and security briefings—all the things that filled her so-called waking hours filled her nights as well. Being asleep only meant they lost what little coherence they had. It didn't feel like sleeping. It felt like going mad and catatonic for a few hours and then regaining enough sanity to push through for eighteen or twenty hours more before collapsing into herself again. It was shit. But it needed doing, so she did it.

At least she had a shower.

"It seems like Bobbie Draper managed to keep Holden from

screwing the mission up," she said, drying her hair. The suite glowed a soft blue, like the promise of dawn. Not that any dawn looked like that on Earth now. But it had once. "I like that girl. I worry for her. She's been sitting behind a desk too long. It doesn't suit her."

She considered the saris in her dresser, running her finger across the cloth and listening to the sound of skin against fabric. She opted for a green one that shimmered like a beetle's carapace. Gold embroidery along the edges that caught the false sunlight made it look cheerful and powerful at the same time. And she had the amber necklace with the jade that went with it. Fashion. All humanity shitting itself to death, and she still had to worry what she looked like going into the meetings. Pathetic.

Aloud, she said, "Gies and Basrat sent word today. Everyone thought they were dead, but they were holed up under a mountain in the Julian Alps. Probably didn't plan to pop their heads above ground until everything was settled, but you know how Amanda is. It's never real with her unless someone knows she has it better. I don't know why you liked them."

She caught her mistake too late, and something vast and dangerous shifted in her heart. She took a deep breath, bit her lip, and went back to wrapping her sari in place.

"Once we have the Free Navy under control, we'll have to do something about emigration. No one's going to want to stay on Earth. At this rate, I may take off. Retire on some alien ocean where I don't have to feel like I'm responsible for making the waves go up and down. Mars will never sort itself out. Smith? He puts a brave face on it, but he's not a prime minister. He's hospice nurse for a republic. Anytime I start feeling like my job's bad, I just have a drink with him."

They were all things she'd said before, in some variation. There were new things every day—reports from the planetary surface, from the surveillance drones around Venus, from her covert service agents on Iapetus and Ceres and Pallas. With the Free Navy busy making the OPA look measured and rational, Fred Johnson could still be of use making contact with the reservoirs of the Belt that understood how dangerous Marco Inaros was and how the damage already done could spiral into something even worse. God knew he never brought in good news. But for everything new, for every irrevocable tick of the clock, there were the things she cycled back to. The ones she revisited again and again like rereading a favorite book. Or poem. Things she said *because* she had said them before.

"There was a thing you read me one time. About jack pines," she said, digging through her jewelry box for her necklace and the gold bracelets that would go with the embroidery. "Do you remember it? All I have is that it ended 'da-*dah*, da-*dah*, da-*dah*, da-*dah*, and paved the way to Paradise.' It was about how the seeds needed a fire before they could spread. I told you it sounded like a sophomore girl trying to make the break up with her abusive boyfriend sound deep. That poem. I can't get it out of my head now, and I can't remember it either. It's annoying."

The bracelets slid into place. The necklace settled too lightly on her collarbone. She sat at her table, touching on eyeliner, tapping a nearly homeopathic bit of rouge onto her cheeks. Just enough to make her look more vital than she felt. Not enough to make it seem like she was wearing makeup. The smell of the rouge reminded her of the apartment in Denmark she'd kept during university. God, her mind was everywhere these days. When she finished, she turned to her hand terminal. The indicator showed she was still recording. She smiled into the camera.

"I have to put the mask on now. Go wade into it all again. They still haven't found you, but I tell myself that they will. That I would know it if you were dead. I don't know it, so it isn't true. But it's getting harder, love. And if you don't come back soon, I'll have saved so many of these messages, you'll spend half a semester just catching up to me."

Except, she thought, there wouldn't be semesters. Or poetry courses. Or any of the things that had made her life hers before the rocks fell. And then, almost as if he was there, Arjun's dissenting voice murmured in her mind, *There will always be poetry.*

"I love you," she said to the hand terminal. "I will always love you. Even ..." She hadn't said it before. Hadn't let herself think it. There was a first time for everything. A last time too. "Even if you're not here."

She stopped recording, repaired the damage her tears had done to the makeup, and lowered her head like an actor preparing to take the stage. When she lifted her eyes again, they were harder. She made the connection request to Said, and he answered immediately. He'd been waiting.

"Good morning, Madam Secretary," he said.

"Cut the bullshit. What fresh hell are we facing today?"

"You have a meeting with Gorman Le from the scientific service in half an hour. Then breakfast with Prime Minister Smith. An interview with Karol Stepanov of the *Eastern Economic Strategic Report*, and then the meeting with the Strategy and Response Committee. That will last until lunch, ma'am."

"Stepanov. He was the one who got the Cigdem Toker Award three years ago for the piece on Dashiell Moraga?"

"I...I can check, ma'am."

"For fuck's sake, Said. Try to keep up here. He is. I'm sure of it. I should talk to his wife before I meet with him," she said. "Is there a place we can push him to in the afternoon?"

"I can make space, ma'am."

"Do that. And make sure Smith is a private audience. I'm sick of every fucking thing I do being under a microscope. If I get an ass polyp, I'll find out about it on *Le Monde*."

"If you say so, ma'am."

"I say so. Send the cart. Let's get this over with."

Gorman Le was a thin man with light brown hair salted with white and jade green eyes that Avasarala guessed were cosmetic.

She hadn't known him before she came to Luna. He'd been pro-
moted above his level of preparation when the rocks fell, and it
showed in his overly somber bearing and the way he cleared his
throat before he spoke.

"The ships that...failed to complete the transition tended to be
larger in mass," he said. "The *Oleander-Swift*, the *Barbatana de
Tubarão*, and the *Harmony* all follow that pattern. The *Casa Azul*
doesn't match that, though."

The science service had always been a large presence on Luna.
It was where the first broad-array telescope had been built, up free
from the interference of atmosphere. The first permanent moon
base had been equally divided between military posturing and
research. But the generations that had risen and fallen since then
had left the Luna science service behind, pressing out to the places
where the action really was: Ganymede, Titan, Iapetus. God help
them all, Phoebe. It left the Luna-based service office hardly
more than admin offices and children's science-fair projects. The
meeting room they were in was gray-green with wall screens left
cloudy by years of fine abrasion and fake leather chairs.

"I'm hearing you say there's no consistent pattern," Avasarala
said.

Gorman Le pressed his jaw tight and flapped his hands in frustration. "There are patterns. There are any number of patterns.
They all had drives built within a twenty-month window. They
were all using reaction mass harvested from Saturn. They all
went missing in high-traffic periods. They all had the sequence
'four-five-two-one' in their long-form registry codes. With this little to go on, I can find as many patterns as you want that match all
the missing ships. But which one matters? No, I can't tell you that."

"Any ships with four-five-two-one in the registry code make it
through?"

Gorman Le made a small huffing sound, like an angry hamster,
then looked down and blushed. "The *Jaquenetta*, registered out of
Ganymede. It went through between the *Oleander-Swift* and the
Harmony. Reported back from Walton with no trouble."

"Well," Avasarala said, amused that he'd actually tracked that down, "we can at least say that one's less likely to be it, then."

"Yes, ma'am," Gorman Le said. "Ma'am, if we could get further data…I'm certain that Medina Station has flight records for all of these. Maybe others. *And* for the ones that didn't have trouble. If we could just—"

"If we controlled Medina Station," Avasarala said, "a lot of things would be different. Do we have anything from our Martian friends about why their rogue navy was so interested in the Laconia gate?"

"Not even confirmation that that's where the breakaway ships went."

Avasarala scowled. "Keeping their knees closed after they're already fucked. Typical. I'll talk to Smith. We can't get Medina, but we should fucking well manage access to all the data we *do* have."

"Thank you, ma'am," Gorman Le said, but he said it to her back. She was already moving on.

Motion helped. The sense of doing things, of progressing, of the problems getting clearer and the solutions—where there were any—getting closer kept the despair at bay. It was harder for Smith. He was a world away from his home and his staff. There just wasn't as much Martian infrastructure on Luna. When he wasn't in meetings or trading messages across twelve minutes of light delay, he sat in his suite and watched the newsfeeds calling him an idiot and a buffoon and the man whose inattention had let the Martian Congressional Republic Navy be sold to terrorists and pirates. He didn't even have managing the worst catastrophe in human history to keep his mind off feeling sorry for himself.

He met her at the door. In simple sand-colored slacks and a white collarless shirt with the sleeves rolled up, he could have been a salesman or a minor prelate. His smile was professionally genuine and warm, the same way it always was. She stepped into the rooms and glanced around. No one. Not even security. A private audience indeed. Score one for Said.

Their breakfast waited in the dining room—poached eggs and thick, buttered toast. The sort of simple, elegant fare that she imagined royalty through the ages had enjoyed while the people they ruled died. She also saw the half-empty bottle of wine on the floor by the sofa, the wall screen tuned to an entertainment feed showing a slightly risqué comedy that had come out three years earlier. Shannon Poe and Lakash Hedayat were naked and trying to cover themselves with the same beach towel without looking at the other or touching skin to skin. In context, it might have been funny. Smith followed her gaze and turned off the screen.

"Laughter," he said. "A balm in hard times."

"I'll have to try it," she said. He pulled her chair out for her, and she let him. "I had a few things I wanted to run past you, but before that? I understand why your intelligence service is hiding information about Duarte, but why the fuck are you keeping the data about the gate-eaten ships to yourself? Are you looking to trade it for something, because unless it's sexual favors, we haven't got jack shit."

"The eggs are good," Smith said.

"You want eggs? I'll have them squeeze a chicken. I want the data on the missing ships."

Smith smiled and nodded as if she'd said something mild and polite. The pale flesh of the egg dripped gold on the way to his mouth. The yolk spattered his shirtfront, but he didn't seem to notice.

"What is it?" she asked.

"I...You'll have to take the matter up with my successor. I've had word today. The opposition is calling for a vote of no confidence. I will be out of office by this evening."

Avasarala took in a deep breath and let it out through her teeth. The silence between them was rich until she broke it. "Fuck."

"They're angry and they're frightened. They need someone to blame. I'm the obvious choice."

"Who are they putting up?"

"Olivia Liu and Chahaya Nelson were both mentioned. It's going to be Emily Richards, though."

Avasarala chewed a bite of egg, but didn't taste it. Richards wasn't bad. She was serious, at least. Liu and Nelson were too entrenched in what Mars had been. They wouldn't be ready for what it was becoming. Richards women made good policy. Always had.

"I'm sorry," she said. "This must be hard for you."

"Politicians are gamblers," Smith said. "We do our best to bend the odds, but the universe does what it does."

Bullshit, she thought. Politicians are the frontal lobes of the body politic. *The universe does what it does.* They'd be better off without him. Only not yet.

"You have a day," she said. "Get me the data before it's too late."

"Chrisjen—"

"What are they going to do? Fire you? Fuck them—give me the data so I can get the problems fixed. If they give you too much shit, I'll offer you asylum."

He laughed and leaned back in his chair. His eyes shifted to the dead wall screen, then back to her. She wondered if the wine by the sofa had been his first bottle.

"Promise?" he asked as if it was a joke. She smiled.

The Strategy and Response Committee. Admirals Pycior and Souther. Parris Kanter from Human Development back at The Hague. Michael Harrow from Aquaculture. Barry Li and Simon Gutierrez from Transportation and Tariffs. Not the dream team she'd have chosen, but the best of who she had left. Sitting around the dark glass table, they all looked as tired as she felt. Good. They should be.

"Mars," Avasarala said. "Smith is out on his ass. Emily Richards is taking over. I'm reaching out to her now. I don't know whether she'll be more open, but I wouldn't assume it. What do you have?"

Li spoke first. Exhaustion made his lisp worse, but the sharpness of his intelligence made his eyes seem brighter. "We're maintaining relief routes in Africa and Europe. Our next area of focus is East Asia."

"There weren't any strikes there," Avasarala said.

"But they took the worst of the ash fall," Li said. "I have my people working out routes and probable needs. Information from the ground is sketchy."

"The Belt?" she said.

"The Belt's the Belt," Pycior said. "There's a wide variety of response. Ganymede is still maintaining neutrality, but it's firmly in the Free Navy's sphere of control. If we could offer protection, it would likely declare for us. The OPA is divided. Tycho Station, Kelso Station, and Rhea are the only ones who've condemned the Free Navy. The Trojan stations and Iapetus aren't declaring any-thing. Most of the rest of the Belt... It's for the Free Navy. As long as they keep promising food, material, and protection, it's going to be hard for moderate Belters to organize, even assuming they want to."

Souther cleared his throat. He spoke in a high voice that reminded her of singing. "We've taken apart the *Azure Dragon*'s comm logs. They indicate that there's a high-level Free Navy meeting on Ceres right now. Inaros and his four captains."

"What are they meeting about?" Avasarala snapped.

"No one seemed to know," Souther said. "But we don't have evidence of a second shepherd vessel. We've identified seven more major rock strikes that are presently en route to Earth. We're tracking them, and we're ready to take them out."

Meaning they were unpinned. Avasarala leaned forward, press-ing her fingers to her lips. Her mind danced across the solar sys-tem. Medina Station. Rhea, declaring against the Free Navy. The food and supplies of Ganymede. The starvation and death on Earth. The Martian Navy divided between the mysterious Duarte and his black market Free Navy and Smith. Now Richards. The lost colonies. Fred Johnson's OPA and all the factions he couldn't influence or command. The colony ships being preyed upon by the Free Navy pirates, and the stations and asteroids gaining the benefit of the piracy. And the missing ships. And the stolen proto-molecule sample.

A dozen possibilities shifted in her mind—redeploy forces to Tycho Station and embolden Ganymede, or blockade Pallas and try to cut off the Free Navy's resupply capabilities, or set up a protected zone for the colony ships out there and running dark. There were a thousand different paths, and she couldn't be sure where any of them would lead. If she guessed wrong, it could mean the collapse of all that was left.

But Marco Inaros and his captains were together in one place, and her ships weren't pinned.

"Fortune favors the bold, yes?" she said. "Fuck it. Let's take back Ceres."

Chapter Eleven: Pa

Seven decades before Michio Pa was born, Earth and Mars rewrote the tariff regulations on raw ore from the Belt. The stated reason was that it would encourage the establishment and expansion of refineries in the Belt and around Jupiter and Saturn. It might even have worked. In the short term, it meant that a wave of Belter prospectors and asteroid miners who'd been living at the edge of survival slipped over into the abyss. Ships were impounded or run illegally or lost from not having the scrip to pay for maintenance and repair. Back then, Earth and Mars had walked in each other's footsteps, and the only option that seemed to have any promise of justice was for the Belt to build a military of its own.

It was never official. The Outer Planets Alliance survived since then by being diffuse and deniable. But the beginnings were there. Choose a faction, find a place in the chain of command, build the thin but resilient structure that would have muscle one day. That would eventually become an answer to the inner planets projecting their power out to where the sun was hardly more than the brightest star.

When Michio Pa turned twenty-two, Fred Johnson—the Butcher of Anderson Station—had seemed like her brightest hope. He was an Earther fighting for the Belt. Fighting against his own natural self-interest. It gave a sense of authenticity to someone young enough and still easily swayed. She'd taken a position on Tycho Station, made her contacts first and then her commitment. Trained in the quasi-military that Johnson was hauling up. Put in her years.

She'd been a true believer, then. She'd been a naïve little prig. But that was before the *Behemoth*.

Getting the XO assignment on the Belt's first genuine warship had been a dream come true for her. The generation ship hadn't been designed for war, but all of her crew had been. That was what she told herself.

Captain Ashford had the command. She had been his second. And slotted in beneath them as head of security, Fred Johnson's personal friend. Carlos C de Baca. Bull. Her babysitter, and the man positioned to step in and take over when she made her first mistake. Her hatred for Bull had been incandescent. Every chance she had to belittle him, she'd taken it. Every misstep he made, she drove a wedge into, prying it open. The *Behemoth* had gone to the ring to face down Earth and Mars. To show that the Belt was a force to be reckoned with. And as above, so below. She'd made it her personal mission to show Bull that she was better than he was.

Which was why it had hurt her so badly when Sam sided with him.

They'd talked about it, her and Sam. How important it was to keep their affair quiet. How not to let anyone—especially anyone in command—guess about them. Sam had agreed, maybe because she actually did agree. Or maybe in order to placate Michio's insecurities. And then Bull and Sam had fucked around with the budget allocations. It had felt like the deepest betrayal possible. Sam—*her* Sam—making common cause with an Earther. With the Earther who'd been sent by Fred Johnson to mind the untrustworthy Belters.

It had been only her first mistake among many. Michio had let her emotions blind her to the wisdom and experience that Bull had offered her until things were badly out of hand. Despite all the casualties after the catastrophe, she hadn't recognized Ashford's volatility and violence as symptoms of brain injury. She hadn't put aside her faith in the chain of command.

And she hadn't made peace with Sam before Ashford killed her.

Fred Johnson had sent her out into the whirlwind because she was a Belter, and he needed a Belter as a figurehead. She hadn't been ready, but she had been convenient. And because of it, people had died.

The *Behemoth* never came back through the gate. They'd stripped her down, spun up the drum, and rechristened her again as Medina Station. Michio Pa, they'd sent back to Tycho on a Martian naval vessel. After the dead had been removed, there'd been plenty of extra space. As soon as she'd gotten back to her quarters, she'd resigned. She didn't even shower first. She quit her official job on Tycho, her militia rank in the OPA, everything. Fred Johnson had sent her personal messages. She didn't know what was in them. She'd deleted them without listening.

And she'd gotten lost, taking one job and another. Trying to keep her nightmares and crying jags to herself. She ran a ship for a salvaging company that sometimes verged over into piracy. She oversaw a trading co-op that didn't announce itself to the tariff boards, which was technically smuggling. She was managing a supply warehouse complex on Rhea for a half-criminal labor union based out of Titan when Nadia and Bertold found her. It had taken six months before she'd realized that she was in love with them and four more before she understood what it meant that they loved her too. The day they first made a home together in a thin, inexpensive hole half a klick below the moon's surface was one of the best she'd ever had.

The others had come in their own way. Laura and Oksana together. And then Josep. Evans. Each new person folded into the marriage had felt like an expansion of her tribe. Her people. Not the politicians, not the war leaders, not the men who loved to wield power. There was a difference between, on the one hand, the Belt and its fight to exist in the face of the gate she'd helped open and, on the other, the voices and bodies of her family.

But the dream didn't die. Somewhere in the back of her mind, the idea of a Belter navy that could stand toe-to-toe with Earth and Mars and demand to be respected lay dormant but alive.

And so when Marco Inaros came with his proposal in hand, she'd heard him out. She was still remembered in Belter circles as the captain who'd stepped up in the slow zone. People respected her name. When the time came, he needed someone who would coordinate rounding up the colony ships he was keeping out of the slow zone and see that the supplies made it to Belters in need. Take from the rich inners and give to the poor of the Belt until things were even. Until they reached the utopia of the void.

But not yet. Now he just needed small favors. Moving some contraband through to Ganymede. Overseeing a prisoner transfer. Helping set up a band of hidden relays outside Jupiter. He had cultivated her with a grand vision and small steps.

And by *cultivated*, she might have meant *seduced*.

"How many ships do we have coming to Ceres?" he asked, walking beside her. The administrative levels of Ceres Station had the smell of living plants, the polished floors and walls that were meant as a boast. Michio felt a little out of place there, but Marco didn't. He managed to make wherever he was feel like his natural habitat.

"Seven," she said. "The closest's the *Alastair Rauch*. It's been braking for a while. Should hit dock in three days. The *Hornblower*'s the farthest, but Carmondy can up the burn if we need him to. I'm trying to have the fleet conserve reaction mass."

"Good. That's good," Marco said, putting his hand on her shoulder. His guards stopped at the door to the conference room, and Michio started past them. Marco held her back. "We're going to need to shift them."

"Shift them?"

"Route them to other ports. Or run them dark and just let them be for a while."

Michio shook her head. It wasn't actual rejection as much as her body expressing her confusion. Half a dozen responses came to her: *They all need to refuel someplace* and *We have stations running low on food and fertilizer that are already coming here to get it* and *Are you kidding me?*

"Why?" she asked.

Marco's smile was warm and charming. Excited and bright. She found herself smiling along with him without knowing why.

"Situation's changed," he said, and then walked into the conference room ahead of her. His guards nodded to her as she passed them, and she wondered for a moment where Marco's son was.

The others were around the conference table. The wall where Marco had spent days outlining his vision of the future Belt had been cleared, and in its place, a picture of an ancient warrior. The man was dark-skinned with an ornate mustache and beard, a turban, a long, flowing white robe, a crimson sash with three swords tucked in it, and an ancient rifle cradled in one arm.

"You're late," Dawes said to Marco mildly as Michio took her seat. Marco ignored them both.

"Consider the Afghan," Marco said. "Lords of the Graveyard of Empires. Even Alexander the Great couldn't conquer these people. Every great power who attempted it exhausted themselves and failed."

"But they barely had a functioning economy," Sanjrani said. Rosenfeld touched the other man's arm and put a finger to his own lips.

Marco paced before the image. "How did they manage it? How did a technologically primitive, scattered people defy the greatest powers in the world for century after century?" He turned to the others. "Do you know?"

None of them answered. They weren't meant to. This was a performance. Marco's grin widened. He lifted a hand.

"They cared about different things," he said. "To the enemy, war was about territory. Ownership. Occupation. To these geniuses, it was about controlling the spaces they did not occupy. When the English armies came to an Afghan city, ready to take the field of battle, they found...nothing. The enemy faded into the hills, lived in the spaces that the enemy discounted. For the English, the city was a thing to be owned. For the Afghan, it was no more sacred than the hills and the desert and the fields."

"That's a bit *romantic*, don't you think?" Rosenfeld said, but Marco ignored him.

"These brave people. They were the Belters of their age and place. Our spiritual fathers. And the time has come for us to honor them. My friends, the *Azure Dragon* has fallen, as we knew it would eventually. Earth is preparing to lash out in its pain and ignorance."

"You've heard something?" Dawes asked. His face was pale.

"Nothing new," Marco said. "We always knew that Ceres was a target for them. They've been biding their time since the OPA's takeover, but our cousin Anderson here was always careful to balance his power with appeasement. It was never their greatest concern. Not until now. The UN Navy is redeploying. They are heading for Ceres. But when they get here...?"

Marco lifted his two closed fists to his mouth, then blew on them and spread his fingers. It was an illusion, but Michio felt she could almost see the ashes blowing off his hands.

"You can't mean..." Dawes choked.

"I've already started the evacuation," Marco said. "All our soldiers and materiel will be off the station well before they arrive."

"There are six million people on the station," Rosenfeld said. "I don't know that we can take them all."

"Of course not," Marco said. "This is a military action. We

take the military ships and supplies that we need, and cede the territory to Earth. They won't let Ceres starve and die. The only thing they have is the chance to play victim and wring sympathy out of the simpleminded. If they don't take care of Ceres, they'll lose even that. And us? We'll be in the emptiness that is our natural home. Unassailable."

"But," Sanjrani said. Almost whined. "The *economic* base."

"Don't worry," Marco said. "Everything we've discussed is coming. Only first, we have to let the enemy overextend itself and collapse. This was always part of the plan."

Dawes rose to his feet. His face was gray as ash apart from two bright red smears on his cheeks. His hands shook. "This is about Filip. You're getting back at me?"

"This isn't about Filip Inaros," Marco said, but the elation and excitement had vanished from his voice. "This is about Philip of Macedon. And about learning the lessons of history." He was silent for a long, terrible moment. Dawes sank back into his chair. "Now. Michio and I have already discussed rerouting the incoming ships. Let's talk about the logistics of emptying the station itself, yes?"

The way that inners fled their own ships when they came to a station fed a certain species of jokes among Belters. How can a Belter choose a ship's dinner menu? Dock. How can you tell an Inner's been away from port too long? They go outside to shit. If you give an Earther the choice of staying on board ship and saving her sweetheart's life or heading out to the docks and never loving again, how do you dispose of the body? It was the way they looked at everything: The ship wasn't real, the planet was. Or the moon. Or the asteroid. They couldn't let go of the idea that life involved rock and soil. It was what made them smaller.

Michio's people weren't all on the *Connaught* when she passed through the docking tube and into her ship's lock, but most were. The ones who were out would likely come back to sleep in their bunks. No one would think it was odd that her whole marriage group was there. Or if it was a little odd, not implausible at least.

She headed down the lift with the weird sense of seeing the ship for the first time. Like stepping into a new station, everything was in sharp focus. Unfamiliar. The green and red indicators of the lift control. The thin, white text printed on every panel to show what was housed behind it and when it had been installed. The subtle MCRN logo still visible on the floor despite their best efforts to buff it away. The smell of black noodles came from the galley, but she didn't pause. If she tried to eat now, she'd only vomit anyway.

They were in the cabins set aside for the family. One of the first things Bertold had done when they got the *Connaught* was take the walls off three of the cabins to make a wider space with crash couches enough that they could all sit together. The Martian designers had made the ship so that people could be alone or else together. It took a Belter to make space to be alone together. Oksana and Laura were sitting on the deck, their harps almost touching as they played through an old Celtic melody. Oksana's paleness and Laura's dark made them seem like something from a fairy tale. Josep lounged in one of the couches, his hand terminal set to some text or another, reading and swaying his foot to the music. Evans sat beside him, trying not to seem nervous. Nadia, looking like the however-many-greats-granddaughter of Marco's Afghan soldier, stood behind one of the other couches, gently massaging Bertold's thinning black hair.

Michio sat in the couch they'd left for her and listened until the melody came to an end in a series of ambiguous fourths and fifths. They put down their harps and hand terminal. Bertold opened his one good eye.

"Thank you for coming," Michio said.

"Always," Laura said.

"Just to ask," Josep said. "Are you our captain or our wife right now?"

"I'm your wife. I think...I think that I ..."

And then she was weeping. She leaned forward, hands over

her eyes. The tight monkey's-fist knot that was her heart blocked her throat. She tried to cough it out of the way, but it sounded like a sob. Laura's hand touched her foot. And then Bertold's arm was across her back and he folded her in against him. She heard Oksana murmuring, "It's okay, baby. It's all right," from what might have been half a world away. It was too much. It was all too much.

"I did it," Michio managed at last. "I did it again. I put us in Marco's control, and he's...He's another Ashford. He's another Fred fucking Johnson. I tried so hard not to do it again, and I did it. And I brought you all along. And I'm so...I'm so *sorry*."

Her family descended on her gently, a hand or an arm, all of them touching her. Offering her comfort. Saying wordlessly that they were there. Evans wept with her, not even knowing why. The tears got worse for a while, confused for a while. And then better. Clearer. The worst of it passed. And when she was herself again, it was Josep that spoke.

"Tell us the story. It'll have less power then."

"He's abandoning Ceres. Getting all the Free Navy out and leave the people for the inners. The colony ships we took? He wants to drive them dark out of the ecliptic for storage instead of delivering the supplies."

"Ah," Nadia said. "That kind, is he?"

"It's hard, changing," Josep said. "Tell yourself you're a warrior long enough, you start believing it. Then peace looks like death. An annihilation of self."

"Little abstract, honey," Nadia said.

Josep blinked wide eyes at her, then smiled ruefully. "More concrete. You're right. You always are."

"I'm so sorry," Michio said. "I did it wrong again. I trusted someone. I put myself in his command, and...I'm stupid. I'm just stupid."

"We all agreed," Oksana said through a scowl. "We all believed."

"You believed because I asked you to," Michio said. "This is my fault."

"Now," Laura said, "Michi? What's the magic word?"

Against her will, Michio laughed. It was an old joke. A part of what made her family her family.

"The magic word is *oops*," she said. And then a moment later, "Oops."

Bertold took a moment to noisily blow his nose and wipe the last of the tears from his eyes. "All right. So what do we do?"

"We can't keep working with the bastard," Oksana said.

Nadia nodded with her hand. "And we can't stay here and wait for the Earthers."

Together, without meaning to, they all looked to her. Michio, their wife. But also their captain. She took a long, shuddering breath. "The thing he asked us for? Gather up the colony ships and spread the food and supplies to the Belters that need them? It still needs doing. And we still have a gunship to do it with. Some of the other ships might see things our way. So either we stick to the mission or else we try to find someplace quiet and sink out of sight before Inaros figures that we're gone."

Her family was silent for what felt like a long time, though it wasn't more than a few breaths set end to end. Bertold scratched at his bad eye. Nadia and Oksana traded a look that seemed to mean something. Laura cleared her throat.

"Being small isn't being safe. Not now."

"Vrai," Bertold said. "I'm for doing what we said we'd do, and fuck the rest. Changed sides before and it didn't kill us."

"Did we?" Josep said. "Would we be changing sides now?"

"Yes," Evans said. "We would."

Josep turned to look Michio full in the eyes. The humor and love in his face was like warmth radiating from a heater. "Fought the oppressor before. Still fighting the oppressor now. Followed your heart then. Still following your heart now. The situation changes, that doesn't mean you do."

"That's sweet," Michio said, taking his hand.

"Abstract, though," Nadia said, and there was love in her voice too.

"Everything you've done," Josep said, "every mistake, every loss, every scar. They all brought you here, so that as soon as you saw Big Himself for what he is, you'd be ready to act. Incapable of *not* acting, even. Everything then was preparation for now."

"That's bullshit," Michio said. "But thank you."

"If the universe needs a knife, it makes a knife," Josep said with a shrug. "If it needs a pirate queen, it makes Michio Pa."

Chapter Twelve: Holden

The wall screen in the dock's public lobby was tuned to an enter-tainment newsfeed. A breathtakingly pretty young woman with one eyelid that was either rouged or tattooed red was being interviewed by someone off screen. The crawler at the bottom of the screen identified her as Zedina Rael. Holden wasn't sure who she was. The sound was on, but incomprehensible over the sound of the people moving through the lobby to or from the docks. The subtitles were in Hindi. On the screen, Rael shook her head, and a thick tear dripped down her cheek as the feed shifted to images of a ruined city under a filthy brown sky. So something about the situation on Earth.

It was easy to forget that the entertainment feeds—musicians and actors and celebrities-for-the-sake-of-celebrity—were all going to be as affected by the catastrophe as everybody else. It felt like that slice of reality should be separate. Inviolate. Plagues

and wars and disasters weren't supposed to impinge on the manufactured world of entertainment, but of course they did. Zedina
Rael, whatever she did that got her a place on the screen, was a
human being too. And had probably lost someone she loved when
the rocks fell. Would probably lose more.

"Captain Holden?" The man was thick-shouldered and dark-
haired with a sharp goatee. He carried an air of exhaustion and
good humor along with his hand terminal. His uniform identified
him as Port Control and his name badge read Bates. "Sorry there.
You been waiting long?"

"Nope," Holden said, taking the proffered terminal. "Just a
few minutes."

"Things are busy," Bates said.

"Not a problem," Holden said as he signed and pressed his
thumb to the reader pad. The terminal chimed. It was a small,
happy sound. Like the terminal was very happy Holden had autho-
rized the delivery.

"Got you in bay H-15?" Bates said. "We'll have that unloaded
for you right away. Who's your repair coordinator?"

"We've got our own," Holden said. "Naomi Nagata."

"Right. Of course," the man said, nodded once, and was gone.
On the screen Zedina Rael had been replaced by a thick-featured
Ifrah McCoy. At least Holden knew who she was. The invisible
interviewer said something, and a lull in the background noise let
him hear the answer: *There must be a response. We have to stand
up.* The frustration and pain in McCoy's voice bothered him, and
he didn't know if it was because he agreed with her or because
he was afraid what that response would lead to. He turned back
toward the docks proper and the work at hand.

In a spin station like Tycho or the Lagrange stations, the ship
would have been parked in vacuum. Luna was another thing
entirely. The shipyard had vast locks dug deep into the lunar
body with tugs to guide ships in and out, retractable seals, air.
The *Rocinante* stood upright, drive cone toward the center of the
moon and chisel-tip upper decks toward the stars, held in a web-

work of scaffolding. The space was large enough to house a ship three times her size, and all of it was filled with breathable air.

Racks of construction mechs stood against the wall except for the four that were on the *Rocinante*, crawling gently over its surface like spiders on a crow. Naomi was in one, Amos in another. The third was Sandra Ip, one of two engineers who Fred Johnson had brought on as the *Roci*'s crew for the flight to Luna when the real crew—less Holden—had scattered to the void.

Alex and Bobbie stood on a raised platform, looking up at the body of the ship. The damage the Free Navy had done was knotted as a scar, and bright. Wide panels—the newly delivered sections of hull—rose up the ship and scaffold, guided by massive waldoes. Alex held out a headset, and Holden connected it to his hand terminal, shifting to the full-crew channel.

"How's it looking?" he asked.

"They did a number on us," Naomi said. "I'm impressed."

"Always easier to break things than put them together," Holden said.

"More evidence for that," Naomi agreed with a Belter nod of the fist. "And these replacement sections ..."

"Problem?"

Sandra Ip's voice answered. It was a little jarring to hear an unfamiliar voice. "They're carbon-silicate lace. State-of-the-art. Lighter, stronger. These things can deflect a glancing PDC round." Defensiveness just below the surface told Holden this wasn't the first time through the conversation.

"They can for now," Naomi said. Holden switched his mic to the *Rocinante*-only channel, but kept listening on the full crew.

"So, just between the family here? What's the issue with the new plates?"

"Nothing," Naomi said. "They're great. Everything it says on the tin. But five years from now? Ten?"

"They don't age well?"

"Well, that's the thing," Alex drawled. "Ain't none of this stuff ten years old yet. The materials-science folks got a kick in the pants after the protomolecule. Bunches of new toys. Lace plating's just one. In theory, it should hold up just like the real thing. In practice, we're the practice. I had a hell of a time convincing the *Roci* I wasn't putting in the wrong mass for them too. It's going to change how she handles."

Holden crossed his arms. Above him, the waldoes shifted the new hull section in, laying it along the *Roci*'s side. "Are we sure we want to do this? We can hold out for the regular kind."

"Not if we want to get out to Tycho anytime soon, we can't," Naomi said. "There's a war on."

"We can turn down the contract," Holden said. "Fred can find another ride."

"I don't know, Cap," Amos said. "Things being what they are, I kind of like that we're getting work. I mean, as long as money still works." He paused. "Hey, does money still work?"

"It does if we win," Naomi said. "Free Navy ports weren't going to refit and refuel us anyway."

"Right," Amos said. "So I kind of like that we're getting work."

Two of the mechs scuttled forward to the edge of the new hull plate. Welding torches like little suns burst into life, cleaving old technology and new together. There was something about it that Holden disliked and distrusted. But there was also something amazing. The very fabric the lace hull was made from hadn't existed when he was born, and now it did.

Vast intelligences had designed the protomolecule, the rings, the weird and implacable ruins that covered all the new worlds. They might be extinct, but they were also being incorporated into what humanity knew, what it could do, how it defined itself. A kid born today would grow up in a world where carbon-silicate lace was as common as titanium or glass. That it was a collaboration between humanity and the ghosts of a massive and alien intelligence would go right by them. Holden was one of the lucky generation who would straddle that break point, that seam between before and after that Naomi and Amos and Ip were making literal right now, and so he could be amazed by how cool it was. Creepy, but cool.

"It's the future," he said. "We might as well get some practice with it."

The rest of Fred Johnson's temporary crew were either already on the *Rocinante* along with Clarissa or on the way from their quarters on Luna. There was an excitement about the coming action. It was the first time that they—Earth, Mars, and even the less radical splinters of the OPA—would work together to take any direct action against the Free Navy. The heavy lifting would be done by Earth and Mars, but the *Rocinante* would be there. An observation ship carrying Fred Johnson. A representative, however imperfect, of the Belt. They were ready.

Except that Holden also wasn't.

Especially now that his parents had come up the well from Earth, the impulse to stay close surprised him. He'd spent most of his adult life off-planet. If anyone had asked, he'd have told them that he didn't miss Earth. Some people, yes. Some places from his childhood, maybe. But there'd been no sense of longing for the planet itself. It was only now that it had been attacked that he wanted to protect it. Maybe it was always like that. He'd outgrown his childhood home, but in the back of his mind, the unexamined assumption was that it would still be there. Changed, maybe. Grown a little older. But there. Only it wasn't now. Wanting to stay was the same as wanting to go back a little in time to when it hadn't happened.

Fred Johnson sent a message. He and weapons technicians Sun-yi Steinberg and Gor Droga were finishing their last meeting. As soon as the new hull was welded into place and the pressure tests complete, they could go. If Holden had any last business on Luna, this was the time for it.

He had some last business on Luna.

The torches flared and died and flared again. The *Rocinante* was remade a little, the same way it had been over and over through the years. Little changes adding up over time as the ship moved from what it had been to what it would be next. Just like all the people she carried.

"You okay?" Bobbie asked.

"What?" Holden said.

"You were sighing," she said.

"He does that sometimes," Alex said.

"I do?" Holden said, realizing as he did that Bobbie was still looped in on the *Rocinante*-only channel. That he was glad she was. "I didn't know I did that."

"Don't worry about it," Naomi said. "It's cute."

"So," he said. "When you're done with that, Naomi? Fred's on his way."

"Yeah," she said, and he was probably just imagining the dread in her voice. "All right."

The cart that drove them down toward the refugee station ran on electromagnetic track that held the wheels to the ground. Part-grumble, part-chime, the sound was loud enough that Holden felt he had to raise his voice a little to be heard over it.

"If she's still being paid through the UN or Mars, that would be different," Holden said. "If we're offering her a place on the ship permanently, I just think we need to be careful about how we do it."

"She's good," Naomi said. "She's actually trained for a ship like the *Roci*, which is more than any of us can say. She gets along with the crew. Why wouldn't you want Bobbie on board?"

The air in the deeper corridors was damp and close. The environmental systems were working at their full capacity, and a little bit more. People shuffled out of the cart's way, some staring at them as they passed, some not seeming to look at anything.

The refugee station stank of loss and waiting. Almost every person they passed was a lifetime that had been severed from its roots. Holden and Naomi were the lucky ones here. They still had their home, even if it was a changed one.

"It's not Bobbie," Holden said. "Of course I want Bobbie. But the terms...Do we pay her? Do we redistribute ownership of the

Roci so that she's got the same stake in her that all of us do? I'm not sure that's a good idea."

Naomi looked at him, her eyebrows rising. "Why not?"

"Because whatever we do with Bobbie sets the precedent for what we do with any other crew we bring on."

"Meaning Clarissa."

"I don't want to give Clarissa Mao ownership of the *Roci*," Holden said. "I just…She's here, and okay, fine. I'm still not sanguine about that, but I can deal with it. And I want to bring Bobbie all the way into the crew, but I just— I can't. I can't agree that Clarissa ever gets to call my ship her home. There's a difference between letting her be there and pretending she's like Bobbie. Or you. Or me."

"No forgiveness?" Naomi asked, halfway between teasing and serious.

"Plenty of forgiveness. Loads of forgiveness. Some boundaries too."

The cart lurched to the left, slowed. The chiming sound cycled lower as it stopped. Father Anton was waiting at the door, smiling and nodding to them as they lifted themselves out and bounce-shuffled forward. The quarters for Holden's parents were better than most. The suite was tight and too small, but private. His mothers and fathers didn't have to share it with anyone outside the family. Mother Tamara's yellow curry scented the air. Father Tom and Father Cesar stood in the doorway to one of the bedrooms, arms around each other's hips. Father Dimitri leaned against the arm of an old sofa, while Mother Elise and Mother Tamara came in from the little kitchen. Father Joseph and Mother Sophie sat on the couch, a thin magnetic chess set between them, the pieces scattered by their game. Everyone was smiling, including him, and none of them meant it.

It was goodbye again. When he'd left for his doomed tour in the Navy, there'd been a moment like this too. A leave-taking that meant something they couldn't be sure of. Maybe he'd be back in a few weeks. Or never. Maybe they'd be here on Luna, or transfer to L-4. Or something else might happen. Without the farm and decades of social inertia to hold them together, maybe they would break apart. A sudden, oceanic sadness washed through Holden, and he had to fight to keep it from showing. Protecting his parents from his distress one more time. Just the way they were doing for him.

One by one, and then in groups, they hugged. Mother Elise held Naomi's hand and told her to take care of her little boy. Naomi solemnly agreed that she'd do what she could. If this might be the last time he had his parents all together, he was grateful that Naomi was there to be part of it, right up until Father Cesar said goodbye.

Cesar's skin was wrinkled as a turtle's, dark as fresh-turned earth. There were tears in his eyes as he took Holden's hand. "You did good, boy. You made everyone proud of you."

"Thank you," Holden said.

"You go give those fucking *skinnies* hell, yeah?"

Over Cesar's left shoulder, Naomi went stiff. Her smile, which had been soft and warm and amused, became polite. Holden felt it like a punch in the gut. But Cesar didn't even seem to know that he'd said something rude. Holden was trapped between asking his father to apologize and preserving this last moment. Naomi, talking to Mother Tamara, plucked at her hair. Pulled it over her eyes.

Shit.

"You know," Holden said. "That's—"

"That's what he'll do," Naomi said. "You can count on Jim."

Her eyes were on his, and they were hard and dark. *Don't make this more awkward than it already is* glowed in them as clearly as if she'd written it. Holden grinned, hugged Father Cesar one last time, and started the retreat to the door, the cart, the *Rocinante*. All eight of his parents crowded outside the door to watch him go. He felt them there even when the cart turned the corner and started up the ramp toward the docks. Naomi sat silently. Holden sighed.

"Okay," he said. "I see now why you didn't want to do that. I'm really sorry that—"

"Don't," Naomi said. "Let's don't."

"I think I owe you an apology."

She shifted to look straight at him. "Your father owes me an apology. One of your fathers. But I'm going to let him off the hook."

"All right," Holden said. The cart lurched to the right. A man with a thick beard trotted out of their way. "I was going to defend you."

"I know you were."

"Just...I would have."

"I know. And then I would have been the reason that everything had gotten weird, and everyone would have gone out of their way to tell me how they respect Belters and how he didn't mean *me*. And you're their son, and they love you. And they love each other. So no matter what anyone said, it would all have been my fault."

"Yeah," Holden said. "But then I wouldn't feel as bad about it. And I feel kind of bad about it."

"Cross you'll have to bear, sweetie," Naomi said. She sounded tired.

At the dock, Fred Johnson's crew was loading the last of the supplies into the cargo airlock. The new lace hull panels stood out on the *Roci*'s side like scars. The cart, having dropped them off, rumbled and chimed itself away. Holden paused for a moment, looking up at the ship. His heart was complicated.

"Yeah?" Naomi said.

"Nothing," Holden said. And then, a moment later, "There was a time I thought things were simple. Or that at least some things were."

"He didn't mean me. No, really. He didn't. Because I'm a person to him, and skinnies and Belters...they aren't people. I had friends on the *Pella*. Real friends. People I grew up with. People I cared about. People I loved. They aren't any different. They didn't kill *people*, they killed Earthers. Martians. Dusters. Squats."

"Squats?"

"Yup."

"Hadn't heard that one."

She put her hand in his, shifted her body against his, reached up to rest her chin on the top of his head. "It's considered rude."

Holden leaned against her as much as the weak gravity would allow. He felt the warmth of her body against his. Felt the rise and fall of her breath.

"We're not people," he said. "We're the stories that people tell each other about us. Belters are crazy terrorists. Earthers are lazy gluttons. Martians are cogs in a great big machine."

"Men are fighters," Naomi said, and then, her voice growing bleak. "Women are nurturing and sweet and they stay home with the kids. It's always been like that. We always react to the stories about people, not who they really are."

"And look where it got us," Holden said.

Chapter Thirteen: Prax

The thing that surprised him the most when it all changed was how little it all changed. At least in the beginning. Between the trailing end of the reconstruction and the rising tide of research projects, Prax sometimes went days or weeks without looking at newsfeeds. Anything interesting in the greater sphere of humanity, he heard about in the conversations of others. When he'd heard that the governing board was putting out a declaration of neutrality, he'd thought it was about gas sequestration and exchange. He hadn't even known there was a war until Karvonides told him.

Ganymede knew too much about being a battlefield already. The collapse was too recent in their collective memory, the scars still fresh and raw. There were ice-flooded corridors still unexcavated after the last outbreak of violence, back before the ring gate, back before the opening of the thirteen hundred worlds. No one wanted that again. And so Ganymede said it didn't care who ran things, just so long as they could continue their research, care for the people in their hospitals, and go about their lives. A massive *We're busy, you figure it out* to the universe in general.

And then…nothing. No one claimed them or threatened them. No one fired nukes at them, or if they had, the weapons hadn't landed and the event hadn't made the news. So much of Ganymede's food was locally sourced, no one worried about going hungry. Prax had some concerns about research funding, but after the first few times he brought it up and had the issue swept aside, he'd stopped trying. They were in a holding pattern. They were keeping their heads down, doing the things they'd always done, hoping no one took notice.

And so Prax's daily trip between his hole and Mei's school and his offices had been weirdly unchanged. The food carts in the station served the same fried corn mash and bitter tea. The project-management meetings continued on Mondays before lunch. The generations of plant and fungus and yeast and bacteria lived and died and were analyzed just the way they would have been if no one had crippled Earth. Or killed it.

When Belters in Free Navy uniforms started appearing on the corners, no one said anything. When the Free Navy ships had started demanding resupply, their scrip had been added to the approved list of currencies and their contracts drawn up. When loyalists who'd filled their boards and feeds with support for Earth and demands that the governing board take a stand went silent, no one talked about it. It was just understood. Ganymede's neutrality was permitted so long as the Free Navy could enforce it. Marco Inaros—who Prax had never heard of before the rocks fell—might not control the base, but he was quite willing to prune away the people who did until the organizational chart had been bonsai'd into the shape that pleased him. Pay tribute to the Free Navy, and govern yourself. Rebel, and be killed.

So nothing much changed and also everything did. The tension was there every day. In every interaction, however mundane. And it came out at strange times. Like reviewing trial-report data.

"Fuck the animal trials," Karvonides said, her face tight and angry. "Forget them. This is ready to go into production."

Khana crossed his arms, scowling at her. Prax, confused, had only the data to turn to, so he turned to it. Harvester yeast strain 18, sequence 10 was doing very well. The production numbers—sugars and protein both—were slightly above expected. Lipids were inside the error bars. It had been a good run. But...

His office was spare and close. The same room he'd taken when he'd brought Mei back from Luna. The first office of his tenure on the Reconstruction Committee. The others on the committee had moved on to larger places with bamboo paneling and augmented-spectrum lights, but Prax liked being where he already was. The familiar had always offered a powerful comfort. If Khana and Karvonides had worked in any other section, there would have been a couch or at least soft chairs for them to sit on. The lab stools in Prax's office were also the same ones he'd had his first day back.

"I ..." Prax said, then coughed, looked down. "I don't see why we'd break protocol. That seems...um ..."

"Completely irresponsible?" Khana said. "I think the phrase is *completely irresponsible*."

"What's irresponsible is sitting on this," Karvonides said. "Two additions to the genome, fifty generations of growth—so less than three days—and we have a species that can beat chloroplasts for making sugars out of light and extends out almost into gamma. Plus the proteins and micronutrients. Use this for reactor shielding and you can shut down the recycler."

"That's hyperbole," Khana said. "And this is protomolecule technology. If you think—"

"It is not! There is literally nothing in Hy1810 that comes from an alien sample. We looked at the protomolecule, said *It can't do that; can we?* and figured out how to make something of our own. Native proteins. Native DNA. Native catalysts. Nothing that traces back to Phoebe or the ring or anything that came off Ilus or Rho or New London ever touched this."

"That...um," Prax said. "That doesn't mean it's safe, though. The animal protocol—"

"Safe?" Karvonides said, wheeling on him. "There are people starving to death all over the Earth right now. How *safe* are they?"

Oh, Prax thought. *This isn't anger. It's grief.* Prax understood grief.

Khana leaned forward, his hands in fists, but before he could speak, Prax put up his palm. He was in charge here, after all. It didn't hurt to actually exercise his power now and then.

"We'll continue with the animal protocol," he said. "It's better science."

"We could save lives," Karvonides said. Her voice was softer now. "One message. I have a friend at Guandong complex. She'd be able to replicate it."

"I'm not going to be part of this conversation," Khana said. The door slammed closed behind him so hard that the latch didn't hold. The door ghosted open again, like someone invisible was coming in to take his place.

Karvonides sat, her hands on Prax's desk. "Dr. Meng, before you say no, I want you to come with me. There's a meeting tonight. Just a few people. Hear us out. Then, if you really don't want to help, I won't bring it up to you again. I swear."

Her eyes were dark enough it was hard to tell iris from pupil. He looked back down at the data. She was probably right, in her way. Hy1810 wasn't the first yeast that had been modified with radioplasts, and Hy1808 and most of the Hy17 runs had been in animal trials for months without any statistically significant ill effects. With things on Earth as bad as they were, the risk of Hy1810 having adverse effects was almost certainly lower than the dangers of starvation. His stomach felt tight and anxious. He wanted to leave.

"It's proprietary," he said, hearing the whine in his voice as he said it. "Even if we could ethically release it, the legal consequences, not just for us but for the labs in general, would be—"

"Just come hear us out," Karvonides said. "You won't have to say anything. You won't even have to talk."

Prax grunted. A little chuffing sound that centered behind his nose. Like an angry rat.

"I have a daughter," he said.

The silence between them went on for the space of a breath. Then another. Then, "Of course, sir. I understand."

She stood up. Her stool scraped against the flooring. It sounded cheap. The urge to say something fluttered in his chest, but he didn't know what it would be, and before he found it, she was gone. She closed the door more gently than Khana had, but with a greater finality. Prax sat, scratching at his arm though it didn't itch, then he closed the report.

The rest of the day was filled with his own work in the hydroponics labs. His new project was a modified fern built for water and air purification. They stood in long rows, fronds bobbing in the constant and well-regulated breeze. The leaves—so green they were almost black—smelled familiar and welcoming. The embedded sensors had been gathering data since the day before, and he looked it over like sitting with an old friend. Plants were so much easier than people.

When that was done, he stopped back by his office, returned half a dozen messages, and reviewed the meetings scheduled for the next morning. It was all routine. All the same things he'd done before the rocks hit Earth. It was like a ritual.

Today, though, he took the extra step of adding an administrative lock on the Hy1810 data. He tried not to think too much about why he'd done it. Something vague fluttered in the back of his mind about being able to show he'd done all he could do. He wasn't sure who he imagined he'd be defending himself before, but he didn't really want to think about that.

He felt nervous during his walk to the tube station. The pale tile walls, the arching ceiling above the platform. All of it was just as it had been ever since the rebuild. It only seemed ominous because of all the things in his own head. While he waited for his tube, he bought a wax-paper cone of fried bean curd with olive oil and salt. The vendor was an Earther, and Prax noted the way the man had kept his hair and beard long, letting them grow out from his skull to mimic the slightly larger heads of true Belters. The man's skin was dark, so the OPA tattoos on his hands and neck didn't stand out as much as they could have. *Cryptic coloration*, Prax thought as the chime announced the tube's arrival. *Probably a good idea*. It was interesting to see how humanity adopted the strategies you saw anywhere in nature. They were part of nature, after all. Red in tooth and claw.

Mei was already home when he got there. Her voice gabbling with and over the slightly higher tones of Natalia's came in from the playroom like music. Prax relocked the door behind him and went to the kitchen. Djuna, making salad for their dinner and reading something off her hand terminal at the same time, paused both activities to smile her greeting. He kissed her shoulder before going to the little refrigerator and plucking out a beer.

"Isn't it my turn to make dinner?" he said.

"You agreed to take tomorrow because of my late meeting—" Djuna started, then stopped when she saw the beer in his hand. "One of those days?"

"It was fine," he said, but he didn't even convince himself. Part of him thought he should tell her, but that was selfish. Djuna had her own burdens and her own work. She wouldn't be able to do anything about Karvonides or Hy1810. If she couldn't fix it, there was no call to burden her. Besides which, then if anyone asked, she'd be telling the truth when she said she didn't know anything.

Over dinner, they talked about the safer parts of work. His plants, her biofilms. Mei and Natalia were having one of their good days when they seemed more like best friends than stepsisters, and they took turns talking about all the things that had happened at school. David Gutmansdottir had gotten sick from the new lunches and had to go to the nurse, and the math test was late, and they'd gotten exactly the same score, but it was all right because they'd missed different questions, so Mr. Seth knew it wasn't that they cheated, and anyway tomorrow was Dress-in-Red Day, and they both had to make sure to put out the right clothes before bed and …

Prax listened to them running together, leaping subject over verb over object like they were running downhill. Natalia had Djuna's brownness, high cheekbones, and thick nose. Beside her, Mei looked as pale and round as old pictures of Luna. After dinner, it was Mei's turn to clean up, and Prax helped her a little. The truth was, she didn't need it. But he enjoyed her company, and it wouldn't be long before she was old enough to start differentiating from the family unit. Then it was homework hour for all of them, and then baths and then beds. Mei and Natalia stayed up talking across their bedrooms to each other until Djuna shut the connecting door. Even then, the two girls talked, like they had to burn through their buffers before sleep could finally come.

Prax lay beside Djuna, his arm as a pillow, and wondered where Karvonides was. If her meeting had gone well. If he hoped it had or not. Maybe he should have accepted her invitation. Even if it was only so that he could know what was going on …

He didn't notice that he was falling asleep until the door chime woke him. Prax sat up, disoriented. Djuna was looking at him, her eyes wide and round and frightened. The chime came again, and his first nearly coherent thought was that he should answer before they woke the girls.

"Don't go," Djuna said, but he was already lurching across the bedroom. He grabbed his robe, knotting the belt as he stumbled into the dimness of the rooms. The system readout said it was just after midnight. The chime came again, and then a deep, soft knocking, like a massive fist using only a fraction of its power. He heard Mei cry out, and knew from long experience that the sound meant she was still asleep, but wouldn't be for long. The skin on Prax's flank puckered into goose bumps that only had a little to do with the temperature of the air.

"Who's there?" Prax said through the closed door.

"Dr. Praxidike Meng?" a man's muffled voice asked.

"Yes," Prax said. "Who is it?"

"Security," the voice said. "Please open the door."

Which security? Prax wanted to ask. Ganymede Station security or Free Navy? But it was too late now. If it was Station, it made sense to open the door. If it was Free Navy, it wouldn't stop them if he didn't. What he was going to do next was the same either way.

"Of course," he said, then swallowed.

The uniforms of the two men in the hall were gray and blue. Station security. The relief that flooded his bloodstream was evidence of how frightened he'd been. How frightened he *always* was these days.

"Can I help you?" he asked.

The morgue smelled like a lab. The chemical reek of the phenol soap bit at his sinuses. The throbbing hum of the high-use air filters. The clinical lights. It reminded him of his years at upper university. He'd taken a cadaver lab then too. The body he'd dissected had been suffused in preservative fluids, though. Not as fresh. And it had been in better condition.

"The identification's solid," one of the security people said. "Metrics and markers sync up. ID matches. But you know how it is. No relatives on the station, and the union has rules."

"Does it?" Prax asked. He meant the question honestly, but when he said it out loud, the words took on nuances he hadn't intended. Can a union still matter when there's barely a government any longer? Are there still rules? The security man grimaced.

"It's the way we've always done it," he said, and Prax heard the defensiveness in the man's voice. The hint of anger. As if Prax was responsible for all the changes they were suffering.

Karvonides lay on the table, her modesty maintained by a black rubber sheet. Her expression was calm. The wounds on her neck and the side of her head were complicated and ugly, but the lack of fresh blood gave the illusion that they weren't serious. They'd shot her four times. He wondered if the others from her meeting were in other rooms, on other tables, waiting for other witnesses.

"I'll attest," he said.

"Thank you," the other security man said, and held out a hand terminal. Prax took it, pressed his palm to the plate. It chirped when it was done recording him, a weirdly cheerful sound, given the circumstances. Prax handed it back. He looked at the dead woman's face, waiting to understand what he felt about her. He had the sense that he should cry, but he didn't feel like it. In his mind, she'd become evidence not of a crime but of what the world had become. Her death wasn't the beginning of an investigation, but the conclusion of one. The data was unambiguous. What happens when you stand up? You're cut down.

"Can we ask you a few questions about the deceased, Dr. Meng?"

"Of course."

"How long have you known her?"

"Two and a half years."

"In what capacity?"

"She was a researcher in my labs. Hmm. I'll have to make sure her datasets get collected. Can I make a note of that? Or do I need to wait until the interrogation's done?"

"This isn't an interrogation, sir. You go right ahead."

"Thank you." Prax pulled up his hand terminal and put an entry on his list for the morning. He thought at first there was something wrong with the display, but it was only his hand trembling. He shoved the terminal back in his pocket. "Thank you," he said again.

"Do you have any idea who might have done this to her? Or why?"

The Free Navy did this to her, Prax thought. *They did it because she was trying to stand against them. She was doing that because people are suffering and starving and dying that might not have to, and she had it in her power to make a difference. They found out, and they killed her. The way they'd kill me if I made things uncomfortable for them.*

He looked into the security man's inquiring eyes. *The way they'd kill you too*, he thought.

"Anything you can offer on the question, sir? Even something small might help."

"No," Prax said. "I don't have any idea."

Chapter Fourteen: Filip

The docks of Ceres Station ran, roughly speaking, along its equator in a wide belt of titanium and ceramic and steel. The dwarf planet's movement made docking difficult, but once the clamps took hold, ships had the advantage of the 0.3g of spin gravity even with the drive off and cold. And with the radius of spin as big as it was, the Coriolis should have been negligible. The *Pella* should have felt like it was under a moderate burn and nothing more, but something kept bothering Filip. A sense that the ship was wrong, or that he was.

Twice, he snuck into the medical bay and had diagnostics run, then deleted the results after he read them. They didn't show anything anyway. But maybe he was just so used to life under thrust that the trace of sideways impulse was enough to unsettle him. Or maybe it was only that the ship was empty except for him. A small, gnawing part of his mind kept suggesting it had something to do with the man he'd shot, but that didn't make any sense. Along with his father, he'd killed billions. Shooting one man— one that didn't even die—was nothing to him. It had to be the Coriolis.

His father had made it very clear that Filip's universe stopped at the airlock. The *Pella* and everything in it was his the same as it always was, but Ceres Station was worse than vacuum. Fair or unfair, Filip was banned from the station for life. It was the deal Marco had struck with the OPA governor, Dawes. The others would be an active part of the evacuation, but Filip could only watch. And so he walked the corridors, went up and down the lift, slept, ate, exercised, and waited while just on the other side of the airlock, all the people he knew best stripped Ceres Station to the studs. He'd have been part of the effort if he could. Maybe that was all it was. Maybe it was just the fact that he'd been left behind and relaxing while the others did the work didn't sit well with him. That seemed more likely than Coriolis. Or the man he'd shot.

The truth was, he didn't remember much of the event. He'd been out with maybe a dozen Free Navy and some local fringe and hangers-on. According to the old laws he was still too young to be in the bars and brothels, but he was Filip Inaros and no one had suggested he leave. There had been music. He'd danced with a local girl, admired her tattoos, bought her drinks. And he'd kept up with her too, drink for drink. She'd liked him, he could tell. And if the music had been too loud for them to talk, that didn't matter. He could tell.

Her interest hadn't been about him so much as about the story of who he was. The son of Marco Inaros. Karal had warned him. Marco had warned him. Some people would be attracted to what they thought he was. He had to be careful always to remember who his family was. Not let himself be baited or seduced. The Free Navy had the power now, but there were still people on Ceres who were more than half loyal to the old ways.

Our enemies, at least you know where they stand, his father had said when they arrived at Ceres. *There's nothing you can trust less than half-Belters.* Marco hadn't said it straight out, but he'd meant Filip's mother and all the people like her. Belters who'd let themselves be turned away from the Belt and the condescending Fred Johnson Earthers who pretended to care about them. *Moderate OPA* was just another way to say *traitor.* So Filip had known not to trust the girl, even while he was drinking with her. Drinking too much with her. When she'd left without telling him, he'd felt humiliated and angry. And then something had happened, he couldn't quite put together, and he'd been carted off by Ceres security and his father called. Which had been humiliating again.

They hadn't talked, not really. Marco had ordered him to stay on ship, so on ship he'd stayed. Maybe they'd never speak of it again. Maybe that conversation was still coming. Maybe not knowing which was what left him feeling wrong. He didn't know. He hated that he didn't know.

He sat in the gunner's station, the screen slaved to his terminal, and sampled the feeds. A man posting under an old-style OPA banner shouting about how the Free Navy was the last, best hope for Belter liberty. A thin-faced coyo sitting too close to his camera talking in halting Farsi about the implications of the biologicals supplied by Earth being cut off. Some high-end pornography in what looked like a water treatment plant and a hotel lobby. An old Sabbu Re movie series, pairing him against Sanjit Sangre back when Sangre had still looked like a badass. Noise. It was all just noise and images, and Filip let them wash over him without noticing what he was taking in. An impressionistic sense of violence and victory, with him and his father at the head of it all. Arousal and anger paired with all the complexity of an old way of life passing into darkness.

When he killed the speakers, the *Pella* was quiet in the never-quite silent way a ship had. The drive was off, so there were none of the low hums or occasional harmonics that made the background of his normal life. But the decking joints still ticked and murmured as the plates warmed or cooled. The air recyclers hissed and huffed and hissed again. So maybe that was part of what felt wrong. The sounds of a ship under thrust were so unlike a ship in dock that the subtle background music of his life had changed and set him on edge. The tightness in his belly, the impatience like an itch in his soul that kept him uncomfortable no matter what position he sat in or stood. The ache in his jaw and across his shoulders. Maybe they were just the natural expression of a man used to being in motion being forced into passivity. That was all. Nothing more than that.

Before you kill yourself, his mother had said, *come find me.*

He stood up, shut down the feeds with a gesture, and stalked down toward the gym. The good thing about being alone was that no one was using any of the equipment. He didn't bother warming up, just brought down the resistance bands, strapped in, and pulled. He relished the way the handles bit into his palms, the sense of his muscles protesting and tearing, each little injury making them grow back again stronger. Between sets, he turned on some music—loud, aggressive dai-bhangra—only to stop in the middle of the next set and turn it off again.

Everything he wanted annoyed him as soon as he had it. He wondered if he'd have felt the same about the girl. If she'd stayed, and they'd fucked, if afterward he'd have wanted her gone. Turned off like the music. He didn't know what it would take to make him feel right. Getting the fuck off Ceres wouldn't hurt, though.

The voices came first, loud and laughing and familiar as Tía Michelle's bread soup. Karal and Sárta, Wings, and Kennet and Josie. The crew, coming back on board. He wondered if his father was there yet, and what he hoped the answer would be.

"Bist bien," Wings said. "Jeszcze seconds more."

The older man staggered a little as he stepped into the gym. His hair was swept up at the sides as it always was, but with a little less crispness than usual. His real name was Alex, but someone had started calling him Wings because of that hairstyle, and his eyes were bloodshot pink, and his gait was a little too relaxed and unsteady. He had a crumpled purple bag under his arm.

"Filipito!" he said, lumbering over. "Bila a ti, I was."

"And now found me," Filip said. "So geht gut, yeah?"

"Yeah yeah yeah," Wings said, not hearing the bite in Filip's words. The older man lowered himself to the deck, and watched blearily as Filip pulled against the bands and trembled with the effort. "Done. Alles complét. Everyone coming home to…to roost. Or…not roost. Fly, sa sa? We're flying out into the big, big empty."

"Good," Filip said. He made the last pull of the set, holding the tension long and hard until his arms shook and burned and failed. The bands snapped back a few centimeters, then slowed and retracted. Filip squeezed his fists. Wings held out the bag.

"Yours," he said.

Filip looked at the bag, then at Wings who shook it at him in a *take it* gesture. It looked like plastic, but it felt and folded like paper in Filip's hands. Whatever was inside it shifted, limp and heavy as a dead animal.

"No point leaving anything for the pinché inners," Wings said. "Confiscations all over the station. Anything they didn't bolt down and half of what they did. Only since tu es lá, I think for you. Yeah?"

He opened the flap. Something dark and textured, regular and irregular at the same time. He pulled the bag free and unfolded the heavy material. It wasn't like anything he'd ever seen before. He unfolded it.

"A…vest?" Filip said.

"For you," Wings said. "Leather, that. Alligát. Real too. From Earth. Took it from a high-end shop by the governor's quarters. Very rich. Only the best for you, yeah?"

Filip gave into the temptation to smell the thing, putting the dead animal's cured scales against his nose and breathing in. There was something subtle and beautiful about the leather—not sweet and not sour, but rich and low and deep. He put it on, settling the weight across his sweat-damp shoulders. Wings clapped his hands in glee.

"You know how much esá cost?" Wings said. "More scrip than you or me would see in five years. For that. Just that. Would be some pinché Inner strutting around the Belt wearing it just to show how he could and we couldn't, yeah? But we're Free Navy now. No one better than. None."

Filip felt the smile on his lips, tentative as a breeze. He imagined himself in the bar now, wearing his leather vest like the richest of the rich from before. Wings was right. This was the kind of thing that no Belter could have had. A symbol of everything that Earth used to remind them that they were less. Small. Not worth. Only who had it now?

"Aituma," Filip said.

"Welcome. You're welcome," Wings said, waving Filip's gratitude away. "The thing for you, the pleasure for me. Good trade à alles."

"How much was it a reál?" Filip asked, part to let Wings brag, part so he could brag himself later. Only Wings had lain back on the deck, his arm over his eyes.

The man shrugged. "Nothing. Everything. For for? Shop's closed. Not like there's going to be another shipment of them, yeah? Esá es the last leather vest out of Earth. *End* point."

The Free Navy left Ceres Station like spores shed by a fungal body. Drive plumes lit and flared and blinked out again like images Filip had seen of fireflies on Earth. If there were still any fireflies on Earth.

And while each Free Navy ship carried a few civilians away toward safety, theirs were far from the only ships leaving. As soon as Marco had made his intentions clear, a wave of civilian refugees had made themselves ready. Rock hoppers and prospectors and shitty half-legal transport ships all filled to the bulkheads with people desperate to get out of the great city of the Belt before it fell back into the hands of Earth and Mars. And in the midst of it all, the great spinning plume of water and ice as the reservoirs vented.

The water reserves spun out from the station, briefly echoing the arms of the galaxy and then stopped, thinned, and spread out into the vast darkness of the Belt. Ice lost among the steady brightness of stars.

The docks, they left in ruins. The reactors, powered down, then either sabotaged or stripped. The power grid and tube systems dismantled. The defense grids stood quiet, their magazines open and empty. Transmitter and sensor arrays were salvaged for parts, then melted to slag. The medical centers had been raided and emptied, leaving only enough to treat the patients already in their care. Taking *those* supplies, Marco said, would have been cruel.

Of the six million people on Ceres, maybe a million and a half would escape before the enemy arrived. The ones that remained would be in a shell of stone and titanium hardly more capable of sustaining life than the original asteroid had been.

If Earth hunkered down and rebuilt, it would take them years to get back to where Ceres had been, pinning them to the station like insects against a board. If Earth chased and attacked the Free Navy, they would be firing on ships carrying refugees. If they abandoned the station, millions of Belters would die under their care and push anyone still sympathetic to the old ways toward the new. Anything they did would be a victory for the Free Navy. They couldn't win. That was Marco's genius.

On the *Pella*, things fell quickly back into their old patterns of duty, but Filip saw differences now. Ways that Ceres Station had changed them. For one thing, the liquor was better. Jamil had his whole cabin stacked with bottles in polished boxes carved from real wood. The packaging alone would have cost more than Filip would have seen in three years' work, to say nothing of the whiskey inside them. Dina came back with half a dozen hand-painted silk scarves confiscated from an Earther's mansion, and she wore them like a bird proud of its plumage.

Everyone wore trinkets of gold and diamond and peridot, but the best was the amber. All the other gems and jewelry could maybe get mined from the Belt. Amber, though, needed a tree and a few million years. It was the one stone that spoke of Earth, and wearing it showed who they'd become better than all the perfumes and spices and leather vests there would ever be. The luxuries that Earth and Mars had bled the Belt to acquire belonged to the Free Navy now. Back to the Belt, as was only just.

It would have been perfect, except for his father.

From the moment Marco had returned to the ship, Rosenfeld at his side, Filip found himself avoiding them. After the first few days spent on the burn, he realized he was waiting to be summoned. Lying in his bunk, trying to sleep, Filip imagined himself under his father's gaze, called upon to justify all that he'd done on Ceres. Murmuring under his breath so that no one passing by could hear it, he rehearsed all the things he would say. It was the security man's fault. It was Filip's own failing, driven by humiliation at the local girl's disrespect. It had been an accident. It had been justified. The image of the girl from the club slowly shifted in Filip's mind until she became something like the devil incarnate. The security man he'd shot grew in his private retellings to become a bumbler and a fool and likely a sympathizer for the inner planets.

When the confrontation he'd dreaded finally arrived, it was nothing like he'd expected. Late at night, his cabin door had simply opened and Marco stepped in as casually as if the room had been his own. Filip sat up, blinking away sleep as his father sat at the foot of his couch. The drive pressed him down at a gentle quarter g. He gestured, and the system brought up the lights.

Marco leaned forward, fingers knotted together. His hair was pulled back in a high, tight bun that drew the skin around his temples tight. Stubble darkened his cheeks and his eyes seemed to have retreated a few millimeters. *Pensive*, Filip thought. He knew that his father would turn in on himself sometimes. This was how he looked when it happened. Filip pulled his legs up, hugging his knees to his chest, and waited.

Marco sighed. When he spoke, his accent was thicker than usual.

"Appearances," he said. "Savvy? War y politics y peace and all in between? It's about appearances."

"If you say."

"Leaving Ceres, it was right. Clever. Genius move. Everyone says it. The inners, though. The old bitch on Earth and the new one on Mars? They'll say otherwise. Call it fleeing, yeah? Retreat. A victory against the Free Navy and all it stands for."

"Won't be."

"I know. But going to have to show it. Demonstration of power. Can't ..." Marco sighed again and leaned back. His smile was weary. "Can't give them the tempo."

"Can't, so won't," Filip said.

Marco chuckled. A low, warm sound. He put his hand on Filip's knee, his palm rough and warm. "Ah, Filipito. Mijo. You're the only one I can really talk to anymore."

Filip's heart swelled in his breast, but he didn't let himself smile. Only nodded the serious nod of a grown man and military advisor. Marco closed his eyes for a moment, leaning back against the bulkhead. He looked vulnerable then. Still his father, still the leader of the Free Navy, but also a man, weary and unguarded. Filip had never loved him more.

"So," Marco said, "we will. Show of strength. Let them take the station and then show that they've won nothing against us. Not so hard."

"Not at all," Filip said as Marco pushed himself back up to standing and stepped to the door. When his father was halfway into the corridor, Filip spoke again. "Is there anything else?"

Marco looked back, eyebrows lifted, lips pursed. For a moment, they considered each other. Filip could hear his own heartbeat. All of his practiced lines seemed to have vanished under his father's soft brown eyes.

"No," Marco said, and stepped out. The door closed with a click, and Filip let his head sink onto his knees. His mistake on Ceres was gone. Forgotten. A disappointment he couldn't explain tainted the relief that flowed through him, but only a little. He'd almost killed a man, and it was okay. Nothing bad was going to come of it. It was almost as good as being forgiven.

Someone should have kept that from happening, his mother whispered in his memory.

Filip pushed the thought away, turned his lights back down, and waited for sleep.

Chapter Fifteen: Pa

The grease crayon was meant to mark decking during construction, and so in a sense Michio was still keeping to its purpose. The marks weren't inventory control or inspection chop, and what she was constructing wasn't a ship, but still. The wall of her cabin had a long rectangular mark where she usually kept a mounted lithograph. An original print by Tabitha Toeava of false coral structures. Part of her *One Hundred Aspects of Europa* series, and it rested in its frame on her crash couch like it was watching her.

Along one side of the wall, Michio had listed the major settlements of the outer planets: Ceres, Pallas, Vesta, Iapetus, Ganymede, and on and on. Some were based on moons, some in the tunnels of well-mined asteroids, and a few—Tycho Station, the Shirazi-Ma Complex, Coldwater, Kelso—were spin stations that floated free. She'd started writing what she thought they needed there: water where there wasn't local ice, complex biologicals everywhere but Ganymede, construction material, food, medical supplies. When it got too dense to read, she cleaned the wall with the side of her fist. The smears were still there.

In the middle column, the colony ships she and her fleet had taken: the *Bedyadat Jadida*, out of Luna. The *John Galt* and the *Mark Watney*, out of Mars. The *Helen R. and Jacob H. Kanter*, sponsored by the Congregation Ner Shalom. The *San Pietro*, sponsored by the DeVargas Corporation. The *Caspian* and the *Hornblower* and the *Kingfisher*, operating under independent charters. All of them stocked to make settlements on new and hostile worlds. Some hardly had enough for a small human toehold. Others, enough to carry a hundred people for three years. Enough to keep the Belt running long enough to remake itself independent of Earth and Mars. Hopefully.

And on the other edge, her own fleet. *Serrio Mal* captained by Susanna Foyle, *Panshin* by Ezio Rodriguez, *Witch of Endor* by Carl al-Dujaili, and so on down the wall. Each of them with their own complement of boarding troops. All of them were hers to command, and would be until it came clear that she answered to herself now. Then...Well. That would be then.

She squeezed the grease crayon and released it. The soft click as it gave up its grip on her fingertips again and again like someone tapping on the door. With every mark she made, the fear in her chest shifted. It didn't leave her—nothing as straightforward as that—but instead of feeling bright and jittery and jagged, her heart folded in on itself and let the crust of a lifetime's failures and pains fall away. At least for a little while. It felt like getting on a treadmill and finding the perfect rhythm. One that brought her breath and her body and her mind together and stilled time.

When she'd started, she'd half hoped to find a reason she couldn't go through with her mutiny. Now that she was engaged, the doubt was forgotten. Somewhere in the process, she'd gone from whether she should to how she was going to. Until Nadia spoke, Michio didn't even notice she was there.

"Bertold still not letting you on the system?"

Michio sighed and shook her head. "Until we make the break, he wants everything off the computers. He's got the local countermeasures ready to update. But you know how it is. Tipping our hand."

"Do you think Marco is monitoring the ship that closely?"

"No," Michio said. Then, "I don't know. Maybe. It's all right. Part of me likes working this way. It's more...I don't know. Tactile?"

"Can see that," Nadia said. "We're getting close."

"I don't want more than a second of light delay," Michio said. "I can't do this trading messages. I have to be able to *talk*."

"We're getting close," Nadia said again, her voice a halftone lower. She understood.

Michio squeezed the grease crayon and relaxed. Tick. "How long?"

"By tonight," Nadia said. She stepped in close, considering the wall and all of its markings. She was half a head shorter than Michio, and the first scattering of gray hair complicated her temple. She sighed to herself and nodded.

"Checking my work?" Michio said, teasing a little.

"Yes," Nadia said seriously. "This was a complicated situation before. We're about to make it much more. Times like this, we check the seals we just checked."

Michio sat on her crash couch and let her wife go over all the ships and stations. Nadia put her hands to her hips in fists and made small sounds in the back of her throat. Michio thought they were approval. It would be easier when she had the ship's system available to plot it all out, place each ship and its vector on a single interface. Even with her wall a mass of careful handwriting, there were other lists—longer lists—of critically important information. The warships under Marco's direct control. The elite guard force that Rosenfeld held in reserve. The thousands of supply containers from Pallas and Vesta and Callisto that had already been scattered to the care of the overwhelming void. Michio stretched her back against the one-third g braking burn, feeling the ache between her ribs.

"When are we going to steal it all?" Nadia asked.

"When I talk to Carmondy," Michio said. "Earlier than that, and Himself might notice. Later, and he might be warned."

"Ah, Carmondy," Nadia said with a sigh. "It bothers me."

"Me too," Michio said. Nadia turned from the wall to consider her. The air of checking for errors didn't change.

"What bothers you?" Nadia asked.

Michio nodded at the wall. "All this. Doing what I'm about to do."

"You don't think it's right?"

"I don't know if that matters. I mean, Marco does what he thinks is right. And Dawes. And Earth. All of them do what they think is right, and tell themselves that they're moral people with the strength to do the necessary things, however terrible they seem at the time. Every atrocity that has been done to us had someone behind it who thought what they did was justified. And here I am. A moral person with the strength to do this. Because it's justified."

"Ah," Nadia said. "You don't think Carmondy will join us."

"I don't. And then I think I'll have to make an example of him so that the others will take me seriously."

"It's not much of a pirate queen who leaves survivors in peace," Nadia said. And then, "You're wrong about one thing, though. Not every evil thing is done by the righteous. Some people do harsh things for the pleasure. But that isn't what bothers me."

Michio lifted her hands, asking the question.

"Working with Carmondy," Nadia said. "I don't know what it is. The man annoys me."

Both of their hand terminals chirped a connection request from Laura on a family-restricted channel. Nadia nodded to Michio to accept and then sat at her side so they could both see the screen. Laura was on the command deck, the backsplash of her control screen lightening her cheeks and dancing in her eyes. Icons of all the others except Nadia appeared along the side.

"What is it?" Nadia asked.

"Newsfeeds just arrived," Laura said. "The inners have Ceres. Making an announcement."

They were all silent for a moment. Knowing that it was coming pulled the punch, but Michio still felt it in her gut. "Play the feed," she said.

Laura nodded, shifted forward to her controls, and blinked out. A feed appeared in her place. Earth and Mars naval ships docked in the berths at Ceres. Seeing them there was disorienting, a juxtaposition of two things that don't belong together. Even though she'd known it was coming, the feeling was strong.

"—estimated at four and a half million, with sufficient reserves to sustain the station for a maximum of two weeks. The combined fleet is presently developing relief strategies including emergency rationing and a call for food and water from other stations in the Belt and the Jovian system."

The image jittered and cut away, a sloppy edit done by an amateur. And then his face filled the screen. Fred fucking Johnson. Michio felt her gut clench. So that was their play. Trot out the Earther to speak for the Belt. Again. His eyes were soft and deep and sorrowful. His hair was close cut and white. A pale stubble stood out against the darkness of his cheeks. The text along the screen's edge said Fred Johnson—OPA Spokesman / Tycho Manufacturing.

Not Colonel Fred Johnson. Not Butcher of Anderson Station. Opportunist. Face of the Belt When Earth's Holding the Camera.

"Michi?"

"I'm fine."

"The culture in the outer planets," Johnson said, "has always been one of mutual support. Conditions aboard ship and on stations have always tested humanity's ingenuity and competence. In the many, many years I've worked with the Outer Planets Alliance, I have never seen that ethos betrayed more profoundly than this."

"You're right," Michio said. "I'm not fine. Shut it off."

Nadia gestured to the screen, and the feed vanished. Michio

stood for a long moment. She didn't remember crushing the grease crayon, but it was a sticky pulp in her hand now. She took a towel from her cabinet and tried to wipe her fingers clean. The crash couch shifted behind her as Nadia sat on it. When Michio had her control back, she turned around. The intimacy of years let her read half a dozen things in Nadia's expression.

"He's not our natural ally," Michio said. "The enemy of my enemy is my friend? That's bullshit. There are always more than two sides. Pretending it's only one or else the other is what let that sonofabitch carry so much weight in the OPA for as long as he did."

"He still does," Nadia said. "Some people will listen to him. He has ships."

"I'll get us ships. We don't need his protection."

"If you say," Nadia said. And then, gently, "Maybe he needs ours."

"He's a big boy. He can take care of himself."

"Four and a half million, though. That's a lot of people."

"Earth wanted the station. They have it. Good for them," Michio said, but her voice sounded less certain in her own ears. "They can take care of it."

"They're going to need food. Water."

Michio pointed to the list she'd scrawled on her wall. Her fingers were dark from the crayon. "Every base on that list is going to need food and water too. Medical supplies. Reaction mass. Construction material. Everything. Everyone is going to need everything. I'm not going to put Ceres at the top of our list. They've got help."

"They got robbed," Nadia said. "By us."

"By Marco."

Nadia smiled and looked off to her left, the way she did when she was ready to end an argument but didn't agree that she'd lost it. Michio couldn't let it go. The words pressed up out of her like Nadia had said them. Had invited her response.

"It's not only that it's Fred Johnson," Michio said.

"If Ceres starts to starve," Nadia said, ending the question as if it had been a statement.

"Fine," Michio said. "If Ceres Station starts going hungry. If they're running out of water. I'll help the people on Ceres. Not for Johnson, not for the OPA. But I'll help the people there."

Nadia nodded, but still looked off to her left, staring at the empty screen like there was a picture still glowing on it. Michio even looked, but there was only black.

"And Earth?" Nadia asked.

"What about it?"

"People are starving there."

"No," Michio said. "I won't send our supplies to Earth. They had centuries to help us, and they didn't."

Nadia's smile widened a millimeter as she rose to her feet. She kissed Michio's cheek and left. A moment later, her voice came from down the corridor with Evans answering. The life of the ship continued, even with everything changing around it. Michio turned back to her lists, but she wasn't sure what she was looking at anymore. Her mind kept sliding back to Fred Johnson's soft, tired eyes. *I have never seen that ethos betrayed more profoundly than this.* She leaned forward and used her thumbnail to scrape a clean line through the center of the word *Ceres*. The gray of the wall showed through the center of the letters. But she didn't rub it out.

When, eight hours later, the *Connaught* finally came within a light-second of the *Hornblower*, the newsfeeds had settled on their narrative about the retaking of Ceres. The phrase *combined fleet* became a kind of catch-all for the patchwork of Earther and Martian naval ships that were clustered there beside a ragged handful of Belter vessels. It was like going back to the days before Eros, when the alliance between the inner planets had seemed unshakable. Certainly there was some nostalgia among the inner planets' commentariat, but the reports from Earth and Mars kept the wailing for the golden age of squeezing the Belt in perspective. Riots had broken out in Londres Nova and scuttled a meeting of the Martian parliament, and the best news from Earth was that the climbing death rate was linear instead of exponential, with hopes that it would level off as the most vulnerable and compromised parts of the globe finished dying.

Marco had gone quiet, though she assumed that meant he was busy planning his next steps with some part of his cabal that didn't include her. That suited her fine. She had enough to think about already.

She had already recorded her message to the other captains under her command. It was ready for tightbeam transmission at her word, and once they went out, there'd be no going back. Nothing else, not even talking to Carmondy, was as irrevocable as that.

So why did putting in the connection request to the *Hornblower* feel like stepping out an airlock?

Carmondy accepted the connection request, and his face appeared on her screen with an icon that showed the communication was secure. His face was broad and placid. On another man, it might have given the impression of harmlessness, but Carmondy had already killed people on her order. She wasn't fooled.

"Captain," he said. "Wondered when I'd hear from you. Alles gut, yeah?"

"Alles interesting anyway," Michio said with a smile that, to her surprise, was mostly genuine. "Looking at some changes to the plan." The message went out to the *Hornblower*, and it came back. One second each way. It made Carmondy's response seem considered and thoughtful. An illusion made from distance and light.

"I heard. Ceres. Hell of a thing."

"Yes," she said. "Ceres. More than Ceres too. Technically, I know you're in Rosenfeld's chain of command, but I'm about to issue some orders to you and your people. I'd appreciate it if you'd follow them."

One second. Two. Carmondy's eyebrows went up. Another second. "Interesting, sa sa? Tell me."

You can turn back. You haven't said it. No one knows but your

family, and they'll still support you if you back away. Put your
faith back in Inaros. Or find another Himself out there to fall in
line behind, since that always works out so well.

"I'm rerouting the *Hornblower* to Rhea. Cutting the prisoners
loose. Redistributing the cargo."

One second. Two. Or was it a little faster this time? How close
were the ships now? "Rhea not one of ours."

"It's not aligned with the Free Navy, no," Michio said. "That's
why I picked it."

One second. No, the messages were definitely coming faster
now. Carmondy nodded and sucked his teeth. A high, hissing
sound as his eyes narrowed. She watched him understand and
waited to see his reaction.

"Mutiny, then?"

"Won't be my first," she said with a lightness that she didn't feel.
"Taking as many ships from my command as will come. Mission's
the same. Get the colony ships and support the Belt. No drift."

The pause seemed to last forever. "No drift," Carmondy said
and shrugged. "Bien. You want us to ride it there, or are we coming back on board?"

Alarms went off in Michio's hindbrain. This wasn't right. She
shook her head. "Ah, Carmondy. We could have been beautiful.
You're coming on board. All your people. But you're sending your
arms and armor here first, and you're coming in pairs."

Pause. "Oh now, Captain, I don't see how that happens."

"I've got two options," Michio said. "Bringing you and yours,
armed and armored, onto the ship because I'm just so sure you're
loyal to me and not Marco? Not one of them."

Pause. A smile she couldn't quite read. Carmondy leaned in
toward his camera. His hands weren't in the square of the screen,
but she imagined them folded together on his table. When he spoke,
his voice was just as friendly but somehow flatter. "Que then?"

"Either you and yours come to me and I send the supplies to the
Belt the way we always said we would, or I kill the *Hornblower*
as a warning to al-Dujaili and Foyle and the rest that I'm serious."

It took longer than two seconds this time. Longer than three. Michio kept her expression calm even while her heart was thudding against her ribs like it wanted out.

"Here's what I say," Carmondy said. "I turn this pinché ship to Pallas. You go your way, I go mine. A que comes between you and Inaros comes between you and Inaros. But you and me walk away, honor on all sides."

Yes floated in the back of her mouth, ready to be said. She wanted this over. She hated conflict. How the hell had she wound up living in the middle of it?

"No," she said. "Your arms and armor in a pack out the airlock within the hour or we break the *Hornblower* again. And we mean it this time." She shrugged. She waited. About a second this time. Closer.

"Kill us to make a point?" he said.

"Kill you so I don't have to kill as many other people later. Rather be loved than feared, but hey. Fallen world." Pause.

"You can't stop me getting the word out," Carmondy said.

Michio sighed, shifted the feed, and sent out her message. The one that began, *You have put yourself under my command out of loyalty to the Belt, and out of loyalty to the Belt I expect you to remain.*

So that was it. Her time with Marco Inaros was over. Michio Pa, once OPA, once Free Navy, now just herself and her ship in a universe all too ready to see her destroyed. For all the consequences that were coming now, for all the pain and loss she'd just invited into her life, she still felt relieved. Like she was where she was supposed to be.

"They know," she said. "Now can we get to the part where you surrender, or are you going to insist that I kill you?"

Chapter Sixteen: Alex

Seriously," Arnold Mfume, one of Fred Johnson's spare pilots, said. "You used a rail gun as a *drive*? To pull a ship up from a decaying orbit?"

Alex shrugged, but the little bloom of pride in his chest was warm all the same. "Naomi did all the math on it," he said. "I was mostly babysitting the *Roci* while it followed her orders. But... well, yeah."

"That is fucking insane," Arnold said through his laughter.

"Didn't really have any other choices," Alex said. "We wind up doin' a certain amount of improvisation, one way and another."

Across the table from him, Sandra Ip smiled. He didn't know if the way her eyes were locked on his was a sign of how drunk she'd gotten, the beginning of an erotic invitation, or a little bit of both. Either way, he found himself smiling back.

"Wish I'd been there," Mfume said.

"I kind of wish I hadn't," Alex said. "It's a lot more fun now that it's not going on anymore. At the time, it was more in the oh-shit-we're-all-going-to-die category."

"That's what adventures are," Bobbie said, and Ip's lazy smile tracked over toward her without changing much. So more about drunk maybe. "Shitty things that make for good stories later."

"I heard *you* went hand-to-hand with a protomolecule soldier," Mfume said.

"That's not even a good story," Bobbie said. Her smile kept it from being awkward, but that path of conversation was definitely closed. Mfume shifted, and Alex could see the temptation to push. To maybe get Bobbie to elaborate, even if it was only a little bit more.

"Now, you want to talk about flying," Alex said, "you should hear about when Bobbie and me were trying to outrun the Free Navy."

"Pretty sure we told that story," Bobbie said.

Alex blinked and looked into his glass. She was right. He had told that story, and since they'd all sat down, Ip might not be the only one well on her way to tipsy. "Right," he said. "In that case, you want to talk about flyin', you should get another drink."

He lifted his arm and leaned back, trying to catch the server's eye.

The Blue Frog was a port bar, and if Alex had to guess, he'd say it had seen better days. The round tables hunched together within larger, swooping, glowing structures that defined the booths that he and the others leaned against. Only the lights seemed dirty and the table was chipped. Different menus detailed the services of the bar: food, drink, pharmaceutical, sex. An empty stage promised live music or burlesque or karaoke, only later. Not right now. And more than that, there was a smell to the place. Not unpleasant, not rotten, but tired. Like spent oil or old sealant.

The expanded crew of the *Rocinante* were scattered among three tables. To Alex's right, Amos sat grinning like a vaguely ominous Buddha with Clarissa Mao, Sun-yi Steinberg, and a shirtless young man who Alex suspected had been ordered from a menu. To his left, Naomi and Chava Lombaugh were locked in a vigorous conversation, while Gor Droga and Zach Kazantzakis leaned back, keeping out of it. The other tables were dominated by a mixture of Earth and Mars navy crews. The crispness of their military uniforms and haircuts seemed out of place, like they were rebuking the architecture for being only what it was. Here and there locals hunched together like they were defending a position against a siege. Covert glances of the natives of Ceres didn't carry a sense of threat as much as bewilderment. The music that leaked from hidden speakers stayed lower than the conversation, shimmering major scale notes making an ambiguous wash of sound, neither celebratory nor sad.

The manager—a dark-skinned man with cold blue eyes and a permanent near-smirk—caught Alex's glance, nodded to him, and sent a server trotting over. The smile on the woman's face seemed almost genuine. Alex ordered another round for the table, and by the time his attention came back to the conversation, the topic had moved on.

"There were rules about that in the service," Bobbie said.

"But there were ways to get around them, right?" Ip said. "I mean, you aren't telling me everyone in the Martian Navy's celibate."

Bobbie shrugged. "If you're in a relationship with someone above you or below you in the chain of command, it's not a joke. Dishonorable discharge, loss of benefits, maybe jail time. That takes a lot of the shine off. But I wasn't Navy. I'm—I was a marine. If there was a little cross-training between services, it wasn't a problem until it started messing up operational efficiency."

"I heard they put chemicals in the food to lower people's libido," Arnold said.

Bobbie shrugged. "If they did, they didn't put in enough."

"What about on the *Rocinante*?" Ip said, turning her full attention to Alex. There was definitely more than just alcohol in the question. "Do you have rules against cheap, sleazy fraternization?"

Alex chuckled, not certain whether he was getting excited or uncomfortable. "Captain and the XO have been together damn near since we got on the ship. It'd be a difficult rule to enforce on the rest of us."

Ip's smile shifted. "You used to be a Navy boy, didn't you? You and the gunny here ever …"

Alex regretted ordering the next round. He was going to need his wits about him pretty soon here. "Me and Bobbie? Nah. That ain't a thing that happened."

"We haven't actually shipped out together that much," Bobbie said. "And anyway…No offense, Alex."

"None taken."

"Really?" Ip said, leaning forward. Her knee pressed against Alex's in a way that was absolutely innocent. Unless it wasn't, in which case it *absolutely* wasn't. "Never even wanted to?"

"Well," Bobbie said. "There was one night on Mars. I think we were both feeling a little lonely. I'd probably have made out with him if he'd asked."

"I can't know that," Alex said, suddenly flushed with heat and unable to look Bobbie in the eye. "You can't tell me that."

Ip kept her leg pressed to his and cocked her head at him. The question was clear. *Is this a thing you're still working out?* Alex smiled back at her. *No, it was never really a thing.*

Naomi's voice lifted, carrying over the murmur of conversation and the music both. She was leaning over her table, finger raised to make some boozy point to Chava. He couldn't make out the words, but he knew her tones of voice well enough to know it wasn't anger. Not real anger anyway. For that, Naomi got quiet.

The server reappeared with a tray of drinks, and Ip leaned across to get hers, then didn't lean all the way back. Alex felt something in the back of his mind relax. It had been a long time since he'd made this particular kind of mistake. Figured he was about due.

"Y'all excuse me for just a minute," he said. "Need to find the head."

"Hurry back," Ip said.

"Count on it."

Walking across the floor, past the bar, and to the back hall, Alex felt like something out of a bawdy joke. Soldiers pairing off after battle was about as old and worn a scenario as there was. But it had gotten that way for a reason. The tension going into battle wasn't like any other feeling Alex had ever had, and the relief when it let up was bone-deep and intoxicating. It wasn't only him or Ip. It wasn't even only sex. He'd known sailors as locked down and shipshape as a training-manual picture who'd come through action and spent the hours afterward weeping or puking. There was one pilot—Genet, her name was—suffered chronic insomnia that even medication could only manage. Every night, she'd be up for an hour between two and three in the morning. Except after an action, when she slept like a baby the whole night through. It was what came of being a primate with a body built for the Pleistocene savanna. Fear and relief and lust and joy were all packed into the same little network of nerves somewhere deep in his amygdalae, and sometimes they touched.

The flight out from Earth had been short and hard and seemed to last forever. The long-range sensors showed no active threats between the ports on Luna and the Belt, but all the way out the thought hung in the air like smoke: Were there rocks falling undetected toward Earth? Toward Mars? Was Marco Inaros three steps ahead of them, the way he always seemed to be? Even Fred Johnson had seemed preoccupied, pacing through the halls with his hands clasped behind his back. The Battle of Ceres was coming. The first fight in the war since the first straight-up ambush. The combined fleet would find out just how badass a bunch of Belters piloting stolen Martian warships really were, and there was reason to expect that would be pretty damned badass.

When the drive plumes had lit up the scans of Ceres, Alex felt it in his throat. Long-range battle. Torpedoes launched at extreme range in unpredictable vectors, designed to come in fast and hard, hoping to slip by the PDCs. He wondered if Mars had ever managed to build a good stealth torpedo, and if the traitors who'd supplied the Free Navy would have traded in them if they did exist. He'd spent hours in his crash couch, chasing every anomaly the *Roci*'s sensor arrays spat out, whether they were above threat threshold or not. When he did sleep, it was all he dreamed about.

When the data came back that the Free Navy ships were burning away, scattered as seeds, he—like every pilot in the combined fleet—looked for the strategy in it. The loops of gravity and thrust that showed where the battle would come together, what the enemy had in its mind. Every time he came up with nothing felt like a threat. The certainty that there was a pattern and he just wasn't smart enough to see it knotted at the base of his skull until his eyes throbbed. His only comfort was that the crews of the Earth and Mars navies, who lived and breathed battle tactics, were as frustrated as he was. When the Free Navy's trap snapped shut, they'd all die surprised together.

Only it kept not happening.

When the first ships reached the docks—two troop carriers from Earth, one from Mars—Alex had held his breath. Ceres was the port city of the Belt, and it was sitting there as unguarded and inviting as bait in a trap. Traffic control gave permission to approach. The combined fleet took berths, soldiers spilled out into the docks, the moment for resistance came and went. Reports started filtering back, many of them to Fred Johnson. The Free Navy was gone. There was no armed resistance. No soldiers, only a handful of booby traps, empty storerooms and reservoirs, and a security force stripped to its skeleton and anxious to surrender to anyone willing to take charge.

The battle for Ceres Station never came. Instead, the combined fleet and the local engineering unions put together an emergency response team that was even now jerry-rigging the environmental systems and recycling plants to keep the station from collapsing. Fred Johnson had spent all his time before the *Rocinante* docked trading tightbeam messages with Avasarala on Luna and whoever would answer back from Mars, where the no-confidence vote on

Smith had ballooned to a full-scale constitutional crisis. After they'd docked, Fred, a security detail in tow, had vanished into a whirlwind of meetings with local OPA groups, unions, and the thin, traumatized remains of the administrative staff.

The rest of the crew went to the bar.

It had been strange at first—still was strange when he thought about it—watching the people of Ceres Station react to their new invaders. Everyone Alex met seemed built out of confusion and relief and anger and a kind of formless grief that spread out through the station hallways like a vapor. Ceres was a huge port, independent of the inner planets for years, and now maybe reconquered by them. Or maybe rescued. No one seemed to know if the combined fleet was the avenging hammer of Earth or the final proof that Fred Johnson's OPA was a legitimate political force. Or if maybe something bigger and stranger had happened.

The smiles of the Ceres natives were tentative, and they carried shards of rage and loss in their eyes. Even here at the Blue Frog, where the crews were welcomed and served the best of what little remained, the fleet and the natives pulled apart, uncertain of each other. Segregated by choice and history. Alex found himself thinking of it as Belters at the bar and inners at the tables, but that wasn't true. Ip and Mfume and all of Fred's people were OPA. Even the divisions between people seemed new, and nobody was quite sure yet which unspoken rules applied.

Alex came out of the men's room to a wall of sound. In the few minutes he'd been indisposed, someone had cranked up the kara-oke and was shouting out a boozy version of Noko Dada's version of "No Volveré" but without any of the harmony parts. He paused at the end of the bar and looked out over the tables, hoping to find a corner where he could have a quiet word with Sandra Ip away from the stage.

Holden was at a table by himself, hunched over a white mug with a ferocious scowl on his face. Alex felt a tug of anxiety. Back at his table, Bobbie and Ip were talking over each other while

Mfume laughed. Ip looked over toward him, grinned, and patted the seat beside her. He held up a finger—one minute—and sloped over toward Holden.

"Hey there, partner," Alex said. "You holding together all right?"

Holden looked up and around like he was surprised to find himself there. Then, after a moment, "Yeah, no. I'm all right."

Alex tilted his head. "Seems like you just said three different things in a row."

"I…ah. Yeah, I did, didn't I? I'm fine." He nodded at the small gold packet in Alex's hand. "What's that?"

Alex held it up. He'd gotten the packet from a dispenser in the men's room. The foil had a dragon's head embossed on it and some nonsense kanji that didn't mean anything.

Holden's brow furrowed. "Sobriety meds?"

Alex felt himself blushing and tried to hide it by smiling. "Well, I'm thinking I may be in a situation here pretty soon where everybody needs to be able to agree to whatever they're agreeing to."

"Always a gentleman," Holden said.

"Mama raised me right. But seriously, are you doing okay? Because you're staring at that coffee like it called you bad names."

Holden glanced down at his cup. The song sloped down to the rough trill at the end. The applause was scattered and weak. Holden turned his coffee mug on the table, setting the black surface dancing. The porcelain scraped against the tabletop until the chords of a new tune crashed out and a woman's voice starting on a Belter Creole cover of Cheb Khaled drowned it out. When Holden spoke, his voice barely carried over the music.

"I keep thinking about my dad calling Belters *skinnies* right in front of Naomi. And the way she took it."

"Family can be rough," Alex said. "Especially when emotions are kind of high."

"True, but that's not what's …" Holden opened his hands. A gesture of frustration. "I always thought that if you gave people all the information, they'd do the right thing, you know? Not always, maybe, but usually. More often than when they chose to do the wrong thing anyway."

"Everybody's a little naïve sometimes," Alex said, feeling as the words passed his lips that maybe he wasn't quite following Holden's point. Maybe he should have taken the first of the sobriety pills before he'd left the men's room.

"I meant fact," Holden went on as if he hadn't heard Alex at all. "I thought if you told people *facts*, they'd draw their conclusions, and because the facts were true, the conclusions mostly would be too. But we don't run on facts. We run on stories about things. About people. Naomi told me that when the rocks fell, the people on Inaros' ship cheered. They were happy about it."

"Yeah, well." Alex paused, rubbing a knuckle across his upper lip. "Consider they might all be a bag of assholes."

"They weren't killing people. In their heads? They were striking a blow for freedom or independence. Or making it right for all the Belter kids that got shitty growth hormones. All the ships that got impounded because they were behind on the registration fees. And it's just the same back home. Father Cesar's a good man. He's gentle and he's kind and he's funny, and to him Belters are all Free Navy and radical OPA. If someone killed Pallas, he'd be worried about what the drop in refining capacity would do before he thought about how many preschools there are on the station. Or if the station manager's son liked writing poetry. Or that blowing the station meant that Annie down in Pallas central accounting wasn't going to get to throw her big birthday party after all."

"Annie?" Alex asked.

"I made her up. Whoever. The thing is I wasn't *wrong*. About telling people the truth? I was right about that. I was wrong about what they needed to know. And…and maybe I can fix that. I mean, I feel like I should at least try."

"Okay," Alex said. He was pretty sure he'd lost the thread of whatever they were talking about a while back, but Holden seemed at least less brooding. "So that means you're about to do something?"

Holden nodded slowly, then drank off all that was left of his coffee at once, put the mug on the table, and clapped Alex's shoulder. "Yeah. I am. Thank you."

"Glad I could help," he said. And then, to Holden's retreating back. "Least I think I am."

Back at the table, Sandra Ip had switched to club soda. Bobbie and Arnold were comparing stories about free climbing at different gravities, and Naomi and Clarissa Mao were at the edge of the stage, getting ready to take a turn singing. Ip caught a glimpse of the foil package in Alex's hand, and her smile was a promise that things were going to go very, very well for him. Still, she must have read something in his expression or the way he held himself when he sat down.

"Everything okay?" she asked.

Alex shrugged. "I'll tell you when I find out."

Chapter Seventeen: Holden

The girl was something like a hundred ninety-two centimeters, and she would have towered over him if she weren't sitting down. Her hair was cut close to her scalp in what Holden figured was fashionable for adolescent Belter girls these days. There were probably hundreds of microfeeds about it, which he didn't follow. Or maybe she was a rebel and the hairstyle was all her own. Either way, it made the slightly enlarged head less pronounced. She sat at the edge of the bench, looking around at the *Rocinante*'s galley like she was regretting that she'd come. The older woman she called Tía stood against the wall, scowling. A chaperone who wasn't impressed with anything she saw.

"I'll just be a second here," Holden said. The software package Monica Stuart had sent him assumed a level of proficiency he didn't have, and he'd managed somehow to turn off some of its intelligence defaults. The girl nodded tightly and plucked at her sari. Holden hoped his smile was reassuring. Or failing that, amusing. "Really. I've just about…Wait, wait, wait. Okay. There."

Her image appeared in his hand terminal with tiny overlays for color correction, sound correction, and something labeled DS/3 that he didn't know what it was. Still, she looked good.

"All right," Holden said. "So, I figure anyone who watches this is going to know who I am. Could you maybe just say your name?"

"Alis Caspár," she said, her voice flat. She could have been a political prisoner the way she spoke. So, it wasn't going too well yet.

"Great," he lied. "Okay, and where do you live?"

"Ceres Station," she said, and then an awkward pause. "Salutorg District."

"And, um, what do you do?"

She nodded, settling into herself. "Ever since Ceres broke away from Earth control, my family has been running a financial coordination service. Converting scrip from different corporations and governments into compatible. Mi family bist peace-loving people. The pressure that the inner planets put on the Belters is not the fault of—"

"Let me break in for just a second," Holden said. Alis went silent, looked down. Somehow Monica made doing this seem really easy. Holden was starting to see how that might actually be the product of years of experience and practice and not something he could jump into without guidance. Except he didn't have time for that, so he forged ahead. "When we met…we met like four hours ago…you were with some of your friends. In the corridor?"

Alis blinked, confused, and looked at Tía. The little incredulous glance was the first time the girl had looked like herself since she'd come on board.

"It was really amazing," Holden said. "I mean, I was walking by and I saw you all there. And I was really impressed. Could you tell me about that?"

"Shin-sin?" Alis said.

"Is that what you call it? The thing with the glass balls?"

"Not glass," Alis said. "Resin."

"Okay, yes," Holden said, pouring enthusiasm out toward her like dropping water onto a sponge. It all seemed to just soak in and vanish. But then Alis chuckled. It didn't matter that it was more *at* him than *with* him. "Could you do it again? Here?"

She laughed, covering her mouth with one hand. For a long second, he thought she might call the whole thing to a halt. But then she plucked a little bag from her hip and took out four brightly colored clear spheres a little larger and softer than the marbles Holden had played with as a boy. Carefully, she set them between her fingers, resting between the second knuckles. She started singing, a high, choppy chant, and then stopped, laughed, and shook her head.

"Can't do this," she said. "I can't."

"Please, just try. It's really great."

"It's dumb," she said. "It's kid thing."

"I'm...really immature."

When she looked at Tía again, Holden glanced too. The old woman was glowering just as deeply as before, but there was a glimmer of amusement in her ancient eyes. Alis settled, laughed, settled again, and started chanting. When the rhythm was established, she started clapping her hands together gently, and passing the spheres from hand to hand, making them seem to dance independently of her. Every now and then the chant would hit a syncopated passage so that one of the balls could drop into her palm and get tossed across to be captured between her opposite fingers. When she reached the end, she stopped, looked shyly toward Holden, and shook her head.

"Better with two people," she said.

"Like partners?" he said.

"Dui." Her glance behind him was no more than a flutter, but Holden knew what it meant, and a touch of glee leapt into his heart. He turned to the stone-faced chaperone, who hoisted an eyebrow at him.

"Do you...Tía?" he said. "Do you know how to do shin-sin?"

She snorted in military-grade derision. When she came forward, Alis made room for her and handed over two of the spheres. They seemed smaller between Tía's thick fingers. The old woman lifted her chin, and for a moment, Holden knew exactly what she'd looked like at Alis' age.

The chant was more complex this time, sung as a round with the rhythms of one part informing and supporting whatever was happening in the other woman's voice. The clear, colored spheres danced between their hands as they clapped palms together, crossing and recrossing, adding their claps to the song. At the moments of syncopation, they tossed the spheres across the space between them and caught them in their knuckles. By the end, both women were grinning. At the end, Tía tossed all the spheres up one after another so quickly they were all in the air at the same moment and then caught them in one hand. It wasn't a trick that could have worked at a full g.

Holden clapped and the older woman nodded, accepting his applause like a queen.

"That is amazing. It's wonderful," Holden said. "How do you learn how to do that?"

Alis shook her head in disbelief at the strange Earther and his childish delights. "Is just *shin-sin*," she said. And then her eyes went wide, and the blood drained from her face.

"Mr. Holden," Fred Johnson said. "When you have a moment?"

"Yes, sure," Holden said. "We were just... Yeah. Give me a second."

"I'll be in Ops." Fred smiled and nodded to the two Belter women. "Ladies."

Holden closed down the software, thanked Alis and Tía, and walked them to the airlock, out and into the docks. After they'd gone, he watched the captured video—girl and woman with their voices and hands playing against each other, the not quite marbles weaving between them like a third player in the game. It was exactly the kind of thing he'd hoped for. He ran the compression and sent it to Tycho Station and Monica Stuart, just the same way he had the others.

He'd hoped to get a lot more done. He'd interviewed a researcher who worked on Ceres Station, self-educated through networked tutorials, plying him with yeasty beer until the older man was loose and comfortable enough to wax passionate about the beauty of tardigrades. He'd talked to a nutritionist from the hydroponic fields who'd only agreed if she could explain the water shortage situation on Ceres, and wound up being the clearest voice of grief and fear that he'd heard. He'd talked to a man who was alleged to be the oldest Belter on the station, who told a long and probably apocryphal story about the first licensed brothel to open there.

And that was all. So far. Four interviews, none of them terribly long. Hopefully it was enough for Monica to work with. She'd promised him that a lot could be saved in editing.

The docks weren't as busy as he was used to seeing them. Especially after the press and barely controlled chaos of Luna, Ceres seemed wounded. Still reeling from the blows it had suffered. The carts and loading mechs stood idle, waiting for a ship to arrive with supplies or some warehouse on the station that still had something worth sending away.

He'd heard once about reperfusion injuries. When a limb had been pressed until all the blood was gone, the flood when it came back could break vessels, bleed into the cellular matrix. He remembered thinking at the time how strange it was for something normal, necessary, and life-giving to cause damage just by showing back up. Ceres was like that now, but he couldn't tell if the combined fleet was the blood returning or if some other flood would have to come before Ceres could take stock of how badly it had been wounded.

On his way back in, he passed Gor Droga and Amos in the locker room running down a short that was making one of the ventilation fans run slow. Clarissa Mao was talking to them both from down in engineering. It was the sort of problem that a ship with a full crew had the spare cycles to address. At the lift, he had to wait for Chava Lombaugh to squeeze past him before he got on.

The truth was that with all of Fred's people and Holden's, the *Rocinante* still had a little less than the full crew she'd been meant to carry. That it felt crowded to him wasn't the ship design, but his own habits and expectations. A full crew would be tighter, more compressed, more like a normal Navy ship. Holden knew that. He even knew that in some ways having the extra people would keep them all safer. The *Rocinante* was built with a lot of redundant backups. The crew was supposed to be the same way. It hadn't worked out that way, though. Another mechanic wouldn't be Amos. Another pilot wouldn't be Alex. People were more than the roles they played in the function of the ship, and they weren't replaceable. And what was true of the *Rocinante* held for the larger field of humanity as well.

The lift stopped. Fred Johnson looked up from the ship controls, nodding to Holden. The lights were at the same dim settings that Alex preferred, and the backsplash from the screens left Fred's skin looking darker than it was. Maura Patel sat across the deck, diagnostics spooling across the communications controls on her screen and headphones over her ears. Holden dropped into a couch beside Fred's and swiveled to face him.

"You wanted me?"

"Couple things. I'm setting up shop on Ceres for now. Avasarala's going to recognize me as acting governor," Fred said. "I'm pulling in all my favors. Everyone I know with any influence from the OPA. I'll bring them here."

"That sounds like an invitation to assassinate you."

"The risk is necessary. I don't know if my crew will be staying here or going to Tycho without me. I'm waiting on word from Drummer about that. One way or the other, I'll get them out of your hair."

"That's...I mean, okay. But they're sort of growing on me. So what did you really want to talk about?"

Fred nodded once, a short, hard motion. "Do you think Draper will be able to speak for Mars?"

Holden laughed. "Like *speak for* ambassador speak for? Negotiate with the OPA? Because I was pretty sure that was up to Mars."

"We may not be in a position to wait for them to get their ducks in a row. Smith's out, and Richards is in, but an opposition coalition's formed that want to put investigating the remaining military ahead of anything else."

"You mean like ahead of fighting the war?"

"For example. Richards and Avasarala are working on it, but I need a Martian face with me if I'm going to make this combined navy hold together. With my background, I can represent the best of Earth to the Belt. I've been doing that for years, and I've built up a lot of trust. But unless I have a representative of Mars, I won't be bringing anything new to the table. Especially with the Free Navy flying Martian ships. Inaros' stock is very high right now."

"Seriously? Because it looks a lot like he just walked away from the biggest port in the Belt."

Fred shrugged eloquently. "His apologists are good at their jobs. And everything is in the shadow of what he did to Earth. Sorrento-Gillis, Gao, all of them. They underestimated the anger in the Belt. And the desperation. People want Inaros to be a hero, and so what he does, they interpret as heroism."

"Even running away?"

"He won't only run away. Don't know what he's got in mind, but he isn't about to retire. And Ceres Station…it's a white elephant now. Just keeping the environmental systems running isn't going to be trivial. We may have to consolidate. Concentrate people physically and abandon parts of the station. Which will be interpreted as Earth and Mars kicking Belters out of their homes by Inaros and his cabal."

Holden ran a hand through his hair. "Yeah, that's messed up."

"It's politics. And it's why we need the OPA. There *is* support for us in the Belt, but it needs cultivation. And we have a few things going for us. They can call themselves a navy, but they're amateurs. The kind of roughshod that thinks discipline is the same as punishment. Rumor is there's already some dissent in Marco's leadership. Probably, it's over his tactics with Ceres. I still don't understand why Dawes would let him walk away from the station, but...well, clearly he did. And Avasarala's keeping a lid on Earth. If the UN had crumbled the way Mars has, I don't know what we'd do."

"This," Holden said. "Try to gather some allies. Pretty much the same thing you're going to do anyway. Only with less hope that it would work."

Fred stretched, his joints popping, then sighed back down into the gel of the couch. The diagnostics on the comm panel flickered, and Patel tapped the run results. As far as she was concerned, the two of them might as well not have been there.

"You're probably right," Fred said. "Still, I'm glad it's not worse. Not yet, anyway."

"Maybe we'll get lucky and Inaros will get himself killed without us."

"It wouldn't be enough," Fred said. "Earth's broken. It will be for generations. Mars may or may not collapse, but there's still the gates. Still the colony worlds. Still all the pressures that keep the Belt on the edge of starvation and even less of what makes it valuable. There's no getting back to status quo ante. We've got to move forward. Which brings us back to Draper. You've worked with her. Can she do the job?"

"Honestly, I think the best person to ask is her. We all know her. We all like her. I'd trust her with my ship, and I wouldn't trust you with that. If she thinks she can, then I think she can."

"And if she thinks she can't?"

"Then ask Avasarala," Holden said.

"I already know her opinion. All right, thank you. And...I'm going to regret asking. Do I want to know what you were doing with those two women in the galley?"

Maura Patel shifted in her chair. The first sign that she was listening to them at all.

"Filming them. That thing with clapping and marbles? It was really visually interesting, and Monica said that was something to be looking for. I'm doing these interviews, and she's helping me edit and distribute them."

"And why are you doing that?"

"It's what's missing in all of this," Holden said. "It's what let things get this bad. We don't see each other as people. Even the feeds are always about weird things. Aberrations. All the times that a Belt station doesn't have a riot? Those days aren't news. It has to be an uprising or a protest or a system failure. Just being here, living a normal life? That's not part of what the people on Earth or Mars hear about."

"So you—" Fred closed his eyes and pinched the bridge of his nose. "You're reaching for more unapproved press releases? You remember starting a war that way once?"

"Exactly. That was talking about an aberration, because I thought that was what people needed to know. But they need all the context too. What it's like to be a teenager with his first crush on Ceres. Or to worry about your dad getting old on Pallas Station. The things that make people here the same as people everywhere."

"Belters rain hell down on Earth," Fred said slowly, "and you respond by trying to humanize Belters? You know there's going to be a raft of people who call you a traitor for that."

"I'd be doing the same thing on Earth, but I'm not there right now. If people call me names, they do. I'm just trying to make it a little harder for people to feel comfortable killing each other."

Fred's screen put up an alert. He glanced at it, dismissed it. "You know if anyone else came up with the idea that they ought to put themselves in the middle of a war so they could sing songs and hold hands and sow peace for all mankind, I'd call it narcissistic opportunism. Maybe megalomania."

"But it's not anyone else, so we're good?"

Fred lifted his hands. A gesture made of equal weights amusement and despair. "I'll want a private word with Draper."

"I'll let her know," Holden said, standing up.

"I can reach her myself. And Holden..."

He turned back. In the dimness, Fred's eyes were so dark the iris and the pupil were the same shade of black. He looked old. Weary. Focused. "Yes?" Holden said.

"The song those two were singing? Get the lyrics translated before you broadcast it. Just in case."

Chapter Eighteen: Filip

The *Pella* coasted through the black, one node in a network of dark ships that traded tightbeams and compared strategies and planned. Stealth wasn't possible in the strict sense. The enemy would be scanning the vault of the heavens for the Free Navy's ships just as much as they were tracking the drive plumes of Earth and Mars and everyone else in the system. The universe was billions of points of unwavering light—stars and galaxies stretching out through time and space, their photon streams bent by gravity lensing and shifted by the speed of the universe's expansion. The flicker of a drive might be overlooked or confused with another light source or hidden by one of the widely scattered asteroids that inhabited the system like dust motes in a cathedral.

There was no way to know how many of their ships the inners had managed to identify and track. There was no certainty that their own sensor arrays had targeted all of the so-called combined navy's vessels. The scale of the vacuum alone built uncertainty.

The inners were easier, since so many of theirs had burned for Ceres. But who was to say there weren't a few scattered hunters, dark and ballistic in the void? Marco had a handful of Free Navy like that, or at least that was what Karal said. Ships that hadn't even been used in the first attacks, cruising in their own orbits like warm asteroids. Sleepers waiting for their moment. And maybe that was even true, though Filip hadn't heard it directly from his father yet. And he liked to think his father would tell him anything.

The days were long and empty, wound tightly around a single, overwhelming question. The counterstrike would come. The attack that would prove that stepping back from Ceres was a tactical choice and not a show of weakness. More than anything that had come before, it would be the event—Marco said this, and Filip believed it—that made clear what made the Free Navy unbeatable. In the gym and the galley, the crew speculated. Tycho Station was the heart of the collaborationist wing of the OPA. Mars had suffered least in the initial attack, and deserved the same punishment as Earth. Luna had become the new center of UN power. Kelso Station and Rhea had rejected the Free Navy and shown their true colors.

Or there were the mining operations scattered throughout the Belt that answered to Earth-based corporations. They were easy pickings and couldn't be defended. Or taking a solid hold on Ganymede, claiming and protecting the food supply of the Belt. There was even some talk of sending recovery forces out through the ring. Take back from the colonies what should never have been there in the first place. Or install platforms above the new planets and extract tribute from them. Reverse the political order and put all the bastards at the bottom of all the wells in chains.

Filip only smiled and shrugged, letting it look like he knew more than he did. Marco hadn't told even him what the plan was. Not yet.

And then the message came.

I always respected you. That was how she began. Michio Pa, the head of the conscription effort. Filip remembered her, but he hadn't had an opinion about her before now. She was a competent leader, a little famous for stepping in when the *Behemoth*'s captain had lost his mind in the slow zone. His father liked her because she hated Fred Johnson, had defected from him, and because she was a Belter and pretty to look at and the face that the Belt would see when the colony ships cracked their guts open and spilled out their treasures. Only now she stared into a camera on her ship, her hair pulled back, her dark eyes serious. She didn't look pretty.

"I have always respected you, sir. The work you have done for the independence of the Belt has been critical, and I'm proud to be part of it. I want to make it very clear before we go forward that my loyalty to our cause is unwavering and complete. On sober reflection and after a great deal of consideration, I find I have to disagree with the change in the plan for the conscription. While I understand the strategic importance of denying materiel to the enemy, I can't in good conscience withhold it from the citizens of the Belt who are in immediate need. Because of this, I have chosen to proceed with the conscription efforts as originally outlined.

"Technically, this is disobeying an order, but I have great faith that when you reflect on how the needs of our people brought us to form the Free Navy, you'll agree it is the best way forward."

She signed off with a Free Navy salute. The one his father had created when he made everything else. Filip queued it up again, watching from the start to the end again, aware of Marco's gaze on him as much as the woman on the screen. The galley around them was empty. No, not just empty. *Emptied.* Whether they'd been ordered to or not, the crew of the *Pella* had evacuated the space and left it for Marco and Filip. If it hadn't been for a smell of curry lingering in the air, the stains of coffee on the table, it might have been their first time on the ship.

He didn't know how many times his father had viewed the message, how he had taken it the first time he'd seen it, or what the mild expression he wore now meant. Filip's uncertainty knotted at the bottom of his abdomen. Being shown the message was a test, and he didn't know quite what he was meant to do with it.

After the second time Michio Pa saluted, Marco stretched his shoulders back, a physical symbol that they were switching to the next part of whatever their conversation was.

"It's mutiny," Filip said.

"It is," Marco said, his voice and expression reasonable and calm. "Do you think she's right?"

No leapt to Filip's throat, but he stopped it there. It was too obvious an answer. He tried *Yes* in his mind, feeling the pressure of his father's attention like it was heat radiating from him. He discarded it too.

"It doesn't matter," he said slowly. "Whether she's right or wrong is beside the point. She broke with your authority."

Marco reached out and tapped the tip of Filip's nose the way he'd done when they were only father and son, not war leader and lieutenant. Marco's eyes softened, his focus shifting elsewhere. Filip felt a momentary and irrational stab of loneliness.

"She did," Marco said. "Even if she were right—she isn't, but if—how could I let this go? It would be an invitation to chaos. Chaos." He chuckled, shaking his head. Anger would have been less frightening.

Filip's uncertainty shifted in his gut. Were they destroyed, then? Was it all falling apart? The vision of the system his father had dreamed—void cities, the Belt blooming into a new kind of humanity free from the oppression of Earth and Mars, the Free Navy as the order of the worlds—stuttered. He caught a glimpse of what the other future could look like. The death and the struggle and the war. The corpse Earth and the ghost town Mars and the shards of the Free Navy picking at each other until nothing was left. It was what Marco meant when he said *chaos*, Filip was sure of that. Nausea welled up in him. *Someone should have kept that from happening.* He shook his head.

"Some day," Marco said, and then again, still without finishing the thought, "some day."

"Do we do?" Filip asked.

Marco shrugged with his hands. "Stop trusting women," he

said, then flicked a foot against the wall, launching himself to the doorway. Filip watched as Marco grabbed a handhold and pulled himself away down the hall toward his cabin. All the questions he hadn't answered floated invisibly behind him.

Left alone, Filip killed the sound to the screen and replayed her message again. He'd met this woman. He'd been in a room with her, and heard her voice, and he hadn't seen her for the traitor she was. For the agent of chaos. She saluted, and he tried to see fear in her. Or malice. Anything more than a professional delivering a message she expected to be badly received. He played the message again. Her eyes were black and hate-filled, or steeled against dread. Her gestures were soaked in contempt, or controlled like a fighter preparing to lose a match.

With a little practice and will, he found he could see anything he chose in her.

A soft sound came from behind him. Sárta sloped into the room feetfirst, and caught herself in a foothold on the wall, locking her ankle in place and absorbing the inertia with her knees. Her smile had the same bleakness that Filip felt, and he suffered a moment's anger that she should feel what he did. Karal's voice came from the lift, talking in low, careful tones. Rosenfeld answered, too low to make out the words. They knew Marco was gone, then. The private audience concluded.

Sárta pointed to the screen with her chin. "Esá es some shit, que?" Fishing for information, looking to know what Marco hadn't seen fit to tell her. Or anyone else.

"He saw it coming," Filip said. He wasn't even lying. Marco might not have said as much, but it was still true. Filip tapped his temple. "Knew to expect it. Everything going to be just fine."

Three more days on the float, and Filip knew it wasn't only the crew of the *Pella* who were feeling anxious. Every hour, it seemed, brought another round of contact requests. Encrypted tightbeam messages flooded into the *Pella*'s queue and waited there for Marco's response. Rosenfeld, as part of the inner circle, stepped in where he could. He went so far as to appropriate the command deck as a kind of private office. The war center in absentia until Marco "came back out of his tent"— whatever that meant.

For Filip, it was all an exercise in projecting confidence. His father had a plan. He'd gotten them all this far, and there was no reason to doubt he would get them the rest of the way. The others agreed with him, or at least seemed to when he was in the room. He wondered what they said when he was elsewhere. They'd all been through battle together. They'd shared their victories and the long, patient hours waiting for their traps to spring. This was different. The waiting was the same, but not being sure what they were waiting for made it feel like maybe they were waiting for nothing. Even for him.

Near the end of the third day, Rosenfeld asked Filip to join him in the command center. The older man looked tired, but his cyst-ridden skin made reading his expressions difficult. Rosenfeld had turned all the screens off. The command center felt smaller without their displays to give the illusion of depth and light. Rosenfeld floated beside one of the crash couches, his body canted a few degrees from the ship in a way that made him seem both taller and subtly threatening.

"So, young Master Inaros," Rosenfeld said, "it seems we have a problem."

"Don't see it," Filip said, but the amusement in the older man's eyes was enough to show how weak his words sounded. Rosenfeld pretended Filip hadn't spoken.

"The longer we go without responding to...call them 'changes in the situation'? The longer we go, the more doubt starts to grow, yeah? Father Inaros is the face and voice of the Free Navy. Has been since the beginning. His skill, yeah? His peculiar gift. But—" Rosenfeld spread his hands. *But he isn't here.*

"He has a plan," Filip said.

"We have a problem. We can't wait for him much longer. Haven't told anyone. Hasn't found its way to the grapevine. But the problem's now, not tomorrow. Even the light lag may make us too late now."

"What is it?" Filip asked.

"*Witch of Endor*. It's at Pallas. All the cache-safes we threw out into the void? Captain al-Dujaili has started gathering them back up. Says it's under orders from his commander, and he doesn't mean us. That's the fifth ship broken for Pa. Meantime, the Butcher's on Ceres, his ass keeping Dawes' chair warm. Calling for a meeting of the OPA clans, yeah? Black Sky. Carlos Walker. Administration on Rhea is looking to send a delegation. Free Navy made a statement when we broke Earth's chains. Statement was, *The revolution is already over.* That we'd won. Inevitable. Already happened, us. Only now, maybe not."

Filip's gut was tight. Anger warmed his throat and shoved his jaw forward like a tumor at the base of his jaw. He didn't know who he was angry with, but the rage was deep and powerful. Maybe Rosenfeld saw it, because his voice changed, became softer.

"Your father, he's a great man. Great men, they're not like you or me. They have other needs. Other rhythms. It's what sets them apart. But sometimes they go so far into the void we lose sight of them. They lose sight of us. That's where little people like me come through, yeah? Keep the engines running. Keep the filters clean. Do the needful things until the great man comes back to us."

"Yeah," Filip said. The rage still shoving its way up his neck, filling his head.

"Worst thing we can do is wait," Rosenfeld said. "Better that we point all our ships the wrong direction than that we leave them too long floating. Change it later, bring them back, they think the situation shifted. Put them on the burn, they know they're going somewhere."

"Yeah," Filip said. "See that."

"Time comes to say it, if it's not him, it's going to be me. *For* him, yeah, but me. Not a bad thing if you stood with. Make everyone know it's me for him, not another Pa."

"You want to give orders to the Navy?"

"I want orders given," Rosenfeld said. "Don't care who does it. Barely care what the orders are. Just there are some."

"No one but him," Filip said. There was a buzz in his voice. His hands ached, and he didn't know why until he looked and saw them in fists. "My father made the Free Navy. He makes the calls."

"Then he has to make them now. And he won't listen to me."

"I'll talk to him," Filip said. Rosenfeld lifted a hand in thanks and blinked his thick, pebbled eyes.

"He's lucky to have you," Rosenfeld said. Filip didn't answer, just took one of the handholds, turned himself, and launched down the throat of the ship where the lift would have risen and fallen if there were any up and down to guide it. His mind was a clutter of different emotions. Anger at Michio Pa. Distrust of Rosenfeld. Guilt for something he couldn't put a name to. Fear. Even a kind of desperate elation, like pleasure without being pleasure. The walls of the lift tube skinned past him as he drifted almost imperceptibly to the port. *If I reach the crew deck without touching the wall, everything will be all right.* An irrational thought.

And still, when he grabbed a handhold and swung into the corridor that led to Marco's quarters without having to correct his path, he felt a little relief. And when he reached his father's door, it was even justified. The fear he'd carried with him of his father wrecked by betrayal—glass-eyed, unshaven, maybe even weeping—were nothing like the man who opened the cabin door. Yes, the sockets of his eyes were a little darker than usual. Yes, there was a scent in his room of sweat and metal. But his smile was bright and his focus clear.

Filip found himself wondering what had kept him locked up so long. If he felt a twinge of annoyance, it was overwhelmed by the warmth of seeing his father back again. Behind Marco, tucked in at the edge of one of the cabinets, a strip of fabric spoke of something light and feminine. Filip wondered which of the crew had been here to comfort his father and for how long.

Marco listened to Filip's report with a gentle attention, nodding with his hands at each point of importance, letting Filip cover everything—Fred Johnson, the *Witch of Endor*, Rosenfeld's half-spoken threat to take the reins—without interrupting him. Filip felt the anger slip away as he spoke, his gut relaxing as the anxiety faded, until by the end he wiped away a tear that had nothing to do with sorrow and everything to do with relief. Marco put a hand on Filip's shoulder, a soft grip that held the two of them together.

"We pause when it's time to pause, and we strike when it's time to strike," Marco said.

"I know," Filip said. "It's only…" He didn't know how to end the thought, but his father smiled anyway, as if he understood.

Marco gestured at the cabin's system, opening a connection request for Rosenfeld. The pebble-skinned man appeared on the screen almost at once. "Marco," he said. "Good to have you back among the living."

"To the underworld and returned with wisdom," Marco said, a sharpness in his voice. "Didn't frighten you with my absence, did I?"

"Not as long as you came back," Rosenfeld said through a rough laugh. "We have a full plate, old friend. Too much needs doing." Filip had the sense that a second conversation was happening between the men he couldn't quite parse, but he kept quiet and watched.

"Less soon," Marco said. "Send me the tracking data for all of the ships still answering to Pa's commands. You tell your guard ships at Pallas *Witch of Endor*'s gone rogue. Jam it, kill it, and send the battle data to us. No mercy for traitors."

Rosenfeld nodded. "And Fred Johnson?"

"Butcher will bleed in his turn," Marco said. "Never fear. This war's just beginning."

Chapter Nineteen: Pa

Iapetus Station wasn't on the moon itself, but in locked orbit around it. The station's design was old: two long counter-rotating arms supporting habitation rings, a central docking station on the axis. Lights glittered on the surface of the moon, marking automated stations where the ice was quarried and split. On their approach, there was a point where the station and moon and the ringed bulk of Saturn behind it were all the same size on the screen. An illusion of perspective.

The docks were almost filled with ancient water haulers that the tariffs had kept from harvesting the moon. No one was enforcing the fees anymore, and all the ships that could were taking advantage of the opportunity. Tugs flying teakettle rose up from the surface or dropped down toward it. Shipping containers filled with ice studded the hulls of the haulers like a crust of salt. The administration of Iapetus hadn't sided with Marco and the Free

Navy or against them, but they weren't losing the chance to shrug off the strictures of Earth and Mars either. Michio watched the traffic control data and tried to see it more as liberty and freedom, less as grabbing what there was to take and getting away while the getting was good.

The comm channel opened. A request from Iapetus control. She could have let Oksana answer it, but impatience won out. "This is the *Connaught*," she said.

"Bien, *Connaught*. Iapetus bei hier. We're slotting the *Hornblower* into berth sixteen. Good to go in half an hour, yeah?"

"That'll do."

"Hear tús have prisoners, yeah?"

"Do. Refugees too. *Hornblower*'s original crew."

"Pissed off, them?"

"Not happy," Michio said. "Think they'll be grateful to be in rooms that aren't welded shut, though. Your supply officer said you'd be able to take them."

"Can take contract here, can book passage to Earth or Mars. Or refugees, can etwas. Prisoners are their own thing."

"Won't have them hurt," Michio said. "Don't want them let free either."

"Guests of the station," Iapetus control said. "All marked. Good and good. And…not official, yeah? 'Gato for the load. Hydroponics were getting mighty strained with the shipments from Earth dead."

"Glad we could help," Michio said before she dropped the connection.

It was true too. There was something in her chest—a soft, golden feeling—that came from knowing that the people who would have suffered without her would at least suffer less. She'd spent more time on Rhea than on Iapetus, but she'd had enough experience to know what shortages of hydroponic equipment meant to a station like this. At the least, her shipments would mean the difference between uncertainty and stability. At most, between death and life.

It wouldn't have been this way if the Belt had been allowed to grow and become independent. But Earth and Mars had kept the labor here on a leash made of soil analogues and complex organics. Now, thanks to Marco, the Belt would have a chance to bootstrap itself up into a sustainable future. Unless, thanks to Marco, it starved and collapsed in the attempt.

She hadn't heard back from him one way or the other since she'd called her ships to refuse his orders. Statements of allegiance had come from eight of her sixteen ships. Acknowledgment from four more. Only the *Ando* and the *Dagny Taggart* had rejected her outright, and even they hadn't taken action yet. Everyone was waiting for Marco to make an announcement. Even her. And every hour he didn't made it seem more possible that he wouldn't.

Other voices, though. Oh, there were others. A collective of independent prospecting vessels out of Titania needed replacement parts for their drives. A cargo ship that was also home to a family crew of twenty people suffered a catastrophic failure of their Epstein drive's power systems and were on the drift. Vesta was putting its population on protein rationing until the food relief Michio had promised them actually arrived. Kelso Station, in an irrational fit of altruism, had sent relief supplies to Earth and was now facing shortages of water and helium-3 for the reactors.

Centuries of technology and progress had allowed humanity to create a place for itself in the vacuum and radiation of space, but nothing had overcome entropy or ideology or bad judgment. The millions of skin-bound complications of salt water and minerals that were human bodies scattered throughout the Belt still needed food and air and clean water, energy and shelter. Ways to keep from drowning in their own shit or cooking in their waste heat. And through accidents of Marco's charisma and her own idealism, she'd become responsible for it all.

But here was her start. The supplies of the *Hornblower*, instead of flying through gates and away forever, would feed Iapetus and give the station there the reserves to help others. The *Connaught* and her sister ships didn't need to solve every distribution issue. Only get the supplies, make them available, and let market forces and the communal nature of the Belt take over from there.

She hoped it was enough.

Oksana, at her station, laughed. It wasn't mirth, so much as a kind of amazed disbelief.

"Que?" Evans asked.

Oksana shook her head. Michio had known her long enough to read the gesture and the ghost of shame that came with it. *Not while I'm on duty.* Keeping that division between being family during family time and crew during crew time had always been important to Oksana. Usually, it was important to Michio too, but between waiting for a berth and dreading news of Marco, any distraction was a gift.

"What is it, Oksana?" Michio said.

"Just something odd on the newsfeeds out of Ceres, sir," she said.

"Well, I don't think it's going to disrupt us. Put it on screen."

"Sir," Oksana said, and Michio's controls vanished, replaced by a professional-looking news video, crawl at the bottom and filtering options along the side. And looking out of her screen, the earnest, open face of James Holden. For a moment, Michio was on the *Behemoth* again, and then she was back. Like a long-forgotten smell or the taste of a food eaten only in childhood, James Holden carried an echo of the guilt and fear, a reminder of violence.

Images flickered as Holden spoke: a terribly old Belter man with merry eyes, two women—one young and one older—clapping hands together in some game like batbat or pattycake or shin-sin, a professionally dressed woman with dark skin and a sober expression standing at a hydroponics tank so long it curved up in the distance with the body of the station. *My name is James Holden, and I want to introduce you to some of the people I've met here on Ceres. I want you to hear their stories. Come to know them the way you do your shipmates and neighbors. I hope you'll carry a little bit of these people with you the way I do now.*

"Fuck is *this*?" Evans asked, laughter in his voice. "Watch the trained Belter dancing for your fun?"

"No, it's Holden," Oksana said. "He's OPA."

"En serio?"

"Johnson's OPA," Michio said. "He works for Earth too. And Mars."

On the screen, Holden was handing a bulb of beer to the ancient-looking man. The Belter's cheeks were already a little flushed, but his voice wasn't slurred at all. *Were five men for every woman on the station, back then. Five to one.*

"You shipped with him, sí?" Oksana asked. "Back in the slow zone?"

"Little bit," Michio said. "He's also waking up next to Filip Inaros' mother. The one Marco didn't manage to kill? That's him."

"And he's announcing to Big Himself y alles where he's bunking?" Oksana said. "So. Brave o crazy, him?"

"Not sure I get to criticize," Michio said, just before the fear hit her system. For a fraction of a second, she didn't know why, and then she realized what she was seeing. In the text crawl at the bottom of the screen, and just marching off the side. *Witch of Endor.* She grabbed the crawl, pulled it back. *Ship destroyed by Free Navy identified as* Witch of Endor.

She selected the feed. Her screen flickered. Holden and the old Belter laughed about Ceres Station before it had been spun up, but she didn't hear them. On her screen, the hyperreal image of an intelligence telescope showed a ship under high burn, streams of PDC fire seeming to bend as the ship accelerated away from the rounds. From the shape of the curve, she guessed it had been pulling almost ten gs. The picture didn't show what she was fleeing from, and the torpedo that managed to penetrate the defenses was moving too fast to see. The ship shifted, spinning for a tenth of a second, and then blossomed into light. *It is unclear*, the announcer said, *why the Free Navy forces appear to have attacked one of their own ships, but reports confirm drive plumes from several other known enemy locations on vectors inconsistent with an attack of consolidated fleet positions—*

"Sir?" Oksana said, and Michio realized she must have said something aloud.

She considered Oksana's eyes, respectful and hard. Evans' soft and alarmed. Her crew and her family.

"We have Marco's answer," she said.

"Shift in language *is* shift in consciousness, yeah," Josep said. He was dressed in his jumpsuit, as was she. But he was strapped into the crash couch. A complex schematic showed the state of the system as best she knew it. The ships loyal to the inners clustered around Earth and Mars and Ceres in red. The Free Navy loyal to Marco in blue. Her own handful of pirates and idealists in green. The independent stations and ships—Ganymede, Iapetus—were white. And a dusting of gold over it all showing where Marco had buried his treasure chests in the void.

"Mind is made from analogies," Josep said, not needing her to contribute to the conversation. "Change in ages, change in the frame. Was *in* against *out* before. Turning into *connected* against *unconnected* now. *Free* Navy. *Consolidated* fleet. The ones who shrug off the chains against the ones who tie themselves together."

A direct one-to-one battle against Marco wasn't plausible. He had too many ships, and Michio's appeals to Rosenfeld and Dawes and Sanjrani hadn't won her any replies. Though they also hadn't been rejected. Marco was the only one calling her traitor to the cause thus far. The others, she assumed, were only following his lead.

Didn't help her in the short term.

She traced routes and burns for her green ships, arcs that would keep them out of range of the Free Navy's wrath and still allow them to send supplies where the need was worst. It was like solving a complex math puzzle without any promise that an optimal solution existed. The search for the least-bad answer.

"Us, freest of the free. Disconnected from the disconnected," Josep went on. "And because of that, coming into connection. Alienated because of our commitment to community, yeah? The yang inside the yin, the growing light from inside the dark. Had to be this way. Rule of the universe. Thermodynamics of meaning, us. Shikata ga nai. So free we have only one option. Because that's how the mind of God is shaped. Minimums and maximums sheeting together like a curve. Like a skin made from interpretation."

Michio moved the tactical display into her personal data and reached out, turning herself with one handhold until she faced the crash couch. Josep gazed at her with an expression of childlike joy. His pupils were so dilated, his eyes looked black.

"Got to go do something," she said. "You going to be all right without a babysitter?"

Josep chuckled. "Been a citizen of the mind since before you were born, child-bride. I can swim in vacuum and never die."

"All right," she said, and set the straps on the couch to restraint with her password as the release. "I'm going to set the system to watch your vitals. May have Laura come sit with you."

"Tell her to bring her go set. Play better when I'm stoned."

"I'll tell her," Michio said. Josep took her hand in his, squeezing her fingers gently. He meant something by it—something deep and subtle and probably not comprehensible by a sober mind. All she saw was the love in it. She dimmed the lights, had the system play soft music—harp and a woman's voice so perfect she assumed it was artificial—and left him alone. On her way up to the command deck, she sent a message to Laura and got a response. Josep probably didn't need a minder, but better to be safe. She laughed at herself as she steadied her ankle against a foothold. Safe in the little things, reckless in the big ones.

Bertold was in Pa's usual crash couch, music leaking from the earphones on his head and the ship's status monitors showing green and happy on his screen. Everything was fine as long as he didn't look out too far.

He lifted his chin to her as she pulled herself into Oksana's customary station instead. It still felt strange, being in a ship designed by Mars. It was all built with a sensibility she couldn't quite put her finger on: military and rigorous and straight. She couldn't help thinking it was because the designers had grown up with a constant gravity pulling them down, but maybe that wasn't true. Maybe it was just Martian because Mars was like that. Not inners against outers, but the rigid and brittle against the flowing and free.

"Matter? Geht gut?" Bertold asked as she retrieved the tactical schematic.

"Fine. But Josep decided to get stoned, and I'm just not doing work that goes well with intoxicated mysticism."

She felt a stab of regret as soon as she'd said it, though she knew Bertold wouldn't take her snapishness as more than it was. Still, if the family fell apart in the middle of everything else failing, she wouldn't be able to do this. She needed her rock.

Good, then, that she had it.

"You mind if I...?" Bertold asked, and she mirrored her display to his. All the ships, all their vectors. The final refutation of the one-ship. Here was humanity in all its fissures and disconnections. She went back to her analysis. Here was how to get a quarter of the lost resources back and only lose two of her ships. Here was how to deliver a tenth, but not to the people most in need. Here was how to keep her ships safe and achieve nothing else.

"Looks like an amoeba giving birth to twins," Bertold said. "Sehr feo."

"Ugly indeed," Michio said, running another scenario. "Stupid, wasteful, and cruel."

Bertold sighed. When they'd first been married, Michio had been deeply infatuated with him and Nadia both. Their shared passions had mellowed since then into an intimacy that she appreciated more than sex. It was the trust that let her say what she was seeing, what she was thinking. Let her hear the hard truth spoken in her own voice. "If we're going to do this, I'm going to have to do some things I don't like."

"Knew that going in, didn't we?"

"Didn't see the details."

"Bad?"

In answer, she flipped a variable in the tactical readout. New options opened that hadn't been there before: Recover sixty percent and lose nothing. Supply the five stations at greatest risk of collapse and keep Marco away from Iapetus. Open and possibly control a path to Ganymede for a few weeks at least. Bertold scowled, working out what she'd done and how she'd done it. When he saw, he grunted.

"That's a dream," he said.

"It's not," Michio said. "It's an agreement, and two enemies willing to respect it as long as their interests align."

"It's putting your back to the Butcher of Anderson Station."

"Well, yes. It is that. But I know what he is. I won't make the mistake of trusting him. He'll use us if he can. I'd be stupid not to repay that in kind. If Marco wasn't putting us as his top priority, it would be different, but he's burning hard for our ships."

"Injured his pride, sa sa?"

"All we need is that the consolidated fleet agree not to fire on us and we don't fire on them, and it opens up zones where Marco won't follow. Safe havens."

" 'Safe' meaning huddled underneath Fred Johnson's guns. Waiting for him to turn them on us."

"I know," Michio said. "And with Johnson, that time will come. When it does, we won't be there."

"This is a bad plan, Captain," Bertold said. His voice was gentle, though. He already understood.

"It is. It's the best bad plan I've got."

He sighed. "Yeah."

"Well," she said. "We could have done things Marco's way."

"Don't think we could have," Bertold said.

"Don't either."

"What about the stations and ships we're giving to? Some of them going to have guns. Have guards."

"Withhold aid unless they agree to fight and die for us?" Michio said. "Let them starve if they won't? No, don't. I'm not saying no to that. I'm asking. Which is worse? Extort people into being soldiers for us, or negotiate with Fred fucking Johnson?"

Bertold pressed a palm to his forehead. "No third side to that coin?"

"Die noble?" Michio said.

Bertold laughed, and then he didn't. "Depends on what the Butcher wants."

"It does," Michio said. "So we should ask him."

"Yeah, fuck," Bertold said. She saw her own dread and anger and humiliation reflected in his eyes. He knew what even considering this was costing her. And the ruthlessness she treated herself with that made it necessary. "I love you. You know that. Always."

"You too," she said.

"Doesn't take much before we have to compromise ourselves, does it?"

"Get born," Michio said, pulling the comm controls and setting the tightbeam for Ceres.

Chapter Twenty: Naomi

The danger is overreach," Bobbie said, hunching over the table and making it seem small. "They sucker-punched us. We got a couple easy wins coming back. It's tempting to drive it as far as we can, and try to break them. Seems like we've got them on the back foot. But the truth is, we're still sizing his forces up. He's still seeing what we do."

"And what are we doing?" Naomi asked, handing across a bowl of scrambled egg and tofu with hot sauce.

Bobbie scooped up a bite and chewed thoughtfully. Naomi sat across from her and tried a bite from her own bowl. Ever since Maura Patel had upgraded the food systems, the *Roci*'s hot sauce tasted a little different, but Naomi was coming to like it. There was a pleasure in the novelty. And also a sense of nostalgia for what had changed. That wasn't only food. That was everything.

"I don't think anyone knows," Bobbie said. "My tactics teacher back in bootcamp? Sergeant Kapoor. He was an entomologist—"

"Your sergeant in bootcamp was an entomologist?"

"It's Mars," Bobbie said, shrugging. "That isn't weird there. Anyway, he talked about shifting strategies like they were the middle part of metamorphosis. Apparently when a caterpillar makes a cocoon, the next thing it does is melt. Completely liquefies. And then all the little bits of what used to be caterpillar come back together as a moth or a butterfly or something. Finds a different way to assemble all the same pieces and make it something else."

"Sounds like the protomolecule."

"Huh. Yeah. Guess it kind of does." Bobbie took another bite of her eggs, her gaze on the far wall. She was quiet for long enough that Naomi didn't know if she'd come back.

"But he meant something tactical?" Naomi said.

"Yes. That pivoting your strategy was like that too. You go into a situation thinking about it a particular way, and then something changes. Then either you stick with the ideas you had before or you look at everything you have to work with and find a new shape. We're in the find-a-new-shape part. Avasarala's busy trying to keep what's left of Earth out of environmental collapse, but once that's stabilized, she's going to try to capture Inaros and everyone else who ever breathed his air and put them all on trial. She wants it to be crime."

Sandra Ip came in from the lift, nodded at the two of them, and pulled a bulb of tea from the dispenser.

"Why, do you think?" Naomi asked. "I mean, why treat it like a criminal act and not war?"

"I think it's a statement of contempt. But in the meantime, Mars is…I don't know. I think it's finding out that for all our strength, we were brittle. I'm not sure how we come back from that, but we'll never be what we were. Not any more than Earth will. And Fred? He's trying to build consensus and coalitions, because that's what he's been doing for decades."

"But you don't think he can." It wasn't a question. Ip left the galley, her footsteps retreating as Bobbie thought.

"I think putting people together's a good thing. Generally useful. But...I probably shouldn't be talking about this. I'm supposed to be his representative for Mars. Junior league ambassador or something."

"But he's trying to rebuild his caterpillar when we need a butterfly," Naomi said.

Bobbie sighed, took a last bite of egg, and tossed the bowl into the recycler. "I could be wrong," she said. "Maybe it'll work."

"We can hope."

Bobbie's hand terminal chirped. She considered the incoming message with a frown. The way she moved, even little motions like this, had the strength and economy of training. And more than that. A frustration.

"Oh joy," Bobbie said dryly. "Another important meeting."

"Price of being central."

"I guess," Bobbie said, hauling herself to her feet. "I'll be back when I can. Thanks again for letting me bunk here."

As Bobbie stepped past, Naomi put a hand on her arm. Stopped her. She didn't know exactly what she was going to say until she said it. Only that it was tied up with the ideas of crew and family and trying not to betray who you were. "Do you *want* to do this junior ambassador thing?"

"I don't know. It needs doing, I guess," Bobbie said. "I've been trying to reinvent myself since Io. Maybe since Ganymede. I really liked working veterans' outreach, but now that I'm not doing it, I don't miss it. I figure this'll be the same. It's something to do. Why?"

"You don't need to thank anyone that you're bunking here. If you like that cabin, it's yours."

Bobbie blinked. Her smile was small and rueful. She took a half step away, but didn't turn her body. The physical expression of hesitation. Naomi let the silence between them stretch. "I appreciate the thought," Bobbie said. "But adding someone into a crew? That's a big deal. I don't know what Holden would think about it."

"We've talked about it. He already thinks you're crew."

"But I'm doing this ambassador thing."

"Yeah. He thinks our gunner is Fred's ambassador from Mars." Naomi knew she was stretching the truth a little there, but it was worth it. Bobbie was still for the space of a heartbeat. And then another one.

"I didn't know that," she said, and then with no other words, stepped back toward the lift, the airlock, Ceres Station. Naomi watched her go.

Fires on shipboard were dangerous. There were any number of ship processes that could rise up past the point of spontaneous oxidation. The trick was knowing when letting a breeze through would start combustion and when it wouldn't. Sometimes talking to Bobbie was like putting her hand on a ceramic panel to see how hot it was. Trying to guess whether a little air would cool the big woman down or start up flames.

Alone in the galley, Naomi went through a little casual maintenance: wiping down the tables and benches, checking the status of the air filters, clearing the recycler feed. Having so many people on the ship left them running through supplies faster than she'd become accustomed to. Gor Droga's fondness for chai drove down their supply of tea analogue. Sun-yi Steinberg preferred a citrus drink that ate into the acids and texturing proteins. Clarissa Mao ate kibble and water. Prison food.

Looking over the supply levels, Naomi had to remind herself that the *Roci* was carrying three times the crew it was used to. Still well within the ship's specs and abilities. The *Tachi* had been designed for two full flight crews and cabins full of Martian marines. Renaming it hadn't changed that. It had only changed her expectations. But they were still going to have to resupply again soon.

The aromatics and spices that kept everyone from eating like Clarissa were going to be hard to get. Supplies were thin on Ceres. Supplies were going to be thin all through the Belt, and now the inner planets too. Any of the complex organics that Earth used to supply could be synthesized in labs or grown in hydroponics on

Ganymede and Ceres and Pallas. The touristy resorts on Titan. The problem, she thought as she replaced the injection nozzle on the coffee machine, was capacity. They could make anything, but they couldn't make it all at once. Humanity was going to get by on the minimum until there was a way to increase production, and a lot of people living on the margin wouldn't make it. They'd die on Earth, yes, but keeping the Belt fed wasn't going to be trivial either.

As she dropped the old injection nozzle into the recycler, she wondered if Marco had thought about that or if his dreams of glory had swept away any realistic plan for taking care of all the lives he'd disrupted. She had a guess about that. Marco was a creature of the grand gesture. His stories were about the single critical moment that changed everything, not all the moments that came after. Somewhere in the system right now, Karal or Wings or—thinking the name was like touching a sore—or Filip might be doing the same kind of maintenance she was doing on the *Pella*. She wondered how long it would take them to realize that the spoils of war wouldn't restock their ships forever.

Probably it wouldn't come clear until they'd used up everything. Kings were always the last to feel the famine. That wasn't just the Belt. That was all of history. The people who'd just been going about their lives were the ones who could speak to the actual cost of war. They paid it first. Men like Marco could orchestrate vast battles, order the looting and destruction of worlds, and never run out of coffee.

When the galley was done, she took herself back to the lift, and up to the command deck. There was new analysis of the ships that had gone missing in the ring gates. No new data, just a rechewing of the old. Her fascination came from a sense of dread. She'd been through those rings, traveled the weird not-space that linked solar systems, and of all the dangers she'd faced, just quietly vanishing away hadn't even been on her scopes. For a few hundred people—maybe more than that—something else had happened. The best minds of Earth and Mars that weren't occupied with trying to deal with their environment and governing bodies collapsing around them were looking at this. Naomi didn't have their resources or the depth of background expertise they did, but she had her own experience. Maybe she'd see something they hadn't.

And so she looked. Like an amateur detective, she followed clues and hunches, and like most investigations like that, she found nothing. The new conversation on the feeds was a theory surrounding the *Casa Azul*'s drive signature showing that the reactor was probably misconfigured, but apart from it being a rookie mistake that transferred a lot of energy into waste heat, Naomi didn't see anything in it. Certainly no reason that it or the other missing ships should have gone dark.

The analysis had just shifted into speculation over the plausibility of failed internal sensors in the *Casa Azul* increasing the pressure from the reactor bottle—which was what she assumed from the start—when her hand terminal chimed. Bobbie. She accepted the connection, and Bobbie's face appeared on her screen. Naomi felt a twinge of alarm.

"What's the matter?" she said.

Bobbie shook her head. It was probably meant to defuse the tension, but it reminded Naomi of a video of a bull getting ready to charge. "Do you know where Holden is? He's not answering his comm."

"Might be sleeping. He was up late going over footage for his broadcast thing with Monica."

"Could you go wake him up for me?" Bobbie asked. The wall behind her was sculpted stone with recessed lighting. Naomi thought it was the governor's palace. Fred Johnson's distant voice, low and graveled by annoyance, confirmed that.

Naomi rose, taking the terminal with her. "On my way," she said. "What's going on?"

"I don't understand why you're part of this," Fred Johnson said.

Across the desk from him, Jim still looked sleepy. Puffy-eyed and his hair still a little mashed from the crash couch. Bobbie, her arms crossed, sat off to one side. Before Jim could come up with an answer, she stepped in.

"He knew this Captain Pa," Bobbie said. "Worked with her on Medina before it was Medina."

"When she was in my chain of command," he said. "She isn't an unknown quantity. She was one of mine. I assigned her to that ship. I don't need anyone telling me about who she is or what they think of her."

Bobbie's face darkened. "Fair enough. I got Holden here because maybe you'd listen to him."

Jim raised a finger. "I don't actually know what's going on here," he said. "So. You know. What's going on here?"

"Michio Pa is one of Inaros' inner circle," Bobbie said. "Only it seems like she figured out that he's a great big asshole, because she broke ranks. Started sending relief supplies places without the Free Navy's say so. And now Inaros is shooting at her and she wants us to help her out."

"Relief supplies?" Fred said, his voice hard as stone. "That's what you're calling them?"

"That's what she's calling them," Bobbie bit back.

Jim glanced at Naomi. His expression said, *This is not going well.*

Naomi smiled back. *I know, right?*

"Michio Pa is stealing colony ships for the Free Navy," Fred said. "Even if she isn't complicit in the destruction of Earth, she has the blood of every colonist lost to her piracy on her hands. Those aren't relief supplies. They're the spoils of *war*. A war against *us*."

"Marco's shooting at her?" Jim said, trying to catch the conversation's reins. But Fred was locked on Bobbie and he wouldn't disengage.

"This is my best-case scenario, Draper. Inaros' coalition is falling apart. They're shooting at each other, not at us. If Pa degrades Inaros' fleet, that means they're that much easier for us to face. Every ship of Pa's that Inaros turns to slag is one less that's hunting down innocent people and stealing their property. There is no advantage to me or to Earth or to Mars that comes of getting involved in it, and I personally resent you calling in your friends here to try to bully me into thinking anything different."

"You aren't the only one here with military training," Bobbie said. "You aren't the only one who's had to weigh taking on problematic allies. You aren't the only one with command experience. But you are the one in this room who's *fucking wrong*."

Fred rose to his feet, and Naomi pushed back into the cushions of her chair. Bobbie stepped toward the man, her hands in fists, her chin jutting. Fred narrowed his eyes.

"I am not interested—" he began.

"If you want me to come here and wear a Martian uniform and puppet back whatever you say, you got the wrong girl," Bobbie half said, half shouted. "You think your magic OPA coalition pajama party is going to step in here and fix this? It's failing. They aren't coming to you anymore. You got Ceres and you got a fleet and you got me as your goddamn window dressing, and it's not enough. Stop acting like it is!"

The words hit Fred like a blow. He rocked back a little on his heels, his lips pressed together. *Was it like this when Marco's coalition fell apart?* Naomi wondered.

When Fred spoke, his voice was quieter, but cold. "I see why Avasarala likes you so much."

"Is that true?" Holden said. This time they heard him. "The OPA isn't coming?"

"It's taking a little longer to arrange than I'd hoped. I may need to change venue for it. Find a place that's neutral territory."

"Neutral territory," Jim said, skepticism in his voice.

"Some of these people are lifelong enemies of the inner planets," Fred said. "The combined fleet makes them nervous. They need to be reassured that our whole focus is on the Free Navy and not them. That's all."

Fred and Bobbie stood awkwardly, the momentum of their anger spent but both resisting being the first one to step back from it. Naomi coughed, though she didn't need to, then rose and went to the sideboard to pour herself a glass of water. It was enough. Bobbie took her seat, and then a moment later, Fred did as well. Jim hunched in his chair. She poured a glass for him too and brought it to him when she sat back down.

"This Captain Pa?" Bobbie said, speaking now to Jim directly. "She's an in. If we can get her to where she's willing to provide intelligence for protection, she might be able to give us something we need to crack Inaros."

Fred shook his head. The anger was gone from his voice, but not the resolve. "Pa is a loose cannon. She has a history of mutiny and defection."

"The last time she mutinied, she saved my life," Holden said. "And just maybe every human in existence. A little context here."

"She isn't coming to us as an ally. She isn't offering to stop her piracy or even slow it down. Cooperating with her means every ship she hijacks from now on will be our fault too!" Fred punctuated the end of his tirade by slapping his thick hand on the table.

"She's offering to give supplies to Ceres," Bobbie said.

"That she stole—maybe killed—to get."

Fred spread his hands, but Jim wasn't looking at him. Naomi sipped her water. It was cold with the bite of minerals, and it did nothing to loosen the lump in her throat. She had to resist the urge to pluck her hair down over her eyes. Bobbie had brought him here as someone to fight beside her. Someone Fred Johnson knew and respected. But the Martian didn't know Jim the way she did. Even loyalty—even love—wouldn't let him compromise his sense of right and wrong. She wondered if Bobbie would stay on the *Rocinante* after this. She hoped so.

Anyone who didn't know him better would have said he looked thoughtful. Naomi could see the grief in the corners of his mouth and the angle of his eyebrows. The sense of loss. She put down her glass. Took his hand. He glanced up at her like he was remembering she was there. She was looking into his eyes, and imagined that she saw a light within them go out. Or no, not out. Not extinguished. Only wrapped in something. Armor. Or regret.

"Okay," he said. "How do we get in touch with Pa?"

Naomi blinked. Fred mirrored her surprise and confusion.

"You're going to try to force my hand?" Fred said. "We aren't going to do it."

"You can pull your people off the *Roci* if you need to," Jim said, nodding as if he were agreeing with something. Fred scowled in a way that said he thought talking to Pa himself might only be the second-worst plan on the table. "If we have to do this alone, we'll be less effective. But we'll do what we can."

"We will?" Naomi asked.

He squeezed her fingers. "We're going to need someone like her," he said so gently it was like someone whispering a love song.

She wasn't sure what he meant, and it didn't make her feel better.

Chapter Twenty-One: Jakulski

Favór," Shului said. "Won't ask you nada alles. Only do this for me, sa sa?"

Jakulski shook his open hands, waving the younger man off. With Kelsey visiting the head, they were alone in Medina's technical command center. Because it was outside the drum, it was one of the only places on Medina that was always on the float. The couches were bolted to what would be the floor if the station ever went under thrust again. Angels wearing blue and gold pushed archways toward a God who, with them on the float, seemed like He was looking at them sideways. The only part that made any sense to Jakulski was the stars.

Shului was a picture of despair: mouth twisted in distress, hands out before him, eyes imploring Jakulski. The thick, crusty sty on the upper lid of his left eye looked like something out of the Book of Job.

"Can't," Jakulski said. "Promised my team I'd buy tonight."

"Will instead. Clear sus tab, y alles la," Shului said. "*Favór.*"

It had been a long shift already, and the truth was, Jakulski was looking forward to sitting down someplace with just a little gravity and a decent scotch. And the white kibble at the café that Salis and Vandercaust usually went to reminded him of his childhood. The prospect of staying another half shift—and worse, another half shift wearing the pinché Free Navy formal uniform—so he could be part of the greeting ceremony in Shului's place had no charm to it.

But the distress in the young man's expression was hard to look at. If he was smart, he'd just keep saying no, and hold to it until Kelsey got back. It'd be easier if there were someone else there. Keep Shului from debasing himself. Can't. Sorry. Be done.

"For for?" Jakulski said. "Just a greeting ceremony, yeah?"

Shului looked embarrassed and pointed to his infected eye. "Rindai gonna be there. She sees this? Favór, brother."

"Che! You still tasting her air? She's not gonna bite you. Talk to her."

"Will, will," Shului said. "Only *after* esá bastard heals up, yeah?"

"Bist bien," Jakulski said, shaking his head. Then, with a sigh, "Favór."

He thought for a moment Shului was going to embrace him, but thankfully the young man only took him by the shoulders and nodded in a curt way he probably thought was manly. Being young was undignified. Being young and in love was worse. He'd been a pup himself once, filled with all the same lusts and fears that every generation suffered. That he'd grown out of them now didn't mean he couldn't remember what it had been like. And fuck, but that pus-caked eye was hard to look at.

He sent a message to the technical team—Vandercaust, Salis, Roberts—that he'd been called on for extra duty and that he'd meet them after it was done if he could. Vandercaust sent back a generic acknowledgment. That was probably all he'd get from them. But maybe he could sneak away from the ceremony quick enough to catch the team. Cover for Shului and not have the tech team feel like he was putting himself above them. Eat his cake and still have it after. It would be a tired night if he could get it all done, but some nights were tired.

People. No matter where he went, no matter what he did, it was all still people.

Kelsey came back from the head and took her place at the main crash couch with the angels looking beneficently down over her shoulder. When Jakulski said he needed to get off shift a few minutes early so he could get back to his cabin and change, Shului jumped in to say how it was all okay and he'd take care of anything that needed doing.

The transition from the command center at the top of the ship into the drum was a long, curving ramp, and Jakulski rode down it in a cart with wheels that gripped the decking at any g, all the way down to the inner surface of the drum, and then down from there, going under the false ground like a caveman driving down into the underworld. His own cabin was back toward engineering. If he'd known he was going to have to go meet the *Proteus* and the grandees from Laconia, he could have brought his good uniform at the start of shift and taken the lift that ran the length of the ship outside the drum, but leaving early was almost as good.

The body of the drum had been built spacious, more like a station than a ship even from the start. Like it knew what it was destined to become. Long corridors with high ceilings and full-spectrum light like what used to fall on Earth before Marco threw a bunch of their mountains into their sky. He caught one of the diagonal halls, curving off toward his cabin on the hypotenuse of the drum's traffic grid, and let himself feel a little philosophical about the way the lights of Medina were like the memory of the species—an idea of brightness that had outlived the light that inspired it. The way Belters had. Belt-light. It was a pretty idea, and a little melancholy too, which made it even better in his mind. All beautiful things should have just a little sorrow about them. Made them seem real.

His cabin had been built for a single young Mormon living alone before marriage, but it was plenty enough for him. He
stripped off his jumpsuit, tossed it in the recycler, combed his
hair, and took his Free Navy uniform out of storage. He threw
his image up on the wall screen to see how he looked. Fucking
uncomfortable piece of cloth, the damned thing was. But for all
that, he had to admit he did come over suave in it. Distinguished
man, elder of his people, him.

To his surprise, he discovered that he was almost looking forward to this.

Medina had been on edge ever since word came through that
Pa and her ships were rogue. But only a little. Everyone here had
been OPA before they were Free Navy. And along with OPA,
they'd been Voltaire Collective. Or Black Sky. Or Golden Bough.
Or Union. Factions within factions within factions, sometimes
with very different groups laying claim to a single name, was as
Belt as red kibble and mushroom whiskey.

There was even a way that the split in the Free Navy was comforting. Not because it meant things were going well, but they
were going to shit in a familiar way. Pa made a play for status;
Marco was going to knock her back. Humanity still worked the
way it always had. All the shooting was happening inside the orbit
of Jupiter anyway. No one wanted it to spill out to the slow zone.
If Duarte got nervous about it all, it was because he wasn't from
here. Whatever he and his were doing on the far side of the Laconia ring, they'd been Martians when they went out and they were
Martians still.

So Duarte wanted to send more resources to Medina? Good.
He wanted to put advisors on the station, make sure the locals
were all trained with the equipment he was shipping in? Good.
More for Medina and everyone happy. And plus all that, the *Proteus* was bringing it in. And everyone wanted to look at the *Proteus*. First ship to come in the gate that hadn't gone out through it
first. A peek at whatever Duarte and his people were building out
there. Given the choice, Jakulski would still have been in the café

with his tech team, drinking a little too much and flirting. But since that wasn't happening, getting to see a little of the advisory force was okay for second place.

The *Proteus* had come through the gate earlier in the day, fast enough to coast to Medina without its Epstein and slow enough that its maneuvering thrusters could bring it into docking position down by the engineering decks. Jakulski'd heard rumors that the Martians were keeping the Epstein at a minimum so that no one could get a good look at their drive signature, but he didn't see how that made sense. Paranoia, rumor, and superstition was all. The *Proteus* might be one of the first ships built at a shipyard on the far side of the rings, but it was just a ship. Wasn't like they were flying there on the back of a dragon.

Captain Samuels—in charge of Medina because she was Rosenfeld Guoliang's cousin, but a good administrator anyway—was at the lock in full Free Navy military dress. Jon Amash representing for security. And there, with her auburn hair in a braid and eyes the same soft brown as her skin, Shoshana Rindai for systems. Shului had a point, that one. If Jakulski had been thirty years younger, he could have seen developing intentions toward her too.

Samuels scowled at him, but not in a way that meant anything. "You're for technical?"

Jakulski lifted an affirming fist and took his place in the line of floating grandees, ready to show the Marteños that the Free Navy was just as much a tight-assed military as the next coyo over. Medina had been meant for a generation ship once, and it still showed in the ship bones. Not much call for greeting visitors out in the wide nothing between stars, so the engineering lock opened onto a bare, functional decking with LED-white worklights and a rack of yellow-and-orange construction mechs on one wall. The air smelled of spent welding fuel and low-foam silicon lube.

Rindai glanced at him, lifting her chin in greeting. "For for Shului not come?" she asked, but before he had to come up with an answer, the lock cycled, and the Martians came in. Jakulski's first thought, quick as a reflex, was that they looked pretty unimpressive for great saviors.

The captain of the *Proteus* was a dark-skinned man with wide-set eyes and broad, expressive lips. His uniform was Martian, except for its insignia. Not taller than Jakulski, probably, and comfortable moving in zero g. The six behind him were in civilian jumpsuits, but the broadness of their shoulders and the cut of their hair said they were as military as the captain no matter what they were wearing. Samuels nodded, but didn't salute. The *Proteus* coyo caught his ankle in a floor hold and pulled himself to a stop as gracefully as a Belter.

"Permission to come aboard, Captain?" he said.

"Glad to have you here, Captain Montemayor," Samuels said. "Esá es my department heads. Amash. Rindai. Jakulski. They're to help you with constructing and arming the security base."

Security base? Jakulski sucked in a long breath. Not something Shului had mentioned. He wondered if not wanting Rindai to see his infected eye had been bullshit and he'd just wanted someone else to pick up the project. Just as likely Shului hadn't even known ...

"Not at all, sir," the *Proteus* man—Montemayor, she'd called him—said. "We're here to help *you*. Admiral Duarte specifically told me to assure you that we have the utmost faith in your ability to address any instability that might come from Sol system. We just want to assist and support our allies in Medina as best we can."

"Appreciate that," Samuels said, and it could just have been Jakulski's imagination, but she did seem to relax a little. Like maybe she'd been expecting this to be less pleasant and was relieved that the Martian coyo had started by showing his belly. Jakulski looked over the other six, wondering which of them he'd be working with and what exactly they'd be working on.

"Come you, have a drink," Samuels said, clapping Montemayor on the arm just as if they were friends. "We'll get you an escort to your quarters."

"It's Callisto all over again," Roberts said.

"You weren't even born when Callisto had trouble," Salis replied. "Que *Callisto all over again*?"

Jakulski leaned back, pressed to the ground by the spin of the drum. Somewhere five levels below their feet, a quarter of a klick aft, and maybe ten degrees spinward, his cabin waited and with it, his comfortable clothes. After the Martians had all been greeted and drunk to and made welcome and all, he'd hurried to the café, thinking maybe he'd be able to catch the technical team before they went home. He hadn't taken the time to stop and change clothes. So now the uniform, even undone at the throat, sanded his neck.

The technical team had all been there, and still were. Planted in their chairs like they'd taken root.

"Don't have to have been there to know what a proxy war is," Roberts said. "My family's Callistan, three generations. I know what it looked like, even if I wasn't there. Earth sends private security. Mars sends advisors. Everybody just there to help out this union or that trade group, but what it came down to was Earth and Mars spending Belter lives so they never had to risk their own."

He'd expected the place to be empty. It was long after his shift, well into when he should have been spinning down for sleep. But the light of the straight-line sun was bright and high, and even after generations in the black, some atavistic part of his brain still told him that meant midday. Drum time was permanent noon, first and last and always. And with the overlapping shifts that kept Medina alive and working no matter what the clock pretended, there were people coming in for an early breakfast or a late lunch, grabbing a quick drink on the way back to their cabin. Or like him and the technical team—burning the midnight oil. All at the same time. It was the drift of humanity left to live on whatever schedule they chose instead of being chained to the twenty-four hours of Earth and Mars. Belter time.

"Maybe if they'd come on their own, yeah," Salis said. "Could see it then. But that's not the way I heard it."

"The way you heard it?" Roberts laughed. "Didn't know you had your cameras in the bedrooms of power. Inside scoop, you?"

Salis made a rude gesture, but he was smiling while he did it. Jakulski took a drink of his beer, surprised to find the bulb so close to empty already.

"Friends in comms, me," Salis said. "What I heard was Marco asked Duarte to come. Not Laconia coming to pull our puppet strings. It's them dancing to a Free Navy song."

"The fuck would they do that for?" Jakulski asked. He sounded like Roberts, like he was busting Salis' balls, but he more than half wanted Salis to talk him into agreeing. In his fatigue, Jakulski couldn't stop imagining the six advisors in their civilian clothes and martial bodies.

"Same reason start storing your casino chips someplace new when your boyfriend moves out," Salis said. "Think on it, yeah? Michio Pa was one of his five. High up. Maybe Marco kept her out of the loop on Medina, only ran that through Rosenfeld. Maybe everyone knew a little of everything. Now Pa's making her play, it's only smart to change it up. She thinks she knows how the rail guns are protected? So he changes how the rail guns are protected. Simple."

"Or now Marco and Rosenfeld and Dawes are distracted, Duarte moves his 'advisors' in place so when he wants to, he can point the rail guns at Medina, tell us all what we should make him for breakfast," Roberts said.

Jakulski lifted a hand, caught the server's eye, and pointed to his spent bulb. One more wouldn't do any damage that wasn't already done. And all of it was going on God-damn Shului's tab anyway. Best make it count. Vandercaust, across from him, noticed and raised his own bulb as well. The server nodded with her hand and went back to what she'd been doing. A bird with wings as wide as Jakulski's outstretched fingers skinned past them, a fluttering and a flash of blue. It rode the breeze like it was still on a planet that curved down at the horizon instead of up. There was something wonderful about air wide enough to fly in.

"Say you?" he asked, looking at Vandercaust.

"Not saying nothing, sa sa?" the oldest tech said, scratching idly at the split-circle tattoo on his wrist. "Drinking."

Jakulski narrowed his eyes. Curiosity shifted sluggishly in his brain. He was too tired. He should go back and sleep. But the server was on her way with two fresh bulbs, and he'd made the trip so he could be with the team. "Best guess, then. Duarte pushing pawns to get control of Medina? Marco using Laconia against Pa? What are we looking at?"

"Best guess is I don't fucking know," Vandercaust said in an amiable voice, and gestured in a controlled way that made it clear he was very drunk indeed. "It's a war. Wars aren't like that."

"Aren't like what?" Roberts said.

"Aren't like stories about wars," Vandercaust answered solemnly. "Stories about wars come after. Like Qin Shi Huang unified China or when you look and say this led to this led to this, and then it was over. How did anything begin? War start when Marco hit Earth? When Earth hit Anderson Station? And it ends when Earth and Mars are dead? When Belters have a home? When everyone agrees it's done?"

Roberts rolled her eyes, but Salis leaned forward, fingers laced across his knee. Jakulski took his new bulb from the server and drank. It was cold and rich, but something made him a little sorry he'd stayed to drink it. Martians on Medina, and Pa running her own crew, and Fred Johnson taking Ceres back. It all felt like someone building the solar system's biggest mousetrap. And Jakulski thought maybe he was living inside the cheese.

Chapter Twenty-Two: Holden

It hadn't really been that long since Fred had crewed up the *Rocinante* for its burn down to Luna, but it had also been a lifetime. Now, with the Tycho-based crew gone, the ship seemed bigger. Emptier. It was like the end of a really long party when all the guests have gone home, and Holden couldn't quite decide if it left him feeling lonely or relieved. When they headed out this time, they'd only have one pilot. One engineer. Still two mechanics, assuming that was Clarissa's official title. After flying with the *Roci* for so many years with just his little family, it was strange to feel the loss of that redundancy, but some deep training was still there in the back of his mind saying that everyone had to be replaceable. As if keeping Chava Lombaugh on the ship would have really made it bearable losing Alex to a badly placed PDC round or a stroke during a high-g burn or any of the other thousand things that could go wrong in space. As if Sandra Ip could ever have taken Naomi's place.

On one hand, it was unthinkable. On the other, it was reasonable. Alex was Alex, and no one else would ever be. If something did go wrong, though, they'd want a pilot. And the chances of things going wrong seemed pretty high.

The *Minsky* had started its life burning out of Luna with colonists funded by Royal Charter Energy. The same company that had landed on Ilus and Longdune and New Egypt. If things had gone the way they'd intended, they'd have passed through the ring gates on their way to landfall in a system called San Esteban. Instead, they'd been taken over by the *Serrio Mal*, looted, and were in a braking burn toward Ceres with what was left of the crew and supplies after Michio Pa and her people were done with it. Food and water, hydroponics and medical supplies, construction mechs and scientific equipment and the people to use them. And burning at its side, a Free Navy gunship as escort. Probably one of Pa's. Probably not a trap.

Probably not going to get reduced to radioactive gas by Fred. But only probably.

Alone on the command deck, he had the *Roci*'s inventory schematic pulled up on the screen and the latest edited piece from Monica spooling on his hand terminal. The inventory chirped and updated. It took him a second to find the new data.

"Alex?"

"Right here, Hoss," Alex replied, his voice coming through the comm and down from the cockpit both.

"Confirm that you're seeing the juice on your couch topped up?"

A moment passed. "I am showing full-on shitty synthetic juice guaranteed to give a migraine and diarrhea if you use it for more than eight hours."

"Seriously?"

"We had better than this on the *Canterbury*," Alex said.

Holden felt a twitch of concern. "Why did we get third-rate juice?"

Naomi answered as if she were beside him instead of strapped into the loading mech on the dock. "Because the alternative was loading the injectors with morphine so you don't care so much about being crushed. There's a war on, you know."

"So there is," he said as the inventory chimed another update.

Amos said, "Should show we're at eighty percent on PDC rounds."

"Showing eighty-one point seven," Holden said.

"Really? I'm pretty sure that ain't right."

"Track it down," Holden said. "I'll let you know if the ship changes her mind in the meantime."

"We're on it," Amos agreed.

We. Meaning Clarissa. He was really going to have to get over that. He felt guilty that he hadn't already, but he didn't have a clear idea how to let his discomfort with her go. He pushed the issue back down his priority list again, the way he always did. And who knew? Maybe they'd all die in a hail of gunfire before it came up again and he wouldn't have to worry about it.

On his hand terminal, the new edit of latest video flickered. This would be the tenth one when it came out. Most of it was an interview with a couple of musicians he'd met up in the shitty part of the station. Two Belters with patois so thick, he'd fed it through a translation program, but their voices were musical and there was an affection in them that transcended the language. Monica had redone the subtitles, putting them at the top of the image, so that the words were beside their faces, close enough to see their expressions as they spoke. They looked like grandfather and grandson, but they called each other "cousin."

As he watched, they talked about the music scene on Ceres, the difference between live music and recordings, between what they called tényleges performance and using microphones. They didn't talk about Earth or Mars, the OPA or the Free Navy. Holden hadn't asked, and the few times that they'd strayed in a political direction, he'd brought it back to the music. Two more reminders that not everyone who lived outside a gravity well had dropped the rocks on Earth. He liked this one a lot, and he wanted to get it approved for release before they left dock. *In case*, without ever quite letting himself think in case of what. Just *in case*.

The first nine pieces he'd released had gotten a little traction. Some of that was, he knew, because his name was on it. Being a minor political celebrity had its perks, and one was a small but reliable audience baked in for this project. Better than that, though, he'd started getting copycats. People with their own feeds on Titan and Luna and Earth doing interviews and slice-of-life bits like the ones he'd put out.

Or maybe they'd always been doing that, and he was copying them. Only he hadn't noticed any of it until now.

"Cap?" Amos said, and Holden realized it wasn't the first time. "You okay up there?"

"I'm here. I'm fine. Distracted. What've you got?"

Clarissa answered. "One of the feeds didn't zero before. We got it. The count's confirmed."

"Great," Holden said. On his hand terminal, the older man struck a chord on his guitar and the younger man laughed. He closed the file. He couldn't tell if it was working or not anymore. His brain couldn't imagine what it would be like to run into it for the first time. Whether the humanity that he saw in it would be there for someone on Earth or Mars or in the colony ships. Or on the far side of the gates.

He heard Naomi coming up before he saw her. He looked back over his shoulder as she stepped off the lift. Her jumpsuit still showed lines of sweat where the loading mech's straps had held her, and when she leaned over to kiss his forehead, he took her arm. Her eyes were a little bloodshot, the way they got when she was tired. She looked back down at him, laughed a little.

"What?"

"You're very beautiful," Holden said. "I hope I tell you that often enough."

"You do."

"Then I hope I don't tell you so often it gets annoying."

"You don't," she said, and sat in the crash couch beside his, stretching her arm as she did so she could keep her fingers twined in his. "Are you all right?"

"A little exhausted."

"Just a little?"

"I'm not hallucinating yet."

Naomi shook her head. Just a few millimeters one way and then the other. "You know you're not responsible for fixing everything."

"Saving humanity from itself is a group project, yes," he said. "Really, all I'm doing is trying to show everyone on Earth and Mars and the Belt and Medina and the colonies that really we're all still just one tribe."

"So just transcend all lived human experience since before the dawn of history?"

"And keep the part where we kill each other to a minimum," he said. "Shouldn't be hard."

"At least you know why you're tired."

She squeezed his fingers and let them go, pulling up a tactical display of Ceres and the space around it. The station itself and the fleet ships that surrounded it like a cloud of blue fireflies were marked as friendlies. The colony ship and its escort slowing toward them were in yellow—status unknown, but of interest. The time to rendezvous was down to hours.

"Part of me hopes that Fred won't let us go out," he said. "We request the clamps come off, and they just say no and we're stuck in here."

"While the colony ship flips at the last minute and accelerates into the port, exploding in a nuclear fireball," Naomi said.

He pulled up his hand terminal and sent his approval to Monica on Tycho. At lightspeed, it would still be minutes before she got it. "It does sound less appealing when you put it that way."

Behind them, the lift cycled down, humming as it went. Alex—his voice still doubled by the headset and the free air—finished his checklist with Amos and Clarissa. Holden stowed his hand terminal in the crash couch's high-g compartment. If things went poorly, he didn't want it zooming around the command deck.

Naomi's voice was low, but focused. "Can I ask you something?"

"Of course."

"Why are we doing this?"

Holden wished his brain had been a little clearer. After a certain point, he felt like his verbal centers ran straight to his mouth without passing through the rest of his brain. "Because we can't just blow up enough things that this becomes a good situation. We're going to need more than that in our toolbox."

Bobbie stepped off the lift. There was something odd about her, but he couldn't put his finger on it. She was wearing simple blacks, but the way she held herself made them look like a uniform. Her hands were in fists at her sides, but she didn't seem angry so much as nervous. That didn't bode well.

"Hey," Holden said.

"Sir."

"Please don't call me sir. No one on the ship does. Everything all right? Fred want something?"

"Johnson didn't send me," Bobbie said. "You're going out, and I'm reporting for duty."

"Okay," Holden said. "You can route tactical and fire control down here, or take the gunner's seat up by Alex. Wherever feels most comfortable."

Bobbie took a deep breath and something Holden didn't understand played out across her wide face. "I'll take the gunner's seat," she finally said, and climbed up to the cockpit. Holden watched her ankles disappear above him, his brow furrowed hard enough to ache a little.

"That was...um," he said. "Was that a moment?"

"That was a moment," Naomi said.

"Good moment or bad moment?"

"Very good moment."

"Well. Shit," he said. "I'm sorry I missed it."

"All right, everyone strapped in?" Alex called.

One by one, the crew answered. They were ready. Or as ready as they were likely to get. Holden let his head sink into the gel of the couch, shifting his screen to match Naomi's. There were an awful lot of ships floating in the vicinity of Ceres right now. He listened as Alex requested that the docking clamps be released. For long, painful seconds, Ceres traffic authority didn't answer. And then, "Affirmative, *Rocinante*. You are cleared to leave."

The ship shuddered and the spin gravity of Ceres vanished as Alex let their momentum fling them out into the vacuum. On his screen, they were a white dot flying off at a tangent to the station's massive curve. He flipped to external cameras and watched the surface of the dwarf planet curve away.

"Well," Naomi said. "Looks like Fred didn't object to this enough to keep us from going out."

"Yeah," Holden said. "I hope he knows what he's doing, trusting delicate work like this to agents of chaos like us."

Amos chuckled, and Holden realized he'd said that on the full-crew channel.

"Fairly sure he's making this shit up as he goes too," Amos said. "Anyway, the worst-case scenario is we all get killed and he gets to feel smart for not having his people on board when we did it. Win-win for him."

When Bobbie spoke, Holden could hear the smile in it, despite the words. "No one dies while standing watch without permission from the commanding officer."

"You say so, Babs," Amos replied.

"Keep braced," Alex said. "I'm gonna have to get us on course here."

Normally the shifting of the ship under maneuvering thrusters was almost subliminal to Holden. The subtle dance of vectors and thrust had been part of his life ever since he'd left Earth. It was only that he was so tired and worried and full of so very much coffee that it bothered him. With every adjustment, up and down changed a little and then went back to the float. When Alex fired the Epstein for a few seconds, the *Roci* sang, harmonics ringing through overtones up and down the hull like a church bell.

"Not too much, Alex," Holden said. "We don't want our braking burn to slag anybody. At least I don't think we do."

"Not a problem," Alex said. "We'll just tap back down to a

good coasting speed until we're right up alongside them. Final braking won't catch anyone in the plume."

"And keep the torpedoes and PDCs hot," Holden said. "Just in case."

"On it," Bobbie said. "We're getting painted by ranging lasers."

"Whose?" Holden asked, dropping the exterior camera and going back to tactical. The scattering of fleet ships. The surface defenses of Ceres. The slowly approaching captured ship and its Free Navy escort.

"Oh," Naomi said, tapping through a list of connection reports longer than her screen. "Pretty much everyone."

"The escort ship?"

"They're painting us too."

On his screen, the incoming ships stuttered, the data around them updating as they killed their braking burns, appearing from behind clouds of superheated gas. The *Roci*'s sensor arrays checked contour and heat signatures, confirming almost instantly. The larger ship matched the *Minsky*—large, blocky, and awkward with communications satellites meant to bootstrap a network around an alien planet covering its sides like warts. The smaller was a Martian corvette, a generation newer than the *Roci*, a little lighter, streamlined for atmosphere and probably loaded with similar ordnance. Its transponder wasn't answering.

"Hate seeing this," Alex said. "Two good Martian-built ships squaring off? It ain't right."

"Well," Holden said. "Who knows? Maybe we're on the same side."

"If it is a fight," Bobbie said, "let's win it. Permission to lock target?"

"Has it locked on us?" Holden asked.

"Not yet," Naomi said.

"Hold off, then," Holden said. "I don't want to go first."

An incoming comm request appeared on his screen from Fred Johnson, and for a confused half second, he wondered what Fred was doing on the gunship, then saw the tightbeam was coming from Ceres. When this was over, he was really going to need to sleep. He accepted the connection, and Fred appeared in a separate window on the side of his screen.

"Regretting this yet?" Fred asked.

"Only a little," Holden said. "You?"

"I want to make something clear. If—*if*—you take possession of that colony ship, under no circumstances does it come within three thousand klicks of my dock. If there are people who need medical assistance on board, they stay on board and we'll send help out to them. Nothing comes off that ship until it's been examined, scanned, reloaded, disinfected, and sprinkled with holy water by whatever flavor of priest I can put my hands on. I'm not running Troy here."

"Understood."

"The only reason I'm letting you do this at all is the chance of recovering prisoners of the Free Navy alive."

"That's the only reason?" Holden said. "So you'll hand all the supplies on the ship back over to the former owners instead of using them to keep Ceres alive?"

Fred's smile was gentle and warm. "Don't be an asshole."

"Okay," Bobbie said. "Now they're painting us. Permission to return the favor?"

"Granted," Holden said.

Bobbie said something under her breath that he couldn't make out, but it sounded happy.

"Be careful, Holden," Fred said again. "I don't like anything about this."

"Well, if it's a trap, you can say I told you so to whatever scraps of us are left."

"I've got thirty ships that'll make sure you have a nuclear funeral pyre big enough they'd see it on Proxima Centauri in four years. You know. If anyone's there."

"That's not comforting," Holden said.

"We should open comms," Naomi said.

"Fred? I've gotta go do this thing. I'll let you know how it went when it's done."

Fred nodded. The connection dropped. Holden swallowed past the tightness in his throat. "How are we for range?"

"Inside effective torpedo range," Bobbie said. "And we'll be good for PDCs in eight minutes and ten seconds."

"Rail gun all warmed up?"

"Oh hell yes."

"All right," Holden said. "Naomi, get me a channel."

A moment later, a new frame appeared on his screen. Dark but with the yellow border of an open connection. They were so close, there was effectively no light delay. That alone made him nervous.

"Attention, unidentified warship. This is James Holden of the independent freighter *Rocinante*. We're here to transfer possession of the *Minsky*. Hope that's what brought you here too. I'd appreciate it if you'd identify."

The screen stayed dark. Anxiety crept up his back. The seconds stretched without a reply. Something was wrong. Without moving, he rehearsed what he'd say to Alex. *Get us out of here. Something's about to blow up.* What he'd say to Bobbie. *Protect the* Roci *first. Disable the gunship if you can. Kill it if you have to.*

The frame flickered. For a fraction of a second, an unfamiliar blond woman with sharp features appeared, and then immediately the image shifted to a woman with dark hair tied back. A small, cynical smile on her lips. Holden realized he'd been holding his breath and exhaled.

"*Rocinante*," she said, "this is Michio Pa of the *Connaught*. Weird to see you again, Captain Holden."

Chapter Twenty-Three: Pa

The *Munroe* died second. Marco's forces caught it near a cloud of machining equipment and medical supplies that had been buried in the void. As best Michio could reconstruct it, a plea for help had come from a mining ship called the *Corvid*. They had five families on the ship, and an outbreak of complex meningitis that had the children in medical comas. The *Munroe*, charging to the rescue, was intercepted by two Free Navy corvettes, and fled from them into two others. Marco had recorded the captain—a middle-aged man named Levi Watts who Michio had hardly known before he was placed under her command—begging for the life of his crew before his ship was overwhelmed.

It hadn't been dignified, and it ended in fire. Copies of it went on a dozen anonymous feeds with an attached listing of all the other vessels that had chosen to follow her.

The *Corvid*'s transponder vanished. The discussions of whether it had also been destroyed or invented as bait for the ambush came to nothing. The message was the same either way: No one could betray the Free Navy, and the Free Navy was Marco Inaros. Evans and Nadia had taken the responsibility of remaking the communication protocols for Michio's remaining fleet. She could see the concern in their eyes and hear it in the timbre of their voices. She loved them for caring, but there was a distance in that love for now. A coldness. She couldn't say how long her rage and grief would stay cold, but for now ruthless analysis was the only way she could mourn.

Maybe that was what worried them.

The *Minsky* had been flying dark outside the ecliptic in an orbit that, given several months, would have taken it near enough to the ring gate that it could have made a break for it, dodged into the slow zone before any of the Free Navy ships could intercept it. So when Foyle and the *Serrio Mal* captured it, she'd also saved the lives of everyone aboard. It would have been a matter of minutes between the ship passing through the gate and rail gun defenses ripping it to pieces. Not that the colonists knew that. Not that Michio had told them.

Even when Foyle learned that the prize ship was being routed to Ceres and into the arms of the enemy, she'd been willing to escort it. Michio had been tempted to let her, but it was the wrong move. Reaching out to Fred Johnson had been her decision. If it was going to go pear-shaped, she should be the one to deal with it.

The transfer had been furtive and quick—high-g, short-burst burns that brought the *Minsky* and the *Connaught* together on an intercept with Ceres that kept away from the bulk of Marco's forces.

When, a lifetime ago, Marco had chosen her to head the conscription arm of the Free Navy, he'd given her the smaller, lighter ships. Armed, certainly, but not built for heavy fighting. She was meant to outrun the vast, bulky ice haulers, converted now to colony ships: massive and easy to overwhelm. Marco and Rosenfeld, the war leaders against the inner planets, had more need of the capital ships. They were the sledgehammer, and she was the scalpel.

And now she was going to find out whether her plan to cut a path where the great Marco Inaros couldn't reach her had worked, or if her rebellion was going to be short-lived and tragic.

The universe has plans for you, Josep said in her imagination. *You couldn't have come this far through so many dangers if there weren't a reason for you to be here.*

The same beautiful bullshit that everyone told themselves. That they were special. That they mattered. That some vast intelligence behind the curtains of reality cared what happened to them. And in all the history of the species, they'd all died anyway.

"Attention, unidentified warship. This is James Holden of the independent corvette *Rocinante*. We're here to transfer possession of the *Minsky*. Hope that's what brought you here too. I'd appreciate it if you'd identify."

"Well, fuck," Michio said.

"Captain?" Oksana said.

James Holden. Probably the most ambiguous man in the system. The Earther who worked for Fred Johnson's OPA. The leader of the coup against Ashford back in the slow zone. The man Marco Inaros hated more than anyone else. Chosen envoy of the Martian Republic and the United Nations to Ilus, and everybody's favorite pawn. If she'd had a dream that his voice would be the one greeting her, Josep would have called it a sign. Of what, she couldn't guess.

Her display showed Ceres Station, the enemy ships arrayed around it like a cloud of insects waiting to attack. And all through the system, she was certain sensor arrays and optical telescopes were focused on her, on the *Minsky*, and on the ship coasting toward her.

Somewhere, Marco was seeing her with the chance to open fire on James Holden. If God had wanted to give her a way to walk back her rebellion, He couldn't have made a better one. She had her ranging laser on him. Even if she died, even if they all died, the other ships in her command would have a chance to sneak back into the Free Navy's fold. No more *Witch of Endors*. No more *Munroes*.

There are no coincidences, Josep said in her mind. Except of course there were.

"Captain, what are your orders?" Oksana asked.

"Open the connection."

Oksana opened the comms, grunted at some small error, and passed the feed to Michio's station. Holden was looking anxiously into the camera. The years had been kind to him. His face had a more comfortable look, and a touch of sorrow and humor that he wore well. She wondered if the others of his crew were still on the *Rocinante* with him or if he'd left Naomi Nagata someplace safely out of Marco's reach.

"*Rocinante*, this is Michio Pa of the *Connaught*. Weird to see you again, Captain Holden."

His lips widened into a boyish grin, and to her surprise, she found herself smiling back. It wasn't pleasure, but the giddiness of fear. Her heart tapped at her ribs like it was impatient. Trying to get her attention. *I could kill him. He could kill me. Either decision would be justified.* The *Rocinante* had a rail gun. By the time she knew he'd fired, she'd already be dead. But he probably wouldn't. And she probably wouldn't either.

"Weird to see you too, Captain Pa. Strange times."

She laughed, and it sounded like someone else. Evans looked at her, concern in his eyes. She ignored him.

"Couldn't help noticing that you've got some ships pointing their guns at me," she said lightly.

"People are nervous," Holden said.

"Was sending you supposed to be symbolic of something?"

"Nope. We just drew the short straw."

It was eerie, speaking to someone on the other side of the fight without so much as a stutter of light delay. She wanted to flip and burn hard, get out. Every second on the float brought her closer to Ceres and the consolidated fleet and Fred fucking Johnson. Every dot on the tactical display made her itch. They were the enemy as much as Marco. But the enemy of her enemy was at least playing nice right now.

No sudden moves. Nothing without warning. They could do this.

"We're ready to transfer control of the *Minsky* to you," she said. "Her passengers are all on board confined to their quarters. I'll send along a manifest with what supplies she's carrying."

Holden nodded. "So. Nothing's going to blow up when we do this, is it? No booby traps? Because there are some smart people who think I'm pretty stupid for trusting you."

"Plenty on my side saying the same of me. Nothing either of us can say right now's going to change their minds. We'll just have to try this. See what happens."

Oksana's voice cut through the air like a wire. "I've got fast-movers coming in from Ceres! Six torpedoes. Fifty seconds to impact."

The breath left Michio's lungs, pushed out by fear so profound it felt like calm. *Open fire, all guns. Get us out of here.* Whatever they were going to do, she had to order it now.

Except she was looking at Holden, and he was surprised too. Shocked, even.

Angry.

She had to give the order. She had to fire. Her family was going to die. If she fired, they'd all fire back. She had to run. Burn hard. Melt everything behind her to slag.

Stop, she thought. *If we die, we die, but right now*, stop.

Why was Holden angry?

"Holden?" she said, her voice trembling. "Do we have a problem?"

"Fuck yes, you have my permission," Holden snapped, and it took her a fraction of a second to realize he wasn't speaking to her.

"The *Rocinante*'s firing its PDCs," Oksana said, her voice high and sharp. Fear was a resonance tone, and the deck rang with it.

"Lighting up our PDCs," Evans said.

"Don't," Michio shouted before she knew she was going to say it. Then, in the stunned silence, "Touch those fire controls, and you will kill us all. Do you understand, Mr. Evans? Everyone you love will die, and it will be your fault." Her husband looked at her, confusion in his eyes. His fingers hovered over the controls, twitching toward them. If she'd shot him, he couldn't have looked more betrayed. "Oksana, what is the *Rocinante* firing on?"

"No no no," Holden said. "We're getting *them*. Not *you*. You don't think we're—"

"They're targeting the missiles from Ceres. Impact in… They're done, sir. The *Rocinante* shot down the attack."

Michio nodded. Her blood rattled in her veins. Her hands shook. She was aware of the panic in her mind like listening to voices in a nearby room, but she didn't feel it. She didn't feel anything.

"Evans," she said. "Put your hands down."

Evans looked at his own fingers like he was surprised to see them there, then slowly lowered them to his sides. She watched the realization bloom in his eyes: If he'd started firing, the enemy fleet would have started firing. Maybe not the *Rocinante*, but everyone else. His instincts had come within a finger-tap of killing them all. He moaned the way he did when he was sick or drunk, unstrapped, and pushed off. His crash couch spun gently on its gimbals as he abandoned his post. She didn't stop him.

On her screen, Holden was bending in toward the camera. Not much, just the little unconscious curve of someone protecting their gut. She forced her own spine to relax. Long seconds passed as she waited for another attack. Heartbeat after heartbeat, nothing came.

"Well," she said.

"Yeah," Holden replied.

Another moment passed. Michio heard another voice behind Holden. Naomi Nagata. The words themselves weren't clear, but the tone of the woman's voice could have stripped paint. So he hadn't left her someplace safe. Fair enough. Safety might not exist now anywhere. The first hints of adrenaline crash haunted the edges of Michio's consciousness: a faint nausea, a deepening weariness, sorrow. She ignored those too.

"Was saying," Michio said, her voice calmer than she'd expected.

"We have the *Minsky* and what she's carrying. Ready to pass control over to you. Then we're backing away before anyone else starts shooting at us."

"That wasn't Fred," Holden said. "I don't know who fired those torpedoes, but we're going to find out."

Michio's lips felt heavy, solid, like she'd been carved from stone. It didn't matter who'd pulled the trigger on the attack from Ceres. Look far enough back, and Marco Inaros would be behind it.

"I appreciate that," she said. "You let us know when you're ready for the remote command protocols."

Marco's response didn't take an hour. He shook his head sorrowfully, looked into the camera with wide, dark eyes. The raw charisma of his presence was banked by being on a screen, but it wasn't extinguished. Proof that the traitor Michio Pa was working with Earth. Undermining the efforts of the Free Navy to protect and rebuild the Belt. Brazenly giving aid and comfort to the enemy. His voice vibrated with indignation on behalf of his people and disgust for her collaboration with the enemy. It didn't matter that the "enemy" included millions of Belters he'd left behind. She wondered whether that would matter to the people who watched him.

He included images of the *Rocinante* defending the *Connaught*. The final proof, if anyone needed it, that she was in bed with the people who most wanted the Free Navy and the Belt to fail.

She watched it on the command deck, a dozen responses competing in her head. She even went as far as recording one, but the words got away from her, tugged along by her anger until the woman looking back at her from the screen seemed almost as crazed as the one Marco described.

They burned away from Ceres, but not hard. The point of the exercise was to put themselves in range of the inners and not be killed. To show the other ships still loyal to her and the handful of independent ships that saw more hope in her path than Marco's that zones of protection were possible. Fleeing her new little zone of safety as quickly as she could was what she wanted down to her marrow, but it wasn't what she'd come here for. Wasn't what she'd risked her ship and her family and her life to get. And so a third of a g, and then the float, reorienting, then another burn. The farther she got from Fred Johnson's guns, the more she tried to make the *Connaught* hard for Marco to track.

When Oksana came to her cabin that night, it hadn't been as her officer but as her wife. She brought a bottle of whiskey with a bright-silver injection tip and two bulbs to drink it from. At first, Michio didn't want the company, but as soon as she did, she was desperate for it. Sex, in Michio's experience, was like music. Or language. It could express anything. Now it was rage and sorrow and need.

Afterward, strapped into the crash couch together, she listened to Oksana's breath, deep and steady as she imagined waves must be. Michio's heart felt fragile and more complicated than it had when she'd woken up that morning. Careful not to wake her wife, she stretched out, caught her hand terminal between her fingertips, and spooled up Marco's denunciation. The light from the little screen filled the room, and she dropped the sound until it was nothing but a distant rhythm of hard consonants. Heard that way, there was a pattern to how Marco spoke. A throbbing in his delivery like he was imitating a heartbeat. She'd never noticed that before.

She shifted over to the cached copies of the community feeds and forums. They filled with reactions and opinions. Judgment of her and her family. Declarations of hatred. Threats of death. Nothing she hadn't expected. These were the people she was risking everything to feed and support. And because she stood against Marco to do it, they hated her. Not all of them, but many. And deeply.

Good thing she wasn't doing it for the popularity.

The alert went on. Attitude adjustment and burn. She shifted the hand terminal to the *Connaught*'s control systems. Nadia had plotted in a complex adjustment, turning on all three axes with a variable burn so that when they were done, only someone with very precise sensor arrays who'd caught them all the way through the maneuver would be able to plot where they were going with any certainty. The countdown came, the burn pressing her and Oksana gently against each other and shifting the crash couch beneath them, swinging one direction and then another and back. The deep rumble of the Epstein was like God apologetically clearing His throat.

Oksana yawned, stretched, put her hand on Michio's shoulder.

"Hoy, Captain," she said, voice slushy with sleep and the aftermath of coupling. Michio sighed, smiled.

"Navigator Busch," she said, matching Oksana's joking formality, and weaving their fingers together. "You should sleep."

"So should you. Can you?"

"No," Michio said. "If it gets to be a problem, I'll hit the autodoc. Get something."

"What's the status?"

Michio almost asked, *The status of what?* But it would only have been so she didn't have to think too much. She knew Oksana meant the Free Navy's reaction. Were there gunships burning for them now? Had long-range torpedoes launched toward them from the ships and stations of the Belt, hoping to come quietly and fast enough to overwhelm their PDCs? Michio shifted to kiss her forehead just at the hairline. Oksana's hair smelled of musk and the fake vanilla she favored. It was a beautiful scent.

"Everyone hates us, but no one's shooting yet," she said.

"They will, though."

"They will. But we've carved little islands of safety. Now that they've accepted our tribute, we can go to Ceres or any other station Fred fucking Johnson takes without Marco following on. Unless he's ready for a full battle with the inners."

"In which case, it won't really matter if we're there or not," Oksana said, her lips against Michio's collarbone. "And you? Are you all right?"

The *Connaught* made a complex corkscrewing burn, the crash couch shifting one way, then another. The universe seeming to swirl around the stillpoint of their bodies. Michio shrugged in the darkness. "I don't know. I know what my project is. Get the things the Belt needs and give them to the people that need them the most. But...no one's going to thank us for it."

"Some will," Oksana said. Then, a moment later, "I mean, no one with *power*."

"Isn't that what we're doing, though?"

"Doing?" Oksana asked, rubbing the sleep out of her eyes.

"If no one with power loves us, let's make our own damn power."

Chapter Twenty-Four: Prax

The morning routine was the same. Prax got up first, padded to the kitchen still wearing his robe and slippers. He started brewing the tea and making breakfast for the family. Pancakes and bacon for the girls. Red rice and eggs for him and Djuna. He played music on the system. Usually something calm and wandering, what Djuna called his getting-a-massage music. And about the time the rice was cooked and the bacon crisped, he heard the sound of Djuna's shower and the voices of Mei and Natalia. This particular morning, the girls were gabbling pleasantly to each other. Other mornings, they would snap and argue.

When Djuna's shower water stopped, he poured the first pancake onto the grill, two eggs beside it. They took almost exactly the same time to cook, so that he could turn them both, one with either hand. It was showing off, but when Mei saw it, it always made her laugh. Djuna's hectoring voice came from the hall, moving the girls through their morning rituals—washing faces, combing hair, getting dressed. When they all came to the table, Prax would be the only one not wearing his work clothes. The girls made fun of him for lazing around in his robe, even though he'd been the one to do the most, and he pretended to be offended even though he really wasn't.

After breakfast, Djuna would take the girls to school on her way to work, leaving him alone to clean away the dishes, take his own shower, and prepare for the lab. It wasn't something they'd ever discussed. It was just the way their own particular domestic habits had formed. Prax liked it like that. He'd had more than enough adventures in his life. He got more work done when things were predictable.

He sweetened his tea with the same syrup he drizzled over the pancakes, put the plates and glasses filled with food in their places, and was just sitting down with his rice and eggs when Djuna came in, driving the girls before her like a cattleman in the tradition of mothers all through history.

Mei was a little quieter than usual, Natalia a little brighter, but both within the error bars. Djuna turned down the music while they ate and talked. When the conversation turned dangerous, Prax didn't notice.

"What does *resistance* mean?" Natalia asked. Her face was serious and sober, and on so small a person, vaguely comic.

"It's a measure of how electrons flow through something," Prax said. "You see, we think about current flowing through wires kind of the same way we think of water flowing through pipes. It's actually more complicated than that when you get down to quantum levels, but it's a very, very good model."

"And models are how we make sense of things," Natalia said. Proud of herself for remembering the catchphrase that he and Djuna had been using with the girls for so long. He didn't think Natalia was old enough to understand it yet, but she would be. And Mei sometimes surprised him with her insights.

"Yes," Prax said. "Exactly. So resistance is about how hard or easy it is for electrons to flow through something."

Natalia's little brow furrowed. Mei was looking away and Djuna had gone very still. Which was odd. But he could tell he wasn't making sense to the girls, so he tried again.

"So imagine you've got a big straw," he said, demonstrating with his hands. "And when you put it in your juice, it's really easy to drink. But then you take a teeny little skinny straw, you have to try really hard to get the same amount of juice up out of the glass. The big straw is like something without much resistance, and the little straw is like something with a lot of resistance."

Natalia nodded very seriously. It was like he could see her trying to solve the puzzle of it. "Is it a good thing or a bad thing?" she said.

Prax laughed. "It's not good and it's not bad. It's just part of how the universe is. Now, if you had a circuit where you wanted really low resistance and you didn't have it, that wouldn't be a very good circuit. But only because it didn't do what you wanted. If you had something where you wanted high resistance, maybe that very same circuit would be perfect. It's not about right and wrong. Just how things work."

"It's time to go," Djuna said, and her voice seemed sharp. It was the voice she used when something was bothering her. And there were still almost fifteen minutes before they really needed to be out the door. Maybe something was going on at the biofilms lab he didn't know about.

When they'd left, he turned his music back on, cleared the dishes, showered, dressed himself for work. The rooms seemed wrong without them, and the extra time by himself empty and somehow ominous. All the way to the tube station, he worried about whether Mei had remembered to take her medicine. He'd planned to use the tube ride to review the new datasets on the harvester yeast, but his eyes kept skipping off his hand terminal and up to the screens across from him. A newsfeed was spooling, but he couldn't hear the words over the rattling of the tube and the voices of the other commuters. Ships were fighting, but he couldn't tell where. Earth. Iapetus. Pallas. Ceres. Mars. In the void between places, far distant from everything. They were all possible. The only thing he could be certain of was it wasn't here, and that only because there weren't any alerts blaring.

At the central station, half the passengers shuffled off into the vaulted transfer chamber, making way for another flood coming on. A half dozen men in Free Navy uniforms were among them. The Free Navy had started wearing sidearms openly now, and they walked with a swagger. Two civilian girls seemed to be with them, laughing and flirting. The oldest of them didn't look much past her twenties. Not *that* much older than Mei. Not really. Prax turned his attention back to the newsfeed, and then his hand terminal. He still wasn't able to concentrate on it, but something about the Free Navy men made him feel more comfortable with his eyes cast down. His heart was pumping a little faster, his back felt tight. He hadn't done anything wrong, but the sense of being threatened and the experience of guilt were so closely related that it was hard to feel one without the other.

When he'd been a student at lower university, he'd had to take a humanities class—literature, drama, art appreciation. Something to make him well rounded. He'd opted for philosophy in hopes that it would have something like rigor to it. Most of the experience had been forgotten, the memories washed away in decades of neuroplastic adjustments. What he did still recall was dreamlike and fragmentary. But sitting there, pressing deeper into the seat as the tube car shifted up toward the surface, the hum and rattle of the tube vibrating up his spine, listening to the too-loud laughter of the soldiers, one moment came back to him vividly. His professor—an overweight, balding man with an alcoholic's complexion and an air of intelligence so profound it seemed to bend space around him—lifting a hand and speaking a phrase: *the terror of the normal.* Prax was almost sure it had been something about Heidegger, but here and now, he thought he understood it better than he had back then.

This was how things were now. This had become normal.

He'd hoped to spend the morning on his own research, but

Khana and Brice didn't even let him get as far as his lab before falling into step beside him.

"I was looking at the open partition, and I think there may have been a problem with the data transfer," Khana said. "The datasets directory only had Hy18 through the ninth run."

"No, no," Prax said. "I know. I didn't get around to transferring them yet. I was going to, but I got distracted."

Brice made a small sound in the back of her throat. Prax understood it, and he didn't envy her. Ever since Karvonides' death, Brice had been in the unenviable position of doing her own work and covering for her dead supervisor. Every day, Prax had intended to move all the critical data out to the open partition. He couldn't even say why he hadn't gotten around to it. It was just that something always seemed to come up.

"Boss," Khana said, "we need the latest on Hy1810 unless you want us to push the new run."

"You can't push the new run," Prax said.

They reached the door of Prax's lab. Khana shoved his hands into his pockets, his jaw set, his eyes focused off somewhere about ten centimeters to Prax's left. "I know. But ..."

"I'll do it now," Prax said. "Give me half an hour."

He ducked into his lab and pulled the door closed behind him. Khana and Brice hovered for a long moment on the far side of the frosted glass and then walked away. Prax sat at his desk. He wanted to check the water levels and pull new samples from the hydroponics. He was tempted to just do that for a few minutes, put off going through Karvonides' partition. But he'd said now, and they really did need to get the animal trials going.

He pulled up the staff directory, keyed in his access code, and let the system do its ritual biometric check. Then, with a deep sigh and a sense of growing dread, he went into the dead woman's partition. It was his job to do this. There was nothing to be anxious about.

Two of the datasets were in editing lock, so he had to close them down before he could move them. Not hard, but it took a few more seconds. He would need to go through her messages too. Make sure anything that needed attention was passed down to Brice or up to McConnell. Anything personal for her, he could ignore. He didn't need to pry, and he probably didn't want to know. Except that one of the messages had James Holden in the subject. NEW JAMES HOLDEN FEED FROM CERES, it said. James Holden, who'd saved Mei. And Prax himself. And everyone. Prax didn't intend to open the feed. It was more like a reflex. *This looks interesting— what is it?*

On the feed, just as promised, James Holden looking ear- nestly into the camera. On the one hand, it looked profession- ally produced. The video didn't stutter or shake. The colors had the carefully modulated look of a newsfeed. Holden's voice when he spoke was clear and sharp without being spiky. But Holden's demeanor had an awkward authenticity that was so familiar and unrehearsed, it was like seeing him in the flesh again.

"This is James Holden from Ceres Station. Today, we're doing the third in this open ended series thing, and I'm really hoping you're all looking forward to this. Especially all my friends and family back on Earth and Mars. I say this every time, but we're doing these clips and interviews so that the folks back home can put faces and voices to the real people out in the Belt. And...yeah. So, let me introduce—"

The image cut to a tall Belter girl sitting in the galley of the *Rocinante*. Prax leaned forward. He'd sat exactly where she was once, during the worst part of his life. He felt a wave of nostal- gia like seeing his apartment from upper university—someplace familiar that had been important to him once—that broke against the novelty of this new girl.

"Alis Caspár."

"Great. Okay, and where do you live?"

"Ceres Station. Salutorg District."

Prax watched the whole feed. The clap-juggling of shin-sin that seemed to delight and fascinate the Earther. The way the girl was embarrassed for him and he didn't seem to notice. The older woman they called Tía flirting with him. It was...charming. With all the news of war and death, with all the images of ships chewing each other to shavings of metal and ceramic, the body bags of Earth, Holden's video was nothing. Pleasant. Meaningless. Sweet, even.

The feed ended. Prax, surprised, found he'd been tearing up. He wiped his cheek with the cuff of one sleeve, and was startled when the next message opened its own feed automatically. A thin-faced woman with skin darker than Djuna's but with the same deep hazel eyes smiled into the camera. The image shook a little and the colors weren't as professionally toned as Holden's had been.

"This is Fatima Crehan, sending back to James Holden and all the good people of the Belt. We're in the refugee camp opened by the governor of Arequipa, and today I want to introduce you to a woman whose causa has been turning heads and filling bellies for, it seems like, everyone in the city."

Prax watched, fascinated. And when it was over, another video feed, this one from Shanghai, where an old man in a yarmulke interviewed a musical band of ethnic Han boys about their music and then watched them in an alleyway with mud-colored clouds churning above them. Prax couldn't look away.

A soft knock came at the door. Brice leaned in. "I'm sorry to interrupt, sir, but—"

"No no no, it's fine. I'm transferring them now." Prax grabbed Karvonides' data reports—none of them edit-locked now—and shifted them into the open partition. "You should be able to access all of them now."

"Thank you, sir," Brice said. And then, "Are you all right?"

"I'm fine," Prax said, wiping his eyes again. "Carry on."

She closed the door. Two hours had gotten away from him somehow, and he was going to have to hurry in order to get all the samples pulled before lunch.

We could save lives. One message.

Prax shut down the dead woman's partition, put it under

administrative lock. There wasn't time to think about anything more. He had work to do. In order to catch up, he ran the samples during his lunch hour, grabbing a few mouthfuls of rice and mushroom before the management team meeting. Afterward, it was time to go and retrieve Mei and Natalia from school, but he sent a message to one of the other parents in his parenting coop. The girls could go play with the other kids until Djuna got home. He stayed, checking in with Brice and Khana. Seeing that everyone who needed access to the datasets could get to them.

Everything felt weirdly dreamlike and light. As if he was watching someone else doing it. In his office, he rechecked the day's sample run. How much dissolved CO_2 in the water, how much nitrogen, calcium, manganese. The plants were doing well, but until the stats were all fed through, he wouldn't know what he was looking at. That was fine.

He resisted the urge to reopen Karvonides' partition. To find the other feeds Holden had made or inspired. It was a bad idea. Instead, he waited, worked, watched through the glass. Only Brice remained, and her workstation was down a long and curving hallway. He closed his terminal, clocked out, went to the men's room, and waited. Washed his hands. Waited. Then casually stepped out to the main floor, swinging by one of the gang stations, opening a terminal with a guest account, accessing the datasets and protocols that Supervisor Praxidike Meng had carelessly put in the open partition without permissions set. The screen showed a pale blue logo, the flag of Ganymede. He sent copies to Samuel Jabari and Ingrid Dineyahze on Earth and Gorman Le on Luna. The only message was PLEASE CONFIRM THESE RESULTS.

Then he shut down the terminal and made his way out to the common corridors. Everything seemed brighter than it should have been. He couldn't tell if he was tired or restless. Or both.

He stopped at a noodle stand between the tube station and home. No-Roof for him and Djuna. Fried tofu for the girls. And—a luxury—rice wine. And a round ceramic container with green tea ice cream for dessert. When he got home, Natalia was whining about having to drill her times tables and Mei had shut herself in her room to trade messages with her friends from school and watch entertainment feeds of boys three or four years older than her. Other nights, he would have insisted that they all come to the table for dinner, but he didn't want to disturb anything.

He served the noodles into recyclable ceramic bowls with a pattern of sparrows and twigs on them, brought one to Natalia at her desk, another to Mei sprawled out on her bed. She was so big these days. Soon, she'd be bigger than his shoulder. His little girl, who no one had expected to live, and look at her now. When he kissed the crown of her head, she looked up at him quizzically. He nodded her toward her screen of soulful-looking young men.

He and Djuna sat at the table together, almost like they were dating again. He looked at her: the curve of her cheek, the little scar on her left knuckle, the gentle fold of her collarbone. Like he was saving it for some coming day when she wouldn't be there. Or else when he wouldn't.

The rice wine bit at his mouth. Maybe it always felt like that— chill and warming at the same time—and he just didn't usually notice. Djuna told him about her day, the office politics and palace intrigues of biofilms, and he took in her words like they were music. Just before he cleared their dishes and broke out the ice cream, she reached across the table and took his hand.

"Are you all right?" she said. "You're acting strange."

"I'm fine," he said.

"Bad day at work?"

"No, I don't think so," he said. "I think maybe it was very good."

Chapter Twenty-Five: Fred

James Holden has just declared piracy legal," Avasarala said from Luna, then paused. Her eyebrows were high on her forehead, and she nodded a little. Like she was encouraging a not very bright child to understand her. "He took in a *pirated* ship. From a *pirate*. And then thanked her for his cut of the fucking booty and waved as she burned away. And you, the Butcher of Anderson Station, grand Whatever-the-Fuck of the OPA? You sat there with your cock in your hand and let him do it. I mean, I understand Holden is Holden, but I let you put your hands on Ceres because I thought you at least were a fucking grown-up."

She leaned back from her camera, shaking her head, and cracked a pistachio.

"I thought better of you, Johnson," she said. "I really did. My life has become a single, ongoing revelation that I haven't been cynical enough."

At this point, he was pretty clear she was talking for the comfort of hearing her own voice. He checked the feed data. Ten more minutes. She might get to something important in the course of it, so he let it play as he walked through the bedroom. Her sharp consonants and scratching vowels made a kind of background music while he dug his evening medications out of his bedside table. Five pills and a glass of water. The pills were chalky and bitter on his tongue, and even after they were washed down his throat, he suffered their aftertaste.

Working twenty-hour days was a younger man's gig. He could still rise to the occasion, but there had been a time his determination against the universe would have felt like a fair fight. Anger alone would have carried him forward, and maybe the scourge of fatigue would have made him feel he was expiating his sins. Now he was surviving on coffee and blood pressure meds and trying to keep the system from falling any further apart. It seemed less romantic.

"It looks like Richards has almost whipped what's left of the Martian parliament into order," Avasarala said, "so hopefully we can get something from her. Just an assurance she won't come piss all over our strategy so it smells more like her would be enough. Souther's pushing for Rhea or Pallas, depending on whether we want to shore up the allies we already have, half-assed as they may be, or deny Inaros a manufacturing base. Admiral Stacey's pushing back against any of it for fear of stretching our ships out too thin."

Both strategies were mistakes. He'd need to make the case for that. She pressed her fingers to her forehead. A short, percussive sigh. For a moment, she seemed smaller. Vulnerable. It was a strange look for her.

"We've had two more rocks. One of them had the stealth coating on it, but we caught it. This time. I've got the deep arrays sifting through all their data looking for more. But it costs so little to push something into an intersecting orbit, Inaros could have done hundreds of these. Spaced them out over months. Years. A century from now, we could see something loop in from out of the ecliptic with a note on it that says, 'Fuck you very much from the Free Navy.' My grandchildren's grandchildren will be cleaning this same shit up."

"Hopefully. If we win," Fred said to the screen. Not that the recording could hear him. He moved to the bathroom, and the display shifted to follow him.

The best thing about the governor's quarters was the shower. Wide as a rainstorm, and the whole floor a grated drain that worked even at a third of a g. Fred stripped and washed the sweat and grime of the day off his skin while Avasarala went over the latest intelligence about the state of affairs on the colony planets (no hard data, but things were probably bad), the reports on the ships that had gone missing passing through the gates (several theories and hope that the flight records from Medina would help if they ever became available), and the situation on Earth (the expected second wave of deaths from collapsed food, sanitation, and medical infrastructure was starting to appear).

After he dried off, Fred pulled on a fresh shirt, clean trousers. Thick, soft socks. The small pleasures of life. Avasarala kept delivering her report, diving into unneeded details and side comments as if she were lonely and didn't want to face the emptiness and quiet of her own rooms on Luna. But even she couldn't last forever.

"I'll expect to hear from you," she said. "And I'm fucking serious about this. Don't let Holden. Make. Any. More. Laws."

Fred sat on the edge of the bed, closed his eyes, and let his head sink into his hands. He'd been awake for over thirty hours now, and was looking down the barrel of another shift. Negotiating with the unions, adjusting decades-old contracts to fit the new situation. Moving Belters out of their holes, shutting down great swaths of the station to conserve the supplies they had. Part of his mind kept treating it like an emergency. A wound that had to be stanched until help could arrive. Three, four times a shift, he'd remember that there wasn't help. That the choices he made today might stay in place for years. Forever.

The temptation to lie back, put his head to the pillow, and let his gritty, tired eyes close was as powerful as hunger and sex had been four decades back. The weight of the idea as much as exhaustion pulled him down. It was stupid for anyone, much less a man his age, to be pushing that hard, and the governor's bed was soft and inviting, the sheets clean and crisp. But if he did, his eyes would open the moment his head touched the pillow. Restlessness would twist him, knotting the sheets around his legs until he gave up, two or three wasted hours later. One more shift, and he'd be spent enough to let the pills work. He'd fall into the blackness behind his eyes, consciousness blinking blissfully out. But not yet.

His first lover—Diane Redstone, her name was—had a phrase for moments like this. *Nice woods*, she'd say, and then get up out of their bed and go to work. He hadn't understood where the saying came from until years after they parted for the last time. Now that he did, he couldn't help harboring an irrational dislike of Robert Frost.

He pulled up his hand terminal, considered himself through its tiny eyes, and pressed Record.

"Message received. I'll do what I can to keep our mutual acquaintance in line. But I'd also point out that he's a resource we'd be foolish to squander. Neither of us is in a position to do some things that Holden and his people can. Speaking of which, I'm including a salvage manifest for the *Minsky*. It's a big ship, and well supplied. It's within my power as acting governor of Ceres to claim emergency powers and seize property for the common good. That's not Holden's law, that's just law. I'll be sending it and a third of its cargo back down to Earth, and the *August Marchant* and *Bethany Thomas* as escort. There's enough in there to keep a midsized city alive. Just a drop in the bucket, I know, but that's how buckets get filled."

He tried to think of anything else he should say, and couldn't decide if there was too much or not enough. Either way, it could wait. He reviewed the message, encrypted and queued it, and then levered himself up off the bed. There'd be time to sleep later.

His security detail met him outside his door and followed him to the carts in the main corridor. His was sheathed in bulletproof glass. Sitting in it made him feel like he'd put his head in a fishbowl. But until he was certain that Inaros didn't have more people mixed in among the millions of legitimate citizens, he was stuck with it. And since he'd never be certain, he figured he might as well get used to it. They lurched out into the corridor—one security cart going before him and another behind, leaving enough room that a bomb would have a hard time taking out all three at once. The logic of the battlefield. And everything was a battlefield now.

The citizens of Ceres made way for them, standing against the corridor walls and staring as they passed. Fred felt like he should genuflect to them. Or wave. Anderson Dawes—his old friend and enemy—had run this station for years. He couldn't imagine the man putting up with this. But Ceres had been a different place then.

The governor's palace was close to the docks, out near the skin of the station where the spin gravity was greatest and the Coriolis least. The *Rocinante* had its own berth in the same dock as the *Minsky*, and when Fred's cart pulled to a stop by the loading dock, James Holden was already there.

"I was wondering if you were going to come over," Holden said as Fred pulled himself out of the cart. "Because I couldn't help noticing that someone shot at us."

"Really? And here, I thought they shot at the pirates."

Holden closed his mouth, his face turning a little darker. But then he shrugged. "Okay, that's a fair point, but it was still a dick move."

"It wasn't my people," Fred said, moving toward the *Rocinante*'s airlock. Holden took the hint and fell in step beside him.

"I guessed that from the way that not every other ship in the fleet followed suit. And thank you for that, by the way."

"You're welcome," Fred said as they passed into the ship's cargo hold. Amos Burton—wide-shouldered and friendly—stopped the mech he was driving and let them pass through with a nod. Fred had never met the infamous Clarissa Mao in person, but the girl who ducked away from the lift and into the machine shop was unmistakable. Wasn't the strangest alliance he'd seen, but it was close. Fred waited until Holden was on the lift too and then set the controls for the crew deck. When they were out of earshot, Fred continued. "There's something I need to discuss with you."

"Is it about how someone shot at us, because I'm still kind of stuck on that."

"I've got a team on it. We know it was Free Navy sympathizers, and we know which supply dump they raided to get the munitions, and no, that's not why I came."

"Are you going to arrest me for aiding a pirate?"

Fred chuckled. "It had crossed my mind, but no."

"Bobbie? Because I'm not sure this whole ambassador thing is working out for her."

"Not that either. You know I've been working on a summit. High-level meeting with the branches of the OPA that haven't declared for the Free Navy."

"The pajama party."

Fred winced. "I wish you wouldn't call it that."

"Sorry. I just like the visual. Your very serious meeting of OPA leaders."

The lift stopped at the crew deck. Fred got off, turning toward Holden's cabin. Their footsteps on the decking sounded louder than Fred remembered, but it was probably just that the full crew wasn't there any longer to provide the background noises of human life. No conversations, no music, no laughter. Or maybe it was only that it seemed that way to Fred.

"They won't come to Ceres." Fred sighed. "Not with the fleet here."

"I can't recommend sending the fleet away, though."

"No, that would be bad. We've agreed on Tycho Station, but only with the provision that no UN or MCRN ships come."

Holden paused at his cabin door. His brow was furrowed. It made him look younger than he was. "We're going to my cabin because I have that whiskey you like, aren't we?"

"We are," Fred said. Holden considered for a moment, shrugged, and led the way in. The captain's cabin was larger than the others on the corvette, but felt smaller by having many of Naomi Nagata's possessions in the space too. Holden opened a locker and pulled a flask and two bulbs out, filling them as he spoke.

"What are the chances of pulling together a meeting like this and not having Marco find out about it?"

"Poor," Fred said, taking the bulb Holden held out to him. "But that's going to be true no matter what we try to organize. The OPA's not an intelligence service. Everything out here runs on gossip and personal relationships."

"Unlike intelligence services?" Holden said, and Fred laughed.

"All right, it's a little like an intelligence service. My point is, yes, the information will leak, if not in detail, at least in broad strokes. Trying to keep it secret would be an exercise in frustration. And counterproductive, really. If we're tiptoeing around the Free Navy, it makes it seem like we're afraid of them. It strengthens my hand if these people see me coming in unafraid. Not foolhardy, but not intimidated."

"Like on a gunship," Holden said. "But not one that works for Earth or Mars. Maybe an independent that's done some work with the OPA on and off. One that Marco has already tried to blow up a couple times and failed."

The whiskey really was very good. Rich and complex, with the aromatics of an oak cask and a pleasant bite. He handed the bulb back over to Holden and shook his head when the captain offered him a second shot. Holden emptied his own bulb, thought for a moment, refilled it, and emptied it again.

"You know," Holden said, putting bulbs and bottle back in his locker, "Inaros is going to disrupt this meeting."

"That's why I'm not sending you messages through the comm system. I don't know how much has been compromised, and I'm a strong believer in the security of the air gap. But the truth is, as much as we'll keep the details away from him, I'm hoping he'll try. There's nothing like attacking in anger to leave you exposed. And if he turns toward us, it gives Pa some breathing room."

"I thought you were against joining forces with her."

"I am. It was a bad move, and I expect we'll pay for it. But since we've done it, we should do the hell out of it. Better to be decisive and wrong than to let them see us wobble."

Holden leaned against the wall, his arms crossed. Scowling. Fred waited.

"How does this end?" Holden said.

"We keep trying to draw him into making a mistake. He keeps doing the same to us. Whoever screws up last loses. Whoever screws up second to last wins. That's what war is."

"Not sure I was asking about the war," Holden said.

"No? What then?"

"You always said you were looking for a place at the table. How do we win the peace? How does *that* end?"

Fred was quiet for a long time, a sense of mourning blooming in his chest, thick and aching. "Honestly, then? I don't know how it ends. I don't even know if it ends. I dedicated my life to this fight. First one side, and then the other. But now, I look at it? What's happened with the gates. What's happened to Earth. I don't recognize this anymore. I keep doing what I can because I don't know what else to do."

Holden took a deep breath and let it out through his teeth. "When should we be ready to go?"

"I told Drummer I'd be wrapping things up here for two weeks. I'd like to leave four days from now. While any of Marco's people who find out about it are still putting together their plans. Make them move before they're ready."

"All right," Holden said. "We'll take you."

"I'll have my people report whenever you need them. I'll see myself out," Fred said with a nod, and headed for the lift.

On the way back down, he closed his eyes and let the thin vibration of the mechanism rattle up through the soles of his feet, up his aching spine, to the crown of his head. There was still so much that needed doing before he left Ceres. He still had to meet with the crew of the *Minsky*, but he'd promised to consult with

Avasarala's solicitor general before he did, so that he didn't acci-
dentally obligate Earth to anything by saying the wrong phrase.
And he wanted patrol rotations set for at least a month, so that his
unexpected absence wouldn't throw anything off. And he wanted
sleep.

As he stepped out the airlock again, his hand terminal chirped.
A new message had arrived from Earth. From Avasarala. He
paused in the wide air of the docks. The roar of the air recyclers
and the clang of the loading mechs. The smell of lubricant and
dust. His security detail was already moving toward him, ready
to usher him back into his fishbowl. He waved them back and
started the message.

Avasarala was in a corridor, shuffling briskly in the lunar
microgravity. She looked as tired as he did, but she had a thin,
amused smile. He'd never known anyone in his life who could be
so cheerfully disappointed in humanity.

"I've run your list past my relief coordinator," she said—what
would it be? Eight minutes ago? Ten? He used to be able to calcu-
late light delay in his head. "It didn't quite bring him to orgasm,
but I think he may want to take you out for drinks when you're in
town. Be careful with him. He's got busy hands."

Someone off screen interrupted. Avasarala's eyes flickered away
from the camera and she shook her head. "Does he want me to
wipe his ass for him too? His job is to make decisions, not ask me
what decisions he ought to make." A curt, deferential voice said
yes, ma'am or something like it, and she started walking again.

Fred found himself smiling. When she'd been his enemy, she'd
been a good one. Now that they were working as allies, the ways
that they were the same almost humanized her.

"Where was I? Oh. Yes, the so-called relief supplies. I'm sending along a list of what we most need on the surface. If you get a
chance to pass it on to Pa, please do. Apparently we're *all* fucking
pirates now."

Chapter Twenty-Six: Filip

The night before the *Pella* left Pallas Station, Rosenfeld hosted a dinner for Marco and the other captains. The hall had been a vast open space designed as a construction compartment, but changed now into a kind of null-g throne room. A soft, chiming music played like flowing water with a melody. Serving platforms bristled with ceramic bulbs brightly colored as oil on water and filled with wine and water. Long ribbons of red and gold shifted in the breeze of the recyclers. Great lengths of gold fibered paper fluttered and bellied against the walls between the hand- and footholds. The crew of the *Pella* and the staff of Rosenfeld's Pallas authority mixed, Free Navy uniforms standing out sharp and martial against the casual civilian clothes of the locals. Young men and women in flowing robes of crimson and blue floated through the air slowly enough to deliver tapas of bean-and-grain cake, curried shrimp fresh from the tanks, and garlic sausage with real meat stuffed in the skins.

No element of the design suggested a consensus up or down. No concession had been made to the architecture of Earth and Mars. The combination of a traditional Belter aesthetic with lushness and luxury left Filip a little intoxicated even before he started drinking.

"I don't know what you could mean by purification," his father said through laughter, "if not 'getting rid of the impure parts.'"

Rosenfeld's answering chuckle was dry. After weeks traveling with the man, Filip still wasn't certain he could read his expressions. "You're saying you planned for this?"

"Anticipated. A change in the system of the greater world always risks having people lose perspective. Get drunk on possibility. Pa rode the wave in; now she thinks she can command the tides. I didn't know she would break, but I was ready if she did."

Rosenfeld nodded. Across the great echoing chamber, two women sang together a few bars of a song that Filip knew, and then dissolved into hilarity. He looked across the open air, hoping that one of them might be looking back. That a girl would be watching him floating in conference with the great minds of the Free Navy. No one was.

When his father went on, his voice was lower. Still conversational, still friendly, but charged. "I had plans in place for anyone that broke. Pa, Sanjrani, Dawes. You. When I make my next strike, everyone will see how weak she is. Her support will burn off faster than breathing."

"You're sure," Rosenfeld said, making the words a statement and a question at the same time. He drank from his bulb, coughed. Filip watched his father waiting for the pebble-skinned man to finish his thought. Rosenfeld sighed, nodded. Filip felt some deeper meaning swim just below his understanding, leaving him bobbing in its wake. "It's only that she's been feeding people. The laity find that sort of thing endearing, sí no?"

"Anyone can buy votes with free ganga," Filip said.

Rosenfeld turned his head then, like he was noticing Filip for the first time. "True, true."

"Johnson and his cobbled-up fleet," Marco said, "have been squatting on Ceres with their eyes wide. Can't move forward without exposing themselves. Can't move back and leave Ceres to us again. They're trapped. Just the way we said they'd be."

"True," Rosenfeld said, and left *True, but...* hanging in the air. All the criticisms trailed behind it like the ribbons in the breeze. *True, but it's been a long time since we left Ceres, and it's left us looking weak... True, but one of your generals broke away and you haven't brought her to heel... True, but Fred Johnson is issuing orders from the governor's mansion at Ceres, and you aren't.* Filip felt every point like a blow to the gut, but because they were unspoken, he couldn't answer them. Neither could his father. Rosenfeld took another drink, accepted a stick of vat-grown meat from a passing server, and steadied his drift with one hand as he ate. His expression was mild, but his gaze stayed locked on Marco.

"Waiting until the perfect moment is the mark of a great strategist," Marco said. "For now, the outer planets are ours to pass through freely. Mars and Earth and Luna—even Ceres. They're hiding behind their walls while we move through the wide plains of the vacuum, masters of the void. The more they realize they don't matter, the more desperate they'll become. All we have to do is watch for the opportunity that's coming."

"Fred Johnson," Rosenfeld said. "He's already reached out to Carlos Walker and Liang Goodfortune. Aimee Ostman."

"Let them talk with him," Marco said, an edge coming into his voice for the first time. "Let them see how little he's become. I know his patterns, and I know what you're saying."

"Not saying anything, coyo," Rosenfeld said. "Except maybe we've been drinking too much."

"I told you before that Johnson would be off the board, and he

will be. We didn't take him at Tycho, and we'll take him somewhere else. He is my white whale, and I will hunt him to the end
of time."

Rosenfeld looked down at his bulb, his body hunching a degree
in submission. Filip had felt his father's victory like it was his own.

"Didn't finish reading that book, did you?" Rosenfeld asked
mildly.

Marco called the ships the three wolves. The *Pella*, of course, was
the leader of the pack, with the *Koto* and the *Shinsakuto* placed in
slow orbit to support her. Moving the ships into position was the
hard part. Marco's trade hadn't included true stealth ships. The
nearest they had were regular gunships with a coating of the stolen radar-eating paint layered over the skin, and without being
designed for it and for holding waste heat, the Martian tech was
less effective.

But the Belt had always had smugglers, pirates, and thieves.
There were ways to hide, even in the abyss. Running without
transponders was only one of them. They'd left Pallas with a
hard burn. Hours of being pressed into the crash couches, juice
burning in their veins and still driven to the edge of consciousness. And then, the coast. With no drive plume to show where
they were, the *Pella* and her fellow hunters were hardly more than
warm rocks, making a traverse of the vastness between Ceres on
the inner Belt and Tycho Station in its own deeper orbit. The *Koto*
risked a braking burn to plant itself alongside a charted asteroid,
using the mass of stone and ice to hide it and explain the ladar
ping responses. The *Pella* and the *Shinsakuto* stayed on the float,
their orbits matching the widespread detritus of the asteroid belt.
No broadcasts. The only communications were tightbeam. They
off-gassed a little to cool the outer hull and complicate its thermal
signature. The emptiness itself was their friend. Even in the most
crowded corners of the Belt, where the asteroids were thickest,

it would have taken a telescope to see the nearest neighbors. The *Pella* was a warm sliver of metal and ceramic in trillions of square kilometers—less than a thumbnail clipping in an ocean.

Even if Ceres saw them—and over the long weeks of their silent hunt, it might—they would be indistinguishable from a thousand other unlicensed prospectors, smuggling ships, and homesteading Belter families. Johnson and his inner planet allies would need to know where to look to find them. And even if they found one, two more waited.

Fred Johnson's desperate meeting to sweep up the shards of the OPA was still weeks away, but Marco put them in and flying dark long before Fred would need to leave the safety of Ceres. *Men have patterns*, he said. And Fred Johnson's were misdirection followed by overwhelming force. Their sources said that the fleet would remain pinned at Ceres. With overwhelming force no longer an option, all that remained was misdirection. And so they floated, their passive sensor arrays pointed at Ceres and Tycho like a too-clever child watching a street magician's other hand. When Fred Johnson went to make his plea to the ragged stragglers of the OPA still willing to listen, Marco said, he would know. And when Johnson's prospective allies saw him die ...

Well, they had lost Michio Pa. But Marco could replace her a hundred times over. Strength pulled people as surely as gravity. More, sometimes.

Marco would wait for hours every day, strapped into his crash couch as if a hard burn could come at any second, his eyes flickering over sensor data, and still end his shifts energized and laughing, excited. Joyful. Filip didn't have his father's raw endurance. For the first several days, he could equal Marco's focus and sense of imminent violence, and even then by the time he went to the gym, to the galley, to his cabin, the brightness in his chest had started to change to something more like anxiety. Or rage. Only he didn't know what he was anxious about or who he was so angry with.

When the *Minsky* came to Ceres, the *Connaught* at its side, Filip had been sure that the moment had arrived. Pa was there, the consolidated fleet watching her inch toward them like a cat hauling a dead mouse home as a love gift. Filip felt it in his blood—the coming violence. The grand and gaudy proof that the Free Navy was stronger than its enemies. He hadn't been the only one either. It was like all the crew of the *Pella*—Josie and Karal and Bastien and Jún—everyone had taken a breath at the same time, steeled themselves for the burn and the battle.

Everyone but Marco.

He'd stayed just the same, watching the datafeeds from his crash couch on the command deck. The attack from Ceres, the *Rocinante*'s defense of the *Connaught*. All of it seemed to wash over Marco like it was nothing. He captured images of the ship transfer. When he recorded his denouncement of Pa and revealed her as a stooge of the inners, he seemed to wake up for a moment, but only while the recording was going on. As soon as the camera shut off, he seemed to fall back into himself. Filip took comfort that this wasn't the same torpor and indifference that had haunted the *Pella* after leaving Ceres the first time. Marco watched like a predator in cover, the *Pella* drifting in its orbit around the distant sun like it was locked to Ceres Station.

Several days after the *Connaught*'s departure, Filip dreamed of Earth—only it wasn't Earth. It was a massive spaceship, layer upon layer of scaffold, reaching down forever. A great fire burned at its core, and Filip was lost in it, trying to find something. Something precious that he'd had and lost or else that had been hidden from him. Also, he was being chased. Sought by something so that he switched from being hunter to prey and back to hunter.

In the dream, he was floating down a long corridor. Purely ballistic. The handholds and footholds skated by on all sides, just beyond his reach. There was a strong smell—mineral and heat. The exposed iron core of the Earth. Its burning heart. And there was something at the end of the passage. Something waiting. His mother and an army of the dead who he'd killed. The rapping of their bone fingers on the deck was a threat and a promise. Filip woke with a shout, grabbing at the straps of his crash couch like they were trying to strangle him.

Then the rapping of fingers came again, and the door of his cabin slipped open. Karal floated in the corridor, his eyes an image of concern. And maybe excitement.

"Hoy, Filipito," he said. "Bist bien?"

"Fine," Filip said. What time was it? He felt like he'd woken in the middle of a cycle, but he couldn't be sure. He'd been sleeping so much lately, it was easy for him to lose track. So long as there was nothing to do but wait, it hardly mattered how the hours passed. But sleeping too long was much like sleeping too little. It left him confused and tired.

"Marco wants you. Command deck, yeah?"

Filip nodded with his left hand while he unstrapped with his right. "Con que?" he said. "Something happened?"

Karal's look of concern eroded into a bestial grin. "Dui," he said. "But let Marco show you, yeah?"

Pulling himself along the lift tube, Filip's heart tapped against his chest. The sense of the dream wasn't quite gone, bleeding into the solid ship under his hands. Excitement and dread wore each other's clothes, spoke in the same voice. When he reached the command deck, the lighting was set for battle, and the crash couches were crewed: Sárta strapping herself down, Wings already in place. Bastien's voice echoed from the cockpit, and the anticipation of thrust made Filip think it was above them. The words were clipped and terse. The air seemed cleaner, as if Filip could see everything for the first time.

Marco reached out and spun his own couch on its gimbals to face him. The light from the screen threw shadows across his father's eyes. Filip saluted, and Marco spread his hands.

"The hour has now arrived, Filip," Marco said. "All of our patience and sacrifice have brought us here to this one, perfect moment." Times like this, he sounded almost like an Earther. Filip nodded, his heart beating faster. He didn't know whether to keep looking at Marco or if it would be all right to turn to the screens. Marco laughed, and pulled Filip close. He gestured to the tactical readout. A dot of light.

If he looked outside the ship, on float with merely human eyes or through the cameras that took in the same spectrum, the star field would have overwhelmed the glimmer from the ship. Even Ceres would have been little more than a bit of darkness where the starlight was blotted out. On the screen, the critical light was brighter, its path sketched in. Filip glanced at Marco for permission, received it in a nod, and then drew back the scale until the full arc of the little ship's pathway was clear.

A single ship, burning hard from Ceres to Tycho.

"Fred Johnson," Filip said.

"More than that," Marco said, and the calm in his voice made him sound almost drugged by pleasure. "Look at the drive signature."

Filip did, blinked. His breath went shallow and tight. It matched the *Rocinante*. James Holden's ship. His betrayer of a mother. The clean, clear center of everything he hated, everything they had to overcome. And here it was, delivered to them like a present.

"I've been tracking them. They've left the effective protection range of Ceres. They're alone in the void, except for us." Marco's smile was beatific, but the expression in his dark eyes changed. Instead of being lost in the gratification of the moment, he was looking at Filip. More than looking at him. Seeing him. Seeing *into* him.

"Karal," Marco said. Half strapped into his couch, the big man paused. Marco shifted a degree. "Need you in engineering. Damage control, yeah?"

Karal shrugged, unstrapped. Marco looked back at Filip, then pointed to the crash couch with his chin. *It's your station. Take it.* As Karal launched down the lift tube, feet vanishing last, Filip pulled himself into the crash couch. Weapons controls filled the screen. Torpedoes. PDCs. The sword of the *Pella* was in his hands.

The warning Klaxon seemed to come from a great distance. The *Pella*, preparing after weeks sleeping on the float. The needle stung when it went into his vein, and the cold, bright flow of military-grade juice lit him from within like he was fire itself, consuming everything he touched.

Two new dots appeared on tactical. New stars in the star-sown blackness, both marked as friendlies. The *Koto* and the *Shinsakuto* leaping from their cover, and announcing their attack. The *Pella* jumped up around Filip, grabbing his crash couch and all the others on the command deck. The gimbals hissed in unison as Bastien brought them around, couches snapping to face the new up and follow it, whichever way the maneuvering thrusters demanded. The rumble of the drive passed through the ship, through Filip's bones. The crash couch gel flowed up the sides of his body. As if he was watching someone else do it, he keyed in firing solutions. One gunship against three. The *Rocinante* couldn't help but die.

"They saw us, them!" Bastien shouted. "We're getting painted!"

"Filip," Marco said.

"Sa sa," Filip said. With a motion, he trained the PDCs toward the distant flicker that was the enemy, ready to chew down any incoming torpedoes. The *Pella* jumped forward again, the hard burn jumping harder. Filip let his arms sink down to his sides, fingers on the built-in controls. He fought to inhale. Five gs. Six, and the acceleration was still going up. The wolves were loose now. The pack running.

His vision narrowed, shadows crowding his peripherals like the dead from his dream. He had the weird sensation that *she* was in the room. Naomi Nagata. But that was only an accident of sleep and high-g blood flow. The crash couch chimed, a fresh infusion of juice brightening him. His lips were growing numb and tingling. He couldn't lift his head from the couch any longer. It was like he was becoming the ship. Or it was becoming him.

He heard his father trying to speak, but the acceleration was affecting him too. The *Pella* groaned, the superstructure settling and flexing under the acceleration. A high harmonic overtone rang through the air like a struck bell.

On Filip's monitor, a message appeared. From his father. His captain. Leader of the Free Navy and liberator of the Belt.

FIRE AT WILL.

Chapter Twenty-Seven: Bobbie

Confirm I've got four more fast-movers," Alex said, his voice tense and calm at the same time.

"Got them," Bobbie said, her jaw aching with the acceleration gravity. The gunner's control identified the new torpedoes, adding them to the six already on her scopes. Three ships converging on them from different angles were identified as the *Pella*, the *Shinsakuto*, and the *Koto*. Marco Inaros' personal ship and two gunships for backup, and nothing for the *Roci* to hide behind but her drive plume. The enemies were a long way off still—millions of klicks—and none on initial vectors that did them any favors. The *Roci* had already gotten past them. They were like a kid on a football pitch, running the ball with three opposing players sprinting to catch up. Except if the opposing players had guns.

When the *Roci* hit the mathematical balance point of velocity, mass, and distance that defined the halfway point, there would be some hard choices to make. Either they'd flip and start braking toward Tycho or commit to letting the chase go on indefinitely. If they let the Free Navy spook them out into the empty spaces between bases and stations, the chase turned into an ugly kind of attrition battle. Who ran out of ammunition or reaction mass first. Given how the outer system looked these days, it would make more sense to brake toward Tycho and hope that backup from the station could reach them before the Free Navy pounded them into scrap metal and blood.

Her job and Alex's were to make sure they lived long enough to have that problem. She tracked the torpedoes. With any luck, they'd all be standard issue. They didn't show the jittering path of point defense countermeasures yet. When they got in effective range, the *Roci* would start chewing them to pieces, streams of tiny tungsten rounds ripping the torpedoes to nothing. If there were only six, she'd have been confident they could do it. Ten at once was a little more complicated, but as long as they didn't all hit at the same time, she was pretty sure they wouldn't be overwhelmed.

Holden's voice in her ear sounded anxious. "How long before we can start shooting back?"

"Fast-movers will be in effective PDC range in sixty-eight minutes," she said. "Do we have any response from Ceres? Because if they could throw a few spare long-range torpedoes at these sons-ofbitches, it wouldn't hurt my feelings."

Fred Johnson's voice answered, calm and businesslike. "I'm working on that now."

"Our new friends are closing," Alex said. "We may have to get a little less comfortable."

"Understood," Holden said.

The *Rocinante* was already under a three-g burn. Bobbie felt it in her joints and eyes. The crappy juice dribbling into her veins gave her a distant, cloudy sort of headache and a taste like form-aldehyde in her mouth. Below her, the rest of the crew—Holden's and Johnson's both—were strapped in for battle. She could hear

Sandra Ip's voice bleeding out from Alex's headset, talking on a private channel. Naomi was talking to someone too, her voice rising from the deck below.

The anxiety and fear in her gut were as familiar as a favorite song. The logic of tactics and violence spread out on the screens, and she found she could see things in them like reading the future. If Ceres fired a barrage of missiles or long-range torpedoes, she knew the *Shinsakuto* would peel off to stop them. She saw how Alex would curve the *Roci*'s path to force a few extra seconds between the Free Navy's incoming torpedoes. The vectors of the enemy ships whispered things in the back of her mind about recklessness and aggression. And she knew that there were other people on each of the incoming ships whose minds were making the same analysis, reaching the same conclusions. Seeing something she didn't or missing a detail that she picked up. All it took was one critical mistake, and they'd be dead or captured. One oversight from the enemy, and they'd get away.

And along with it all—the shitty juice, the battle fear, the desperate effort of keeping her mind clear while all the blood tried to pool at the back of her skull—there was something else. A warmth. A sense of being where she belonged. Her team was counting on her, and her life depended on all of them doing their jobs with efficiency and professionalism and an unhesitating competence.

When she died, she wanted it to be like this. Not in a hospital bed like her grandmother. Not in a sad little hole on Mars with a gun in her mouth or a gut full of pills like the failures of veterans' outreach. She wanted to win, to protect her tribe and wipe the enemy into a paste of blood and dismay. But failing that, she wanted to die trying. A snippet of something she'd once read popped in her head: *Facing fearful odds protecting the bones of her fathers and the temples of her gods.* Yeah. Like that.

"Shit," Alex said. "I've got six more. We're up to sixteen fast-movers."

"I've got 'em," Bobbie said.

"Why are they spacing them out like that?" Holden asked.

"The *Shinsakuto*'s getting ready to flip and burn," Bobbie said. "I'm guessing Fred talked Ceres into helping."

"I did indeed," Fred said. "Just got confirmation."

"If our PDCs are going to have a chance chewing these fuckers up, I've got to punch it," Alex said.

"Everyone in your couches?" Holden said. There was a chorus of response. No one said no. "Do what you need to do, Alex."

He looked over at her. Pilot's and gunner's stations were the only ones in the cockpit. It was designed that way because if systems started failing, they could shout to each other. They had to be able to coordinate, because from now to the end of the battle, no one else mattered. Every other life on the ship was about to become cargo.

"You good for this, Gunny?"

"Let's kill these assholes," she said.

The *Rocinante* jumped forward, hitting her in the back like an assault. Her arms slammed into the gel, her fingers against the control barely able to move. The images on the screen went fuzzy, her eyes deforming past her ability to refocus them. She tensed her legs and arms, pushing the blood back to her core. The couch chimed and a fresh blast of cheap juice hit her bloodstream. Her gasps sounded like someone choking. Eight gs, maybe? Maybe more. It had been too fucking long.

An endless time passed, and then a chime told her the first round of torpedoes were in PDC range, and her targeting solution kicked in. Alex bent the *Roci*'s path, forced the attackers to shift. Gave her an extra fraction of a second between them. The PDCs lit up, going gold on her display as they fired. The deep chattering tapped through the deck with each one like she was playing music. Four torpedoes flamed out at once, but the other six danced away from the streams of metal, then spiraled closer to the ship. Alex banked hard, catching one with the edge of the drive plume, making the other five maneuver. She caught four. The fifth shifted, evaded, streaked close—

Alex tried to yell, but it came out as little more than a high squeak. The ship turned the extra three degrees to bring another PDC arc into play, and the enemy torpedo died, falling behind them in bright shards and melting in their plume.

A message appeared on her screen from Alex. TAKE IT TO THEM?

The two ships were bearing down on the *Roci*, pushing hard to narrow the distance. She didn't know if that was bold or foolhardy. Probably they didn't either. Ships full of Belters weren't known for loving high-g burns, but this was war. You took the risks you had to take. But the third ship had peeled off. And two points, her old sergeant used to say, defined an opportunity. Those bad guys were awfully close to each other.

DONNE, she typed back, and didn't bother fixing the error.

She routed the five torpedoes between the *Pella* and the *Koto* in a starburst. The Free Navy ships were firing PDCs at the *Rocinante* now, the rounds coming like ropes of pearls on the screen. Alex maneuvered around them easily. Range was too far still for close-quarters battle tactics to apply, but maybe the Belters didn't know that. Or just meant it as an insult.

She watched the curving arcs of PDC fire shift to find her torpedoes as they burned for the abstract line between the two ships. Two of hers died. Three. Four. But the fifth curved into the space between the *Koto* and the *Pella* where their tracking software would recognize that the PDC fire that would stop the torpedo would also riddle the friendly on the other side. The two ships lurched apart, and the *Koto* dropped a torpedo that took out Bobbie's attacker just a few seconds before impact.

The maneuver had bought them a few moments, but at the cost of one-quarter of their total torpedo stores. It wasn't a game she could afford to keep playing when the ante was so high. But by then she'd put in her next firing solution and passed it to Alex.

To his credit, he didn't question her. In a single instant, the gravity vanished, the *Roci*'s Epstein dropped to zero. Her couch slammed to the side, the hard spin of the maneuvering thrusters whipped them around. The custom-built keel-mounted rail gun made the ship jump as it fired. It was the one weapon the *Roci* had that wasn't standard for a Martian corvette. The rotation continued until they were back on their old course, and then ten gs slammed her back into her couch as the Epstein drive kicked back on and the counterthrusters killed the spin.

A high-speed three-sixty with a precision-timed rail gun shot halfway through the spin wasn't exactly standard combat tactics for Martian frigates, but she thought her old combat-tactics instructors would have approved.

The sudden crushing weight of thrust brought a wave of nausea, and her heart stuttered in a confusion of fluid dynamics and pressure. She must have blacked out for a moment, because she didn't see the *Koto* hit. Only the glowing plume of superheated gas expanding behind it where it had dropped core. Even pressed into the crash couch, she managed a smile. She waited to see if the *Pella* would break off, go to the aid of her fallen comrade.

It didn't.

Bobbie fed a new firing solution, passed it to Alex, and they tried again. A weightless, spinning moment, the kick of the rail gun, and slammed back into the couch like an assault. The *Pella* knew now. At the vast distances between them, even the fraction of a second that it took to spin the *Rocinante* around was enough for the enemy to anticipate them and dodge. She threw two more torpedoes at the *Pella*, but they were shot down well before they could do damage.

The *Pella* launched another round of torpedoes, but without the *Shinsakuto* and the *Koto* to box them in, Bobbie wasn't worried. The complexities of the battle looked to be over. Now it became longer and simpler and worse. Something in her trachea slid where it wasn't meant to be and she forced out a cough, her head spinning a little when she did.

This was how they'd end now. A long, desperate race to see who ran out of PDC rounds or torpedoes first. Who had allies near enough to complicate the situation. But before any of that, there was the braking threshold. The point of no return at which they wouldn't have enough reaction mass left to match the thrust they'd already pumped into their vector. They'd be trapped in a desperately long orbit, at the mercy of whoever came for them. *That* was her hard deadline.

Fighting to move her fingers against the built-in controls, she sent a message to Holden: DISTRACT THEM.

A moment later, a reply arrived: ???

DISTRACT THEM.

Bobbie waited for the inevitable calls for clarification, but was pleasantly surprised when instead the comm array went active. A tightbeam. To the *Pella*. She saw the connection accepted. Good. She tried to count down from five, but got lost somewhere around three. She breathed through gritted, aching teeth, and re-sent the firing solution. Float, spin, fire, and slam back into the couch, spine shrieking and mind fluttering on the edge of blackness. It hadn't done any good. The *Pella* had dodged again.

There had to be a way. She couldn't let the enemy run them out. She couldn't let her team down again. There had to be a way. They could fire a fraction of a second earlier... but the keel mount meant the *Roci* could only fire straight ahead. A tear pressed out of her eyes, slamming to the gel beside her ear like a stone. Were they still at eight gs? She looked at the firing solution through blurred eyes. There had to be something. Some other way to draw a straight line between two points.

She could try again, but the *Pella* would dodge the way it had before. The rail gun could only draw perfectly straight lines, and now that the *Pella* knew what their spin meant, its computers would be very good at predicting the slug's flight path and adjusting.

Something. Something there. The tiny, shining limn of an idea. The *Pella* would dodge the way it had before.

So how did it dodge before?

Her wrist creaked as she pulled the battle record up, moving back second by second. Twice the *Pella* had dodged the rail gun. Both

times by firing all her port maneuvering thrusters—sidestepping—
and then correcting on the starboard. It kept her pointing the same
direction, not veering away. But if it was a habit …

She fed the firing solution in again. The moment of sicken-
ing spin, the bang of the rail gun, the crack of the couch taking
her in. But the *Pella* did it again. It dodged the same way. It was a
pattern, and patterns were gaps in the armor. She could fit a knife
in there.

The formaldehyde taste in her mouth was heavy and chemical.
They were out of PDC range, but that was only convention. PDC
rounds didn't magically evaporate or slow down. Every tungsten
slug that hadn't hit its target in battle was still out there in the
black somewhere, speeding on as fast as the moment it had left the
barrel. It was only the overwhelming vastness of space that kept
every ship out there from being holed at random.

This wasn't fucking random, though.

Her fingers ached. Her head ached. She didn't care. She pulled
up the speeds of everything she had—PDC rounds at so many
meters per second. Torpedoes started slower, but followed a sharp
acceleration curve. Rail-gun rounds…she rechecked the number.
Okay. Rail gun rounds went really fast.

It was a puzzle. It was only a puzzle. There was an answer, and
she could find it. There would be one chance. She keyed in the
new firing solution, everything tied together.

You are mine, you piece of shit. You are mine now.

She passed it over.

The *Rocinante* shuddered, the vibration of the PDCs made
more violent by the high-g burn. On her screen, it looked like a
cloud of gold. Thousands of rounds spinning out to kill torpedoes
that weren't there. Too imprecise to hit the *Pella* at this range, and
not in the right place anyway. It looked like a misfire. A malfunction. It looked like nothing. Then the torpedoes launched. Three
of them, spitting toward the *Pella* in tight curves. The obvious
danger. Shards of white showing internal strain, vector, guiding
themselves toward their target and accelerating toward the *Pel-*

la's port side. The *Pella*'s PDCs opened up, spraying toward the incoming, evasion-drunk torpedoes. For long, terrible minutes, the pieces of her puzzle moved into place.

It wasn't going to work. They were going to see it. As clear as it was to her, they had to be able to see it too.

The torpedoes sped in, driving toward the *Pella*'s flank and the withering fire of her PDCs. The *Pella* dropped three torpedoes of her own. Bobbie's golden cloud of PDC rounds was almost in position.

Alex killed the engine as he had before. Spun them. The rail gun fired in the split second it came to bear on the *Pella*, the spine of the ship creaking. Before Bobbie could see what had happened, the *Roci* completed her arc, her drive returning as it had before. And the *Pella*—flagship of the Free Navy and private gunship of Marco Inaros—dodged the rail gun round just as it had before. *Just* as it had before. By sidestepping away from the torpedo battle to its port.

And into the path of the oncoming cloud of PDC rounds.

There was no way to know how many hit, but the *Pella* veered off course, its main drive still firing full out even as it turned almost orthogonally to the direction of the *Rocinante*. Alex eased off, and a mere three-g acceleration felt like being light as a balloon. Bobbie checked the stores and noted she'd already fired half her torpedoes, so she fired half of what was left, sending five more after the *Pella*, one after the other streaming toward the wounded ship's drive cone. The *Pella* had lost at least one thruster on her starboard and struggled to bring PDCs to bear.

And then it got hard to see what happened, because the enemy drive plume was pointing straight at them, the *Pella* retreating up out of the ecliptic and toward the uncaring stars. Alex cut the drive, leaving them on the float. The back of Bobbie's head was wet. Either she'd been sweating or the tears pulled from her eyes had pooled. Or her skin split and she was in her own blood. No matter what, it felt great.

Alex was staring at her, his eyes wide, shaking his head. Slowly a grin pulled at his lips. He started chuckling, and then she did too. Her ribs hurt. Her throat hurt. When she tried to move her left arm, the elbow protested like it had been dislocated and shoved roughly back into place.

"Holy shit," Alex said. "I mean just holy fucking *shit*."

"I know," she said.

"That was *great*!" Alex whooped, and punched the air. "We did it! We kicked their butts!"

"We did," Bobbie said, closing her eyes and heaving a deep, slow breath. Her sternum popped like a firecracker, and she started laughing again. A thin sound, distant as home, plucked at her awareness. She realized she'd been hearing it for a while, but hadn't registered it in the heat of battle. Now that she heard it, she recognized it at once.

It was a medical alarm.

Chapter Twenty-Eight: Holden

When Holden left the Earth Navy, he'd had a dishonorable discharge on his record and a sense of relief and righteous anger stiffening his spine. He'd thought at the time that the greatest irony of his newly fallen position in life was that, while his career options were now substantially narrowed and his status in the world dimmed, he felt freer. Looking back at it now, that freedom only earned second place after the subliminal, barely expressed relief that he wouldn't see any more ship-to-ship fighting.

Since the *Rocinante* had become his home, he'd tracked down pirates for the OPA. Battled over Io. The slow zone. Ilus. If he'd sucked it up and stayed in the service, he'd have been a thousand times safer. It wasn't something that had occurred to him before. In all the previous battles, he'd been in charge. Working for so many years with a skeleton crew of only four made frantic action the norm. Between his crew and Fred Johnson's now, every station had someone in it, and a backup ready to step in besides. Even with the high burn pressing him into the couch so hard he could barely breathe, there was a deeper urge to do something. To take control of some corner of the action. To have an effect.

The truth of the matter was that anything he did now would get in someone else's way. Watching the tactical map and trying not to pass out were literally all he could usefully manage. Even calling Ceres for help had been someone else's job. And Fred, in the couch at the far side of the command deck, had done it better than he could have. When a power exchange blew out and switched to the fallback, Amos or Clarissa had flagged it for repair before he could remember how to pull up the damage control schedule. Mfume and Steinberg were at stations amidships, Lombaugh and Droga down in engineering, two teams of pilot and gunner ready to take over if the Free Navy cleaved the cockpit off the ship. So he watched the *Shinsakuto* falling away to intercept the long-range torpedoes from Ceres and then shifted to the *Koto* and the *Pella*—Marco Inaros' ship—as they raced up at them from below like sharks.

Naomi was in the next couch over, breathing in ragged gasps. He wanted to talk to her, to ask if she was okay, to offer her some sort of comfort. He tried to imagine her response. Something that meant, *I appreciate that you care, but the time to talk through my emotional well-being isn't during a firefight.* It was just another way that he could try to control something. Make something better. Anything. She was less than a meter from him, and a million klicks away.

When the drive cut out and the ship spun hard, he knew they were dead. Then thrust slammed him back into his couch. For a few seconds he'd wondered whether it had actually happened, or if he was starting to hallucinate, but then he saw the *Koto* falling away beneath them. Even then it took a few seconds to understand what had happened, just in time for it to happen again. He heard Naomi cry out as the impact of the couch hit them all again.

He wanted to shout up to Bobbie that she had to stop it. That there were people in the ship—some of them Belters. And anyway no one had grown up in gravity hard enough that they could shrug off eight-g impacts all day, crap-ass third-rate juice or not. But he couldn't even do that, because if she was doing it, she probably was right to. The best he could do was hate it and endure.

All of which was why, when something finally did arrive that he could do, he was practically giddy with relief.

DISTRACT THEM.

He stared at the words with blurry, aching eyes. Who was Bobbie asking him to distract? The crew? The enemy? He forced his fingers to the controls, managing ??? only with some effort.

The answer came back just the same. DISTRACT THEM.

Holden stared at the words. As much as he wanted to help, there really wasn't much he could do that the ship wasn't already doing. The ECM package was spraying radio chatter at the pursuing ship, doing its best to blind the enemy torpedoes. The comm laser was throwing as much high-frequency light into the *Pella*'s sensors as it could pump out. As far as distractions went, the *Roci* was already doing her best. He forced another painful breath.

On the other hand, what else was he doing? And thinking about the comm laser gave him an idea.

He grabbed the comm control and put in a tightbeam-connection request to the *Pella*. Maybe they'd think he was asking for their surrender. Or offering his. Intellectually, he knew there had to be some anxiety in him. This was Marco Inaros. The man who'd killed the Earth. Who'd tried to capture Naomi and kill him. But between the ache of the burn and his juice-regulated heartbeat, he didn't feel it.

The tightbeam picked up carrier, paused while it negotiated wavelength and data protocol, and then the connection was accepted, and Holden was looking up into the eyes of Marco Inaros. He'd seen pictures of the man. Watched the videos of his press releases. He knew the face as well as he might any third-rate celebrity. Thrust had pulled back Marco's hair, stretched his skin, pushed his cheeks back and in. It made him look younger than he was. Holden hoped it was doing the same for him.

He hadn't assumed that the *Pella* would brake enough to make conversation possible. Whatever he was going to do, he'd thought it would be in text. But now that they were facing each other, he thought this might be enough. The monitor was only about sixty centimeters from Holden. Marco's would be about the same. It created the illusion that they were close to each other. He could see the little flaw in Marco's hairline where it curved back at the right temple. The blood vessels in his eyes. It felt intimate. Almost embarrassing. And, motionless as they were, there was also an uncanny feeling, like looking into the mirror and seeing someone else looking back. Here was a man who'd taken on the fate of humanity like it was a part-time job, right here in front of him. Close enough to touch.

It was hard to be certain what emotions were actually in Marco's expression and what Holden only imagined. A defiant sneer. Then confusion. Maybe they were there; maybe they were only what he expected to see. He was certain, though, that a malicious gleam came into the man's eyes at the end. The effort of working his controls showed in Marco's face, and Holden expected a message to come through. A taunt, an accusation. He was wrong.

Marco clicked away, and a new face appeared. Younger. Darker. As crushed by the acceleration, but unmistakable. Filip Inaros. The boy didn't look at Holden, didn't seem aware of him. Holden, it seemed, wasn't showing on his monitor. Marco was only giving Holden a moment to look at the boy.

He didn't know what he was supposed to see there. Maybe it was a vulgar masculine boast. *She may be with you now, but I fucked her first.* That seemed about Inaros' level. Maybe it was to show that the son hated them as much as the father. But where looking at Marco had felt awkward, seeing Filip was actually fascinating. Holden couldn't help searching for traces of Naomi in the younger, masculine face. The epicanthic fold at the corner of his eyes. The angle of his cheeks and the shape of his lips. The way he moved reminded Holden of Naomi struggling under a burden.

What struck him most was how young the boy looked. At that

age, Holden hadn't left Earth yet. Had still been waking up at the ranch in Montana, having breakfast with his many parents before going out to mend fences and check the turbines at the wind farm. Thinking of the Navy because Brenda Kaufmann had broken up with him, and he was sure he'd never get over her.

There were mistakes you made because you were young. Everyone made some of them.

Thrust cut out. Holden's couch snapped to the side again, bucked as the rail gun fired, and slammed back into him. On his screen, the boy's eyes widened as his couch swiveled. Something loud happened on the *Pella*. Someone shouted. The high whine of a medical alert. The tightbeam dropped as the thrust gravity on the *Roci* dropped back. Still more than usual, but after that long pushing at eight gs, his body's response was profound and visceral. Naomi's moan was half pain, half relief. People were shouting in his ear: delight and exaltation. His mouth tasted like blood. His elbow ached as he reached for the monitor, switching to tactical without the in-couch control. Alex's voice, muffled like they were both underwater, reached him. *That was great. We did it. We kicked their butts.*

The *Pella* was burning away, still under high thrust, but racing away. A wave of the *Rocinante*'s torpedoes raced after them. Without thinking, he disarmed them.

His fingers hesitated above the screen, his mind falling apart and coming back together and falling apart again the way it did at the end of a long burn. The blood reperfusing through his brain carried strange, fleeting sensations. His left leg cold and wet, like he was standing in a river. The smell of burning hair. A sense of unfocused moral outrage that flickered and went out as suddenly as it had come. He pressed his hands to his eyes and coughed. Pain shot down his spine. His ears rang. Tinnitus.

No, not tinnitus.

"*Jim.*"

He wrenched himself around, fighting against the unnatural weight of his body. Naomi was struggling in her couch, futilely trying to rise in the heavy g. Her face was ashen. His half-functioning brain leaped to panic. She was hurt. *Something's wrong. This is my fault.*

"What?" he said, his voice rough and phlegmy. "What happened?"

Bobbie came down from the cockpit, muscles straining on the ladder rungs. Naomi looked from him to her and back again. She was pointing at something, gasping to get words out.

"Fred," Naomi said. "He's having a stroke."

"Oh," Holden said, but Bobbie had already surged forward, undoing the straps and half lifting Fred out of his couch. At their current acceleration, the old man had to weigh over two hundred kilos. Bobbie nearly collapsed but stayed on her feet, her arms wrapped around his upper body, trying to pull him free of the restraints. Holden staggered to the lift and shouted up. "Alex! Cut thrust. Put us at a third of a g."

"Hostiles are still—"

"If they shoot at us, do something clever. We've got an emergency."

The gravity let go again. Holden's spine lengthened. His knees felt like they were swelling. Bobbie, now carrying Fred in her arms, was on the lift, dropping toward the medical bay. Fred looked tiny cradled against her, his eyes closed. Holden told himself that the old man's arm draped around Bobbie's shoulder was clinging to her. Had strength. He didn't know if it was true.

A cacophony of voices shouted in his ear. Everyone asking what had happened. What was going on.

"Steinberg!" he barked. "You're on weapons. Patel, take the comms." Then he pulled off his headset. The lift was coming back up for them, the gentle hum barely audible in the noises of the ship, and the only thing he had ears for. He willed it to go faster.

Naomi put a hand on his shoulder. "It's going to be okay."

"Really?"

Naomi shrugged helplessly. "I don't know."

The lift came. They loaded on, descending for the crew deck. If the *Pella* got itself back under control, it could loop around. The fight could start again at any second, catching them away from their crash couches. Holden knew they should be burning hard, rushing toward Tycho as fast as they could. He walked through the tight, military corridor, into the medical bay. It felt like he was in a different ship. Everything was just where it always was, but it seemed new. Fresh. Foreign.

Fred lay on the table, stripped to the waist. The autodoc was strapped to his arm, needles inserted into the veins. He looked weirdly vulnerable, as if he'd physically shrunk between the time he'd gotten into the crash couch and now. Bobbie stood over him, arms crossed, glowering like an angel out of the Old Testament. One of the scary kind. The kind that kept you out of paradise and killed armies in a single night. She didn't look up as they came in.

"How bad is it?" Holden asked.

Somehow Bobbie made her shrug an expression of rage. "He's dead."

He didn't know how Amos and Clarissa got the duty of preparing the body, but whatever the mechanism, it turned out to be a good fit. Amos stripped him, and Clarissa cleaned Fred's skin with a damp cloth. Holden didn't need to be there for it. Didn't have to watch. Except that he did.

They didn't talk. Didn't make jokes. Clarissa swabbed Fred's body with a calm, businesslike intimacy. Compassionate and unsentimental. Amos helped when Fred needed to be moved and dressed in a fresh uniform and when she needed to slide the body bag under him. It took a little less than an hour from start to finish. Holden didn't know if that seemed like too long or not long enough. Clarissa hummed something as she worked. A soft melody he didn't recognize, but one that didn't seem to rest in either a major key or a minor one. Her thin, pale face and Amos' thickness seemed perfectly matched. When the bag was sealed, Amos hefted it. Easy to do. They were still barely above a third of a g.

Clarissa nodded to Holden as they passed out of the medical bay. Her skin was bruised at the back of her neck and all along the arms where the blood had pooled during the burn. "We'll take care of him," she said.

"He was important," Holden replied, and wasn't ashamed at the catch in his voice.

Something like sorrow or amusement flickered in Clarissa's eyes. "I've spent a lot of time with the dead. He'll be okay now. You go take care of the ones that lived through it."

Amos smiled amiably and carried the bag out. "You need to get drunk or in a fistfight later, just let me know."

"Yeah," Holden said. "All right."

After they left, he stood beside the empty medical table. He'd been on it more than once. Naomi had. Alex. Amos. Amos had regrown most of a hand in this room. That death had come randomly—stupidly—seemed obscene even though it was mundane enough. People stroked out. Fred was older than he'd once been. He was dealing with high blood pressure. He'd been going without sleep, pushing himself. The juice they had was lousy. It had been a long battle and a hard burn. All of it was true. All of it made sense. And none of it did.

The others were still at their stations, but the word had gotten out by now. He was going to have to face them at some point. He didn't know what he'd say to Fred's crew. *I'm so sorry*, but after that?

He brushed his hand on the mattress, listened to the hiss of skin against plastic. It felt colder than he'd expected. It took him a second to realize it was the dampness from Clarissa's cloth evaporating. He recognized Naomi by her footsteps.

"Do you remember when it came out he was working with the OPA?" Holden asked.

"I do."

"It was the only thing on any of the newsfeeds for...I don't know. A week. Everyone saying he was a traitor and a disgrace. Talking about whether there should be an investigation. Whether he could still be brought up on charges even though he'd resigned years before."

"What I heard was more equivocal," Naomi said. She came into the room, leaned against one of the other tables. She pulled her hair down over her eyes like a veil as she spoke, then scowled and brushed it back. "The people I knew assumed he was a mole. Earthers trying to Trojan horse their way into our organization."

"Was it still your organization back then?"

"Yeah. It was."

He turned, pulled himself up to sit on the table. The autodoc, sensing his weight, pulled up the start screen, glowed hopefully for a few seconds, and turned back off. "I just can't remember a time when Fred Johnson wasn't someone important. It's just …"

Naomi sighed. He looked at her. The lines on her face that hadn't been there when he'd met her. The way the line of her jaw had changed. She was beautiful. She was mortal. He didn't want to think about it.

"Every faction of the OPA Fred could bully or beg or cajole into coming together is waiting for us at Tycho," Holden said. "And we're going to have to tell them Marco won."

"He didn't win," Naomi said.

"We'll have to tell them we were ambushed and Fred died, but Marco totally didn't win."

Naomi smiled. Laughed. It was strange how it made the darkness better. Not less dark. Just better, even though it still was what it was. "Well, all right, when you put it that way. Look, worst-case scenario is we don't get them on our side. I'm not saying it wouldn't be great to have more of the Belt on our side. But if we don't have them to work with, we don't. We can still win."

"Only the war," he said. "Not the part that matters."

Chapter Twenty-Nine: Avasarala

Gorman Le blinked, rubbed his entirely-too-green eyes, and waited for her to respond.

"And you don't know where it came from?" Avasarala said.

"Well, Ganymede," he said. "The transmission records are clear. It definitely came from Ganymede."

"But we don't know who on Ganymede."

"No," he said, nodding to mean yes, she was right. Fucking confusing way to express himself.

The meeting room was a smaller one in Nectaris facility. The lights were cold, the walls a brushed ceramic that hadn't been fashionable in thirty years. It was on a physically separate environmental system, so the air didn't have the recently rebreathed smell that most of Luna suffered these days. If the gunpowder stink of lunar fines was there, she'd gotten so used to it that she couldn't tell.

Gorman Le sat hunched forward like a schoolboy, a glass of water forgotten in his hand. He was wearing the same suit he'd had on yesterday and the day before. She was starting to think he kept it in a closet and threw it on whenever he had to talk with her. Weariness radiated from him like he was a medic on the last hour of a four-day shift, but there was something else in him. Something she hadn't seen recently. Excitement, maybe. Hope.

That was bad. Lately, hope was a poison.

"So the report schema or whatever the hell you call it could be real," she said. "Or it could be the Free Navy trying to fuck with us. Or it could be...what?"

"Nutritional yeast with advanced radioplasts. We've been looking at how the protomolecule was able to grow based on some kinds of ionizing radiation?" The rise of inflection at the end made it a question, as if he were asking her permission instead of debriefing her. "Nonionizing too, but that's really easy. Light's nonionizing radiation, and plants have been harvesting that since forever. But—"

Avasarala raised her hand, palm out. Le's mouth kept moving for a few seconds, part of him still speaking while the rest was reined in. "I care deeply about all the fine details," she said, "only actually, I don't. Sum it up."

"If the numbers are right, we could feed maybe half a million more people on this base right now. The first runs we did looked really good. But if it's something that doesn't scale and the farms crash, we could lose days cleaning it back out."

"And then people starve."

Gorman nodded some more. Maybe he didn't mean anything by it. "Resetting would definitely mean missing some production goals."

She leaned forward, plucked the glass from his hand, and looked into his eyes. "Then people starve. We're grown-ups here. You should be able to say it."

"Then people starve."

She nodded and leaned back. The terrible thing was that her

back felt better. She'd been at one-tenth of a g for so long, she was getting used to it. When she went back down the well, she'd have to reacclimatize. When. Not if. Gorman was looking at her, his jaw set, his nostrils flared like a panicky horse. She had to restrain herself from patting his head. She wanted some fucking pistachios.

"What's your doctorate in?" she asked.

"Um. Structural biochemistry?"

"Do you know what mine's in?"

He shook his head for a change.

"Not structural biochemistry," she said gently. "I don't know anything about whether this magic yeast recipe is bullshit or not. So if you can't tell, I'm less than fucking useless. So what are we here for?"

"I don't know what to do." He looked young. He looked lost.

The impulse to snap at him fought with the impulse to hug him. She closed her eyes, and damn it but they felt good closed. This morning, it had been a coordination meeting with the Lagrange stations talking about refugee loads, then security and resources talking about policing guidelines for the people still coming up the well. Over lunch, reports of an armed uprising in what was left of Sevastopol—people panicking as food and water ran low. It was all bleeding together in her mind, one long, ongoing, weary sense of urgency.

She wanted to be angry with Le, but either she understood his frozen panic too well or else she just didn't have the energy anymore. "Is it a good bet?"

"I think so," he said, almost at once. "The data looks—"

"Then implement it. If it doesn't work, you can blame me."

"That's not what I was...I mean...If a larger scale production run works here, we should really look at sending this down the well." *Down to Earth. Where they were even hungrier.*

She opened her eyes. Something in them made Gorman look away.

"Yes, ma'am. I'll see that it's done."

She rose. The meeting was over. Only when she was out the

door and shuffling across the yellow-gray paving toward her cart did she think about giving Le some kind of encouragement. A pat on the shoulder. A gentle word. She'd backed him down out of habit, not because he needed to be brought into line. She used to be better at this.

As the cart lurched forward, she pulled up a connection to Said. He appeared in a half-sized window that left room for her calendar and notes, almost too small to make out more than his V-shaped face and high, curly hair floating above a collarless blue shirt. "Ma'am?"

"Where do we stand?"

"You have a report from Admiral Pycior on the Enceladus situation waiting for review."

"Is it going to say anything besides 'The Free Navy fucked off before we got there and now we have more people we need to feed,' or do I already have the gist of it?"

"That's the gist. There were some casualties on our side. The *Edward Carr* is also going to need extensive repairs."

She nodded. Another fucking battle like trying to grab water in her fist. The cart turned, dipped into an access tunnel. Two security guards saluted as she passed. The cart turned down another ramp, slotted itself into the highspeed toward the government and administration centers at Aldrin, and turned again so that she could look back down the throat of the passageway. Gray walls with white archways retreating back and up. The air like an eternal exhalation. The architecture seemed small in context. Insignificant against the tremendous scope of Luna and Earth. She clung to it like a lifeline. "Reports from Ceres are that the *Rocinante* was ambushed, but escaped. It's on course toward Tycho Station."

"Small favors," she said.

"You also have a personal meeting on the schedule, ma'am."

Personal meeting? For a long moment, she couldn't remember what it was, but as the highspeed line lurched, pulled her cart in, and began its acceleration run, she remembered that Ashanti had been asking to see her. Somehow, her daughter had wheedled Said into putting her on the calendar.

"Cancel that," Avasarala said.

"Are you certain, ma'am?"

"I don't want to spend half an hour listening to a girl whose diapers I changed lecture me about taking care of myself. Tell her I'm tired and napping."

"Yes, ma'am."

"Do you have something you want to say, Mr. Said?"

Said coughed. "She's your daughter, ma'am."

Avasarala smiled. It was the first time Said had pushed back at her. Maybe there was hope for the little fucker yet. "Fine. Give her the first dinner slot that's still open."

"That's three days."

"Three days, then," Avasarala said. The highspeed stopped accelerating, leaving her rocketing through the evacuated tunnel at however many hundreds of kilometers per hour it went. Enough to take her halfway across the face of the moon in half an hour. A body in motion remained in motion. It was a metaphor as much as anything. Stay in motion, because once she rested, she didn't know how she would bring herself to ever start again.

She couldn't remember how long it had been since she'd meditated. It used to be that when things were bad at work, she spent more time sitting, not less. Listening to her own breath rattle through the complex spaces at the back of her nose, being with her body in a deep and connected way that let all the shit settle. If she'd been keeping up, she'd have remembered to encourage Gorman Le, for instance. She hated to guess how many other little fuckups she'd passed by without even noticing.

The highspeed tunnel curved, pushing her gently against the cart's door. She told herself that between the war and the recovery, there was just too much to do. That was accurate as far as it went, but she'd spent too many years becoming familiar with her own mind to entirely ignore the fact that she was bullshitting herself. Meditation was there so that she could be with herself, experience what it meant to be Chrisjen Avasarala more deeply. And since she was fairly certain Chrisjen Avasarala was a bag of sorrow and glass right now, fuck that. Meditating deeply so that she could really, clearly experience being angry and lonesome and hurt and horror-struck never seemed as good as a strong gin and tonic and another hour of work.

She could be a basket case later. When things were under control.

The highspeed had just started slowing down when her hand terminal chimed. Said looked contrite, but not so much that he'd left her alone.

"Priority message for you from the *Rocinante*, ma'am."

"The fuck does Johnson want now?"

"It's not from Colonel Johnson. Captain Holden sent it."

She hesitated. In his window, Said waited. "Send it to me," she said.

Said nodded as she closed his window. She threw the readout to the cart's screen. Whatever was going on, she wanted to be able to see it without squinting. The message appeared, flagged with red. As soon as she opened it, she knew. Death was on Holden's face as clearly as if it had been written there. When he spoke, his voice was careful and controlled. Hospital tones. Funeral.

He laid out what had happened briefly, not giving any details she didn't need. The *Pella* had led the attack. They'd managed to fend off the Free Navy. Fred Johnson was dead. And then, as if Holden were having a stroke of his own, he stared for a long moment into the camera. Into her eyes, without seeing her.

"All the OPA groups Fred called together at Tycho are waiting there. We're on course and starting our deceleration burn. But I'm not sure if we should still be going there or if there's someone you want to send. Or how long they'll wait. I don't know what to do next."

He shook his head. He looked young. Holden always looked young, but usually it was young and impulsive. The lost expression around his eyes was new. If it was even there. Maybe she was only seeing it because she felt it in her own heart, her own belly.

The message ended. The terminal prompted her for a response, but she only sat with it in her hand as the highspeed came to a halt, the cart pouring itself into more familiar corridors. She looked at her hands, and they seemed to belong to some other woman. She tried sobbing, but it seemed forced and inauthentic. More like playacting than grief. If she'd been in control of the cart, she might have let it drift into the wall or down any random corridor, all unaware. But it knew where to go, and she didn't think to take it to manual.

Fred Johnson. Butcher of Anderson Station. Hero of the UN Navy and traitorous voice of the OPA. She'd known him in person and by reputation for decades. He'd been her enemy and opposite and occasional untrusted ally. The part of her that was still thinking noticed how odd it was—how implausible—that his death should be the drop that made her cup overflow. She'd lost her world. Her home. Her husband. If she'd kept any of those, maybe this wouldn't have destroyed her.

Her sternum ached. Actually ached. Like there was a physical bruise there, and not only emotion left too long pressing at her flesh. She probed it with her fingertips, tracing the boundaries of the pain like a child fascinated by a dying insect. She didn't notice the cart had stopped until Said opened the door.

"Ma'am?" he said.

She stood. The lunar gravity seemed less like a force of nature and more like a suggestion. As if she could rise against it through simple force of will or the beating of her heart. She noticed Said again, noticed that she'd forgotten he was there. He looked distressed in an officious, too-pretty way.

"Please cancel everything," she said. "I'll be in my rooms."

"Do you need anything, ma'am? Should I get a doctor?"

She frowned at him, the muscles in her cheeks seeming to exist at a distance. She was piloting her body like it was a mech with failing controls. "What would that help?"

In her rooms, she sat on the divan, her hands cupped in her lap, palms up. Like she was holding something. The air recycler's fan had a little noise to it, resonant and unsteady. Wind passing over a bottle's mouth. Mindless, idiot music. She wondered if she'd ever noticed it before, and then forgot it. Her mind was empty. She wondered if there was something coming. Some overwhelming flood that would carry her away. Or if this was simply who she was now. An empty woman.

She ignored the knock at her door. Whoever they were, they'd go away. Only they didn't. Her door slid a few centimeters open. And then a few more. She thought it would be Said. Or one of the admirals. Some functionary of governance come, like Gorman Le, to ask her to carry the weight of loss and uncertainty for them. It wasn't.

Kiki wasn't a little girl anymore. Her granddaughter was a woman in her own right, though a young one. Her skin was deep brown like her father's, but she had Ashanti's eyes and nose. A glimmer of Arjun in the color of her eyes. As much as Avasarala tried to hide it, Kiki wasn't her favorite granddaughter. The girl always had an air of observing judgment that made being with her difficult. Kiki cleared her throat. For a long moment, they looked at each other.

"What are you doing here?" Avasarala asked. She'd meant it to drive the girl away, but it didn't. Kiki came in and closed the door behind her.

"Mother's hurt that you rescheduled us again," Kiki said.

Avasarala twitched her hands, fingers splayed, palms up. Exasperation without the energy behind it. "Did she send you to lecture me?"

"No," Kiki said.

"What, then?"

"I was worried about you."

Avasarala snorted in derision. "Why would you worry about me? I'm the most powerful person in the system right now."

"That's why I'm worried about you."

That's not your fucking job floated at the back of her throat, but she couldn't say it. The ache in Avasarala's sternum sank deeper, pressing in past bone and cartilage. Her vision went blurry, tears sheeting across her eyes with too little weight to pull them down. Kiki stood by the doorway, her face expressionless. A schoolgirl before her principal, waiting to be scolded. Without speaking she shuffled forward in the scant gravity, sat at Avasarala's side, and lowered her head to her grandmother's lap.

"Mother loves you," Kiki said. "She just doesn't know how to say it."

"It was never her job to," Avasarala said, her fingers smoothing her granddaughter's hair the way they had her daughter's once when they'd all been younger. Some other time before the world had shattered under them all. "Love was always your grandfather's work. I loved"—her breath caught—"I loved him very much."

"He was a good man," Kiki said.

"Yes," she said, running her fingertips through the girl's hair. Tracing the paler line of her scalp.

Minutes passed. Kiki shifted a little, but only a little. Grandmother and granddaughter were quiet. The tears in Avasarala's eyes weren't thick. Didn't fall. When she blinked them away, none rose to take their place. She considered the curve of Kiki's ear the way she once had Ashanti's, when her daughter had been a little girl. And Charnapal, when he'd been a child. Before he'd died.

"I do the best I can," Avasarala said.

"I know."

"It isn't enough."

"I know."

A weird peace seemed to flow over her. Into her. For a moment, it was as if Arjun were there. As if he'd spoken some perfect bloom of a poem to her instead of only her least favorite granddaughter bearing witness to her failures. Everyone had their beauty and their way of expressing it. It was only hard for her to love Kiki because they were so much like each other. Exactly alike, if she were being honest. That made loving her too much dangerous sometimes. She knew what being herself had cost her, and so seeing herself in Kiki made her so very afraid for the girl. Avasarala heaved a great sigh, plucked at the girl's shoulder.

"Go tell your mother I had something fall through, and we should eat together. Tell Said too."

"He was the one that let me in," Kiki said, sitting up.

"He's a fucking busybody and he should stop putting his fingers in my shit," Avasarala said. "But this one time, I'm glad he did."

"So you won't punish him?"

"Fucking right, I'll punish him," she said. Then, almost to her surprise, she kissed Kiki's smooth, unlined forehead. "It's just this time I won't mean it. Go now. I have something I need to do."

She'd expected her makeup to be ruined, but it really wasn't. A touch of eyeliner and a stray lock of hair tucked down was all she needed to look like herself again. She pulled Holden's message back up, let it play while she composed herself in the eye of her terminal's camera.

When the prompt to reply came, she squared her shoulders, imagined herself looking into Holden's eyes, and started the recording.

"I'm sorry to hear about Fred. He was a good man. Not perfect, but who is? I'll miss him. What we do next is simpler. You get your sorry ass to Tycho Station and make this work."

Chapter Thirty: Filip

The *Pella* limped along at a third of a g. After so long on the float, Filip felt even that in his knees and spine. Or maybe it was only that he was still bruised by the god-awful forces of the battle now behind them.

The battle they'd lost.

He stood in the galley, a bowl of Martian-designed rice noodles and mushrooms in his hand, and looked for a place to sit, but the benches were all filled. The *Koto* had taken it worse than the *Pella*—a rail gun round holing the reactor and cracking the hull from stem to stern. Most of the ships Filip had lived on would have died in that same second, but the Martian Navy had built with battle in mind. In a slice of a second so thin you could see through it, the *Koto* had registered the hit and dropped core, leaving the crew trapped and helpless, with only the battery backups to keep them alive.

The *Shinsakuto* had been driven away from them, hounded and harassed by fighting ships and torpedoes from the consolidated fleet and Cercs. If the *Rocinante* had finished its job on the *Pella*, the crew of the *Koto* would still be out there on the float. Or maybe they'd be dead by now, the air recyclers finally failing and leaving them all to gasp and choke and claw each other in their death panic. Instead, they were all on the *Pella*, hot-bunking with the usual crew, taking up space on the galley and pointedly not making eye contact with Filip as he looked for his place among them.

His own crew was there too. Men and women he'd been shipping with since before it all began. Aaman. Miral. Wings. Karal. Josie. They were looking away as much as the others. Only about half of them were wearing their Free Navy uniforms. *Koto* and *Pella* both had dropped back to the simple functional clothes that any crew might wear, and some of the ones still in uniform had rolled up their sleeves or left their collars open. Filip felt his own uniform, crisp and fresh and done to the neck, and for the first time he felt a little foolish in it. Like a kid dressed in his father's clothes as a costume.

The murmur of conversation was a wall that excluded him. He hesitated. He could just take the bowl back to his quarters. It wasn't really that they were keeping him apart. It was only that they were so crowded now, and stung from having lost a fight. He took a step toward the corridor, intending to go. Meaning to. And then stopping and looking back in case there was some slot, some corner of bench, that he'd overlooked. Some place for him.

He caught Miral's eye. The older man nodded, and—Filip thought with a sigh—shifted to open a little room beside him. Filip didn't run there like a little boy, but he went quickly, worried that the gap might close again before he reached it.

Karal was sitting across from Miral, and all of them sandwiched by unfamiliar bodies. A woman with dark skin and a scar across her upper lip. A thin man with a tattoo on his neck. An older woman—white, close-cropped hair and a crooked, unfriendly smile. Karal was the only one of them to acknowledge Filip, and that only with a grunt and a nod.

When the older woman spoke, it seemed like she was picking up the thread of a conversation that had been going on before Filip had taken his seat, but with a studied casualness of someone with an agenda. "Con mis coyo on the *Shinsakuto*, the Ceres fleet's there forever. Earth away from Earth."

"Forever's a long time," Miral said, considering the table like he was reading it. "Can think we know what a year, two years, three years down looks like, aber that's only shit and guessing."

"Can't see the future," the woman said. "Can see what's there now, though, que no?"

Filip took a mouthful of too-salty noodles. He'd waited too long to start eating, and they were more than halfway to paste. The older woman grinned like she'd won a point, leaned in, put her elbows on the table so the split-circle tattoo of the OPA on her wrist showed. Almost like she was displaying it.

"All I'm saying is maybe time we start winning something, yeah? Ceres. Enceladus. Seems like las sola cocks we kick anymore are Michio Pa's, and not so much hers even."

"We beat Earth," Filip said. He'd meant it to seem like an off-hand comment. Something thrown into the conversation almost at random. Instead, he sounded shrill and defensive, even to himself. The words lay there on the table like something broken past fixing. The older woman's smile was thin and nasty. Or maybe he only thought it was. One way or the other, she leaned back, took her elbows off the table. When she stood, when she walked away, it was with the air of having made her point, whatever it had been.

Karal coughed, shook his head. "No te preoccupes, Filipito," he said.

"Why would I worry?" Filip asked around another bite of the noodles.

Karal made a circling motion with his hand. *All this and everyone.* "After a fight it's the story about the fight, yeah?"

"Yeah," Filip said. "Bist bien. I understand."

Miral and Karal glanced at each other, and he pretended not to notice. The other crew from the *Koto* kept their silences to themselves. "Hoy, coyo," Miral said, touching Filip's shoulder. "Finish that and come help me with some repair work, yeah? Still tracking down some ganga between the hulls."

Filip pushed the bowl away with his fingertips. "This is done already," he said. "Let's go, us."

The strike that had crippled the *Pella* hadn't been one thing, but a tight cluster of PDC rounds. If they'd hit straight on, it would have been better. The top of the ship above the cockpit and command deck was angled and reinforced against exactly that kind of impact. Maybe it would have peeled back a section of the hull and made a hell of a bang, but kept the guts of the ship safe. The way it had happened—the rounds raking down the side of the ship in a stream—was worse. The housings of the *Pella*'s maneuvering thrusters and PDC cannons, sensor arrays and external antennas had suffered. It was like someone had taken a scraper along all the exposed parts of the ship and taken off whatever could be removed. The damage had left a blind spot in their PDC coverage, but the torpedo that came through it had malfunctioned. If it had detonated, it could have cracked the ship in two, and the old bitch from the galley would have had to hope for the mercy of the inners to keep her leathery ass from drowning in her own waste air.

The torpedo had still hit hard enough to breach the outer hull, though. And the long, tedious work of finding each bit of scrap shaken loose needed to happen. Leaving a handful of metal and ceramic shards to rattle around between decks whenever they fired the maneuvering thrusters was begging for death. So Filip and Miral suited up, checked each other's seals and bottles and rebreathers, and crawled into the space between the hulls. The Martian designs were elegant and well ordered, everything labeled along with inspection and change-out dates. In the white flare of light from his lamp, Filip considered the bent plate of the outer hull, the jagged gash where the stars showed through. The galactic plane glowed white and gold and rose against the black. It was hard not to stop and stare.

It was different looking at the stars as stars and not dots on a screen. He'd spent his whole life in ships and stations. Seeing the billions of unblinking lights with just his own eyes only happened when he went outside on a repair or an operation. It was always beautiful, sometimes alarming. This time, it seemed almost like a promise. The endless abyss opened around them, a whisper that the universe was larger than his ship. Larger than all the ships put together. Humanity could put its flag on thirteen hundred of those dots and not be a percent of a percent of a percent. That was the empire the inners were fighting and dying to control. A hundred more planets a dozen times over, and less than a rounding error of what was out there staring back at them.

"Hoy, Filipito," Miral said on the suit's private channel. "Come around. Think I've got something."

"Commé. Moment."

Miral was crouched down beside the power conduit for the sensor array. His light was playing over a bit of inner hull. A short, bright line showed where something had scratched it. Miral ran his glove over it, and it smeared. Ceramic, then.

"Okay, you little shit," Filip said, playing his lamp down the conduit. "Where'd you go?"

"Follow on," Miral said, scrambling down the handholds.

When they reached Pallas, the crews could do a more complete inspection. There were tools to blast nitrogen and argon into every crease and curve of the ship and blow out anything stuck there. Better, though, to have as much done before they arrived. And, Filip thought, there weren't any other people out between the hulls. As jobs went, it was the most isolated one that the *Pella* had to offer. All alone, that was reason enough to work it.

Miral's little gasp of victory caught Filip's attention and brought him down close to where the other man was hunched. Miral took a pair of pliers from his belt, applied himself to a section of conduit where the weld had left a gap, then sat back with a grin Filip could see through the suit's helmet mask. The chip was the size of a thumbnail, jagged along one side, smooth on the other.

Filip whistled appreciatively. "Big one."

"Si no?" Miral said. "Leave esá bastard la bouncing around like shooting a gun in here, yeah?"

"One less," Filip said. "Let's see how many more we find."

Miral made a fist and agreed, then tucked the shard into a pocket. "You know, when I was about your age? Drinker back then, me. Spent my time with this coyo always talked about fights he'd been in. Got in them a lot. Liked them, I guess."

"Yeah," Filip said, lowering himself farther down, playing his light across the housing of a maneuvering thruster. He didn't know where Miral was going with this.

"This coyo, he said mostly when things spun up, it was from the other bastard getting embarrassed, sa sa? Maybe didn't want to throw knuckles, but couldn't find a way to push off without his crew seeing him weak."

Filip scowled behind his faceplate. Maybe Miral was talking about what had happened on Ceres? It still bothered Filip sometimes. Not the violence itself, but little flashes of the humiliation left over from realizing the girl he'd been with at the Ceres bar had gone. It wasn't something he wanted to spend more time with. "Que sa, es," he said, hoping that would be enough.

But Miral went on. "Only saying, a man who's feeling like he lost face, yeah? He'll say things he doesn't mean because of it. Do things he doesn't mean."

I meant all *what I did*, Filip thought but didn't say. *Would mean it again, to do it over.*

But it had the bright, painful feel of touching a fresh scrape, and he'd already come across like a shitty little kid once today. Better to keep his own counsel. And as it turned out, that wasn't what Miral meant at all.

"Your father? He's a good man. Belter to his bones, yeah? It's just this Holden bastard's a sore for him. Getting knocked back, happens a alles one time and another, y alles talk a little bigger afterward. Not a good thing, not a bad thing. Just the way men get made. Don't take it too close."

Filip paused. Turned back.

"Don't take it too close?" he repeated, making it a question. A demand that Miral say what he meant.

"That," Miral said. "Your dad doesn't mean what he says."

Filip turned his light on Miral, shining it through the older man's faceplate. Miral squinted, put a hand up to shade his eyes.

"What does he say?" Filip asked.

Marco's quarters were past clean to spotless. The walls shone in the light, freshly polished. The dark smudges that always built up beside handholds nearest the door—evidence of the passage of hundreds of hands—had been scraped away. The monitor didn't carry so much as a fleck of lint. Fake sandalwood from the air recycler didn't quite bury the ghost of disinfectant and antifungal wash. Even the gimbals on the crash couch sparkled in the gentle light.

His father, watching the monitor, was also groomed to an eerie perfection. His hair clean and perfectly in place. His beard soft and brown and trimmed so well it seemed almost false. His uniform looked like it had never been worn before. Crisp lines and clean folds. The seams set perfectly, as if by his own precision and the force of his will, he could haul all the rest of the ship up to his standards. Like all the control Marco had spread across the system had been concentrated in one place. Not an atom in the air was out of place.

Rosenfeld was on the monitor. Filip caught the words *other eventualities* before Marco stopped the playback and turned to him.

"Yes?" Marco said. Filip couldn't tell what was in his voice.

Calm, yeah. But Marco had a thousand varieties of calm, and not all of them meant things were okay. Filip was too aware that they hadn't really spoken since the battle.

"Was talking to Miral?" Filip said, crossing his arms and leaning against the doorframe. Marco didn't move. Not a nod, not a glance away. His dark eyes left Filip feeling exposed and uncertain, but there wasn't a way to step back from this. Not without asking. "Said you were telling how what happened was my fault?"

"Because it was."

The words were simple. Matter-of-fact. There was no heat to them, no sneer or accusation. Filip felt them like a blow to the chest.

"Okay," he said. "Bien."

"You were the gunner, and they got away." Marco spread his arms in a quick, surgical shrug. "Was it a question? Or maybe you're saying it was *my* fault for thinking you could do it?"

It took Filip an extra try to talk past his throat. "Didn't drive us into those rounds, me," he said. "Gunner, me. Not the pilot. And didn't have a rail gun, yeah? Pinché Holden had a rail gun."

His father tilted his head to one side. "I just told you that you failed. Now you're giving me reasons why it's okay that you failed? Is that how it works?" Filip knew the kind of calm now.

"No," he said. Then, "No, sir."

"Good. Bad enough that you fucked it up. Don't start bawling over it too."

"Not," Filip said, but there were tears in his eyes. Shame ran through his blood like bad drugs and left him shaking. "Not bawling, me."

"Then own it. Say it like a man. Say 'I fucked it up.'"

I didn't, Filip thought. *It wasn't my fault.* "I fucked it up."

"All right, then," Marco said. "I'm busy. Close the door when you go."

"Yeah, okay."

As Filip turned, Marco shifted back to the monitor. His voice was soft as a sigh. "Crying and excuses are for girls, Filip."

"Sorry," Filip said, and pulled the door to behind him.

He walked down the narrow corridor. Voices from the lift. Voices from the galley. Two crews in the space of one, and he couldn't stand to be near any of them. Not even Miral. Especially not Miral.

He put me up, Filip thought. It was like Miral said. They hadn't kept hold of Ceres, and then Pa had insulted him by breaking away. This was supposed to be the thing to show the Free Navy couldn't be fucked with, and all three of their wolves together hadn't been able to stop the fucking *Rocinante*.

Marco had been humiliated. And shit floated against the spin, that was all it was. Still, the space below Filip's ribs ached like he'd been punched. It wasn't his fault. It was his fault. He wasn't bawling out excuses. Except that was absolutely what he'd done.

He turned on the light in his cabin. One of the engineering techs was hot-bunking there, blinking up into the light like a baby mouse.

"Que sa?" the man said.

"I'm tired," Filip said.

"Be tired somewhere else," the tech said. "I've got two more hours down."

Filip put his heel against the crash couch and spun it. The tech reached out a hand, stopped it, and unstrapped. "Fine," he said. "You're so fucking tired, sleep then."

The tech took his clothes, muttering under his breath, and left. Filip locked the door behind him and folded himself into the couch, still in his uniform that stank of sweat and the vac-suit seals. The tears tried to come then, but he bit them back, pushed the hurt down into his gut until it settled into something else.

Marco was wrong. His father had embarrassed himself because Holden and Johnson and Naomi got past them. It was like Miral said. Men got like that, and they said things they didn't mean. Did things they wouldn't do if they were thinking straight.

Filip hadn't fucked it up. Marco was wrong, that was all. This time, he just got it wrong.

Words came into his mind, as clear as if they'd been spoken. Though he'd never heard her speak them, they came in his mother's voice. *Wonder what else he got wrong.*

Chapter Thirty-One: Pa

Eugenia was a terrible place to put a base of operations. It was less an asteroid than a complex pile of loose scrap and black gravel traveling in company. Neither the asteroid itself nor the tiny moon that circled it had ever suffered the gravity to press them together or the heat it would take to fuse them. Eugenia and other duniyaret like it offered nothing solid to build on, no internal structure to shore up. Even mining it was hard, the tissue of the asteroid too fast to shift and fall apart. Build a dome there, and the air would seep out through the ground it was built on. Try to spin it up, and it would fly apart. The science station that Earth had built there three generations ago and abandoned was little more than a ruin of sealed concrete and flaking ceramic. A ghost town of the Belt.

The only things it had to recommend it at all were that it wasn't inhabited already and its orbit wasn't too distant from Ceres and the questionable protection of the consolidated fleet. And even that proximity was only temporary. With Ceres' orbital period a couple percent faster than Eugenia's, every day added a little bit to the distance between them, stretching the bubble of safety until it would eventually, inevitably pop. In fairness, if they were still using it to escape the Free Navy when Eugenia and Ceres drifted to the far side of the sun from each other, they'd have bigger problems.

Instead of trying to build on the surface of the asteroid, Michio's little fleet had begun assembling a nakliye port that orbited around Eugenia's main body: shipping containers welded one to another to make passageways, warehouses, airlocks. A tiny reactor was enough to keep the air circulating and enough heat to balance what was lost to radiation. It was temporary by design. Inexpensive, fast to assemble, and made from material so standardized and ubiquitous that a solution discovered once could be applied in a thousand other situations. It grew from a seed of three or four containers, spreading out, connecting, reinforcing, making distance where distance was needed, bringing together where it was not, spreading like a snowflake the white of rotting sealant.

There were stories of the poorest Belters living in nakliye stations for years, but more often they were used as Michio used them: storage and refueling stations. Floating warehouses without taxes or tariffs to bite into the operating budgets of the prospector. Hyperdistilled water to give pirates reaction mass and potables and oxygen. The older siblings to the scattered supply dumps the Free Navy had consigned to the void. On her monitor, it looked like some ancient sea creature, still experimenting with multiple cells. And beside it, the *Panshin*, compact and sleek.

The ship had matched orbit so precisely it seemed motionless beside the port, as if the two were connected. The flares of working lights and welding torches studded the station's skin, and the spidery shapes of mechs shepherded supplies to it from the *Panshin*. The *Connaught* had shut down its Epstein hours before to keep from slagging the port and the *Panshin* besides, and eased into her own gentle orbit on maneuvering thrusters. The deceleration burn was less like thrust gravity than a suggestion that Michio snuggle into her crash couch.

"They're painting us. Should I acknowledge?" Evans asked.

Everything was a question with him now. Ever since the scare at Ceres Station, his confidence had shattered. It was a problem, but like so many of her problems, she wasn't sure how to fix it. "Please do," she said. "Let them know I'll be coming over."

"Yes, sir," Evans said, turning to his monitor. Michio stretched, forcing her blood along its course. She didn't know why she should feel anxious about seeing Ezio Rodriguez again. She had known him for years, on and off. Another partner in the ongoing struggle to keep the Belt from being used and discarded by the inners and their allies. Only now, he'd taken her side against the Free Navy. This would be the first time she'd breathed his same air since her relief effort had become what it had become. And what did you take to a meeting with a man who'd agreed with you enough to risk his life and the lives of his crew? A thank-you card?

Michio laughed, and Oksana looked over. Michio shook her head. It wouldn't be funny out loud.

"The *Panshin* acknowledges, sir," Evans said. "Captain Rodriguez is on the port."

"Then the port it is," Michio said, unstrapping herself. "Oksana, the ship's yours."

"Sir," Oksana said, but there was a little disappointment in the word. She'd wanted to come along too, but someone had to keep an eye on Evans, and those two had been coming closer of late. Maybe having some time alone with Oksana would put Evans in a place where he could talk about what was bothering him. Better if the impulse came from him. Ordering someone to disclose their private fears wasn't good leadership. And no matter how much Michio was his wife, she was also his captain.

The *Connaught* came to her place less than a kilometer from the *Panshin* and Eugenia port. That was Oksana showing off a little, but Michio didn't mind. It made her transit short and easy.

The vac suit was Martian, armored but not powered. Well-made, like everything Marco had bartered for. Bertold and Nadia came with, each carrying a sidearm. They passed out of the *Connaught*'s airlock and into the gap, moving slow to conserve fuel and talking about whose turn it was to cook that night while the stars slid between their feet. Michio felt the unexpected tug of happiness. It was amazing to think that people lived their whole lives on a planet's surface and never had even one moment like this one, the closeness of intimate family and a vastness to rival God in the same breath.

The airlock was set halfway into one of the shipping containers, the walls cutting off the spread of the galaxy before they reached the door. All three cycled in together. As soon as the indicator went green, Michio checked her suit to confirm and then turned off her own oxygen supply and cracked open her seals.

The air inside the port stank of spent oxy-fuel and overheated metal. The percussion of someone's music carried farther than the rest of the song, making the port throb a little. A steady, mechanical heartbeat. The lights were all unsoftened LEDs, sharp-edged shadows creeping along the ceramic walls as they pulled themselves through the long corridors. Magnetic pallets clung to the surfaces, making no distinction between wall, floor, and ceiling. Old hand terminals had been fixed to each, showing what it contained, where it had come from.

A woman in a transport mech shifted away to the side as they passed, the arms of the mech pulling in close like a spider. She saluted to Michio and Bertold and Nadia equally, with an air that said she didn't know who they were and didn't care. So long as they were on the same side, they were good with her.

They found Captain Rodriguez in one of the hubs. Nine containers opened their mouths in each of the six directions, fifty-four in all, and were meant to be packed full. Michio could tell at a glance that they weren't. Ezio Rodriguez was a thin-faced man with a trim beard streaked with white, though the rest of his face looked young. He wore his hair cut to the scalp. His suit, like hers, was Martian design. Unlike her, he'd customized it: a star-burst blazon on the back between his shoulder blades and the split circle of the OPA as if it were on an armband. Half a dozen other people were moving pallets in the containers around them, shouting to each other through the free air instead of using their radios. Their voices echoed.

"Captain Pa," Rodriguez said. "Bien avisé. Been too long."

"Captain," Michio said. "The *Connaught*'s come to relieve you. Take our turn building and standing guard, sa sa?"

"Welcome to it," Rodriguez said, spreading his arms. "Not much, y not nothing."

Each of Michio's little fleet—alone or in pairs—had taken turns building and guarding the port while the others hunted colonists or gathered the supplies scattered into space, dodging Marco's ships while they did it. The *Solano* had taken another of the colony ships—the *Brilliant Iris* out of Luna—and was escorting it toward Ceres to pay their dues to Caesar. Eugenia port was too small to accommodate a ship that large anyway. The *Serrio Mal*, on the other hand, was picking up the dark containers flung off Pallas and Ceres. Those were destined for Eugenia, and from there to wherever they were needed most. Delivering the supplies to Kelso and Iapetus was the most dangerous duty, and Michio reserved it for herself.

Worse than that would be not going.

"Looks thin, que," she said.

"Looks because is," Rodriguez said. "Gathering up's been ralo these last times. Not getting what we were before. Some though."

"Enough?"

Rodriguez laughed like she'd made a joke. "Got something interesting, though. Something for you."

Michio felt the hair at the back of her neck stand up. This felt wrong. She smiled. "You shouldn't have."

"Couldn't pass it by," Rodriguez said, firing his suit's thruster toward an access way. "Over this way. I'll show."

He didn't tell her to leave Bertold and Nadia, which was good.

She wouldn't have. But she didn't know whether to be reassured that he hadn't tried to peel away her guards or frightened that maybe they didn't matter.

"Bertold," she said as they followed the other captain.

"Savvy," he said, his hand on the butt of his gun as if it had only happened to come to rest there. Nadia was the same. They fell into a guarding formation as naturally as blinking. When Rodriguez reached the walls of the port, he landed with a clank, turning on his mag boot and killing his momentum with his knees. The music they'd heard before was gone now, and Rodriguez looked behind them, as if making sure they weren't followed. Or else that they were.

"Making me nervous, coyo," Michio said, walking after him. "Something you want to say?"

"Bon sí, aber not here," Rodriguez said, the lightness gone from his voice and a grim tension in its place. "Smuggled past the smugglers, this one."

"Not feeling better."

"You will or you won't. Come alles la."

The container he took them to had a little office built out from the side. Scrapwelded together with its own airlock. Rodriguez keyed in a passcode by hand. Bertold stretched his arms, blew out his breath, like a weight lifter about to try more than his usual load.

"Love you," Nadia said, her voice calm and conversational as if she wasn't saying it in case they were her last words.

The airlock opened, and a man popped out. Thin frame, dark hair in curls. "Is she here?" he said, and then, "Oh. There you are."

A shock of surprise, the uncertainty of whether this was a threat or something more interesting. "Sanjrani."

"Nico, Nico, Nico," Rodriguez said, pushing Sanjrani back through the airlock. "Not here. Didn't sneak through te ass end of nothing to wave you like a flag. Get back safe in." When Sanjrani had retreated, Rodriguez turned to Michio, motioning that she should follow. When she hesitated, he lifted his arm to his sides, cruciform. "Got no guns, me. Esá goes bad, la dué la can shoot me."

"Can," Bertold agreed. His sidearm was drawn, but not pointed. Not yet.

"All right, then," Michio said, clomping forward in her boots, the magnets dragging her down against the floors, holding her, and letting her go again with every step.

In the little office, Sanjrani sat strapped onto a stool before a thin desk. Another waited across from him. She didn't see a trap. Didn't know what she was looking at. "Are you looking to change sides?" she asked.

Sanjrani made a deep, impatient cough. "I'm here to tell you why you're killing everyone in the fucking Belt. You and Marco both. You two should be on *my* side."

"Does he know you're here?"

"Am I dead already? No, he doesn't. That's how desperate I've gotten. I try to talk to Rosenfeld, but he's only talking to Marco. No one knows where Dawes got to. They won't *listen*." There was a desperation in his voice, high and thin as a bow against a string.

"All right," she said, moving to the stool, pulling the belt across her lap. "I'll listen."

Sanjrani relaxed and pulled up a diagram from the desk's display. A complex series of curves laid over x and y axes. "We made assumptions when we started this," he said. "We made plans. Good ones, I think. But we didn't follow them."

"Dui," Michio said.

"First thing we did," he said, "was destroy the biggest source of wealth and complex organics in the system. The only supply of complex organics that work with our metabolisms. The worlds on the other side of the ring? Different genetic codes. Different chemistries. *Not* something we can import and eat. But that was okay. Projections were clear. We could build a new economy, put together infrastructure, make a sustainable network of micro-ecologies in a cooperative-competitive matrix. Base the currencies on—"

"Nico," she said.

"Right. Right. We needed to start building it all as soon as the rocks fell."

"I know," she said.

"You don't," he said. Tears sheeted across his eyes, clung to his skin. "*No recycling process is perfect.* Everything degrades. The colony ships? The supplies? They're all stopgap. They're the measure of how long we have to make a living Belt. Look here. This green curve is the projected output of the new economic models. The ones we're not doing, yeah? And this"—he pointed to a descending red curve—"is the best case of how long the conscripted supplies will last. Equilibrium is here. Five years out."

"All right."

"And this line here, the base we would need between them to keep the present population of the Belt alive."

"We stay above it."

"We *would* have," Sanjrani said, "if we'd kept to the plan. Here's where we are now."

He shifted the green line. Michio felt her throat tighten as she understood what she was looking at.

"We're fine now," Sanjrani said. "We'll be fine for three years. Maybe three and a half. Then the recycling systems stop being able to meet demand. We won't have infrastructure in place to fill the gaps. And then we'll starve. Not just Earth. Not just Mars. The Belt too. And once we start, we'll have no way to stop."

"All right," Michio said. "How do we fix it?"

"I don't know," Sanjrani said.

The *Panshin* left a day later, taking Sanjrani and what little remained of Michio's peace of mind with it. Her crew did their part, building out the port, ringing the new wires. Messages seeped into the *Connaught*'s antennas, some of them for her. Iapetus needed more food-grade magnesium. A collection of prospecting ships had exhausted their filters and needed replacements. The

Free Navy poured out what they called news, some of it about how much Belter material she'd given over to the enemy.

Whenever she tried to sleep, the sense of dread welled up in her heart. When the hard times came, when the starving began, it would come like a ratchet. It was hard to make a new, shining city in the void when the people designing it, building it, living in it were dying from want. When they were dying because she and Marco were at each other's throats instead of following the plan.

She had to remind herself that she hadn't been the one to change things. Marco had gone off script before her. She'd made her break because he had. She was trying to help. Only when she closed her eyes, she saw the red line sloping down toward nothing, and no upward green swoop to answer it. Three years. Maybe three and a half. But to make it work, they had to start now. Had to have started already.

Or they had to make a very new plan, and neither she nor Sanjrani knew what that was.

The others avoided her, giving her food and water and space to think. She woke alone, worked her shift, slept alone, and didn't feel the loss of company. And so she was surprised when Laura came to find her in the gym.

"Message came for you, Captain," she said. Not Michi, but Captain. So Laura was not her wife then, but her comm officer on duty.

Michio let the tension bands slide back into their housings and wicked the sweat off her skin with a towel. "What is it?"

"Tightbeam relayed through Ceres," Laura said. "It's from the *Rocinante* en route to Tycho Station. It's flagged captain-to-captain."

Michio considered telling Laura to play it. That they were family, and didn't have any secrets. It was a dangerous impulse. She stifled it.

"I'll take it in my quarters," she said.

When she opened the message, James Holden looked out from the screen. Her first thought was that he looked like crap. Her second thought was that she probably did too. She tucked her sweat-damp towel into the recycler. *No recycling process is perfect.* She shuddered, but Holden had started talking.

"Captain Pa," he said. "I hope this gets to you quickly. And that everything's all right with your ship and your crew and... Well. Anyway. I'm in kind of a weird situation, and to be honest, I was hoping I could ask you for a favor."

He tried a smile, but his eyes looked haunted.

"I'll tell you the truth," he said. *"I'm kind of desperate here."*

Chapter Thirty-Two: Vandercaust

When the guards got bored kicking him, they rolled Vandercaust into the cell and sealed the door.

He lay in the dark for some stretch of time—five minutes, an hour. Not more than that. When he sat up, his ribs and back ached, but not with the deepness or grinding sensation that broken bones carried. The only light was a single recessed LED at the joint where the back wall and ceiling met. Its dimness stole the color from everything, so the little streaks of blood on his shirt only looked black.

With nothing better to do, he took a slow inventory of his body: bruised ribs and cheek, swollen eye, abrasions at his wrists where they'd cuffed him. Nothing bad, really. He'd suffered worse, and sometimes at the hands of his friends. Wasn't like this was the first time he'd been arrested. Not even the first time he'd been arrested for something he didn't do. It had always been inners that did it before, though.

The more it changes, the more it's still the same, he thought. He found a comfortable spot in the corner where he could rest his head, close his eyes, and see if the anxiety was enough to keep him awake. It was, mostly, but he did manage a little doze before the door broke seal and swung open. Two guards in armor and side-arms. A higher-up in armor too. All Free Navy colors.

Probably that was good. People didn't generally dress up for a murder.

"Emil Jacquard Vandercaust?"

"Aquí," he said.

The higher-up was a thick-faced boy with a brown complex-ion that matched his eyes. Handsome, in his way, but too young for Vandercaust's tastes. He'd come to an age when sex was less about who he fell into bed with and more about who he woke up next to, and the set of people he considered children extended to include men in their early thirties. The pretty child scowled, maybe at Vandercaust and maybe at how he'd been treated. For a moment, the silence in the room made him wonder if they'd leave again. Lock the door and stick him in the dark. The idea made him aware of his thirst.

"Agua, yeah?"

"Commst," the boy said. Vandercaust levered himself up to his feet, his abused muscles shrieking, but not badly enough to stop him. The guards fell in, one ahead and one behind, and the boy leading them all like a sad little parade. The room they took him to was brighter, more comfortable, though not by much. A low metal stool was welded to the deck, short enough that sitting on it made Vandercaust feel like he was in some school for children, expected to take a desk meant for a six-year-old. He'd been ques-tioned by security enough in his life to recognize the little humili-ation as the tactic it was. A guard brought him half a bulb of tepid water, watched him drink it, and took it back.

The guards stepped out, the door closing behind them. The boy stood at a desk, looking down at him through a floating display. Seeing the display from behind was like seeing someone through a bright mist.

Vandercaust waited. The boy took a flat yellow lozenge out of his pocket. Focus drugs, or what Vandercaust was supposed to assume were. The boy put the lozenge under his tongue, sucked thoughtfully for a moment. Shuddered.

"You missed the battle alert yesterday," he said.

"I did."

"Can you explain that?"

Vandercaust shrugged. "Deep sleeper when I'm drunk, me. Didn't hear it. No se savvy what happened before it was over, yeah?"

"Savvy tú now?"

"Heard some things, yeah."

"Let's go over what you heard, then."

Vandercaust nodded, as much to himself as to the boy. Time to pick his handholds careful. Whatever they were spun up over, this was the time he'd land in it if he spoke the wrong words.

"Was a bunch of ships came from the colonies, what I heard. Fourteen, fifteen ships all through rings at the same time. Fast too. Trying to get to Medina before the rail guns took them out, yeah? Only didn't so much. What the guns didn't put holes in, station defenses took out. Some debris hits on the drum hull, aber nothing can't be fixed."

The boy nodded, made some notation in the bright air between them. "Fourteen or fifteen?"

"Yeah."

The boy's eyes hardened. "Was it fourteen you heard, or fifteen?"

Vandercaust frowned. There was something about the boy's reaction that didn't sit right. If they'd been playing poker, he'd wait to see if the boy's hand was particularly strong or weak, then spend the rest of the night cleaning him out over that hardness. Only there weren't any cards to come down here.

"Heard fourteen or fifteen. A phrase. Eight or ten. Six or seven. Didn't hear a number."

"What rings did they come through?"

"Don't know."

"Look at me," the boy said. Vandercaust looked up into the boy's light-brown eyes. "What rings did they go through?"

"No savvy. I don't know."

The boy's eyes flickered, looked away. Vandercaust scratched his arm even though it didn't itch. Just to be doing something.

"They all came through within fifteen seconds of each other," the boy said. "And they *were* going fast. Any thoughts about that, Mister Vandercaust?"

"Coordinated," he said. "Sounds like they been talking con alles, sa sa? Making plans."

Which—ah, yes—meant they'd found some way to break light-speed, bend time, and locate each other in the vastness of the galaxy, or else that conversation had been passing through the rings. Through Medina. It meant somewhere on Medina Station, somebody had been working against the Free Navy. He'd known that the arrest couldn't just be for missing an emergency shift. Now it came a little clearer what the boy was looking for. Watched the boy watch him understand.

"Who told you about the attack?"

"Heard about it in my workgroup. Jakulski. Salis. Roberts. Just chap-chap over coffee, yeah?"

Another notation made. "Anything you think of I should know about them?"

A coldness that had nothing to do with the temperature ran up Vandercaust's back, lifted his skin in bumps. Maybe it wasn't only that he'd slept through the alarm. He'd been drunk. Drunk men could sleep through anything. But if he hadn't made the call *and* he was near to someone with something worth hiding …

Salis had friends in communication. Bragged about them all the time, how he knew what was going on with Duarte and Inaros, what kinds of barks and whines were floating through the rings.

Someone was coordinating an attack on Medina, wouldn't they be in communications? Have to be, ne? And Roberts talking about Callisto and proxy wars. How Duarte's people were maybe using them against Earth and Mars, about how much she hated being caught between the powers like that. She'd been the first one Vandercaust knew to squint hard at the advisors from Laconia setting up defenses on the alien station where rail gun housings were. Possible that she'd work with the colonies if it meant shrugging off Laconia and keeping Medina independent. And hadn't Jakulski been at the greeting when the advisors came? He said it had been as a favor to one of the other supervisors, but what if he'd been engineering a chance to put eyes on the enemy?

Thousands of people on Medina, living and working. All of them Belters, more or less. Most of them OPA before and Free Navy now. But there were some that hadn't known what was coming. Maybe some with family still on Earth, dying under the rockfalls. He didn't know anything about Jakulski's mother, Salis' siblings, Roberts' old lovers. Any of them could just be acting like Free Navy because it was asking for hell to be anything else.

The boy cocked his head, sucked at the focus drugs. Vandercaust laced his fingers together and forced out a little laugh. "Easy to see how a coyo could get paranoid."

"Why don't we go over this from the start?" the boy said.

It went on for hours, it felt like. No hand terminal. No screens that he could see. All Vandercaust had to judge by was the animal rhythms of his body. How long it was before he got thirsty again. Hungry. When he started feeling sleepy. When he needed to visit the head. He walked the boy through his whole night before the attack. Where he'd been. Who else had been there. What he'd drunk. How he'd gotten back to his quarters. Over and over, pushing at anything he said a little different from another time, pushing him to remember things he didn't really remember and then coming at him when he got some detail wrong. The boy asked about Roberts, Salis, Jakulski. He asked about who else Vandercaust knew on Medina. Who he knew on the Sol side of the

ring. What he knew about Michio Pa and Susanna Foyle and Ezio
Rodriguez. When he'd been at Tycho Station. At Ceres. At Rhea.
At Ganymede.

They showed him images of the attacks. The ships emerg-
ing through the gates all around the great sphere of gates. He
watched them die as tactical images. As telescopic records of real
people, really dying. Then they talked more, and showed it all to
him again. He had a sense that the readouts were subtly different the second time out—another attempt to catch him out on
something—but he couldn't say what the changes were.

It was exhausting. It was meant to be exhausting. After a while,
he stopped trying to keep his answers safe. He'd known enough
about interrogation to see that this—wearying and harsh and dull
though it was—was on the gentler end of that spectrum. He had
no reason to protect his friends beyond the vague tribalism of
being on a workgroup with them. If they were innocent, the truth
would have to be armor enough. For them, and for him too.

They took him back to his cell. No beating this time. Just a
hard shove through the door that left him sprawling and knocked
his cheek against the wall hard enough to split it. He slept for a
while, woke in darkness, slept again. The second time he woke,
there was a bowl of beans and mushrooms congealing beside the
door. He ate them anyway. No way to know how long he'd be
there. How long it would all go on. Whether it would get worse.

When the door opened again, five people in Free Navy uniforms came in. The brown-eyed boy wasn't among them, and for
a moment, that made Vandercaust very nervous. Like looking for
a friend and not finding them. The leader of the new group was
laughing with one of her subordinates, checked her hand terminal
by holding it up beside his face without paying much attention to
him, tapped her screen.

"You should go, pampaw," she said, walking out. "Late for
your shift, you."

They left the door open behind them, and after a moment,
Vandercaust walked out of the cell, out of the security station, into

the wide corridors of the drum. His body felt like a rag used for too long. He was certain that he smelled like sick primate and old sweat. The guard had been right. It was almost time for his shift, but he still went back to his hole, showered, shaved, changed into new clothes. He spent a few long minutes admiring the bruises on his face and sides. On a younger man, they could have been badges of endurance. On him, they just looked like an old man who'd caught the toes of a few too many boots. So he was late. He had reason to be. Little rebel, him.

He found Salis and Roberts deep in the service passageways, testing flow on the sewage intake for the backup recycling plant. Roberts' eyes lit up as he approached, and she threw her arms around him.

"Perdíd," she breathed against his ear. "Are you okay? We were *worried.*"

"Es dui?" Salis said, reaching across the table for the wasabi-flavored soy nuts. "They beat you up à nothing?"

The shift done, the three had retired to their usual bar. The breeze from spinward was as it always was. The thin line of sunlight stretched above them. Vandercaust pushed the bowl toward Salis' fingers. "Security is police, and police are the same everywhere."

"Still," Roberts said. "Why bother pushing off the inners if it's just to have a Belter foot stepping on our necks instead?"

"Wouldn't talk like that," Vandercaust said, then drank. Water tonight. Might be some time before he went for a long, solid drunk again. "Anxious times, these."

"Talk how I want to talk," Roberts said, but softly. She turned to her hand terminal. He could see the green and silver of the station feed, same colors it had been before the Free Navy took over. He wondered why they hadn't changed it. A way to give a sense of continuity, maybe. Anything on the feed would have been vetted, of course. The power of Medina Station was that it was so much not a part of any of the systems on the far sides of the gate. The price of it was that information came from a single source. Back in Sol system, there would be any number of feeds and subfeeds. Some broadcast, some left in storage to be queried and mirrored. Hard to control what got out. Maybe impossible. Medina, one set of jammers blocked every unlicensed receiver and transmitter at once.

The server came with his gyro—textured fungus and soybean curd instead of lamb and beef. Cucumber yogurt. A sprig of mint. He reached out for it with a little grunt and a sudden ache. It wasn't the worst beating he'd ever suffered, but he'd still be sore for days.

"Why they set you out?" Salis asked. "Sprecht el la?"

"No, they didn't say," Vandercaust replied. "Or that they wouldn't be back. Maybe they just needed someone to keep you two on schedule."

He'd missed two full shifts and come in during the middle of the third. Three days, almost, lost in the darkness of the security cell. No lawyer, no union representative. He could have asked for one—should have, by the rules and customs—but the certainty was solid as steel that it would have only meant more bruises. Maybe a broken bone. Vandercaust knew enough of history and human nature to know when the rules weren't the rules anymore. He took a bite of his sandwich, then put it down while he chewed. After this, he'd go home. Sleep in his own bed. Sounded like the promise of paradise. He traced fingertips over the split circle on his wrist. It had been a statement of rebellion once. Now, maybe it only made him seem old. Still taking sides in the last generation's fight.

"My friend in comms?" Salis said. "You know what they say? Found a hidden dump in the data core. Walled off. Think it was what they used to coordinate with the colonies. Confirmations came in from all the gates just before the attack hit. Only funny thing? Two ships didn't come through."

Salis cranked his eyebrows up toward his hairline.

Vandercaust grunted. "Were asking me about how many ships came through. Like they wanted a number."

"Probably why. See if you knew how many came through or how many were supposed to, yeah? Trip you up if you were in on."

"But didn't have nothing," Vandercaust said, tapping his forehead with two fingers. "Bon besse for me."

Salis put a hand on his arm. The young man looked pained. Aching, but not in the muscles and joints. Not the way he was. "You should let me buy you a drink, coyo. You had a shit week."

Vandercaust shrugged. He didn't know how to explain himself to Salis or Roberts. They were young. They hadn't seen the things he'd seen. Hadn't done the thing he'd done. Being picked up by security, locked away, beaten, interrogated. They didn't scare him in themselves. They scared him for what they said about how it came next. They scared him because they meant that Medina Station wasn't a new beginning in history. It was and would be as red in the gutter as everyplace else humanity had set its flags.

Roberts sat up, her eyes going wide. "They got!"

Salis let his hand drop, turned to her. "Que?"

"The mole? The coordinator. They got."

She turned her hand terminal toward them. On it, station security in Free Navy uniforms were walking, eight of them, around a broad-shouldered, squat man with dark hair and a scruff of beard. Vandercaust thought he looked familiar, but couldn't place him. The image jumped to Captain Samuels, with Jon Amash standing behind her on one side. Political power and security service, one beside the other, and no light between them.

Samuels' lips began to move.

"Turn it up," Salis said. Roberts fumbled with her terminal, then shifted around between them so they could all see the screen.

"—ties not only to the settlements that chose aggression against us but also with regressive forces back in Sol system. He will be questioned fully before execution. While we have to keep eyes open and alert, I am convinced, given all I have seen, that the immediate threat to Medina Station is under control."

"Execution," Roberts said.

Salis shrugged. "You put the ship at risk, that's what happens. Those colony bastards weren't coming to play dice and make happy."

"Least it's over," Vandercaust said.

"Is why they let you go," Roberts said, shaking her hand terminal. "Found him. Saw you weren't involved."

Or picked someone to play the goat, Vandercaust thought. *Only I got lucky enough it wasn't me.* It wasn't the sort of thing you said out loud. Not at times like these.

Chapter Thirty-Three: Holden

The room they were using as an anteroom was larger than the *Rocinante*'s galley. Wide tables with built-in monitors and tall metal stools. Soft, indirect lighting in a manipulated spectrum that reminded Holden of early mornings in his childhood. He didn't have a rank or a uniform, but the ship jumpsuit had seemed wrong for the occasion. He'd decided on a dark, collarless shirt and pants that echoed the sense of a military uniform without making any specific claims.

Naomi, pacing now along the wall by the yellow double doors, had matched him, but he had the creeping sense that they looked better on her. So of the three of them, only Bobbie was in uniform, and hers had the insignia left off. The cut and the fitting all screamed Martian Marine Corps. And the people they were going to meet with—the ones gathering right now down the hall—knew who she was anyway.

"You keep pulling at that sleeve," Bobbie said. "It bothering you?"

"It? No, *it's* fine," Holden said. "I'm bothering me. Do you know how many times I've done this kind of diplomatic work? I've been in battles and I've put together video feeds, but to walk in, look down the table at a bunch of OPA operatives, and tell them how they all need to listen to me? I've done that exactly no times. Never."

"Ilus," Naomi said.

"You mean when that one guy killed the other guy in the street and then burned a bunch of people alive?"

Naomi sighed. "Yeah. Then."

Bobbie flexed her hands, put them palm down on the table display. The monitor glowed for a moment, waiting for a command, then dimmed again when nothing came. Muffled voices came through the doorway. A woman with a Belter's accent asking something about chairs. A man replying, his voice too low to make out. "I've been in rooms like this before," Bobbie said. "Political work. A lot of different agendas and no one saying out loud what they were actually thinking."

"Yeah?" Holden said.

"It sucked."

The *Rocinante* had decelerated toward Tycho harder than they'd planned, burning off the speed they'd poured on during the battle and pressing them all down a little more than usual, like an illness or a regret. Holden held a little ceremony in the galley where each of them shared some memory of Fred Johnson and they let their various griefs blur together. The only ones not to speak were Amos, smiling his amiable and meaningless smile, and Clarissa, her brow furrowed in concentration like it was all a puzzle she was trying to solve.

When they broke up, Holden noticed that Alex and Sandra Ip went off together, but he didn't have time or enough moral high ground to worry about fraternization. Every hour that passed had taken them a few thousand klicks closer to Tycho and the meeting there. All of his spare time was in his cabin with the door closed trading messages across the emptiness of the system. Michio Pa. Drummer on Tycho. A man named Damian Short, who'd taken the reins on Ceres. But mostly Chrisjen Avasarala.

Every long, heavy day, he traded messages with Luna. Long lectures from Avasarala on how to conduct a meeting, how to present himself and his arguments. More importantly, how to listen to what the others said and didn't say. She sent him dossiers on all the major OPA players who would be there: Aimee Ostman, Micah al-Dujaili, Liang Goodfortune, Carlos Walker. Everything Avasarala knew about them—who their families were, what their factions within the OPA had done and what she only suspected they'd done. The depth of background was overwhelming, group loyalties intersecting and drawing apart, personal insults affecting political agreements, and political agreements shaping relationships. And along with it, Avasarala pouring the distilled insights of a lifetime of political life into his ears until he was drunk with it to the edge of nausea.

Strength by itself is just bullying, capitulation by itself is an invitation to get fucked; only mixed strategies survive. Everything is personal, but they know that too. They can smell pandering like a fart. If you treat them like they're a treasure box where if you just tweak them the right way, the policy you want falls out, you're already fucked. They'll misjudge you, so be ready to use that.

By the time he walked into the meeting room on Tycho, he intended to have a little, simplified version of Avasarala that lived in the back of his mind. It felt like doing a decade of work in a few days because it sort of was. He got to where he couldn't sleep and he couldn't stay awake. When they finally reached Tycho Station, it was hard to say whether the dread was more powerful or the relief.

Walking the habitation ring of Tycho the first time after their return had been eerie. Everything was perfectly familiar—the pale foam of the walls, the slightly astringent smell in the air, the sound of bhangra music leaking from some distant workroom—but it all meant something different now. Tycho was Fred Johnson's house, only now it wasn't. Holden kept having the nagging sense that someone was missing, and then remembering who it was.

Drummer had done her mourning in private. When she escorted them in, she was the head of security that she'd been before: sharp and aware and businesslike. She'd met them at the docks with a convoy of carts, each one with a pair of armed guards. That didn't make Holden feel better.

"So who's in charge here now?" he'd asked as they paused at the bulkhead that marked the administrative section.

"Technically, Bredon Tycho and the board of directors," she said. "Except they're mostly on Earth or Luna. Never been out here. Always pleased to keep their hands clean. We're here, so until someone comes and makes a strong opposing case, we run it."

"We?"

Drummer nodded. Her eyes got a little harder, and he couldn't say if it was grief in them or anger. "Johnson wanted me to keep an eye on the place until he got back. That's what I plan to do."

There were supposed to be four people waiting for him.

There were five.

He recognized all the faces that Avasarala had prepared him for. Carlos Walker, wide shoulders and face, even shorter than Clarissa, had an uncanny air of stillness. Aimee Ostman could have passed for a middle-grade science teacher, but was responsible for more attacks against inner-planet military targets than all the rest combined. Liang Goodfortune, who Fred had only managed to lure to the table by offering amnesty for their daughter, a former OPA hitter still housed in a numbers-only prison on Luna. Micah al-Dujaili, with his fat, red-veined drunkard's nose, who'd spent half his lifetime coordinating free schools and medical clinics throughout the Belt. Whose brother had been captain of the *Witch of Endor* when the Free Navy destroyed it.

The fifth person had the white hair of an old man, pocked cheeks, and a deferential smile that was almost an apology, but not quite. Holden recognized him, but wasn't sure from where. He tried to keep his poker face, but the fifth man saw through the effort without seeming to realize it was there.

"Anderson Dawes," the man said. "I don't think we've ever met person to person, but Fred talked about you often. And, of course, your reputation."

Holden shook hands with the former governor of Ceres Station and master of Marco Inaros' inner circle, his mind racing. "I was wondering if you'd be here," he lied.

"I hadn't announced myself," Dawes said. "Tycho's a risky place for a man in my position. I was relying on Fred to vouch for me. We worked together for many years. I was sorry to hear about him."

"It's a loss," Holden said. "Fred was a good man. I'll miss him."

"As will we all," Dawes said. "I hope you don't mind my arriving unannounced. Aimee reached out to me when she knew she was coming, and I asked her to let me follow along."

Good, great, the more the merrier, Holden thought, but the little version of Avasarala in his imagination frowned. "I'm glad you're here, but you can't be in this meeting."

"I can vouch for him," Aimee Ostman said.

Holden nodded, tried to imagine what Avasarala would say, but it was the old, almost-forgotten voice of Miller that came to him. "There's a way we do things. This isn't it. I hope you don't mind waiting outside, Mr. Dawes. Naomi, could you see that our friend here finds someplace comfortable?"

Naomi stepped forward. Dawes shifted his weight to the back of his feet, surprised. *This is your house*, Avasarala said in Holden's mind. *If they don't respect you here, they won't respect you anywhere.* Dawes gathered up his hand terminal and a white ceramic cup, nodding to Holden with a tight smile as he left. Holden took his seat, grateful for the solid and looming presence of Bobbie at his side. Aimee Ostman's lips were pressed thin. *If you're looking for mutual respect, you can start by asking before you invite people to my secret meetings.* It seemed like a rude thing to say out loud.

"If you're looking for mutual respect, you can start by asking before you invite people to my secret meetings."

Aimee Ostman cleared her throat and looked away.

"All right," Holden said. "This was supposed to be Fred Johnson's presentation, but he's gone. I know you all came here on the strength of his word and his reputation. And I know you're all concerned about Marco Inaros and the Free Navy. But I also know this is the first time any of you have met me, and I may not have your full confidence."

"You're James Holden," Liang Goodfortune said in a tone that meant *Of course you don't have our full confidence.*

"I took the liberty of arranging an introduction," he said, shifting the message from his hand terminal to the monitors on the table.

Michio Pa looked out at each of them. The command deck of the *Connaught* glowed behind her. "Friends," she said. "As you know, I was not long ago in the inner circle of the Free Navy, and what I saw there convinced me and many of those in my command that Marco Inaros is not the leader that the Belt needs. As the Free Navy has abandoned its original purpose of supporting and rebuilding the Belt and keeping the industry that feeds Belters from shifting out to the new colony worlds, I have stayed true. You all know this. I have lost friends to this effort. I have risked my life and the lives of those I care most deeply for. I serve with the true heroes of the Belt. My credentials are beyond reproach."

Bobbie nudged him and nodded toward Micah al-Dujaili. Tears were shining in the man's eyes. Holden nodded. He saw it too.

"Since my parting of ways with the Free Navy, I have been working with Fred Johnson toward a comprehensive plan that will guarantee the safety and well-being of the Belt." Pa paused, took a deep breath. Holden wondered whether she did that every time she lied, or just when it was a whopper. "This meeting was intended to be an introduction of that plan and of Captain Holden as integral to it. Unfortunately, while Fred Johnson was able to see the path forward, he isn't able to make that journey with us. As a dedicated citizen of the Belt and a servant of our people, I'm asking you to hear Captain Holden out and then to join with us for a living future. Thank you."

Everything about her statement had been negotiated. He'd lost track of the number of times they'd traded back and forth, Pa asking for something, Avasarala explaining what it really meant, him running between the two of them like a messenger, but learning a little more with every pass. Pa would agree to say they'd been working toward a plan, but not that they'd been working on a plan. She would say that Holden was integral to it, but not that he was central. The whole process had been everything he hated—niggling on details and nuances, fighting over turns of phrase and the order information was presented in, fashioning something that, even where it wasn't outright false, was tailored to be misunderstood. Politics at its most political.

He looked at the four faces sitting around the table and tried to judge whether it had worked. Aimee Ostman looked thoughtful and sour. Micah al-Dujaili was still composing himself, moved by the reminder that his brother had already sacrificed himself in the cause. Carlos Walker, still and silent and unreadable as language in an unknown alphabet. Liang Goodfortune cleared their throat.

"Looks like Inaros has a habit of losing women to you, Captain," Goodfortune said. Walker chuckled. *They'll try embarrassing you a little to see how you react. Don't try to one-up them, or they'll try to escalate out of conflicts later. Stay on point.* Naomi stepped back in, came to sit at his side.

"Losing Fred is hard because it's sad," Holden said. "He was a friend. But it doesn't change the situation. He formed a plan, and my intention is to follow it. Fred called on each of you because he felt you had something to offer this and also something to gain by it."

Carlos Walker's eyes shifted, as if he'd heard something interesting for the first time. Holden nodded to him, an intentionally
ambiguous gesture. Then he turned to Bobbie. Her turn to take
the floor.

"There will be a military aspect to this," she said. "We're not
getting through any of this without some risk, but we're confident
that it is more than outweighed by the rewards."

"You say that as a representative of Mars?" Aimee Ostman
asked.

"Sergeant Draper has worked as a liaison between Earth and
Mars on several occasions," Holden said. "She's here today as a
member of my crew."

That was odd. Bobbie seemed to grow tenser at the words,
gather herself, sit up straighter. When she spoke again, her tone
was almost exactly the same as it had been before—no louder, no
rougher—but something about it had grown fierce. "I have experience in combat. I've led teams in battle. It is my professional
opinion that the proposal Fred Johnson put together is the best
hope for the long-term stability and safety of the Belt."

"Find that hard to believe," Aimee Ostman said. "Looks to me
like the captain here's been getting all the women and Inaros has
been taking all the stations."

Before Holden could answer, Micah al-Dujaili snapped back.
"Looks to me like Inaros is as bad at keeping territory as he is at
keeping women."

"Stop it with the 'women' bullshit," Carlos Walker said. His
voice was surprising. Reedy and musical. A singer's voice. The
accents of Belter cant were almost absent from it. "It's juvenile.
He lost Dawes too. He lost everyone in this room before he even
began, or none of us would be here. Inaros has an open sore where
his heart should be, and we all know it. What I want to hear is
how you intend to change the dynamic. Every time you move
toward him, he's pulled you into overreach. Your consolidated
fleet is going to be stretched too thin soon. Is that what you want
us for? Cannon fodder?"

"I'm not ready to discuss the details," Holden said. "There are security issues we all have to address first."

"Why did you bring us here if it wasn't to tell us what you intended?" Aimee Ostman said.

Liang Goodfortune ignored her. "Medina. You're going for Medina."

Something will go wrong. Something always does. They'll see something you didn't mean them to see; they'll have a trap set you didn't know to expect. These are intelligent people, and all of them have their own agendas. When it happens—not if, when—the worst thing you can do is panic. The second worst thing you can do is engage. Holden leaned forward.

"I'd like to give all of you the opportunity to consult about this before we talk about any of the tactical options," Holden said. "I've spoken to the security chief. You are all welcome to stay here on the station or else return to your ships. Feel free to talk among yourselves or with anyone you think might be useful. You can have access to the station comms unmonitored, or if you'd rather use the systems on your own ships, you won't be recorded or jammed. If you are interested in being involved with this, we'll reconvene here in twenty hours. I'll be ready to go through all the details then, but I will expect your loyalty and commitment in return. If you aren't comfortable with that, you have safe passage away from Tycho anytime within that window."

"And after that?" Carlos Walker asked.

"After that's a different country," Holden said. "We'll be doing things differently there."

Holden, Naomi, and Bobbie all stood. The other four rose a moment later. Holden watched how each of them said their good-byes or else didn't. When the doors closed behind the four emissaries, leaving him alone with Naomi and Bobbie, he slumped down in his chair.

"God *damn*," he said. "How does she do this all day, every day? That was maybe twenty minutes start to finish, and I already feel like I should dip my brain in bleach."

"Told you it sucked," Bobbie said, leaning against the table. "Are you sure it's a good idea giving them free rein of the station? We don't know who they're talking to."

"We couldn't stop them," Naomi said. "This way it looks like a gesture on our part."

"So theater and palace intrigue," Bobbie said.

"Just for now," Holden said. "Just until they buy in. Once they commit, we can get down to our plan."

"Johnson's plan," Bobbie said. Then a moment later, "So, just between us. Did Fred Johnson really have a plan?"

"I'm pretty sure he did," Holden said, sagging into himself. "Don't know what it was."

"So this one we're selling?"

"I'm kind of making it up."

Chapter Thirty-Four: Dawes

There was no viewing of the body. Fred Johnson—the Butcher of Anderson Station—had requested that his body be recycled into the system of Tycho Station. Water that had been his blood was likely already coming through the taps and faucets throughout the station. His chalk bones would reenter the food cycle in the hydroponics pools. The more complex lipids and proteins would take longer to become humus for the mushroom farms. Fred Johnson, like all the dead before him, fell to his component parts, scattered, and entered the world again, changed and unrecognized.

Instead, there were printed images of him on the chapel wall. A portrait of the man as a colonel in the service of Earth. A picture of him as an older man, still strong in his features but with a weariness creeping in at his eyes. Another of a ridiculously young boy—not more than ten years old—holding a book in one hand and waving with the other, his face split by a massive and child-like grin. They were the right ears, the right spacing of the eyes, but Dawes still had to work to believe that happy child had grown into the complex man he'd known and called friend and betrayed.

The memorial was in a small chapel so aggressively nondenominational that it was hard to tell the difference between it and a waiting room. Instead of religious icons, there were sober, abstract shapes. A circle in gold, a square in forest green. Intentionally empty symbols meant as placeholders for where something with significance might have been. The Tycho Manufacturing logo in the hallway outside held more meaning.

The pews were bamboo textured to look like some sort of wood—ash or oak or pine. Dawes had only ever seen pictures of live trees. He wouldn't have known one from another, but it gave the little room some sense of gravitas. Still he didn't sit. He walked past the pictures of Fred Johnson, looking into the eyes that didn't look back. The thing in his chest, the one making it hard to breathe, felt thick and complicated.

"I had a speech ready," he said. His voice echoed a little, the emptiness giving it depth. "Well practiced. You'd have liked it. All about the nature of politics and the finest of humanity being our ability to change to match our environment. We are how the universe consciously remakes itself. The inevitability of failure and the glory of standing back up after it." He coughed out a chuckle. It sounded like a sob. "What I really meant was I'm sorry. Not just sorry I backed the wrong horse. Am sorry about that. But I'm sorry I compromised you while I did it."

He paused as if Fred might answer, then shook his head.

"I think the speech would have worked. You and I have so much history behind us. Seems strange. I was a mentor to you once. Well. Feet of clay. You know how it is. Still, I really think you'd have seen the value in having me back. But this Holden prick?" Dawes shook his head. "You picked a shit time to die, my friend."

The doors opened behind him. A young woman in an oil-stained Tycho Station jumpsuit and a deep-green hijab stepped in, nodded to him, and took a place in the pew, her head bowed. Dawes stepped back from the pictures of the dead man. There was more he wanted to say. Apparently there always would be.

He took a seat across the aisle from the woman, folded his hands in his lap, lowered his head. There was a profound mundanity in shared grief. A set of rules as strong as any human etiquette, and they didn't allow for him to keep up his one-sided conversation. Not aloud, anyway.

The Free Navy could have been—ought to have been—a glorious moment for the Belt. Inaros had conjured up a full military for them out of nothing. Dawes had told himself at the time that Inaros' failings as a political animal weren't a problem. Were an opportunity, even. As a member of the Free Navy's inner circle, Dawes could exert his influence. Be kingmaker. The cost was high, yes, but the rewards were nothing short of visionary. An independent Belt, cut free of the inner planets. The threat of the gate network under their control. Yes, Inaros was a peacock who made his way through life on charisma and violence. Yes, Rosenfeld had always had a whiff of brimstone about him. But Sanjrani was smart, and Pa was capable and dedicated. And if he'd said no, it would all have gone ahead without him anyway.

It was what he'd told himself. How he'd justified it all. The best would have been that someone besides Inaros had acquired the ships. The second best was that Inaros' circle of advisors and handlers include him. So what was third?

After the abandonment of Ceres, Dawes had gone on playing the role of elder statesman for a while, even as Pa's rebellion made it impossible to pretend things were on track. When Aimee Ostman had found him, told him that Fred Johnson was putting together a meeting on Tycho, it had looked like an opportunity to broker peace. If not between Earth and the Free Navy, at least with the remains of the OPA. It had been the perfect way to leverage his relationship with Fred into a place at the table.

Another woman came in, sitting beside the one in the hijab. They exchanged soft words. Two men came in together, sat in the back. Change of shift was coming. Mourners would be stopping in on their way to work, or on their way back from it. Dawes felt a twinge of resentment that they should interrupt his time alone in the chapel. It was irrational and he knew it.

And anyway, Fred Johnson had made his wishes clear, even if he hadn't meant to. And Dawes still owed the colonel something.

"Is fucking bullshit is what it is," Aimee Ostman said. "James pinché Holden can fuck himself."

Dawes sipped his espresso and nodded. Holden's first move had been to humiliate her. For reasons Dawes understood. But still, for her to begin by losing face was hard.

"Forgive him for it," Dawes said. "I have. You should too."

"For for?"

Aimee Ostman scowled and scratched her chin. Her quarters in the station were wide and luxurious. One wall was taken entirely by a screen tied to an exterior camera, the resolution so fine it was indistinguishable from a window into space. The divan was spotless cream, the air scented with volatile molecules that mimicked sandalwood and vanilla. Dawes gestured at it all with his demitasse.

"Look at this," he said. "Room for an ambassador. For a president."

"And?"

"And he gave it to you," Dawes said and took another sip. "Thought it was doing you honor. Best suite in the station."

"He spat in your face," Aimee Ostman said, pointing index and middle finger at him together like the barrel of a gun. "Kicked you out."

Dawes laughed, shrugged. Invited her to laugh and shrug with him. It bit at his soul, but it was the thing to do. "I showed up unannounced. It was rude of me. Holden was in the right. How would you have been if I'd brought him to the back room at the Apex without telling you first?"

She scowled, her eyes tracking low and to the left. "Should have been more polite about it."

"Maybe. But he's new at this part."

She sat across from him, folded her arms. The clouds in her eyes weren't gone. He wouldn't have expected them to be. But they weren't thick with thunderbolts either. "Maybe," she said. Grudgingly. "But I'm not staying. Not after that."

"You should reconsider," Dawes said. "If the plan came from Fred Johnson, it will be solid. And better that you be part of it than not."

She grunted, but there was a hint of a smile at the corner of her mouth. That one found home. Dawes leaned into it a little, pressing his advantage.

"There has to be a grown-up in that room," he said. "Holden's a puppy. We both know that. We need you there to keep him from fucking everything up."

"Holden's the most experienced man in the system," Dawes said. "He's been on Medina. He's been past it to the colonies. He walked off Eros Station before it woke up. He fought pirates for us. He went on diplomatic missions for us. His ship has berthed at Tycho Station more than anyplace else since the day he stole it from Mars. Holden has *years* working with the OPA."

"There's OPA," Liang Goodfortune said, turning left down the corridor so that Dawes had to trot to keep up with them, "and there's OPA."

Tycho Station didn't have the same breadth and depth as Ceres. Everyone here had a job or access to one. The brothels were all licensed, the drugs all from a dispensary, the gambling all taxed. But the station was also a home to people who'd lived their lives in quiet rebellion against the inner planets, and that meant a kind

of demimonde had existed there too. Workers for an Earth corporation whose first loyalty was to the Belt. And so there were
clubs where the music had lyrics shouted in Belter cant, where
the drinks and food called back nothing to a farmland under the
bare sun, where the games were shastash and Golgo instead of
poker and billiards. Liang Goodfortune fit in there like they'd
never left.

"So it was Johnson's OPA," Dawes said. "He was a good ally."

"He was useful for an Earther," Liang Goodfortune said.
"That's not saying much. And Holden's just the same. Another
Earther for us to rally around? You know better than that, Ander-
son. Holden's worked for Johnson and Earth."

"On behalf of the Belt," Dawes said. "UN Navy kicked him
to the curb before any of this began. His career was with a water
hauler *because* he couldn't stomach being part of imperial Earth.
Coyo can't change where he was born, where he grew up, but he's
lived on float. His lover's one of ours."

"Savvy you he's loyal to the Belt because he's sleeping with
Naomi Nagata? Or you think maybe she's *dis*loyal à the Belt
because she's with a squat? That knife cuts from the grip."

"Holden has been making a one-man propaganda campaign on
behalf of the Belt," Dawes said, raising his voice over the ambient
musical shout of the nightclub.

"His amateur anthropology feed? It's insulting y patronizing y
shit," Liang Goodfortune said.

"It's well meant. And it's more than other people in his position
have done. Holden's a man of action."

They came into the larger room, lights swirling around the bar,
music thudding hard enough to press his lungs. Dawes had to lean
in until his lips were almost brushing Goodfortune's ear. "I think
if there's anyone in the system better prepared to stand against
Inaros, you can't find them and neither can I. Either you make
cause with him, or you go hat in hand to the Free Navy and say
you're ready to take their table scraps. But do it soon, because I will

wager everything I have that even if he has to go to war by himself, James Holden will *destroy* Marco Inaros before this is done."

"He can't do it alone," Dawes said, spreading his hands wide.

The *Desiderata of Bhagavathi* had been Carlos Walker's ship for thirty years, and it bore the stamp of his peculiar aesthetic sense in every detail. The anti-spalling covers on the walls were gray, but textured to catch the light in smooth curves that rose and fell like the hills of a vast desert or the not-quite-identifiable skin of nude bodies. The crash couches on the command deck weren't simple, utilitarian gray but a sculpted bronze that had nothing to do with the actual metal and ceramic that made them up. Music played on the speakers so softly it might almost have been Dawes' imagination: harp and flute and a dry, hissing drum. It felt less like a pirate ship than a temple. Maybe there was room for both.

"That isn't an argument that I should do it with him," Carlos Walker said, handing over a drinking bulb. The whiskey that flooded Dawes' mouth when he sipped was rich and deep and complicated. Carlos Walker smiled, watching him appreciate it. "I came out of respect for Johnson. I am staying out of respect. That respect doesn't extend to dying on Holden's errands. You say yourself that Medina is too well defended."

"I say it's well defended," Dawes said.

"The rail guns will kill any ship that comes through the ring."

"Perhaps," Dawes said. "But keep in mind, this is Fred Johnson's plan. And that Fred had access to Michio Pa and all that she knows about the station defense."

Carlos Walker hesitated, though with him it expressed itself only as a slightly longer silence. He shook his head. "There's risk in leaving Marco Inaros and his Free Navy to play themselves out. There's danger in taking them on. But only one requires that I drive my ship into rail gun fire. I can't agree to it."

"Not every battle is won on the battleground," Dawes said. "I respect your caution, but Holden hasn't asked you to be vanguard.

Hasn't even asked you to go through the ring gate. Don't assume he's going to demand heroism and sacrifice. I know his reputation, but no one survives the things he's survived without having a deep capacity for thoughtfulness and foresight. And more than that, strategy. Holden comes across feckless sometimes, truth, but he's a thinker. What he's doing? It's all from the head."

"You think he's not angry?" Dawes said. "Holden is here as much for vengeance as you are. This is a man who acts from the gut, from the heart, before his head gets in the way."

They were alone in the chapel, except for the images of Fred Johnson. It felt wrong to bring talk of violence and revenge into even as milquetoast a holy place as this, but grief came in all kinds of clothing. And this had begun as a moment to show respect for the dead. Micah al-Dujaili hunched forward, his arms resting on the back of the pew in front of him. His eyes were bloodshot.

"Carl talked to me," he said. "Said he couldn't stand by while the Belt starved. And Inaros killed him for it."

"Tried to kill Holden's wife too," Dawes said. He knew that wasn't quite true, but this was a moment for broad strokes. "Not because she was a threat. Not because she was of any sort of strategic value. Just because she'd embarrassed him, and he could."

"Inaros isn't who we thought he was. Everyone, they still call him a hero. They look at Earth and they look at Mars, and they cheer. They still cheer."

"*Some* still do," Dawes said. It was true. All through the system, Inaros had as many that loved him as had turned away. More, maybe. "It's not him, though. It's the idea of him. The man who stood up for the Belt. Only that man hasn't risen up yet. They only think he has."

"Will this Holden hurt him?"

"Every time Holden takes a breath, Marco Inaros suffers," Dawes said. And that was probably as close to truth as anything he'd said in the last two days.

Micah nodded slowly, then stood, wavering drunkenly, and threw his arms around Dawes. The embrace went on longer than Dawes felt comfortable with. Just as he began to wonder if the other man was starting to black out, Micah stepped back, gave a sharp OPA salute, and walked out of the chapel, wiping his eye against the inside of his wrist. Dawes sat back down.

It was midshift, and almost midnight for him. The three Fred Johnsons still graced the front wall. The child, the adult, and the man who, all unknowingly, was at the end of his struggles. Fred Johnson as he had been. The way Dawes remembered him best was tied up and spitting angry the first time they'd met, and the flicker of disappointment in the man's eye when he realized Dawes wasn't going to kill him.

They'd fought a hell of a fight together, against each other and side by side. And then against each other again. The clash of empires, only he wasn't sure what the empires were any longer. Everything they'd done had brought them here, one dead, the other living a life he barely recognized or understood.

Humanity hadn't changed, but it had. The venality and the nobility, the cruelty and the grace. They were all still there. It was just the particulars he felt shifting away from under him. Everything he'd fought for seemed to belong to a different man in a different time. Well. It was in the nature of torches to be passed. Nothing to be sad about in that. Except that he was sad.

"Well, there you have it," he said to the empty air. "The king-maker's last hurrah. I hope to hell you knew what you were doing. I hope James Holden is what you thought he could be."

It was almost an hour later that the door opened and a young man came in. Tight dark curls, wide-set warm eyes, a thin apologetic mustache. Dawes nodded to him, and the man nodded back. For a moment, they were both silent.

"Perdón," the man said. "Not rushing, me. It's only I'm supposed to take this one down now. It's...it's on the schedule."

Dawes nodded and waved him forward. The man moved hesitantly at first, then reached a point of commitment where the work was just the work. The corporal came down first, then the head of the OPA. The young boy with the book and the grin stayed until last.

There had been a moment when that child had waved into a camera, decades ago, not knowing the gesture was also his last. The boy and the Butcher were both gone now. The man took the picture down, rolled it together with the others, and slid them all into a sleeve of cheap green plastic.

He stopped on his way out. "You all right, you? Need something?"

"Fine," Dawes said. "I'm just going to stay here a little longer. If that's all right."

Chapter Thirty-Five: Amos

Sex was one of those things where the way it was supposed to work and the way it worked for him didn't always match up real well. He knew all the stuff about love and affection, and that just seemed like making shit up. He understood making shit up. He also understood how people talked about it, and he could talk about it that way, just to fit in.

In practice, he recognized there was power in being with another living body, and he respected it. The pressure built up over the weeks or months on the burn kind of like hunger or thirst, only slower and it wouldn't kill you if you ignored it. He didn't fight against it. For one thing, that was stupid. For another it didn't help. He just noticed it, kept an eye on it. Acknowledged it was there the same way he would anything powerful and dangerous that was sharing his workspace.

When they got into port someplace big enough to have a

licensed brothel, he'd go there. Not because it was safe so much as it was an environment where he knew what all the dangers looked like. Could recognize them and not be surprised. Then he'd take care of what needed to be taken care of, and afterward, it wouldn't bother him for a while.

Maybe that was different from everyone else, but it worked for him.

The thing was, he'd usually be able to sleep afterward. Really sleep. Deep and dreamless and hard to pull up out of until he was done. And right now, he was mostly just looking at the ceiling. The last girl—the one called Maddie—was curled up next to him, the sheets draped around her legs, her arm under one pillow, snoring a little. One of the good things about getting a room for the whole night is they'd give you a quiet one away from the front. Maddie was someone he'd used and been used by before when the *Roci*'d been on Tycho, and he liked her as much as he liked anyone that wasn't in his tribe. That she felt safe sleeping next to him warmed something in his stomach that usually stayed cold.

She had a little gap between her front teeth and skin as pale as anyone he'd ever met. She could blush on command, which was a pretty good trick, and she'd been in the life since she was a kid. Before she'd come to Tycho for the legal trade. His own childhood in the illegal trade meant they had context that made the talk before and after more comfortable for him, and she knew he wouldn't pull any of that "you're better than this" soul-saving bullshit. He also wouldn't start calling her a bitch and being abusive out of shame the way some johns did. He liked shooting the shit with her afterward, and usually the way she snored just a little didn't keep him from drifting off.

Only that wasn't what was keeping him awake. He knew what was keeping him awake.

He got out of bed quietly so as not to wake her up. He'd paid her and rented the room for the whole night, and the house wasn't about to give him a refund for leaving early, so she might as well get the rest herself. He gathered up his clothes and slipped out into the hallway to get dressed. A john on his way out passed by as he was pulling on his jumpsuit, made brief and awkward eye contact, nodded curtly. Amos smiled his amiable smile and made room for the guy to go past before he zipped himself in and headed out toward the docks.

The *Roci* had spent more time in Tycho than any other port, usually getting put back together after the last whatever went wrong. It wasn't home—nowhere outside the *Roci* was home— but it was familiar enough that he could feel the differences. It was in the way people talked to each other in the hallways. The kinds of images that played on the newsfeeds. He'd seen what it was like for a place to change in ways that didn't change back. Earth was like that. Now Tycho. Kind of like a big, slow wave coming out from where the rocks had hit Earth and spreading through every-place humans were.

There were people on Tycho who recognized him too. Not like they knew Holden. Holden, he couldn't walk through a room anymore without people staring at him and pointing and making a fuss. Amos had the sense that was going to be a problem even-tually, but it wasn't one he knew how to fix. He wasn't even sure what it implied at this point.

Back at the ship, he headed down to the machine shop and his workstation. The *Roci* told him that Holden was in the galley with Babs, Naomi was catching some bunk time, and Peaches was at work replacing the hatch seals they'd been talking about. He made a note on his work schedule to double-check them when she was done, even though he knew they'd be fine. Peaches turned out to be a pretty good worker. Smart, focused, seemed to really enjoy fixing things, and never bitched about the stresses of shipboard life. Perspective, he figured. Shittiest ship there was still had to be better than the best cell in the pit, if only because you got to pick that you were in it.

He shrugged into his couch, pulled up the technical reports, and spooled through the way he had before. Not that he expected to find anything different. Just to see if there was any reaction when he got to the weird bit. He got to it and looked at the data for a while. The torpedoes Bobbie had fired off. Their trajectories. The error logs. And he had the same reaction. It was bugging him.

He shut the workstation down.

"Hey," Peaches said, coming up from engineering with an ARL polymer tank slung over one shoulder.

"Hey," he said. "How's it going?"

She was still too skinny. The smallest standard jumpsuit still left her swimming in it. They'd had to adjust the code to convince the *Roci* that anyone flying on her could be so slight. Working made her look healthier, though.

She thumbed open a storage locker, slid the tank into place, and dropped into her couch. "I got the seals replaced, but I don't like the inner airlock door in the cargo bay. It's not throwing errors, but the power's dirty."

"Dirty dirty? Or inside the error bars but it pisses you off dirty?"

"Second one," Peaches said, and then grinned. But her grin faded fast. "You all right?"

He smiled. "Why do you ask?"

"Because you're not all right," she said.

Amos leaned back, shifted to crack his neck. Part of him wanted to talk to her about the torpedoes, but he couldn't picture Holden doing it. And this was kind of a Holden thing, so he only shrugged. "Need to talk to the captain about something."

"Then we're back to the 'throw ships at them until they run out of ammunition' plan," Bobbie said. Her voice was clear and sharp. Someone who didn't know her might have thought she was pissed, but Amos was pretty sure that was her having a good time. He hesitated in the corridor outside the galley. Truth was, even if they decided to go after Medina like they were stomping snakes to death, they'd be in port for a couple more days. There'd be time to ask the question later that didn't mean putting his elbow in the planning. But he also wanted to get some decent sleep, so he went forward anyway.

They were sitting across the table from each other, leaning in like two kids dissecting the same frog. The display between them glowed blue and gold. Holden looked tired, but Amos had seen him looking worse one time and another. Holden was the kind of guy who smoked himself down to the filter if he thought it was the right thing to do.

"We should talk to Pa again," Holden said, looking up at Amos and nodding. "If we go for the station, we risk losing a lot of people."

Amos ambled to the food dispensers. They were topped up fresh, so he had a lot of choices. There was a part of him that liked it better when it was just a few.

"It's called war for a reason, sir," Bobbie said. Even though she didn't hit it, the *sir* had a sting. A reminder that it wasn't just them anymore. "We know the fire rate. We know the retrain rate. We can do the math. If we can get even a small team onto the surface—"

"Of the alien station that we totally don't understand but strapped a bunch of artillery to anyway," Holden said. Bobbie wouldn't be interrupted.

"—we can take control of them. The lack of protection on the station is the best shot I have."

Amos keyed in *noodle soup*. The dispenser hummed and chugged for a second while Holden raised his eyebrows.

"Best shot *you* have?"

"I'll lead the team," Bobbie said.

"No. Look, I'm not getting you into this just because you want a fight."

"Don't be insulting. Name one other person you know you'd rather combat-drop onto a hostile station and I'll bow out."

Holden opened his mouth to reply, then just froze, gaping like a fish. When he finally closed it, his only reply was a shrug of defeat.

Amos chuckled. Both of the others turned to look at him as the bowl popped out, steaming and smelling like salt and recon-

stituted onion. "Anyone who can shut the cap'n up like that wins
the ass-kicking contest every time," he said, taking a spoon. "I'm
not the boss of anything, but seems to me like having Babs here
and not putting her in the front line? You use a welding rig to weld
things. You use a gun to shoot things. You use a Bobbie Draper to
fuck a bunch of bad guys permanently up."

"Right tool for the job," Bobbie said, and it sounded like
thank you.

"You're not tools," Holden said. Then sighed. "But you're not
wrong. Okay. Just let me consult with Pa and Avasarala and the
OPA Council, or whatever we're calling it. In case someone has a
better idea."

Amos took a spoonful of noodle, sucked it up, and smiled
while he chewed.

"All right," Bobbie said. "But guideline? A decent idea now is
way better than a brilliant plan when it's too late."

"I hear you," Holden said.

"All right," Bobbie said. "What about this Duarte asshole?
What's Avasarala's guess on his reaction?"

"You know," Amos said around his noodles, swallowed, "I
hate to bust in, but you think I could borrow the cap'n for a few
minutes?"

"Problem?" Holden asked at the same moment Bobbie said,
"Sure."

"Just need to check something," Amos said, smiling.

Holden turned to Bobbie. "You should get some rest. I'll fire
off our notes. If we get enough sleep and eat breakfast after, we
might even get some replies back."

"Fair enough," Bobbie said. "You're going to sleep too, right?"

"Like the dead," Holden said. "Just got to finish the stuff first."

Bobbie rose up and headed out, tapping Amos' shoulder with
her knuckles as she passed. A silent *Thanks for having my back*.
He liked her, but that's not why he'd agreed with her. When you
got a nail to drive, use the fucking hammer. Just made sense.

Amos sat down in her vacated spot, but sideways, with his

back against the wall and one leg running along the bench. His hand terminal chimed. Some update that Peaches had been running sending its system clear message to the team. As he watched, the *Roci* updated him: Alex was back on board. Amos shut the alerts off.

Holden looked like shit. Not *just* tired, exactly. His skin got waxy and his eyes sort of sank back in the sockets when that happened. Not exhaustion, then. Something else. He looked like a kid who just realized he'd jumped in the deep end of the pool and was trying to figure out whether he should embarrass himself by shouting for help or drown with a little dignity.

"You doing all right?" Holden asked before Amos had quite gathered his thoughts.

"Me? Sure, Cap'n. Last man standing. That's me. What about you?"

Holden gestured, hands out to the walls and bulkheads, the dock and station beyond it. The universe. "Fine?"

"Yeah, so. Peaches and I were doing the post-fight spit and polish."

"Yeah?"

"I went over the battle data. You know, usual thing. Make sure the *Roci* was doing all the stuff we expected her to do. Didn't need anything pinched or crimped or whatever. And, you know, part of that's looking at the armament performance."

Holden's jaw shifted just a little. It wasn't much. Probably wouldn't even have lost him a hand of poker, except Amos had known when to look for it. So that was something to remember. He took another spoonful of his soup.

"Those torpedoes that Bobbie fired off at the end," he said. "One of 'em scored a direct hit."

"I didn't know that."

"Okay."

"I didn't check."

"It hit," Amos said. "But it didn't go off. A dud is a serious problem. So I started looking at why it failed."

"I disarmed them," Holden said.

Amos put down his bowl, abandoned his spoon in it. The display Holden and Bobbie had been looking over shifted, trying to guess what Holden wanted to be shown.

"But that was the righteous thing to do," Amos said. He didn't make it a question, exactly. Just a statement that Holden could agree with or not. He didn't want it to sound like anything was riding on it. Holden ran his hands through his hair. He looked like he was seeing something that wasn't in the room. Amos didn't know what it was.

"He showed me her kid," Holden said. "Marco? He showed me Naomi's son. Showed me that he was on the ship right then. Right there. And...I don't know. He looks like her. Not *like her* like her, but family resemblance. In the moment, I couldn't take that away from her. I couldn't kill him."

"I get that. She's one of us. We take care of us," Amos said. "I'm only asking because those are the bad guys we're planning to go up against again. If we're not willing to win the fight, I'm not sure what we're doing in the cage."

Holden nodded, swallowed. The display gave up and shut down, leaving the galley just a little bit darker. "That was before we got here."

"Yeah," Amos said carefully. "Who your tribe is got kind of weird all of a sudden. If you're the new Fred Johnson, that's going to change what it means when you decide not to blow people up."

"It is," Holden said. The distress in his expression was like the growl of a power coupler starting to fail. "I don't know that I'd do it differently if we were back there, in that same moment. I don't regret what I did. But I know next time can't be like that."

"Naomi should probably be good with that too."

"I was planning to talk to her about it," Holden said. "I may have been putting it off."

"So I gotta ask this," Amos said.

"Shoot."

"Are you the right guy for this job?"

"No," Holden said. "But I'm the guy who got it. So I'm going to do it."

Amos waited for a few moments, seeing how that answer sat with him.

"Okay," he said, and stood up. The soup had gotten cold enough to have a little film forming on the top. He dropped it and the spoon into the recycler. "Glad we got that cleared up. Anything me and Peaches need to put on the schedule? Feeling like we should maybe give Bobbie's stuff the once-over."

"Pretty sure she's already done that a few hundred times," Holden said, forcing a smile.

"Probably true," Amos said. "Well, all right, then."

He started out the door. Holden's voice stopped him. "Thank you."

He looked back. Holden looked like he was hunched, protecting something. Or like someone had kicked him in the chest. Funny how everyone else's image of the guy got bigger and it made the real one seem small. Like there was only so much food to share between the two of them. "Sure," he said, not certain what he was being thanked for, but pretty solid this was a good answer. "And hey. If you want, I can change the permissions so that you can't disarm the torpedoes next time. If taking it out of your hands would help."

"No," Holden said. "My hands are fine."

"Cool, then." He headed out.

In the machine shop, Peaches was putting away her tools and running the closing sequences for her diagnostics. "Tested the new seals," she said.

"They good?"

"Within tolerance," she said, which was as close as she was probably ever going to get to saying they were good. "I'll check them again tomorrow when the polymerization's totally done."

"Okay."

The system chirped. She checked the readout, okayed it, and closed the display. "You heading out to the station?"

"Nope," Amos said. Now that he bothered to notice, his body was feeling heavy and slow. Like coming out of a hot bath he'd stayed in a little too long. He wondered if Maddie was awake yet. If he got there quick enough, maybe he could finish up his night there. Except no. She'd be going on shift again about the time he was nodding off, and then it wouldn't be clear if he'd come back to screw again, and that'd just be awkward. Unless...He considered intellectually whether he wanted to screw again, then shook his head. "Nah, I'm just coming in. Going to grab some sack time now."

Peaches cocked her head. "You came back early?"

"Yeah. I couldn't sleep," he said. "But I can now."

Chapter Thirty-Six: Filip

Fixing your ship was what it meant to be a Belter. Earthers lived lives eating off the government dole and fucking each other into torpor by exploiting the Belt. Dusters sacrificed themselves and anyone else they could get their hands on for the dream of making Mars into a new Earth, even while they hated the old one. And Belters? They fixed their ships. They mined the asteroids and moons of the system. They made every scrap go longer than it was designed to. They used their cleverness and resourcefulness and reliance on each other to thrive in the vacuum like a handful of flowers blooming in an unimaginably vast desert. Putting hand to the *Pella* was as natural and proper as breathing in after breathing out.

Filip hated that he didn't want to do it.

In the first days, it was simple on-the-float work. Even then, he felt the eyes of the others on him, heard their conversations go quiet when he came in earshot. Josie and Sárta welding in the space between the hulls had said something about the dangers of nepotism, not knowing he was on the frequency, and then pretended they hadn't when he showed up. In the galley, newsfeeds from the crippled Earth were his best companions. His father didn't call for him or restrict his duties. Either would have been better than this nameless limbo. If he'd been cast down, he could at least have taken some pride in having been wronged. Instead, he woke for his shift, went to help with the repairs, and wished that he could be someplace else.

It was only when it came clear that the dead thruster was going to need a new housing that they burned for a shipyard. In other lives, they'd have tried for Ceres or Tycho, but the second-string yards were still decent. Rhea. Pallas. Vesta. They didn't use any of those. When his father's order came down, it was for Callisto.

A new escort came, guns bared, to keep the *Pella* safe from the torpedoes and attack ships of the enemy. But while Earth and Mars and Fred Johnson's OPA probably had their eyes on the *Pella*, they didn't let themselves be pulled out from their bases and fleets. They were a prize, but not one worth risking for.

Lying in his crash couch, watching feeds of neo-taarab bands from Europa and half a dozen bad sex comedies because Sylvie Kai had roles in them, Filip fantasized that there would be an attack. Maybe a little fleet led by the *Rocinante*. James fucking Holden and Filip's own traitorous whore of a mother in command, screaming out after him with their rail gun and torpedoes. Sometimes the fantasy ended with someone else getting the *Pella* beat up even worse and everyone seeing how hard it was to win that fight. Sometimes it ended with them killing the *Rocinante*, blowing it into glowing gas and shards of metal. Sometimes he imagined that they'd lose and die. And the twin points of light in that last and darkest daydream fit together like a clamp bolt in its housing: It would be an end to working on the ship, and also they would never reach Callisto.

The surviving shipyard on Callisto stood on the side permanently locked facing away from Jupiter. Its floodlights cast long,

permanent shadows across the moon's landscape and the ruins of
its sister yard, a Martian base shattered years ago. Shattered in one
of the first actions by the Free Navy. In Filip's first command. The
dust and fines stirred up by the actions of human commerce fell
slowly on Callisto, giving an illusion of mist where there was no
free water and only the most tenuous atmosphere to carry it. He
watched the scattering of floodlights on the moon's surface grow
larger as they came in, white and bright and random like a handful of the star field had been grabbed and mashed into the dirt.
When the *Pella* tipped down into a repair berth, the sound of the
clamps coming into place was deep as a punch. Filip unstrapped
and made his way to the airlock as soon as he could.

Josie was there—long, graying hair pulled back from his narrow, yellow-toothed face. Josie who'd been on the Callisto raid
with him. Who'd been under Filip's command. He lifted his eyebrows as Filip started to cycle the lock.

"Not wearing tués uniform," Josie said, only the smallest sneer
in his voice.

"Not on duty."

"Hast shore leave, tu?"

"No one said no," Filip said, hating how petulant his voice
sounded in his own ears. Josie's gaze hardened, but he only turned
away. The pressures went equal, or nearly so. When the *Pella*'s
outer doors slid open, there was still a little pop. Enough to make
Filip feel the change from one place to another, but not so much
that his ears hurt from it. A security detail waited on dock wearing light armor with raw places on the shoulder and breast where
the indistinct outline of the Pinkwater logo could still be seen like
a shadow. He nodded to them with his hands and walked forward,
half afraid they'd call him to stop and half hoping for it.

He'd never been to Callisto before his raid. Never seen it before
he called the strikes down. He didn't know what it had looked
like before, and he could still tell that the surviving half showed
the scars. Walking past the dock and into the commercial district,
Filip could pick out which walls had been replaced. Here and

there, a run of decking had a slightly off color, the sealant not as aged as the runs around it. Little scars. He might not even have noticed if he hadn't known to look.

It had been justified, though. It had been to get the radar-eating paint from the Dusters so that the rocks they threw at Earth would be hard to see. It had been part of the war. And anyway, he hadn't tried to hurt them. It was only they were right beside the enemy. Their fault. Not his.

Voices wove a rich and shifting murmur through the wide, tall main hall. A cart blatted for people to clear its path. Work crews in gray jumpsuits wore Free Navy armbands and split-circle OPA tattoos on their wrists. The air smelled of urine and cold. Filip found a place against one wall, set his shoulders against it, and watched like he was waiting for something. Someone to see him, stop, and point an accusing finger. *You were the one who tried to kill the yards! You were the one who cracked our seals! Do you know how many of us died?*

He waited for something to happen, but no one took any notice of him one way or the other. He was no one to them. A kid with his back against the wall.

The bar he ended up in was at the far end of the shipyard complex, close to the tunnels down to the deeper-level neighborhoods and the fast transit to the Jovian observatory on the far side of the moon. It wasn't only yard hands at the pressed-polymer tables. There were girls his own age in bright clothes come up from the residential levels below. Older people in academic-looking rumple hunched over their hand terminals and their beers. He'd known vaguely that there was a good upper university somewhere on Callisto, something associated with the technical institutes on Mars. Somehow never put it together in his mind with the place he'd been set to raid.

He sat apart, at a bright-pink table with a bowl of living grass as a centerpiece. From there he could watch the oversized wall screens with their scroll of newsfeeds muttering to themselves like angry drunks or else look over the finch-bright girls talking to one another and managing to never glance his way. He ordered black noodles in peanut sauce and a stout from the table display and paid with Free Navy scrip. For a long moment, he thought the table might refuse payment—if it said his money was bad, that would be when the girls looked over at him—but it chimed pleasantly, accepting, and threw up a countdown timer to when his order should come. Twelve minutes. So for twelve minutes, he watched the feeds.

The Earth still dominated, even in its suffering. Images of devastation mixed with earnest-looking newsreaders staring into the camera or else interviewing other people, sometimes earnest as sycophants, sometimes yelling like the other coyo'd been fucking their sweethearts. The bright girls ignored the screen, but Filip's eye kept wandering back to it: a street covered in ashes so deep the woman cleaning it had a scarred snow shovel; an emaciated black bear lurching one direction and then another in distress and confusion; some official of the half-dead Earth government surveying a stadium filled with body bags. The beer and noodles came, and he started eating without quite noticing that he had. He watched the march of images, chewed, swallowed, drank. It was like his body was a ship, and all his crew were about their work but not talking to each other.

The pride in the devastation was still there. Those dead were because of him. The ash-drowned cities, the blackened lakes and oceans, the skyscraper burning like a torch because not enough infrastructure still existed to extinguish it. These were the temples and battlements of his people's enemy, fallen into dust and ruin, and thanks to him. The raid he'd done here, at this yard, had let it happen.

And now here he was with the end and the beginning, one seen through the other like two sheets of plastic laid one on the other. Like time pressed flat. Still a victory and still his, but maybe there was a little aftertaste now, trailing just after like milk on the edge of sour.

Say it like a man. Say I fucked it up. Only he hadn't. It hadn't been *his* mistake.

The shining girls rose in a flock, touching each other's hands, laughing, kissing each other's cheeks, and then scattered. Filip watched them walk out with a kind of forlorn lust, and so he saw it when Karal walked in. The old Belter could have been a mech driver or a drive tech or a welder. His hair was white and thinning and cut close to the scalp. His shoulders and hands and cheeks showed a lifetime of scars. He stood for a moment, looked around with an air of not thinking much of what he saw, and then lumbered over toward Filip's booth and sat across from him like they'd planned to meet there.

"Hoy," Karal said after an awkward moment.

"He send you?" Filip asked.

"No one send me, aber se savvy I ought to come."

Filip stirred his noodles. The bowl was hardly half empty, but his appetite was already gone. The slow, rolling anger in his gut seemed to take up all the space that food might want. "No need. Solid as stone, me, and twice as hard."

It sounded like a boast. Like an accusation. Filip wasn't even sure what he'd wanted the words to be, but not this. He ground his fork into the mash of noodles and sauce, shoved the bowl to the edge of the table for the server to take away. He kept the stout, though.

"Not throwing signs, me," Karal said. "But was a time I was your age. Long time, but I remember it. Me y mis papá used to have it out sometimes. He'd get high and I'd get drunk and we'd spend the whole day sometimes yelling at each other about who was the dumbest asshole. Throw punches sometimes. Pulled a knife once, me." Karal chuckled. "He cracked my ass the other way for that one. All I'm saying, fathers and sons, they fight. But you and yours? It's different, yeah?"

"If you say," Filip said.

"Your da? He's not just your da. Marco Inaros, leader of the Free Navy. Big man, him. So much on his shoulders. So much he's thinking on, worrying on, planning on, and it's not like tu y la can scrap it out like the rest of us."

"That's not what it is," Filip said.

"No? Bist bien, then. What's it?" Karal said, and his voice was soft and warm and gentle.

The anger in Filip's gut was shifting, unsteady as a scab on an infected wound. The rage and righteousness started to feel less authentic, like a wrap tied around something that wasn't either. That was something worse. Filip gripped his hands in fists so tight they ached, but he lost his hold. The anger—not even anger, *petulance*—slid to the side and an oceanic sense of guilt rose up in him like a flood. It was too big, too pure, too painful to even have a single event to focus it.

It wasn't that he regretted leaving the ship without permission or missing his shots on the *Rocinante* or killing Earth or wounding Callisto. It was larger than that. Regret was the universe. Guilt was bigger than the sun and the stars and the spaces between them. Whatever it was, all of it, was his fault and his failing. It was more than he'd *done* something bad. Like the fossil of an ancient animal was flesh that had been replaced by stone, whoever Filip had been once had kept his shape but been replaced by a raw and rising sense of loss.

"I feel...*wrong*?" Filip said, scrabbling for words to describe something so much bigger than language. "I feel...I feel like—"

"*Fuck*," Karal said, breathy and sharp. His eyes were fixed behind Filip. Caught by something on the newsfeed. Filip turned, craning to see the screen. Fred Johnson looked out from the wall, dark-eyed, calm, somber. A red banner beneath him read, *Confirmed Dead After Free Navy Attack*. When he turned back, Karal had already pulled out his hand terminal and was shifting through newsfeeds as quickly as his crooked fingers could manage. Filip waited, then took his own terminal out. It wasn't hard to find. It was all over the feeds—Belt and inner planets both. Sources from Tycho Manufacturing Collective on Earth were confirming the death of Frederick Lucius Johnson, formerly of UN Navy and longtime political activist, community organizer, and spokesman of the Outer Planets Alliance. He'd died as a result of injuries sustained during an ambush by forces of the Free Navy...

Filip read it all, aware that there was something to it he wasn't understanding. It was only a wash of words and images, disconnected from his life, until Karal, across the table from him and grinning, spoke.

"Gratulacje, Filipito. Guess you got him after all."

Back on the *Pella*, music was playing over the ship system. A bright mix of steel drum and guitar and men's ululating voices raised together in celebration. Sárta, one of the first to see Filip when he came down the corridor from the airlock, scooped him up in her arms, pressing his cheek against hers and leaving him uncomfortably aware of her breasts. When she kissed him— briefly, but on the lips—she tasted of cheap mint liquor.

The galley was packed like a party. The whole crew, it seemed, gathered together in front of the newsfeeds that announced the death of the Butcher of Anderson Station. The heat of their bodies made the room feel stifling. His father was in among them, smiling and strutting and clapping people on the shoulder like the groom at a particularly fortunate wedding. All the sulking and menace were gone from his expression. When he caught sight of Filip across the crowded room, he put his hands together in front of his heart making a celebratory double fist.

This was, Filip realized, the first real victory since the first attack on Earth. Marco had been claiming success after success, but they'd all been for retreats and scuffles or the discipline killing of mutineers like the *Witch of Endor*. From the moment they'd left Ceres, the Free Navy had needed a solid, unequivocal success, and this was it. No wonder even the sober seemed drunk with it.

The newsfeed shifted, a Free Navy logo appearing in its place, and the roar of the group grew even louder as each told the others to be quiet. Someone cut the music and put the audio for the newsfeed in its place. When Marco appeared on the screen, more dignified and statesmanlike than the actual grinning man in the room, his voice rang all through the *Pella*.

"Fred Johnson claimed to speak for the same people he oppressed. He began his career by slaughtering Belters, then pretended to be our voice. His years as a representative of the OPA were marked by pleas for complacence, patience, and the constant deferment of the freedom of the Belt. And his fate will be the fate of all who stand against us. The Free Navy will defend and protect the Belt from all enemies, internal and external, now and forever."

The speech went on, but the crew began cheering so loudly, Filip couldn't hear it. Marco lifted his arms, not to quiet them but to bathe in the noise. His shining eyes found Filip again. When he spoke, Filip could read the words on his lips: *We did it*.

We, Filip thought as Aaman jostled into him, pressed a bulb of something alcoholic into his palm. We *did it. When it was a mistake, it was mine. When it was a victory, it was ours.*

In the center of the joyful storm, Filip felt himself growing still. A flicker of memory came to him, strong and rich with import as an image from a dream. He couldn't place its source. A film he'd watched, he thought. Some drama where a stunningly beautiful woman had looked into the camera and in a voice made from smoke and muscle had said, *He put blood on my hands too. He thought it would make me easier to control.*

Chapter Thirty-Seven: Alex

Good morning, Sunshine," Sandra Ip said.

Alex blinked, closed his eyes, cracked open just the left one. He'd been in the middle of a dream where apple juice had gotten into the coolant feeds on a ship that was both the *Rocinante* and his first ship back when he'd been in the Martian Navy. The sense that he was supposed to fix something lingered even as the details faded. Sandra, naked, smiled down at him and he stopped trying to hold on to the dream.

"Hey to you too, Pookie," he growled. The night's sleep left his voice deep and gravelly. He stretched up his arms, palms flat against her headboard, and pressed to stretch down between his shoulder blades. His toes reached out past the edge of the blanket, and she pinched them playfully as she walked back toward the shower. He lifted his head to watch her retreat, and she looked back to watch him watch her.

"Where you headed?" he asked, partly because he wanted to know, partly just to keep her in the room a few seconds more.

"I've got a shift on the *Jammy Rakshasa* today," she said. "Drummer's making sure all these OPA bigwigs feel like we're taking care of them."

"*Jammy Rakshasa*," Alex said, laying his head back down. "That's a weird name for a ship."

"It think it's some kind of in-joke with Goodfortune's people. Decent ship, though." Her voice echoed a little from the bathroom. "The weirdest ship I ever worked was called the *Inverted Loop*. Gravel miner made out of a salvaged luxury yacht. The captain had this thing about open space, so they'd cut all nonstructural walls and decking out."

Alex frowned up at the ceiling. "Seriously?"

"When that thing was under thrust, you could drop a bearing in the cockpit and listen to it hit every deck down to the reactor. It was like flying in a balloon full of sticks."

"That ain't right."

"The captain was a guy named Yeats Pratkanis. He had some issues, but his crew loved him. Nothing like the stupid shit people do for a captain when they're really invested in not seeing how fucked up he is."

"S'pose that's true."

The sound of water splashing against metal announced the shower, but Alex could tell by the music of it that her body wasn't in the flow yet. He looked up again, found her in the doorway, her arms lifted above her to rest against the frame. She was only a little younger than him, and the years showed on her body. Silver ghosts of stretch marks just visible along her belly and breasts. The fuzzy tattoo of a waterfall down the side of her left leg. A jagged scar that puckered the flesh of her right arm. Hers was not the beauty of youth but of experience, same as his. Still, he could see the girl she'd been in the way she lifted her eyebrows, shifted her weight into her hip.

"You want to take a shower, Sunshine?" she asked with false innocence.

"Oh hell yes," Alex said, hauling himself up from the bed. "Yes, I do."

Ever since that first night on Ceres, he and Sandra had been spending a chunk of their off hours in each other's company this way. When they'd been on the *Roci*, they'd split their time between his cabin and hers. Here on Tycho, her quarters had become their default. She'd been on the station long enough for her seniority and union rules to land her two rooms, a private bath, and a bed that was a lot more comfortable for two than trying to fit into the same crash couch.

As love affairs went, Alex had been surprised at first and a little wary. Sandra's sexuality was joyful and unrestrained. It had taken him a little time to knock the rust off and join her in it. He'd had a few lovers before he'd gotten married, one—shamefully—while he was, and a couple dalliances afterward. A woman's full and delighted attention wasn't something he'd ever expected to have again. Once he convinced himself that, yes, this was really happening, he fell into it like he was sixteen.

After the shower, they toweled each other dry and he helped put lotion on her back where she couldn't reach, and a little where she probably could too. She put on her uniform, tied back her hair, then brushed and gargled while he crawled back into the bed.

"Another day of sloth for you?" she asked.

"I'm a pilot with nowhere to go," he said, stretching his arms out in a gesture that said, *It's not my fault*. She laughed.

"This is why I'm not one," she said. "Engineers always have something to do."

"You need to learn to relax."

"Well," she said, her voice taking on a low purr that was come-on and laughing at the come-on both, "you keep setting me an example and maybe some of it'll rub off on me."

"Maybe when your shift's over, we could order in."

"It's a plan," she said, then checked the time on her hand terminal and grunted. "Okay. I've got to run."

"I'll lock up when I go," Alex said.

"You'll sleep in my bed all day like a lion."

"Or that."

She kissed him before she left. He let himself sink into the pillows after the door closed, rested there for a long moment, then stood up and gathered his clothes from the floor. Sandra's quarters were soft and welcoming in a way he wasn't used to. The comforter wadded and shaped at the foot of the bed was a pale blue with a pattern of lace at the edges. Sandra had hung draping cloth at the corners of the room to soften the light and disguise the edges. Her desk had a small glass vase with dried roses arranged in it. The peppery smell of spent perfume sank into his clothes when he was here, so that hours later he'd walk through a draft and be suddenly and viscerally reminded of her. The women he'd lived with these last years—Naomi, Bobbie, even Clarissa Mao now—weren't the sort for frills and softness. Plush pillows and rosewater. Being around that particular kind of femininity was familiar enough to be comfortable, exotic enough to make this time, this moment, this relationship something all his own. Turned out some part of him had wanted something all his own.

Or maybe—pulling on the same sock he'd worn yesterday—it wasn't even that. Maybe it was only that he knew how much the war might take from them all, and Sandra Ip was his chance to refill some cistern of his heart and body that there wasn't going to be time for later. A place of gentleness and affection and pleasure like a hurricane eye. He hoped she felt the same about him. That they were stocking up good memories, him and Sandra both, against the history that was about to unfold around them.

It was getting harder and harder to shrug off the sense of dread back on the *Rocinante*. The days since they'd arrived on Tycho had been one endless meeting for Holden. When he wasn't fencing with Carlos Walker about what supplies and support the OPA could provide, he was trading long recorded messages with

Michio Pa about the firing rate of the Free Navy's rail gun artillery in the slow zone. When he wasn't reporting to or getting reports from Avasarala, he and Naomi and Bobbie were comparing positional maps of the system with Aimee Ostman and Micah al-Dujaili. Holden never seemed to lose his temper, never seemed to rest. Every time Alex saw him, Holden smiled and was pleasant and upbeat. If he hadn't spent years with the man, he might almost have been fooled into thinking things were going well.

But the man in the meetings, pacing the corridors of the *Rocinante* or the docks outside them, sitting hunched over his flickering hand terminal, wasn't really James Holden at all. It was like Holden had become an actor and his role was *James Holden*. The surface was whatever it needed to be at the moment. That wasn't the man he knew. Alex could feel the howling void of desperation and despair behind everything he said.

It showed in the others too. Naomi had become quieter, more focused. Like she was always in the middle of puzzling through an impossible problem. Even Amos seemed on edge, though what it was about was so subtle that Alex couldn't have said for certain if that was even true. It might just have been his own fears projected against Amos' blank slate. And if Bobbie and Clarissa seemed immune from it all, it was only because they were relatively new to the ship. They didn't know the feel and rhythm of the *Rocinante* well enough yet to hear when she went slightly out of tune.

And every story of the Free Navy—another ship captured or killed, another Earth spy caught and executed on Pallas or Ganymede or Hall Station, another rock intercepted before it could hit Earth—turned the ratchet one more notch. The consolidated fleet was going to have to do something. And soon.

The little restaurant just off the main hall. Bright lights, a little redder spectrum than the sun. Syncopated harp-and-dulcimer music, which was apparently in fashion these days. Tall stools around a white ceramic bar. A plate of something not entirely unlike chicken in a vindaloo that was better than it had any right to be. Sandra had introduced the place to him the first night on Tycho, and he'd become a regular since.

His hand terminal chimed the connection request, and Alex accepted it with his thumb. Holden appeared on the screen. It might just have been the dim light on the command deck or the blue of the monitor the captain was sitting in front of, but his skin looked waxy, his eyes flat and exhausted. "Hey," Holden said. "I'm not interrupting anything, am I?"

"Thanks for askin'," Alex said, maybe a little too heartily. He felt like he needed to haul the energy of the conversation up when he talked to Holden these days. As if he could inject health into the man by being so damned chipper at him. "I'm just finishing some breakfast. What's up?"

"Um," Holden said, and blinked. For a moment, he looked surprised. Like what he was about to say seemed a little implausible to him. "We're looking to ship out in about thirty hours. Clarissa and Amos are in the middle of their sleep shifts, but I'm calling an all-hands meeting in four hours so we can make sure we've got everything in order."

The way he said it sounded like an apology. Alex felt the words land like he was drinking something cold on an empty stomach. "I'll be there," he said.

"We're good?"

"Cap," Alex said, "this is the *Roci*. I made sure we were topped up and ready as soon as the docking clamps were in place. We could take off five minutes from now and be fine."

Holden's smile said he'd understood all Alex's subtext. "Still, good to get everyone together and double-check."

"No argument," Alex agreed. "Four hours?"

"Four and change," Holden said. "If Amos sleeps in, I'm going to let him."

"See you on board then," Alex said, and they dropped the connection. He took another bite of the vindaloo. It didn't taste as good. He slid bowl and fork to the recycler, stood up, waited a few seconds just so he wouldn't be going to find Sandra quite yet.

He went off to find Sandra.

Despite its name, the *Jammy Rakshasa* was an unexceptional-looking ship. Wide at the front, boxy, with a random studding of PDCs and thrusters scattered over her skin in a way that spoke of generations of use and modifications, the design growing and changing and leaving artifacts of its previous incarnations like a house altered by tenant after tenant until the original architecture was all but lost. A Belter ship. If it hadn't been for the high security presence, both on the dock and floating around the ship itself, he'd have wondered if he was looking at the right one.

He waited outside the utility airlock, holding on to the wall with one hand as he floated. He saw Sandra before she saw him. A cluster of engineers and mechanical techs in environment suits floating together at a wall display, four different conversations going among the seven of them. Her hair was in a ponytail that waved like a flag when she shook her head, impatient with what the man beside her was saying. When she glanced in Alex's direction, she did a quick double take. He saw the smile start on her lips, saw it wilt. She finished her discussions, pushed herself off, gliding through the air toward him. By the time she grabbed a handhold and pulled herself to a halt, the knowledge was already in her eyes.

"Well," she said. "Orders came through?"

"Yeah."

Her expression softened, her gaze tracing the curves of his face. He looked at her, memorizing the shape of her eyes, her mouth, the little scar at her temple, the mole tucked almost behind her ear. All the details of her body. A bad habit in the back of his head fed him all the wrong things to say: *You should ship out with us* and *I can resign and stay here with you* and *I'll come back if you wait for me.* All the things that would make her feel better right then in the moment and break her trust in him later. All the things he'd said to women he loved before and not meant then either. She laughed gently, like she'd heard him thinking.

"I was never looking for a husband," she said. "I've had husbands. They're never what they're cracked up to be."

"My track record is I make a pretty shitty one anyway," Alex said.

"I am glad you're my friend," she said. "You make a great friend."

"You make a great lover," Alex said.

"Yeah," Sandra said. "You too. So how long?"

"Captain's called a meeting in"—he checked the time—"a little over three hours. Says we're heading out in a little less than thirty."

"You know where?"

"I expect he'll tell me when I get there," Alex said. He took her gloved hand. She squeezed his fingers gently and then let them go.

"So I get a lunch break in about an hour and a half," she said. They were casual words, spoken carefully. Like if she bit down too hard, she might break them. "I could take it a little early. You want to meet up at my place? Freshen up the luck one last time before you go?"

Alex put his hand to her cheek. She braced a leg against the wall so she could press into his palm. How many millions of times had people had this exact conversation before? How many wars had put two people together for a moment and then washed them apart? There had to be a tradition of it. A secret history of vulnerability and want and all the things that sex promised and only occasionally delivered. They were just one more couple among all the countless others. It only hurt this time because it was them.

"Yeah," he said. "I'd love that."

The galley of the *Rocinante* smelled like coffee and maple-flavored syrup. Naomi shifted when Alex came in, making room for him on the bench. Amos sat on her other side, looking into nothing and scooping scrambled eggs from a bowl with two fingers. His eyes were still puffy from sleep, but he seemed alert otherwise. Clarissa stood in the doorway, uncertain but present. Alex thought about getting some food, but he wasn't hungry. It would only have been so he had something to do with his hands.

A conversation between Bobbie and Holden echoed down the lift as they approached, their voices hard and competent and businesslike. Maybe even a little excited. There was an anticipation in the air that didn't feel like joy, but wasn't entirely unlike it either.

The melancholy in Alex's chest and throat eased a little as they came in, Bobbie taking the bench across from him while Holden headed for the coffee. When he'd left Sandra's quarters to come here, he'd carried a sense of loss with him. He still felt it. Would feel it for maybe days, maybe weeks, maybe forever. But not as strongly. And his people were here. His crew, his ship. The worst of the sting was already over and the sweet, he thought, would last. For him. Hopefully for Sandra. It was great sharing a moment with a genuinely good woman. There was a pleasure in coming home again too.

Holden took a sip of his coffee, coughed, and took another one. Clarissa slid in and took a seat behind Amos as if she could hide behind him. As Holden ambled over—head down, expression distracted—Bobbie reached across and tapped Alex on the wrist.

"You good?"

"Right as rain," Alex said. "Said my goodbyes."

Bobbie nodded once. Holden sat down facing them all, sideways on the bench. His hair was unkempt, his eyes focused on something only he could see. The attention of the room—Naomi's, Amos', Alex's own—turned toward him. An ancient and barely familiar anticipation shifted in Alex's chest, like a fragment of childhood beginning of school year.

"So, Cap," he said. "What's the plan?"

Chapter Thirty-Eight: Avasarala

Avasarala screamed.

Her breath ripped out of her throat, abrading her flesh as it passed. She tasted bile in the back of her mouth, and her legs trembled, ached, burned as she tried to push the steel plate another centimeter away.

"Come on," Pieter said. "You can do this."

She screamed again, and the plate moved away. Her legs went almost straight. The impulse to push through and lock her knees took effort to resist. It might snap her knees back the other way, but then at least this would be done.

"That's eleven," Pieter said. "Go for twelve. One more."

"Fuck your mother."

"Come on. Just one more rep. I'll be here to help."

"You're an asshole and nobody loves you," she gasped, lowering her head. The worst was the nausea. Leg day always seemed to mean nausea. Pieter didn't care. He was paid not to care.

"You're going down the well in twelve days," he said. "If you want the leader of Earth, the hope and light of civilization, to get wheeled off the shuttle in a chair, you can stop. If you want her to stride out in front of the cameras like a Valkyrie returned from the underworld and ready for battle, you'll go for twelve."

"Sadistic fuck."

"You're the one who fell behind on your exercise schedule."

"I've been saving the fucking species."

"Saving humanity doesn't prevent bone-density loss or muscular atrophy," he said. "And you're stalling. One more."

"I hate you so much," she said, letting her knees bend, easing the steel plate back closer to her. She wanted to cry. She wanted to puke all over Pieter's pretty white exercise shoes. She wanted to be doing anything else at all.

"I know, sweetie. But you can do this," he said. "Come on."

Avasarala screamed and pushed the steel plate away.

Afterward, she sat on the fake-wood bench in the locker room with her head in her hands until the idea of moving didn't disgust her. When she did finally stand up, the gray-clad woman in the mirror seemed unfamiliar. Not foreign precisely, but certainly not her. Thinner, for one thing, with sweat stains at the armpits and under the breasts. White hair that didn't fall to her shoulders so much as flow out, the thin lunar gravity too weak to pull it down. The woman in the mirror looked Avasarala up and down with dark, judgmental eyes.

"Some fucking Valkyrie," Avasarala said, then headed for the shower. "You'll have to do."

The good news was that Mars had finally slogged its way through its constitutional crisis, done the obvious thing, and put Emily Richards in as prime minister. No, that wasn't fair. There was more going well than just that. The rioting in Paris was under control now, and the racist cells in Colombia had been identified and isolated without any more murders. Saint Petersburg had fixed its water-recycling problem, at least for the moment. Gorman Le's mystery yeast was doing everything it had claimed on the tin, which increased the overall food supply for the survivors, and the reactors in Cairo and Seoul were working again so they could make use of it. Fewer dead people. Or at least fewer dead right now. Next week was always next week, and always would be.

The bad news still outweighed the good. The second wave of deaths hadn't slowed yet. The medical infrastructure was saturated. Thousands of people were dying every week from conditions that even a year ago would have been easily treated or cured. The violence over resources hadn't by any means stopped either. There were vigilante raids in Boston and Mumbai. Reports of whole police forces going rogue and hoarding relief supplies in Denver and Phoenix. The oceans were being choked. The sludge of dust and debris wasn't sinking as quickly as the models had suggested, and the light-eating plants and microbiota were dying off as a result. If there hadn't been so many fucking human beings stressing the food webs over the last few centuries, the system might have been more robust. Or it might not have. It wasn't as though they had a second Earth to use as a control. History itself was a massive n=1 study, irreproducible. It was what made it so difficult to learn from.

After her shower, she changed into a lime-green sari, did her hair and her makeup. She was starting to feel a little better. It was the pattern she was noticing. The actual exercise left her miserable, but once she'd recovered, the rest of her day seemed to go a little better. If it was only the placebo effect, that was enough. She'd take what she could get, even if it was only tricks of the mind.

When she was almost ready to face the rest of her day, she opened an audio-only connection to Said. "Where do we stand?" she said instead of hello.

"The security group from Mars is finishing their meal," Said answered without missing a beat. "They'll be in the conference hall in half an hour. Admiral Souther will be there with you if you need him."

"Always good to have a penis in uniform in the room," Avasarala said sourly. "God knows they might not take me seriously otherwise."

"If you say so, ma'am."

"It was a joke."

"If you say so, ma'am. There's also a report in from Ceres Station. Admiral Coen has confirmed that the *Giambattista* is under burn just the way Aimee Ostman promised."

Avasarala held a pearl earring to her left ear, considering it. Nice. Understated. Didn't go with the sari, though.

"I'm sorry, ma'am?" Said's voice was confused.

"I didn't say anything."

"You…ah…you growled."

"Did I? Probably just an editorial comment about how pleased I am that we're trusting the fucking OPA now. Ignore it and continue."

"That's all you have on the schedule for today," he said, almost apologetically. "You did ask me to keep the afternoon clear in case the security briefing went long."

"So I did," she said, trying a pair of aquamarine studs that were much better. "Word from The Hague?"

"They say your office will be ready and the critical staff will be in place. We're on track to move the seat of governance back to the planet surface on schedule."

She imagined she heard a certain pride in Said's voice at that. Well, good. He ought to be proud. They all ought to be. Earth might be a pile of corpses and shit, but it was *their* pile of corpses and shit, and she was tired of looking up at it from the moon.

"About fucking time," she said. "All right. Tell Souther I'm on my way. And to bring me a sandwich or something."

"What sort would you like? I can meet you with—"

"No, tell Souther to do it," she said. "He'll think it's funny."

The conference room was the single most secure chamber in

the solar system, but it didn't wear that on its sleeve. It was small enough for six people to sit comfortably. Red curtains on the walls to hide the air recyclers and the heaters. The table was wide, dark, and set just a little low to give a few centimeters more room for the holographic display. Not that anyone ever used holographic displays. Showy, but not functional. The Martian military attaché wasn't here to be wowed by graphic design, and Avasarala liked him for that.

The man himself—Rhodes Chen—sat on one side of the table with his secretary and assistant to either hand. Souther was already there too when she arrived, leaning back in his chair and laughing with Rhodes. A small tin plate waited at her chair—white bread and cucumbers. When Chen saw her, he stood, and all the others with him. She waved him back down.

"Thank you for coming," she said. "I wanted to be sure our allies on Mars were entirely up-to-date on the situation with the Free Navy."

"Prime Minister Richards sends her regrets," Chen said, taking his seat. "Things are still unsettled back at home, and she didn't feel comfortable being physically absent from the government building."

"I understand," Avasarala said. "And your wife? Michaela? Is she feeling better?"

Chen blinked. "Why...yes. Yes, she's doing much better. Thank you."

Avasarala turned to Souther. "Admiral Chen's wife went to the cooperative school with my daughter Ashanti when they were girls," she said. Not that Chen remembered that, or had even known. In fairness, the girls hadn't been particularly close, but you played the angles the universe gave you. She picked up her sandwich, took a bite, and put it back down to give Chen a moment to hide his discomfort.

"I'm going to have to ask your staff to leave," Avasarala said.

"They can be trusted," Chen said, nodding as if he'd agreed.

"Not by me, they can't," Avasarala said. "We won't hurt them. But they can't stay."

Chen sighed. His secretary and assistant politely gathered up their things, nodded to Souther and Avasarala, and left. Souther lowered his head, waiting for the system to report whether either had left anything behind. It would be sad to come this far and have a bug in the room. A moment later he shook his head.

"Now then," she said. "Shall we get down to business?"

Chen didn't object, and Souther pulled up a schematic of the solar system in its present state. The sun and the ring gate as the major axis, and the planets and moons, stations and asteroids, scattered as the laws of orbital mechanics had placed them. As with any tactical map on that scale, the proportionality had suffered a little in favor of visibility. In truth, all of humanity's children lived on scattered stones smaller than dust on the face of the ocean. They hid the fact with graphics and highlighted lists of ship names and vectors. Had the map matched the territory, there would have been nothing to see. Even the Earth with her suffering billions would have been less than a pixel.

But the Free Navy showed there in yellow. The consolidated fleet in red. Michio Pa's breakaway ships and their new OPA let's-call-them-allies in gold. It was rough and ugly. Souther pulled up a pointer, and drew the room's attention to the ring gate at the system's edge.

"Our target is Medina Station," he said in his oddly high-pitched, musical voice. "There are several reasons for that, but critically, it's the choke point for passage through to the colony systems, including Laconia, where former Martian naval officer Winston Duarte appears to have set up shop. Whoever has possession of Medina and its defenses controls the ring gates and traffic through them. It will reopen trade and colonization ships for us, and cut Inaros' supply lines from his ally."

Chen leaned forward, his elbows on the table, eyes glittering with the reflection of the display. He hadn't reacted at all to

Duarte's name. Good poker face, and he'd expected to hear it. Richards wasn't trying to deny the Martian Navy's role in this clusterfuck. That was good. She took another bite of the sandwich and wished she'd thought to bring some pistachios. She didn't have much appetite right after lifting weights, but when it returned, she was ravenous.

"Inaros' method of operation up to now has relied on strategic retreat," Souther continued. "Stripping and abandoning territory rather than trying to hold it and leaving the support of the people left behind to the consolidated fleet. It has served him well in that we have been reluctant to overextend our defensive force, and the Free Navy has been able to carry out raids and attacks of opportunity on both Earth and Martian forces and dissenting factions on their own side."

"The pirates," Chen said.

"The pirates," Avasarala agreed. No need to beat around that particular bush.

"We believe that strategy will fail with Medina," Souther said. "Its importance is too great to abandon. And if we're wrong and the Free Navy does abandon it... Well, then we have all the advantages we were hoping for and he looks like a joke."

"He won't abandon it," Avasarala said.

"What about the rail guns?" Chen asked. An interesting move, showing that Mars already knew about the defensive artillery. She wasn't quite certain what letting her know they knew that was meant to achieve. Souther glanced at her. She nodded. No reason to pretend ignorance.

"Our best intelligence on that comes from the defectors from the Free Navy. Captain Pa of the *Connaught* was one of Inaros' inner circle. Our understanding is that the rail guns set up on the alien station are Medina's first line of defense. The station proper also had PDCs and a supply of torpedoes left by Duarte, but the rail guns are set to defend and destroy any unauthorized ships that pass through the ring gates."

"That seems like a problem," Chen said. "Your thoughts on how to overcome that?"

"We're going to send a shitload of ships through the ring gates," Avasarala said as Souther shifted from tactical to an image of the *Giambattista*. It wasn't a pretty ship: large, boxy, and awkward.

"This is a converted water hauler crewed by the Ostman-Jasinzki faction of the Outer Planets Alliance," Souther said. "It has been loaded with slightly under four thousand small craft. Breaching pods, small transports, prospecting skiffs. A devil's brew. We're calling it our Surinam toad, but the ship's registered as the *Giambattista*."

"That thing has four thousand reactors in it?" Chen said.

"No," Souther said. "Most of the engines are chemical rockets or compressed-gas thrusters. Many of them are hardly more than environment-suit thrusters welded to a steel box. That is part of the reason they're being carried to the edge of the ring before they're ever deployed. These aren't long-range craft. At a guess, I'd say half of them would be hard-pressed to make the trip from the ring gate to Medina under the best of circumstances. There are also several thousand torpedoes with a mixed but generally low-yield assortment of warheads."

"So, chaff," Chen said. "Cannon fodder."

"We're not putting people on all of them," Avasarala said. "Even the OPA's not that suicidal."

Souther went on. "A fraction—the best ships—will carry a ground-attack group, whose mission will be to take control, not of Medina but of the rail-gun emplacements themselves. Once our forces control those, we expect Medina Station to capitulate. And since the rail guns were intended to defend Medina from more than thirteen hundred gates, and we're only going to focus on the Sol and Laconia gates, we have reason to expect a relatively strong defensive position, which we can reinforce not only from Sol but with the colony ships that have already passed through and are willing and able to come to our assistance."

"All right," Chen said.

"You sound skeptical," Avasarala said.

"No offense, ma'am," Chen said. "But I'm looking at this, and it doesn't square. If Inaros has been trying to tempt the fleet into overreach—spreading our forces too thin—then this run out to the edge of the system seems like his dream scenario. Unless you're planning to send it unescorted, in which case you might as well not send it at all."

"The escort will be a salvaged Martian corvette with a keel-mounted rail gun of its own," Souther said. "The *Rocinante* is already burning on an intercept course. It's going from Tycho Station, so it's in the neighborhood. Relatively speaking."

"There are also advantages to having that particular asset in place on Medina when we take it," Avasarala said.

Chen's laugh was thin and despairing. Avasarala stretched her right leg, feeling the ache in it. It would be worse in the morning. Lifting weights was an argument against a benign God. As if that needed more evidence.

"Why bother, then?" Chen asked. "A single escort ship and an old ice hauler heading out to the most sensitive strategic position in the system? I don't mean to be rude, but I have to think you don't like the people in those ships very much. They're going to have the whole Free Navy chasing them out and turning them to slag before they're a million klicks from the ring gate."

"That," Souther said, "remains to be seen."

If Chen had been a dog, his ears would have gone up just then. Avasarala saw it in his face and the set of his shoulders. "This," she said, "is why we need to talk. In private. Securely. I need assurances, Mr. Chen, that the rot at the heart of your navy was well and truly burned out. I trust Emily Richards to look out for her own best interests and Mars' too. In that order. And I've done a deep background check on you."

"You've...excuse me?"

Avasarala put out her hands, palms facing each other about a meter apart. "I've got a report on you this thick. I know every pimple you've popped since your voice broke. Everything. Praise-worthy, shameful, indifferent. Everything. I have violated your privacy in ways you can't imagine."

Chen went white, then red. "Well," he said.

"I don't give a shit about any of it," she said. "The only thing I cared about was whether you had the stink of Duarte on your fingers. You don't. It's why you're in this room. Because I trust you to take this back to Richards and no one else. And I need to know if you trust Mars."

The silence in the room was profound. Chen pressed his fingers to his lips. "With this? Maybe. I get the sense you're making some kind of request here. You should be very clear and explicit if that's the case."

"I want Richards to instruct the remnants of the Martian Navy—the ships in the consolidated fleet and the ones you have in reserve as well—to coordinate closely with Earth and the OPA and the fucking pirate fleet."

"To do what?"

"Run a distraction campaign," Souther said.

Avasarala waved him back, leaned in toward Chen, a smile on her lips. "Inaros isn't going to chase after the *Giambattista* and *Rocinante*, because he'll be distracted by the largest and most aggressive fleet action in history kicking his balls up into his throat. By the time he understands what we were really after, it'll be too late for him to do anything but hold his dick and cry. But I need to know that you're in."

Chen blinked. His reserve cracked, just a little.

"Well," he said, "when you put it like that."

Chapter Thirty-Nine: Naomi

The *Rocinante* burned, but not straight for the ring gate. That would have been too obvious. The intention was to rendezvous with the *Giambattista* in an ambiguous orbit, leaving it unclear to anyone watching whether they were looking to position themselves in a long burn spinward toward Saturn, turn out toward the science station on Neptune, or make for the gate. Let Marco wonder a little bit, and be in position when the distractions started pulling his attention away. Assuming he was even watching where the *Roci* went.

Naomi assumed Marco was watching where the *Roci* went. She assumed everyone was. She understood how much her old friends hated her now.

Even in this moment of relative calm, Jim was spending ten- and twelve-hour shifts on the comms. When he wasn't sending out or receiving messages, he'd watch newsfeeds. The Free Navy presence was growing on Ganymede and Titan. The consolidated fleet splitting its forces in order to send guard ships to Tycho. Angry voices coming off Pallas to denounce the traitors who'd colluded with the inner planets; not just Michio Pa and her pirate fleet anymore but also the OPA factions that Fred Johnson had put together. It was how Jim tried to have control over something he couldn't actually control. The messages he watched and sent out were a kind of prayer for him, though he wouldn't have said it that way. Something that brought peace and the illusion that what they were caught up in wasn't so massively bigger than their own individual wills and hopes and intentions.

So even though it set her teeth on edge, she let him go on with it. She got used to falling asleep to the musical voices of Earth newsfeeds, waking up to the hard cadences of Chrisjen Avasarala and Michio Pa in her cabin.

"We will burn after we see the consolidated fleet commit," Pa said, her distant, muted voice sliding into Naomi's half-dream. She sounded so weary, it made Naomi want to go back to sleep in sympathy. "I understand that's not a popular decision, but I'm not interested in having my people be the worm on Earth's hook."

"I never understood that," Naomi said. Jim closed his hand terminal display and settled the earphones down around his neck, his expression guilty. Naomi shifted, and the crash couch swung under them like one of the hammocks she'd grown up sleeping in. "How do hookworms figure into catching fish, anyway?"

"Not hookworms," Jim said. "Worms, like earthworms. Or insects. Crickets. You'd put them on metal hooks with a barb on the end, tie a really thin line to the metal hook, and throw the whole thing out into a lake or a river. Hope that a fish would eat the worm, and then you could haul the fish out with the hook that was caught in its mouth."

"Sounds inefficient and needlessly cruel."

"It really sort of is."

"Do you miss it?"

"The fishing part? No. The standing out on the edge of a lake or being in a boat while the sun's just coming up? That a little bit."

This was the other thing he did. Reminiscing about being a boy on Earth, talking about it as if she'd ever had experiences like his. As if just because she loved him, she'd understand. She pretended that she did, but she also changed the subject when she could.

"How long was I asleep?"

"It's still six hours until we're close enough to start docking," Jim said, answering her real question without having to check. "Bobbie's down in the machine shop with Clarissa and Amos doing some last-minute fixes to her combat armor. I get the feeling she's looking to suit up and stay suited up until she's on Medina."

"It has to be strange for her to lead OPA fighters."

Jim lowered himself to the gel of the crash couch, one arm bent behind his head. Naomi put her hand on his chest, just under his collarbone. His skin was warm. In the shadows, he looked vulnerable. Lost.

"Did she say something to you about it?" he asked.

"No. I was only thinking. She's spent so much of her life with Belters as the enemy, and now she's going to an OPA ship filled with OPA soldiers. We aren't her people. Or we weren't before now."

Jim nodded, squeezed her hand, and then slid out from under it. She watched him dress in silence for almost a minute.

"What is it?" she asked.

"Nothing."

"Jim," she said. Then, gently, "What is it?"

When he did his little, percussive, surrendering sigh, she knew he'd given up trying to protect her from whatever it was. He pulled on his undershirt and leaned against the wall.

"There was something I meant to talk about with you. About the ambush where Fred died?"

"Go ahead."

He did. Connecting to the *Pella*, trying to distract Marco, seeing Filip, disarming the torpedoes. He told it all with a sheepishness like a kid confessing that he ate the last bit of sweet. Even when she turned up the cabin lights and started pulling on her own clothes, he didn't meet her eyes. Amos had called him on it, offered to lock him out of the torpedo controls. Jim had said no. His silence was the only sign that he was done.

Naomi stood for a moment, watching her emotions like they were objects scattered by an unexpected turn. Horror at the idea of Filip's death. Rage at Marco for putting their child in harm's way. Guilt, not only for Filip but for Jim too. For the position she'd put him in and the reflexive compromises he'd made on her behalf. All those she'd known to expect, but there was an impatience too. Not with Jim exactly, or herself, or Filip. With the need to mourn again what she'd mourned so many times before.

"Thank you," she said, her heart thick and heavy. "For caring. For trying to watch out for me. But I lost Filip. I couldn't save him when he was a baby. I couldn't save him now that he's essentially a man. That's twice, and twice is always. I can't stop hoping that he'll be all right in all this. But if he's going to get saved, he's going to have to do it himself."

She pushed away a betraying tear. Jim took a half step toward her.

"He'll have to do it himself," she said again, her voice a degree harder to keep him from touching her or saying something soft and consoling. "Same as everyone."

When the *Giambattista* got into clear visual range, she wasn't a pretty ship. Longer than the *Canterbury* had been back in the day, thicker through the middle, with a score of massive storage cells open to the vacuum where it had stored the ice harvested from Saturn's rings or captured comets or any of the other sources around the system. Between the floodlit work shelves, the external mech storage sheds, attitude thrusters and sensor arrays and antennas, there were so many sources of drag that even the thinnest atmosphere would have ripped the ship to scrap. But no torpedo tubes.

No PDCs. There were thousands of tiny boats tucked into the huge ship, and nothing more than a winsome smile and a handgun to protect them.

On the command deck, Bobbie put one hand on Naomi's shoulder, another on Jim's. "Freaking out yet?"

"I'm fine," Naomi said in the same moment that Jim said, "Yes."

Bobbie's chuckle was warm. She was as happy as Naomi had seen her since she'd come back to the ship. She walked across the deck, mag boots clicking with each contact and release. It made Naomi nervous. If something happened to make the *Roci* move suddenly, either the boots would hold the deck and break her shinbones or they'd release and leave her bouncing against the walls of the ship. Not that the danger was real. It was only that, like Jim, she was probably freaking out. At least a little bit.

She watched the *Giambattista*'s braking pathway. The main engines turned off, the plume cooling and speeding away from the ship. It coasted toward them. Six thousand klicks. Five and three-quarters. Five and a half.

"All right," Alex said across the ship's comm. "Everyone hold on to your feathers. We're maneuvering to dock."

To Naomi's relief, she heard Bobbie strapping into a couch behind her as Amos and Clarissa announced that they were secure.

"Can you knock?" Jim asked.

She opened a tightbeam connection. Waited a long moment, and found herself face-to-face with a man whose white beard and salt-and-pepper hair made him look like something out of a children's story about wolves in human skin.

"Que sa, *Giambattista*," she said. "*Rocinante*, wir. Go es gut alles la?"

The wolf grinned. "Bist bien, sera Nagata suer. Give us your warriors girl, and let us kick these cocks à l'envers a pukis."

Naomi laughed, less at the vulgarity of the image than at the glee with which the old man said it. "Bien. Prepare for docking." She cut the connection and called up to Alex. "We have permission to dock."

Behind them, Bobbie was humming a melody Naomi didn't recognize, but it was syncopated, upbeat, even playful. The *Roci* lurched, the couches all shifting a few degrees to compensate. They were almost in matching orbit. Only a few meters' drift, and the thrusters under Alex's care were drawing that down to nothing.

"He knew your name," Jim said.

"You're not the only one people recognize," she said as the docking tube extended from the *Roci* and fixed itself to an outer airlock on the *Giambattista*. So close in, the hauler dwarfed the corvette. A horsefly and a horse. The scale of what they were about to try came home to her then and took her breath away. These two ships were the stealthy, small force. Easy to overlook in a system wracked with violence. Tiny to the point, they all hoped, of insignificance. And still huge.

"Are we going to be knocking around anymore?" Bobbie asked. "Because otherwise, I'm going to go get dressed and head over."

"You wearing your power armor just walking across the tube?" Alex asked.

"You know how it is," Bobbie said. "Never get a second chance to make a first impression."

"Awesome," Alex said.

"I'll meet you in the lock," Amos said.

Naomi looked over to Jim. He was frowning. "Say again, Amos?"

"Yeah," Amos said. She could hear the smile in his voice. "I thought I'd head over with Bobbie. These OPA fuckers are our best buddies and all, but we're still us and they're still them. Someone oughta watch Bobbie's six while she's out among them English. Besides which, I'm going to be as good as any of them at breaking heads."

"Might need you on the *Roci*, big guy," Jim said, his voice light. "With the whole heading-into-battle thing, I'd kind of like to keep my mechanic close to hand."

Bobbie retreated down the lift tube, pulling herself hand over hand, her floating feet disappearing last.

"That's sweet, but you don't need me, Cap," Amos said. "Peaches here knows the ship as well as I do. Anything you need done, she can do it."

Jim grunted, and she put her hand out, grabbing the edge of his couch and spinning it until they were facing. Jim saw the message in her expression. "Copy that, Amos," he said. "Bobbie? Make sure you bring enough of him back we can regrow the missing bits."

"Roger. Wilco," Bobbie said. Her voice sounded close and echoing. She already had her helmet on. Naomi wanted to be reassured by the joy that Bobbie took in the anticipated violence, but she couldn't quite manage. All she could do was hunker down and endure and see what happened next. At least she had practice with it.

Over the next hours, Bobbie and Amos inspected their new allies—the ship's reports and logs, the ships in their berths, the OPA fighters they'd be leading on the attack—while Naomi, watching through Bobbie's suit camera, cataloged it all. Racks of guns and boxes of ammunition. The motley assortment of boats and soldiers. Bobbie's assessments were calm, rational, professional, and fueled the dread growing in Naomi's gut.

Her mind wandered a little bit during the slow moments. Human violence as a kind of fractal—self-similar on all scales from bar fight to system-wide war. The buildup of insults and lost face that swelled over the course of an evening or a century. The shoving and shoving back, neither side sure they wanted to escalate and uncertain how to back down. All of that was the history of the inner planets and the Belt since the beginning. Then Marco had thrown his sucker punch and sent the system reeling back. Since then, feints and evaluations, flurries of violence that weren't meant to end anything so much as find position, test the opponent.

Everything since the rocks fell on Earth had been preparation for this: a counterattack made in earnest and without reservation. Each side hoping to engineer a punch that the other didn't see coming. Forgotten arm. Maybe it was in their blood, their bones. A shared human heritage. The pattern they were exporting to the stars now. It left her tired.

"Well, it's not what I'd pick, but it's better than I'd hoped," Bobbie said from her new, cramped quarters on the *Giambattista*. In the background, Naomi could make out Amos' voice, lifted and laughing among others. Fitting in with the new group. Or no, that wasn't right. Letting the new group think he fit in. She had a terrible sense that he wouldn't come back on the *Rocinante*; the empty premonitions of anxiety and impatience.

"Do you want to check the boats in more depth?" Naomi asked.

"No," Bobbie said. "I can do that on the way. Pull the trigger. Let's get this apocalypse on the road."

"All right," Naomi said. "Stay safe."

"Good hunting. We say, 'Good hunting.'"

"Good hunting, then."

The words were powerfully inadequate. She dropped the connection, unstrapped, braced herself against the handholds on the wall, and stretched her arms, her legs, worked the kinks in her spine. When she was done, she realized it was the same routine she did before she worked out. Preparing for great effort.

She went down to the galley where Alex and Jim and Clarissa were eating together. They all looked over at her as she pulled herself into the room. "Bobbie says we're good to go."

"Well, shit and yahoo," Alex said.

Jim pulled his hand terminal out of his pocket, tapped through a set of commands including one with a double password, then pressed a button.

"Okay," he said. "Signal's out. As soon as the attack's under way, we'll burn for the ring and hope no one notices us."

They were all quiet for a moment. Naomi felt like there should have been some kind of fanfare. Gongs and trumpets to announce the coming death and destruction. Instead, it was just the galley, the four of them, the sound of the air recyclers, and the smell of chicken.

"Looks like a shit night for sleeping," Naomi said. "I'm going to be up watching the newsfeeds." Jim didn't say anything. His eyes were sunken with exhaustion and something else. Not fear. Worse than fear. Resignation. Naomi pushed off, braced beside him, and put her hand on his. He managed a smile. "I'll bring drinks and snacks. We can watch the fireworks start."

"I don't know," Jim said.

"It ain't sulking if we all do it together, Hoss," Alex said. And then, to Naomi, "Count me in."

"Me too," Clarissa said, and then didn't add *if I'm invited*. Against the backdrop of the war, it was such a small thing, and Naomi was still glad to see it.

"Yeah," Jim said, "okay."

It took hours. All across the system, drive plumes flared. Around Ceres and Mars and Tycho, the consolidated fleet leaped away from their defensive positions and into the Belt. The scattering of Michio Pa's pirate fleet joined in, and the OPA. By the time the last of them reported that they were on the burn, the ships of the Free Navy were starting to react. The *Rocinante* traced vectors and travel groups, threads of light tangling the emptiness between stations and planets. Battle lines. The newsfeeds lit up— civilian, government, corporate, and union all becoming aware that something was happening and leaping to make sense of what it could be.

It was just after midnight, ship time, that the *Roci* raised the alarm.

"What do we have, Alex?" Jim asked.

"Bad news. I'm seeing a couple of fast-attack ships headed our way out from Ganymede."

"Well, so much for not being noticed. How long before they reach us?" Jim asked, but Naomi had already queried the system.

"Five days if they're just buzzing us and looping back," she said. "Twelve if they try to match orbit while we're on the burn."

"Can we take them?" Clarissa said.

"If it was just us, might could," Alex said. "Problem is we're guarding this cow. But if we burn hard enough, we might make the ring before they get us."

"Figure it out on the way," Jim said. "Right now, we need to get the *Giambattista* up and burning as hard as it can and still let Bobbie do her inspections."

"No plan survives contact with the enemy," Alex said, unstrapping and pulling himself up toward the cockpit. "I'm warming her up."

"I'll tell our friends across the way to do the same," Holden said, taking comm control.

On Naomi's monitor, the thousands of hair-thin lines marked where the battles were, and where they were expected to be. On impulse, she took down the tactical display, leaving just the wide scatter of drive plumes all around the system, and then added in the star field.

It was the widest concerted attack ever. Hundreds of ships on at least four sides. Dozens of stations, millions of lives.

Among the stars, it didn't stand out.

Chapter Forty: Prax

The more time passed, the clearer it became how little Ganymede's official neutrality meant. The ships in the docks and orbiting the moon were more and more Free Navy ships, fewer and fewer anything else. The soldiers in Free Navy uniform appeared more often at the tube stations, in the markets, in the public halls and corridors, first with the apparent casualness of citizens, then in larger groups with more aggressive demeanors. Then with armored emplacements that would allow them to shoot in safety whoever happened by.

Djuna had stopped letting him watch the local newsfeeds at breakfast on the weekends. Too many stories about bodies being found in unfortunate conditions. Too many missing people, too many espionage claims, too many reminders from the still-official security apparatus that Pinkwater was an unaffiliated corporate entity with no political litmus tests and only the safety and well-being of the citizens of Ganymede at heart. The sorts of things people said because they weren't true.

For Prax, the official news and the gun-wielding soldiers weren't the most disturbing things. There were smaller things that he noticed. The way that the girls didn't fight against being home by curfew anymore. The wistful conversations Djuna would start about taking positions somewhere else, emigrating off Ganymede entirely, and then end without ever drawing a conclusion. The small things carried more weight. Yes, a dissident circle was killed. Yes, people disappeared. But—apart from Karvonides—they weren't people he knew. And the change in the station was also changing his family. It was also changing him.

Prax went about his work because there was nothing else to do. It wasn't as if things would be made better by hiding in his bed. And the appearance of normalcy was sometimes almost as good as the real thing. So he went to the meetings in the mornings, worked with his plants in the afternoons. Some of the runs had to be scaled back. Research and development weren't a priority as much as generating food to resupply the warships. Prax thought that was shortsighted. If anything, disruptions like this were an argument for more research, especially with the radioplast work that Khana and Brice had under proposal. He tried bringing the point up now and again. He'd even gone so far as to ask whether there was a contact with the Free Navy that the labs could talk to about it. No one was enthusiastic about it, though. So that was something else the occupation had taken away.

Under it all, the fear of what he'd done in sending the data to Earth hung over him. It was almost a relief when the security forces finally came.

He was in the overflow hydroponics lab at midafternoon. Rows of black-leaved plants rose up from the tanks toward the light banks. The roots that pushed through the underlying aqueous gel were pale as snow. Prax was moving from plant to plant, his hands in light-blue NBR gloves. He checked each leaf gently, looking for sprays of yellow and orange where the radioplasts were dying. Until the man called his name, his afternoon had been going pretty well.

"Dr. Meng?"

There were four people, all of them men. Two wore simple uniforms with the Pinkwater logo on the breast and shoulder. The other two were Free Navy. Prax felt his heart thud against his chest as the adrenaline hit, but he tried not to look more than a little uncomfortable. Anyone would be a little anxious when the Free Navy came asking for them. Even the innocent. He thought that was right.

"Can I help you?"

"We need you to come with us now," the taller of the two Free Navy men said.

"I can't," Prax said, gesturing toward the plants he hadn't checked. As if that were explanation enough.

They stepped closer, moving around him. They all had sidearms. Handcuffs. Canisters of restraint spray.

"You have to come with us now," the tall man said again.

"Do...do I need my union representative?" he asked, but he wasn't surprised when the shorter of the Free Navy men pushed him in the small of the back. *I could run*, he thought. *It wouldn't help, but I could do it.*

They marched him out through the front office. When they passed Brice in the hall, she looked away, pretending not to notice. The front desk was abandoned, everyone suddenly called to the restroom or a coffee break at the same moment. None of the people he worked with would actually see him leave. That's how quickly the right kinds of power could make someone disappear. Walking out the front door for what he had to assume was the last time, it felt like an epiphany. He'd wondered, watching the newsfeeds, how so many could go missing in a station with people and cameras everywhere. He understood now.

All they had to do was make it too dangerous for others to watch.

They loaded him into a cart, drove off down the main corridor, down the southern exchange ramp, and into a well-lit concrete hallway. He had the sudden, visceral memory of waiting here back after the mirrors fell, when the survival of Ganymede Station had been an open question. He'd waited in line right there, trying to find Mei. It would be her turn now to wonder what had happened to him. Symmetry.

At the Pinkwater office, they took him to a small, cold room. Green walls. Green floor. Everything stank of industrial cleaner. The kind they used to clean up blood and spit. Biohazard stuff. A chair bolted in place in front of a cheap, plastic desk. Black dots along the wall shifted toward him like the eyes of a spider. Not cameras, but the same multifrequency image arrays he used in the labs. They were sensitive enough to pick up his heart rate from changes in his skin and track the heat in every part of his body. He'd used them extensively on last year's soybean experiments, and seeing them here felt almost like betrayal.

The taller Free Navy man came in. A dark-skinned woman in a Pinkwater uniform with him. Prax looked up. He'd imagined this moment so many times in the middle of dread-soaked nights that now that it was happening he was almost curious to see how well it met his expectations. Would they beat him? Threaten him with violence? Would they threaten Mei and Djuna and Natalia? He'd heard that sometimes they would addict prisoners to drugs and then threaten to withhold their supply and let withdrawals do the work.

"Dr. Meng," the tall man said, sitting across from him. Did they take focus drugs? Prax had heard of focus drugs, but he didn't know how they worked. "You were supervisor for Quiana Karvonides? You're on record as identifying her body."

"I am," Prax said. Was there a way to pretend his way out of this? Would they believe him if he denied everything he could deny? Or would he give himself away? All the black, mechanical eyes on him, and the tall man's pale-brown ones too. Only the Pinkwater woman was looking at her hand terminal. "I did. Karvonides didn't have family on the station, I think. I'm not sure about that, though. Is something wrong?"

"She was working on proprietary yeast? Is that right?"

"That's one of the projects we do," Prax said, nodding. He was being too anxious. They'd know.

"She was working on it particularly?"

Prax's mouth was dry, and the cold of the room seemed to creep up his legs and into the base of his spine. What had he done? Why hadn't he kept his head down? But no, that wasn't right. He had reasons for taking every action he took. And he'd known there were risks. Being here in this room was one, even if he hadn't known which room in particular. He wondered whether there were other people watching him, or if the spider eyes fed into some sort of software that analyzed him and fed them the answers.

"Dr. Meng?"

"Yes, sorry. Yes, she worked on the harvester yeast. It's an organism, um, that harvests a very broad range of electromagnetic radiation, the way that a plant uses light. It's reverse-engineered from the protomolecule data. It lets the yeast generate its own sugars from the radioplasts, and then, um, its native systems can convert that into higher-complexity nutrients."

The two shared a look. He couldn't tell what its significance was. How would Mei do without him? She was older now. Nearly adolescent. She was going to start pulling away from the family unit soon anyway. Maybe that wasn't such a bad time to lose him. Would they put his body back in the recycler? He couldn't think like that. Not now.

"What can you tell us about Hy1810?" the woman asked, and Prax felt like she was looking through him. Seeing his bones and the shape of his blood vessels. He'd never felt more naked. He tried to lean back in his chair, to rock it a little back and forth, but the bolts only grated a little. There were notches and scrapes on the wall he hadn't noticed until now. Painted over, yes, but there. He didn't want to think about what had made them.

"It's the tenth variation using protocol eighteen," he said. "It's proprietary. I'm not supposed to talk about that. I'm sorry."

"Why did you move the Hy1810 data out of Karvonides' partition?"

And there it was. They knew. He took a breath, and he could hear it shaking in his throat. They wouldn't need focus drugs or psych computers. He was readable as plain text. It had been a dream that he might avoid the worst. All that was left was watching it play out. He felt a vestigial, unreasoning hope. There had to be a way. He had to get back home, or else who would make pancakes for the girls?

"I moved it on the request of some of the other project engineers. With Karvonides' passing, they needed to have access to the run data. Otherwise there was no way to move forward. So, yes, I put it in a partition where they could reach it."

"Did you review the permissions on that partition?"

"The information was proprietary," Prax said, clinging to the idea like it was the last, water-logged fragment of the ship that had sunk beneath him. It sounded weak, even to him.

The man leaned forward. "That data was sent to Earth. We've isolated the tracking data on it, and it came from the partition *you put it in.*"

Lies and denials bubbled in his mind. *Anyone could have accessed that data. I was sloppy. Careless with security, maybe. That's all. I didn't do anything wrong.*

In his mind's eye, he saw Karvonides again. The wounds on her neck and head. Yes, he could deny her again, but it wouldn't make any difference. They already knew, or near enough. They'd push him, torture him, and he would break. It didn't matter what he said now. He was dead. No more pancakes. No more evenings coaxing the girls into doing their homework or Sunday mornings waking up late with Djuna. Someone else would have to take over his research. Everything he'd loved, everything he'd lived for, was gone.

To his surprise, it felt less like fear than a sort of terrible freedom. He could say anything he wanted now. Including the truth.

"The thing you need to understand," he said, an irrational, intoxicating courage blooming in his heart. "Biological equilibria? They're not straightforward. Never."

"Equilibria," the man repeated.

"Yes. Exactly. Everyone thinks that it's simple. New, invasive species comes in and it has an advantage and it outcompetes, right? That's the story, but there's another part to that. Always, *always*, the local environment resists. Yes, yes, maybe badly. Maybe without a clear idea of coping with novelty. I'm not saying it's perfect, but I am saying it's there. Even when an invasive species takes over, even when it wins, there is a counterbalancing process it has to overcome to do that. And—" The tall man was scowling, and his discomfort made Prax want to speak faster. To say everything he had in his heart before the hammer fell. "And that counterprocess is so *deep* in the fabric of living systems, it can never be absent. However well the new species is designed, however overwhelming its advantages seem to be, the pushback will always be there. If one native impulse is overcome, there will be another. You understand? Conspecifics are outcompeted? Fine, the bacterial and viral microecologies will push back. Adapt to those, and it'll be micronutrient levels and salinity and light. And the thing is, the thing is, even when the novel species *does* win? Even when it takes over every niche there is, that struggle alone changes what it is. Even when you wipe out or co-opt the local environment completely, you're changed by the pushback. Even when the previous organisms are driven to extinction, they leave markers behind. What they are can never, *never* be completely erased."

Prax sat back in his chair, chin high, breath deep and fast, nostrils flared. *You can kill me. You can wipe me from the rolls of history. But you can never change the mark I've made. I stood against you, and even when you've killed me, it won't undo the things I've done.*

The man's scowl deepened. "Are we still talking about the yeast?"

"Yes," Prax said. "Of course we're talking about the yeast."

"All right," the man said. "That's great, but what we need to know is who had access to that partition."

"What?"

"The partition you put the data in," said the Pinkwater woman. "Who could have linked to it from there?"

"Anyone with access to the workstations in the research group *could* have," Prax said. "What does that have to do with it?"

The man's hand terminal chimed, and he pulled it out from his pocket. The red backsplash on an alert made him look almost like he was blushing, but when he put the hand terminal away, his face had gone pale.

"I have to step back," the Free Navy man said. "You finish this, yeah?" His voice was tight. Prax thought he was shaking. The woman nodded and checked her own hand terminal. Prax watched him go, confused. Wanting, almost, to call him back and insist that they finish. This was important. This was his martyrdom in the cause of freedom and science. The interrogator couldn't just walk away in the middle of it. When the door closed, he turned to the woman, but she was still looking at her terminal. A newsfeed with something about the war.

She whistled softly, her eyes going wide. When she looked up at him, it was like she was surprised to see him.

"The yeast data," he said, reminding her.

"Dr. Meng, you have to be more careful. You can't do that anymore."

"Do what?"

The woman's impatient smile didn't reach her eyes. "You can't put data that might help the enemy into an open partition. I know it's proprietary, but someone leaked it, and we have an active investigation now into who that might have been."

"But— No, you don't understand."

"Dr. Meng," she snapped. "I know you don't like us coming in and telling you how to run your lab, but these are delicate times. I'm asking you to take a long, careful look at your lab's security hygiene so that we don't have a less pleasant conversation next time. You understand that?"

"Yes. Of course."

"All right, then," the woman said with the air of having won an argument. "You can go now."

Prax didn't know what to do. He sat quietly for a moment, waiting for clarification he didn't know how to ask for. The woman checked her hand terminal, looked back at him, annoyance in her expression.

"Dr. Meng? We're done for now. If we have any further questions, we'll find you."

"I should leave?"

"Yes," she said.

And so he did. Walking through the halls and up to the public carts felt like moving through a dream. His stomach felt empty. He wasn't hungry, there was just a massive bubble in his gut where something—pain, despair, hope, fear—was supposed to be. He rented a cart, took it to the tube station. The whole incident had been so brief, his shift wasn't even done. It would be, though, by the time he got back to the lab. So he went home instead.

The newsfeeds on the tube were alive with whatever military action had been on the security woman's hand terminal. He tried to make sense of it all, but the words seemed to lose their meaning somewhere between the screen and his senses. He caught himself staring emptily at a young man sitting across from him and had to make a conscious effort to look away. All he could think was the dark-skinned woman saying *You can go now*.

Djuna was home when he got there, sitting on the couch with her head in her hands, her eyes bloodshot and her cheeks blotchy from crying. When he stopped in the entryway from the kitchen and lifted his hand in greeting, she stared at him for a moment, stunned, and then leaped up, ran to him, and wrapped him in her arms. After a long moment, he hugged her back, and they stood in their rooms, the way he never thought they would again.

"Leslie sent me a message," Djuna said, her voice still thick with tears. "She said they came for you at the office. That the security people took you away. I was trying to find a lawyer who would talk to me. I sent the girls to Dorian's. I didn't know what to tell them."

"All right," Prax said. "It's all right."

Djuna leaned back, searching his eyes like there was something written in them. "What happened?"

"I confessed," Prax said. "I told them…I told them everything. And then they let me go."

"They did what?"

"They said I shouldn't do it again, and that I should leave," he said. "It wasn't at all the reaction I expected."

Chapter Forty-One: Pa

I've got fast-movers," Evans said. "Five, wait…Seven."

"Coming from?" Michio asked, though she was already certain of the answer. The assaults throughout the Belt had already pulled the Free Navy's fighters to other conflicts, thinning the defenses at Pallas. She had to give Holden his due. He hadn't tried to use her and her ships as bullet sponges.

"Pallas Station," Evans confirmed. "No one's shooting out in the black."

"PDCs have them," Laura said. "Permission to fire?"

"You have permission," Michio said. "Oksana, evasive maneuvers at will. Let's show these fuckers we can dance."

"Yes, Captain," Oksana said between teeth bared in concentration and joy. A moment later, the *Connaught* lurched, shifted. Over the system, Josep howled a wordless battle cry.

The Four Horsemen, Foyle called them. The *Connaught*, the

Serrio Mal, the *Panshin*, and the *Solano*—the most experienced of Pa's breakaway fleet. They fell toward Pallas Station from four different directions, spreading the local defenses as thin as they could. If there had been time, maybe Marco would have pulled resources off Pallas too, sabotaged the manufacturing infrastructure, and left anyone who couldn't escape on their own for Pa to rescue or let starve under her name.

But that assumed there was someplace for the Free Navy to run to.

"Two down," Laura announced. "Five to go."

"Sooner's better than later," Michio said.

Metal and ceramic creaking and singing from the strain, the *Connaught* turned and accelerated, then cut power and went on the float, whipping around to give the PDCs a wider field of fire. Laura's guns buzzed, vibrating the ship and killing three more of the station's torpedoes even as the *Connaught* sped in toward them flank-first. The surface of the asteroid glittered ahead of them, her target and her enemy and the home to tens of thousands of the people she'd thrown her safety and career aside to help and protect.

"Keep the rounds from hitting the station if you can."

"Do my best, Captain," Laura said, but her subtext was clear— if it gets down to them or us, it's them. Michio couldn't disagree.

"*Panshin*'s taking fire," Evans said. "*Serrio Mal* too."

"*Solano*?" Michio asked.

The *Solano* had taken the most damage in the raids and scuffles since she'd broken ranks with Marco. Enough that it was chosen to be the sacrifice ship, emptied of her crew and all useful material. It was the hinge point of her battle plan. Three of her ships to distract and disarm Pallas, to the point that, even if they shot it full of holes, they couldn't scatter the *Solano* into a debris field thin enough to keep the docks from crippling damage.

"Still far enough back it's not being targeted," Oksana said.

"Four more down," Laura said. "That last one's being a booger... Got it!"

"Captain," Oksana said. "We're going to need to return to braking burn if we don't want to get very close and personal with the station."

"Do it," Michio said. "I'm taking comms."

"Understood," Evans said. "I've got another wave of torpedoes coming in. And we are nearing effective PDC range."

Michio set for broadcast. So close to the station, there'd be no light delay. Everyone listening would hear her almost as she spoke. After so long at high-lag distances, it felt odd. She considered herself in the camera as Oksana spun the ship and punched the deceleration. She started the broadcast.

"This is Captain Michio Pa of the *Connaught* to all citizens of Pallas Station. Be advised, we are here to remove the false governance of the Free Navy and return control of the station to its citizens. Evacuate the docks immediately. I repeat, evacuate the dock levels immediately for your own safety. We call on the Free Navy administration for immediate and unconditional surrender. If we do not have that confirmed in the next fifteen minutes, it will be too late to save the docks and shipyard. For your own safety, evacuate now."

The comms display threw up an error alert. Her signal was being jammed. She boosted it as much as the *Connaught*'s transmitter allowed and set it to loop. She hadn't had much hope of a peaceful ending, but she'd tried.

The ship lurched again and burned hard, pressing her back into her couch. Laura shouted something obscene, but the ship didn't detonate. They'd dodged whatever it was.

"*Panshin* took a hit," Evans reported. "PDC. They look all right. The *Solano*'s still not top of the Pallas threat index." He paused, rechecked his monitor. "It's working."

"Thank you," Michio said. "Let's start taking out their PDCs."

"Already on it," Laura said. "Just as long as I can keep these torpedoes from flying up our ..." She trailed off, lost in concentration. Michio didn't interrupt.

This wasn't what she wanted. Wasn't what she'd ever wanted.

She'd begun this whole fallen, fucked-up process because the dream of a Belt for Belters—a life that didn't depend on being used and exploited by the larger powers in the system—had meant something. And now here she was, fighting alongside Earth and Mars. Against Belters.

Three years, Sanjrani gave them. Three and a half. And then starvation. And she was about to break the docks at a major port so that James Holden could open the way to the colony worlds again and leave them all behind. This was what she'd agreed to do. It was her part in stopping Marco and trying to save the Belt, even if it was the Belt three years from now.

Every step along the way had made sense, except that they ended up here. Everyone she'd allied with her whole life had started by seeming to be good, competent, and loyal. They'd all disappointed. And now, she was going to do the same. She'd changed sides so many times, she didn't know who she was anymore.

If she changed the plan now, if she backed away ...

Fought the oppressor before. Still fighting the oppressor now. Followed your heart then. Still following your heart now. The situation changes; that doesn't mean you do.

Fuck.

"Evans," she said. "What's the status of the *Solano*?"

"On course, Captain."

"Do we have control of it?"

Evans looked over at her. His eyes were wide and uncertain. Panicky. "I have telemetry, yeah."

"Slow it down," she said, pulling up tightbeam connections to the *Panshin* and the *Serrio Mal*. "Give us more time to kill the defenses."

Captain Foyle accepted the connection first, then a moment later, Rodriguez. In the separate windows of her display, they looked like negative images of each other. His pale skin, her dark, but with the same thinness and close-cropped hair. The images shook under different strains as the *Panshin* and the *Serrio Mal* suffered their own separate evasions.

"We have a change of plan," Michio said. "The *Solano* isn't ramming the station. We're going to park it, ass-end at the ports, inside safety range, warm up the Epstein, and melt anything that comes out to slag. Blockade."

Foyle's eyes could have been cast iron for all that her expression changed. She'd be hell at the poker table.

"Con que?" Rodriguez said, his lips narrowing. "Is late à diffe the plan."

"Late's better than too late," Michio said. "The Belters of Pallas aren't the enemy. I'm not going to make them the enemy. I need slow passes from both of you. Every PDC gets dusted. Every gun and torpedo emplacement, we break. Then sensor arrays. I need this station blind and declawed."

For a moment neither one of her captains spoke. She could hear all the objections in her own voice. She was tripling the risk of the mission. She was spending an order of magnitude more ammunition—torpedoes and PDC rounds—than a simple escort of the sacrifice ship required. She was putting them, her commanders and their crews and their families, at risk to preserve a station that was actively trying to kill them all.

"I need you to trust me," she said. A loud pop announced a stray PDC round had holed the *Connaught*. Oksana shouted something about sealing the deck. Michio didn't look away from the screen. Let them see these were her risks too.

"Dui," Foyle said in her whiskey-and-cigar voice. "You say it, bossmang, and we get it done."

Rodriguez, shaking his head, muttered something obscene, looked into the camera with tired eyes. "Fine."

She dropped the connection. When she checked in with fire control, Laura had already changed the profile. On the display, every weapon on the face of the station was marked in red, targeted for destruction. But not the docks. Evans was out of his couch and pouring sealant on the hole where the PDC round had punched through the hulls. The slug had passed through the command deck maybe a meter from her head. She could have died.

Any of her people could have died. Knowing it was like being two different people at once. One, horrified at the idea that it could have hit Laura or Evans or Oksana. The other, shrugging away what hadn't happened. This was the work. This was the choice she'd made, and it was the right one.

For two long hours, the *Connaught* dodged, strained, poured rounds down onto the surface of Pallas. What had originally been a fast, sharp attack turned into a long, bloody bout more about endurance and supplies than clever tactics. The *Panshin* and the *Serrio Mal* matched her blow for blow, hammer strikes against an anvil. The jammers were set too deep in the stone for even her torpedoes to reach, and every time the curve of asteroid cut off her line of sight to the other ships, Michio was afraid something would happen. That she wouldn't see them again. And once, the *Panshin* emerged from a long pass with a bright scar and section of her hull peeled back.

Slowly, a blindspot appeared around the docks. Parts of space leading to Pallas that had been defended, weren't. Evans brought the *Solano* into it kilometer by kilometer, then meter by meter until it had locked to Pallas' orbit with only an occasional little push from the maneuvering thrusters to keep it stationary.

"They're going to find a way to kill it, sir," Oksana said. "May take them days, may take them hours, but this isn't a blockade that can hold for long."

"Get me line-of-sight on the *Panshin*, Oksana."

"Sir."

Rodriguez, when he appeared on the screen again, was grinning. So that, at least, was a good sign.

"How's your ship, Captain Rodriguez?" Michio said, returning his smile despite herself.

"Esá bent, broken, fucked, flustered, and far from home," Ezio said, laughing. "Got a couple in the med bay and one in the morgue, but we done the thing, que sí? Pulled a whole station's teeth and half their eyes too, account son los *champions*."

"I think we are," Michio said. "I'm going to need you to stand guard on this. Pull back far enough that you're out of range of anything Pallas puts together. Take control of the *Solano*."

"Babysit?" Rodriguez said.

"Got your hull pulled back like a condom wrapper, Ezio. I'm not putting you in at Titan."

God bless the man, he looked disappointed. "Bist bien," he said. "We'll hold the line. But you and Foyle take the torpedoes we've still got, yeah? Stock up. Anything we do, we can manage con PDCs and my winning smile."

"Won't say no to that," Michio said.

"Que tu trigger?" he asked. "When do I light it up and slag the fuckers?"

"When you know it's Free Navy you're burning down. Not if just people. Lose the ship before you hurt civilians. Killing people because they got in the way is inner-planets bullshit. It's Free Navy bullshit. We're better than that."

"Damn right we are," Rodriguez said and signed off. When he saluted, he had blood on his fingers.

She pointed a tightbeam connection request at one of the less damaged comm arrays, unsure if it would do any good. Even if the equipment was limping along well enough to function, there was no reason for the connection to be accepted. Only it was.

A familiar dark, pebbled face appeared on her monitor. From what she could see behind him, he was in a well-appointed office, brightly lit and probably somewhere deep enough in the station that she couldn't have reached him without nukes or a reactor set to critical and crashed into the station.

"Captain Pa," he said. "You seem to be moving from one shitty decision to another."

"Rosenfeld," she said.

"When you broke with Inaros, I understood it. Respected it, even. I was disappointed when you turned to Fred Johnson. But this? Playing marionette to Chrisjen Avasarala and Emily Richards. And Holden?" He shook his head. "Something happened to you, Michio. You've changed."

"Context changed," she said. "I'm still the same. And here's what happens next. I have a live, warmed-up Epstein drive pointed at the docks. If I see any activity there? I slag them. If I see any shuttles or boats taking off from the surface, I'll shoot them down and slag the docks. If I see anything that looks like an attempt to sabotage the *Solano*, I'll slag the docks. If any Free Navy ship comes within a hundred thousand klicks of Pallas, I'll slag the docks. You will find yourself governor of an old, broken station that can't move supplies in or out."

"Duly noted," Rosenfeld said dryly.

There didn't seem anything more to say, but she didn't kill the connection. Not yet. And then, "Use this."

"Excuse me?"

"You're a political animal. Use this opportunity. I'm giving you an excuse to drop out of the fighting. You can tell Marco that I pinned you down. You won't even be lying. Even if he beats us all, you know he can't govern the system. And your plan?"

"My plan? What plan?"

"The one where you're the man behind the throne. The real power while Marco's the public face and figurehead. That won't work either. He can't be controlled. He can barely be predicted. I'm not blaming you. I made the same mistake. I saw what I wanted to see in him. But I was wrong, and you are too." Rosenfeld's face was unreadable and still. Michio nodded. "Do you know the magic word?"

"No," he said, his voice rich with disdain. "What's the magic word?"

"*Oops.* You should say oops, Rosenfeld. Own it that you made a mistake. That ship I have with its ass pointed at you? It's your chance to do something about the fact that you picked the wrong side."

"You want me to thank you for that?"

"I want you to make sure all the people in there get food and water, and I want you to keep them safe until this is over."

"And when's that going to be?"

"I don't know," she said, and dropped the connection.

For a long moment, she rested in her couch, held in place by the straps and the familiarity of the voices and sounds around her. Her jaw ached where she'd been clenching it. She had a bruise across her collarbone, and she couldn't remember which maneuver might have caused it. She closed her eyes, letting it all wash over her. Laura talking through the headset with Bertold about how many PDC rounds they had left. Oksana and Evans laughing over nothing, releasing tension, quietly celebrating that—on some level, by some measure—they'd won. The smell of the portable welding rig burning off the emergency sealant and closing the punctures in the hull. Her home. Her people. She filled her lungs with them all.

The comm display chirped. A request from the *Serrio Mal*. She accepted it. Susanna Foyle appeared on her monitor.

"Captain Pa," she said.

"Captain Foyle."

"Rodriguez tells me we're not taking three ships to Titan after all."

"That's right."

"Used up a lot of ordnance on this mission that wasn't in the specs," Foyle said.

"Also true," Pa agreed.

"Going to leave us outnumbered and outgunned." It wasn't an accusation. Just an observation.

"We won't be the only ships there," Pa said. "We'll have backup."

For the first time, Foyle's face lowered its dignity to have an expression. "Squats and Dusters. No one we can count on."

"We're all in this together," Pa said, and Foyle coughed out a single laugh.

"As long as you're going first, we'll follow. Didn't get this far by taking the easy way. We've got our patches in place and our bandages on. You're ready to burn, then so are we."

"Thank you."

Foyle nodded, dropped the connection. Pa pulled up a system-

wide tactical map with all the fighting that was going on throughout the system. A cluster of updates from Vesta. A chase between
Free Navy fighters and a dozen Martian warships as Marco's forces
tried to loop around toward Mars itself. The guard force left behind
at Ceres tracking four Free Navy ships. The orbital defense of Earth
on high alert, most of its patrol ships away from their posts and on
the attack. The sum of all of humanity's presence in the solar system, bent on violence and spectacle. And at the edge of the display,
almost off it, *almost* forgotten, the *Giambattista* and the *Rocinante*,
already decelerating toward the ring gate, and two fast-attack ships
burning hard to intercept.

Good luck, you bastard, she thought, putting her hand over
the tiny gold dot marked *Rocinante*. *Don't make me sorry I
trusted you.*

And then, over the ship-wide system, "All stations report.
We've got another fight to get to. Don't want to be late."

Chapter Forty-Two: Marco

"Son coyo, son *tod*!" Micah al-Dujaili shouted out from the screen. "You and all your ti-ti soldat! I am here for you, Inaros. What *you* did to my family."

Marco muted the broadcast. Somewhere nearby, someone else was watching it. Al-Dujaili's rant still nattering in the distance as the *Pella* rose off Callisto, a half dozen ships arrayed behind her. "Do we have target lock?"

Josie lifted a hand in affirmation, his eyes firmly on the monitor. They were only at a single g, but Marco felt a headache beginning at the base of his skull. It didn't matter. It was only a little pain, after all. There'd be time to take something for it when his enemies weren't wasting good air. Around him, the command deck of the *Pella* was tight and bunched. Josie with weapons. Karal at the comms. Miral muttering into his headset to someone down in engineering. They were wolves. A band of predators ready to strike. Al-Dujaili shouted something about vengeance. Something about betraying the Belt in the name of glory.

"Let's shut this fucker up, then," Marco said casually. "Fire everything."

The warning had come to the Jovian system in time for him. Earth, Mars, the traitor Michio Pa, Holden. Naomi. All his enemies had lit their torches and hoisted their pitchforks for him and taken to the road. Marco wasn't surprised. He'd known to watch for them, and when they came, he was ready. True, he hadn't expected it to come from everyplace at once the way it had. The consolidated fleet had come boiling out of Ceres, up from Earth and Mars. They'd burned hard and taken some of the nearest of the Free Navy's forces by surprise. But space and distance were Marco's natural allies. It took time to burn across the half-billion kilometers from Mars, and the Jovian system was Belters' land. And Belters meant Free Navy, no matter what yapping little pups like Micah al-Dujaili and Aimee Ostman wanted to pretend. By the time their Earther allies made it to al-Dujaili's side, the man would be a corpse, and all the ships traveling with him dead at his side.

"Firing now," Josie said.

The *Pella* rang with the mechanisms of torpedo and PDC, the vibrations traveling through the hull and making the whole ship chime like a war bell. Marco could taste the sound—ice and copper. It was beautiful.

"Hoy, Captain," Karal said. "Got messages coming in. Other ships que savvy if they should be firing too?"

"Yes," Marco said. "Tell them all to open fire."

"The ones kommt de Ganymede too? Not in effective range, them."

Marco shifted to stare at Karal. The ache in his brain grew a degree worse. He'd known Karal for decades, trusted him. In his voice now, though, Marco heard doubt. More than doubt. Insolence.

"All. Fire. Let al-Dujaili spend his rounds plucking their torpedoes out of the black. It'll shut his nattering mouth."

"Dui," Karal said, turning back to the comms and speaking in a voice too low and urgent for Marco to bother listening.

It was happening everywhere. Vesta. Pallas. Titan. Hygeia Station. Thisbe Yards. Europa. Large targets and small, the enemy was coming at him thinking they would wash the Free Navy aside like a wave. And there was damage, yes. Pallas blockaded. Vesta fallen. The battle forces burning toward Titan alone might make one of the largest in history, and he couldn't say how decisive his victory there would be. It almost didn't matter. The important thing was that he had goaded them into action. Into reaching out in anger and fear. It was a recipe for overreach. After the careful, turtle-meek response of Earth and Mars to this point, it was a relief.

Let them come. Let them win their little victories. The Free Navy would hold what it could, scatter into the dark where that was wiser, and loop back to crush the unguarded targets left behind. It was the mistake he'd known they would make. The inner planets with all their centuries of dominion still dreamed that they could fight a war and win. Marco knew better. War was never won and never lost. Until now—until *him*—Earth and Mars had thought they were at peace because the violence had all poured out on the Belt and not back at them. Their fault. Their shortsightedness. They'd had their age of victory. It was over now. And this paroxysm, this grand mal seizure of a battle plan, promised a thousand more like it to come.

The Belt would take its hits. But it would never take them passively again. That was his victory.

"First wave's down," Josie said. "They got all our torpedoes. No hits. Try again?"

"No," Marco said. "We wait. Let them think they can handle us. Then crush them."

"Bien," Josie said. Karal muttered into the comms, passing the word along. Without the weapons fire, the ship still wasn't quiet. It only felt that way. Marco stretched his neck, craning it to try to relieve the tension there, but everything in him was straining out toward al-Dujaili. He'd killed Fred Johnson with his own hands already, and now all the OPA factions that had been stupid enough to follow an Earther would see what crop they'd sown.

He pulled up the tactical display. The eight enemy ships led by al-Dujaili's *Torngarsuk* were scattered enough to make taking two down with a single torpedo impossible, but near enough that their PDC fire could reinforce each other. For all al-Dujaili's ranting and venom, he hadn't lost his temper enough to abandon good sense.

The *Pella* and the six other Free Navy ships from the Callisto shipyards held a looser formation but a wider surface. Outnumbered for the moment, but with ten Free Navy ships on hard burn from Ganymede, they wouldn't be for long. Marco grinned.

"Cut to a quarter g," he said. "Tell the Ganymede ships to coordinate braking burns and watch close. If the enemy waits, we outnumber them. If they attack now, be ready to turn. Draw them out of their formation."

"Bien," Josie said. "Aber... They're firing."

"Go!" Marco shouted, willing the *Pella* like it was part of his body. Like he could bend its path with pure force of his intention.

"At a quarter?" Karal yelped, and Marco shouted wordlessly and grabbed the pilot's controls. Under his command, the *Pella* leapt forward, pushing him back. The hull creaked and groaned, but he saw Josie's targeting solution feed in, heard the great and glorious rumble of the weapons, watched the arcs of PDC fire still too distant to pose a real threat but near enough to disrupt the enemy and then the spread of torpedoes. And the spreads from the others in his group. And far distant, but drawing close, a woven cluster thick as a rope—torpedo tracks from the Ganymede ships. All converging, all falling in to the enemy. Fire and metal and blood. It was like joy. Like music.

He bent the *Pella*'s course, firing thrusters at a hundred percent or not at all, feeling the glorious torque of the turn in his blood and the aching pressure of his crash couch trying to hold him. Someone shouted, but Marco was past listening now. This was battle. This was glory and victory and power.

A proximity warning, and the *Pella*'s PDCs shifted automatically, splashing an enemy torpedo that had been lost among the cloud of converging fire. Marco laughed. His other ships had taken his cue, turning toward the *Torngarsuk*. One of al-Dujaili's ships misjudged, took a torpedo from the Ganymede ships in her side, and crumpled, venting air. One of Marco's ships lost a thruster to a torpedo, and three of the remaining enemy coordinated to mow it down with PDC fire like lions descending on a crippled gazelle. Even in that moment of loss and rage, Marco felt the joy of the fight.

It was ugly, brutal, direct. They were past clever solutions and elegant traps now. This was toe-to-toe throwing punches until someone fell to the ground. This was the urge that had put mankind on the battlefield with stones and lengths of wood, beating each other blood on blood on blood until only one side remained. And that side was Marco's. The Free Navy, and fuck all the rest.

The *Torngarsuk* died last, dancing around arcs of PDC fire while al-Dujaili shouted defiance and obscenity over the radio. And then didn't. The *Torngarsuk* lost power, drifted, and detonated. Its own tiny, brief sun. Marco fell back into his crash couch, aware for the first time in he couldn't say how long of the thrust gravity pulling at him. The tactical display showed two of the enemy ships fleeing. He hadn't noticed when they'd left, but it hadn't been recent—they were already far outside his effective range. Farther and faster with every breath. He smiled, noticed the taste of blood on his lips. He'd bitten his cheek. He didn't remember that either.

Slowly, his consciousness seemed to broaden. Not just his monitor and his couch and his body. There was an alert sounding somewhere. A smell of smoke and the bright scent of fire suppressants. His headache had bloomed without him noticing into a throbbing unpleasantness, and his hands felt like his fingers had gesturing at the wall screen as he listed his suggestions and plans. Marco kept his gaze on his son and let the others pretend nothing was happening but the meeting. *If you act like a child, you will be treated like a child. Embarrass me and I will embarrass you.*

Filip swallowed, turned, and walked out of the room, shoulders back and head held high. Marco laughed as the door shut, just loud enough he was certain Filip would hear him.

He turned to the wall screen. "You don't list Tycho," he said. "Why not?"

Chou looked at his list, then back at Marco. "You want to take Tycho?"

"Why not?" Marco said. "These battles we're fighting now? They're the inners turning us against each other. Tricking us into killing our own. Belter against Belter, and for what? We can never win Earth and Mars over. They'll never see us as people. But Aimee Ostman? Carlos Walker? They should be on our side. Would be, if they weren't still stuck in a past that's gone, gone, gone. Yeah?"

"You say it," Chou said, nodding but dour.

"Tycho has always been a jewel of the Belt. A source of our pride and a symbol of our success. It's why Fred Johnson squatted on it all those years. Now another Earther who thinks he's the savior of the poor backward Belt. Why should we let James Holden keep what was never his?" Marco grinned and let the syllables drip out of his mouth. "*Tycho Station.* Gather up all the ships we can, and burn there in force before the inners can regroup. We're faster than them. Smarter. And when we reach Tycho, we will see them rise up to greet us and toss Holden out the airlock, I will guarantee that."

Lister cleared his throat. "*Rocinante*'s not on Tycho, though."

Marco frowned. A little stab of confusion and resentment pricked his heart. "What?"

"Los dué ships we sent after Ostman's ice hauler? *Giambattista*? No transponders, but came close enough they got drive signatures off the escort ship. Esá es la *Rocinante*."

bent backward and were only just coming back to true. He looked around the deck. Josie and Miral and Karal, all looking back at him. He lifted a fist.

"Victory," he said, and coughed.

But the victory came at a price. Two of his reinforcements from Ganymede were done, the crews dead, the ships hardly more than scrap. Three of the ships from the Callisto yards would need repair. The *Pella* had suffered a breakdown in the air recycler that was annoying but trivial. Enough that they had to land in the shipyard again for a few days while it was repaired and tested. Johnson's lickspittle OPA had taken worse, died in greater number, but still, this wasn't the sort of success Marco could afford many more of.

And add to the injury the insult of being lectured by Nico Sanjrani.

"This has to stop," the little economist said from the screen. "The damage to infrastructure is getting worse, and the more the curve deflects, the harder—the more nearly *impossible*—it's going to be to pull it back up."

Marco, in the office he'd appropriated for Free Navy's command on Callisto, leaned back in his chair, closed his eyes. The message had been sent with heavy encryption, its origin path and return hidden in layers of mathematics. All he knew for certain was that Sanjrani was far enough away that the light delay and the limitations of equipment kept him from a real-time conversation. For that, Marco was profoundly grateful.

"I can resend the analysis," Sanjrani whined. "But this situation is making things worse than the numbers show. *Worse.* Whatever it takes to stop it, you need to do that. If we don't start building a separate exchange economy soon—and by soon I mean weeks or months ago—we may have to reimagine the whole project. We may not be able to get away from inner-planet-backed scrip at all, and then we can be as politically independent as we want, only it will still devolve back to financial constraints by the inner planets, which was what we were trying to get away from in the first place."

Sanjrani looked tired. Stressed. There was an ashy tone to his skin, and his eyes seemed sunken. Given that he was holed away somewhere safe from battle, it seemed more than a little histrionic. Marco stopped the message—there was another twenty minutes in the spool—and composed his reply. It wasn't a long one.

"Nico," he said gently. "You give me too much credit. None of us have the power to control what atrocities Earth and Mars and their misguided allies in the Belt will commit to stop us. We can only hold to our principles and our dreams. We will absolutely prevail, in time. When the inners put down their arms and leave the Belt in peace, we will have the power to end this. Until then, our only options are to defend ourselves or let our people die. I won't compromise on that, and I know you won't either."

There. Thirty seconds to answer thirty minutes of alarmist maundering. That was what efficiency looked like. He sent the message back on its looping way, checked the newsfeeds—the battle at Titan was entering a second day with heavy casualties on both sides, and still too early to know what he'd won or lost in it—and the work reports on his ships—the *Pella* was ready to launch, but not with any size of escort for at least another three days—and then heaved himself up and walked through to the meeting room.

Whatever it had been before—engineers' workspace, security building, storage—the room was now the war council of the Free Navy. Karal, Wings, Filip, Sárta from the *Pella*. Captain Lister from the *Coin Silver*, Captain Chou from the *Lína*. They sat on white upholstered chairs, their uniforms lending them a formality. They stood and saluted when he entered the room. Except for Filip who nodded as a son to his parent.

"Thank you for coming," Marco said. "We have plans to make. This assault must not go unanswered. We have to mount a counterstrike and show the inners that we aren't intimidated. Show our strength."

A murmur of agreement passed through the room, ally speaking loud enough to be heard. Only not to be

Except, to his surprise, Filip.

"Another one?" his son said. "The last grand gest well, que?"

Marco froze. The anger in Filip's voice—more th *contempt*—was like being slapped. All around the room, ers went silent and still.

"Something to say, Filipito?" Marco asked, his voice l calm and rich with threat. But Filip chose not to hear it.

"Yeah, something. We had this conversation before, Walked away from Ceres and said we needed to plan a sh strength. Counterattack. Keep them afraid of us. We did *before*, and now we're here *again*." Filip's face was flushed, breath fast and heaving like he'd run to get here. "Only last tim wasn't esá coyos la, was it? It was Dawes and Rosenfeld and S jrani. And Pa, yeah? Inner circle. Heart of the Free Navy. Part the plan."

"You're tired, Filip," Marco said. "You should go rest."

"How does this get different from last time you said it?" Filip said. "Tell me that."

Rage rose up in Marco's breast, filling his head with heat and fumes. He could smell it like a chemical fire.

"Want to know, me," Filip said, voice trembling. "This plan we've got. And the last plan before it. And the one before that. Which one's the real plan? Is there? Or are we just falling down and pretending we meant to?"

Marco smiled. When he stepped toward his son, Filip braced against a blow. Jaw tight. Hands in fists. Marco tousled his hair.

"Boys, eh?" he said to the others. "Boys and their tantrums. Captain Chou. Can we hear your report?"

Chou cleared his throat. "We have a few targets might serve," he said, pulling up his hand terminal and sending a data file to the wall screen. "Depends how it fits with the larger strategy."

Filip went white, his jaw jutting out. Chou went on talking,

The room was silent. Marco felt something crawling up the back of his neck. All the years he'd kept quiet track of where Naomi was, what she was doing, and now she and her lover had slipped away without his knowledge. It felt like a threat. Like a trap.

"The *Rocinante*," he said, speaking each word carefully, "is running escort on Ostman's old, broken-down ice hauler?"

"Looks like," Lister said.

Something was wrong with the air mix. Marco wasn't getting enough oxygen. His heart was beating fast, his breath coming faster.

"Where are they going?"

Chapter Forty-Three: Holden

Inertia was one problem. Location was the other.

The *Giambattista* was a massive ship, hard to bring up to speed and hard to slow down. A testament to the inconvenience of mass and Newton's first law. It was already braking toward the ring gate, pouring out energy and reaction mass in order to bring it to an orbit matching the gate. Between those two datapoints—where it was going and how quickly it was shedding momentum to get there—the fast-attack ships knew within a narrow range of possibilities where they would be and when they would be there.

Holden's calculus was built from unknowns. How many gs could the *Giambattista* endure during a hard brake? How many of the ships she carried in her vast belly would fail under that strain? The cold equations of velocity, energy transfer, and relative motion could draw idealized curves to describe any number of scenarios, but experience added on a permanent and indelible *unless something unexpected happens, and then who the hell knows.*

"Best guess, Alex," Holden said. "What are we looking at?"

Alex rubbed a hand over his thinning hair and made a distressed chuffing sound under his breath. The galley smelled like chamomile tea and cinnamon, but Naomi and Clarissa were both empty-handed. The *Roci*'s deceleration was about a g and a half, matching the *Giambattista*. It made Holden feel like he was tired even though he wasn't.

"If I was them," Alex said, "I'd plan to overshoot. Time my braking run so that I'd go by just before that big bastard out there got to the ring. Group both ships together, because there's an attack opportunity during that pass. Drop a shitload of torpedoes that could use my velocity as a boost, hope I got a few good hits in. Once I'd passed, my torpedoes would be fighting against my velocity instead of building on it, so I'd likely save my powder until I could kill off what was left of my speed. Then come back to finish up anything that survived that first pass."

"Sounds plausible," Naomi said. "And what would you do if you were us?"

"Get to the ring as quick as I could," Alex said, more quickly this time. "Make them hurry to catch up to us so that the loop back took as long as possible. Then use whatever that window was to get Bobbie and her forces in through the gate, let her take over the rail guns, and get our butts into the slow zone so she could splash those bastards when they got back."

"Going to be unpleasant trying to keep the *Giambattista* alive once they get back," Clarissa said. "Two of them. One of us. That boat's a big target."

"All right," Holden said. "What about their drive plumes? If they're braking toward us, how big a threat are they?"

Alex shook his head. "The speeds we're looking at, if we get in their plume, we'll be in their laps."

Clarissa's voice was small, calm. "If it's a suicide mission?"

Alex sobered. "Well, ah, then... Yeah, that would suck."

"If we break the *Giambattista* with too hard a burn," Naomi said, "we can still stage the attacks from out here. We're already unloading the first wave from outside the gate. There's no reason we can't launch the second one from here too. The command crew can't be much larger than the *Canterbury*'s was. We'll evacuate them on the *Roci* if we have to."

"Unless whatever we break interferes with us deploying the boats," Clarissa said. "Then Naomi and I are out there with welding torches trying to pop Bobbie's stuff loose when the attack ships get back, and everyone has a bad day." It was weird hearing Amos' idioms spoken in her voice. The two had spent a lot of time together, though. So maybe it wasn't.

Holden rubbed his palm across the cool surface of the table. The weight of the moment pressed on his shoulders. "I'll talk to Bobbie and Amos. They're there. They can make our case. Cut the deceleration now, go on the float until the last minute, and then burn like hell to brake. Make them chase us."

"Going to be hard selling that to Belters," Naomi said. "My people aren't fans of high g."

"Alternative being torpedo strikes makes a compelling argument, though."

Naomi shrugged. "It does."

After that, the hours stretched. Sleeping would have been a good idea, but it wasn't possible. He hit the gym, pulling against resistance bands until the ache distracted him from the attack ships bearing down on them. But as soon as he stopped, it flooded back in on him. Wondering whether the enemy would target the *Giambattista* because it was the larger target or the *Rocinante* as the bigger threat. If the plan to take Medina would work. If it would work in time. What the Free Navy would do if it worked, if it failed.

If they won and the passage to the colony worlds opened again, what it would mean for the Belters, for Earth, for Mars. What the shape of human history would look like if the Free Navy beat them. Anticipation soured to anxiety and fear, and then impatience and back to anticipation again. Usually, the *Roci* was comfortable as an old shirt. Under the guns this way, he felt closed in. Claustrophobic. He couldn't quite forget, the way he usually could, that they were a bubble of air and metal in an unthinkably huge emptiness.

Naomi found him in their cabin after his exercise. Her hair was tied back, away from her face, and her eyes were calm and serious.

"Was looking for you," she said.

He waved a little gamely. "Present."

"You doing all right?"

"I don't know. Yes?" He held out his hands, a gesture of helplessness. "I don't know why I'm having such a hard time with this. Not like it's the first war I've started."

Her laugh was rueful and warm. She launched across the room, caught onto the handholds where she could look over his shoulder at the monitor. The two enemy ships on approach. The *Giambattista* and the *Roci*. A red field where the braking burn would start. A white line where the *Roci* thought the attack would come. The first attack. Violence reduced to spare and well-presented graphic design.

"You didn't start this one," Naomi said. "Marco did that."

"Maybe," Holden said. "Or maybe Duarte did. Or the protomolecule. Or Earth and Mars over the last couple of centuries of not giving a shit about the Belt. I don't know anymore. I feel like I understand what I have to do in the next…I don't know. Five minutes? Maybe ten? Then after that, things get muddy."

"Next is enough," Naomi said. "As long as you always see the next step, you can walk the whole way."

She put a hand on his shoulder, her palm warm against his skin. He laced his fingers with hers and braced as she pulled herself down beside him. A simple maneuver they'd done a million times before. The long practice of trivial intimacy.

"I keep wondering if this was inevitable," he said. "There are so many things we could have done differently. Maybe we could have kept this from happening."

"We you-and-me, or we humanity?"

"I was thinking humanity. But you-and-me too. If you'd killed Marco when you were kids together. If I'd kept my temper and not gotten kicked out of the Navy. If... I don't know. If any of the things that got us here hadn't happened, would none of this be happening?"

"Don't see how it could."

On the screen, the two enemy ships ticked closer to them while they shifted—not as quickly—toward the red warning of the hard burn. "I keep thinking it would have, though," Holden said. "If it wasn't me or you or Amos or Alex, if it wasn't the *Roci*, it would be someone or something else. The Belt didn't get screwed because of you or me. Whatever it was that made the protomolecule didn't throw it at us because of anything that we'd done."

"Seeing as we were single cells at the time."

"Right? The details would be different, but the... the shape of it all would be the same."

"That's the problem with things you can't do twice," Naomi said. "You can't ever know how it would have gone if it had been the other way."

"No. But you *can* say that if we don't do something different, it'll happen again. And again. And again, over and over until something changes the game."

"Like the protomolecule?"

"It didn't change anything," Holden said. "Here we are, still doing all the same things we did before. We've got a bigger battleground. Some of the sides have shifted around. But it's all the crap we've been doing since that first guy sharpened a rock."

Naomi pulled herself closer, tucked her head against his shoulder. Probably people had been doing that since the dawn of time too, just not in freefall.

"You've changed," she said. "The man I met on the *Canterbury* wouldn't have said that it was everyone's business. That whatever anyone did counted."

"Well. I've had really a lot of people shooting at me since then."

"And you've grown up some. It's all right. I have too. We're both still doing it. That's not something you stop. Not until you're dead."

"Mm," Holden said. Then, "So I'm guessing this kind of thing doesn't bother you?"

"Nature of history? No, it doesn't."

"Why not?"

He felt Naomi's shrug against his body, familiar as if he'd done it himself. "I know what I need to deal with next. I've got two attack ships crawling up my ass, ready to kill me and all the people I love most in life. And if they manage it, my evil ex-boyfriend may very well grind all human civilization in the system into a new dark age."

"Yeah. That guy's an asshole."

"Yup."

They watched it coming, knew it would come. It didn't make it any less frightening when it came.

Alex put the *Roci* just ahead of the *Giambattista*'s nose, offset enough not to melt her with their exhaust, but close enough to maybe stop the enemy torpedoes before they hit. The two incoming plumes were like stars—fixed and steady. Holden remembered being a boy in Montana, learning to catch a baseball. The way that the ball seemed to float almost motionless when it was coming straight for him. This was the same.

"Status?" Holden said.

"Sixty-three seconds to effective range," Naomi said. "*Roci*'s watching them."

Holden breathed out. The captain of the *Giambattista* insisted that her ship wouldn't suffer more than three and a half gs, so that's what they were at. The enemy was slowing at a little over eight, but still going so fast that they would only spend a fraction of a second in range.

"Forty," Naomi said, and coughed. A painful sound that made Holden aware of the weight on his own throat. Maybe they should have gone on the juice after all. Behind them, the ring gate would have been visible to the naked eye by now. Even a very low-power scope would be showing the weird, almost organic, moving-but-stationary nonmaterial of its frame. Signal was leaking through the bare thousand kilometers of its diameter, distorted like ocean waves seen from beneath—radio, light, all the electromagnetic spectrum, only warped and made strange. And beyond that, the rail guns waiting to kill them all.

"Starting to think this may not have been a great plan," he said.

"Five seconds. Four …"

Holden braced. Not that it was going to help, just that he couldn't keep from doing it. On the external cameras, the enemy drive plumes grew larger, thicker, brighter, and then in a blink, faster than the frame refresh, they were gone and the *Rocinante* bucked hard around him, slamming him into his crash couch like he'd fallen off a ladder. The ship rang like a struck gong, deafening. For a confused second, he thought they'd been thrown around by the enemy's wake. That they were going to capsize.

The *Roci* steadied. An alarm was sounding, brash and demanding.

"What have we got?" Holden shouted.

"I don't know," Clarissa shouted. "I haven't been looking at this any longer than you. Just…All right. Looks like we ate a couple PDC rounds or…No, hold on. That doesn't make sense."

The alarm shut off. The silence seemed more ominous. Maybe the shaking hadn't been the *Roci*'s maneuvering thrusters getting them out of the way. They'd been hit. They might be spewing out their spare air into vacuum.

" 'Doesn't make sense' is not good, Clarissa," he said, trying to make his panic sound cheerful. "Something that made me feel like we weren't dying would be really nice."

"Well, we got a little beat up," Clarissa said. "I thought it was PDCs, but…No. We took out a torpedo close enough that we caught some debris."

"They launched four torpedoes at us and two at the *Giambattista*," Naomi said from behind him. "We got them all, but there

was a little damage to both ships. I'm waiting to get a solid report
from Amos."

In that blink, Holden thought. That moment of shaking had
been a whole battle too abrupt for a human mind to follow. He
wasn't sure if that was amazing or terrifying. Maybe there was
room for both.

"Not dying, though," Holden said.

"Not any faster than usual, anyway," Clarissa said. "I'll need to
swap out some sensor arrays and plug a couple holes on the outer
hull when we get a chance."

"Alex?" Holden said. "What's it look like up there?"

"I got a bloody nose," Alex said. He sounded affronted. Like
bloody noses were something you got when you were a kid and
beneath his dignity now.

"I'm sorry about that, but I was thinking more about the ships
that were trying to kill us?"

"Oh. Right," Alex said, sniffing back the blood. "Like I said,
that first window's closed. Anything they throw at us now, we
can knock down easy. And it doesn't look like they're changing
much about their burn."

"How long does that give us?"

Alex sniffed again. "We'll get to a matching point beside the gate
in a little less than an hour. If our little friends do a straight-line
burn to come back to us and don't change their burn rate? We'll
have six and a half hours. If they loop around so they can come at
us from different directions, a little more."

"What's the most?"

"Eight," Alex said. "Best-case scenario, we're going to need to
get all our folks through that gate and under protection of our
shiny new rail gun artillery inside of eight hours. Seven's more
realistic. Six would mean we didn't have to sweat it."

"Amos is saying they got knocked around a little, but only lost
some plating in the storage decks and maybe half a dozen boats,"
Naomi said. "Bobbie's calling it a win, and they're scrambling the
first wave."

Between the three and a half gs and the violence of the *Roci*'s defense, Holden's jaw and back ached. He couldn't imagine how unpleasant this had to be for Naomi and the Belters in the *Giambattista*. Including the first-wave team that Bobbie was about to lead down the enemy's throat. One wave to take the rail guns, then a second to secure Medina. By then, maybe he'd know what he needed to do next.

If it didn't work out, they'd try to keep the *Giambattista* and the OPA soldiers still on her alive long enough to come up with some other plan.

The ring gate grew larger on the scopes, looming up until they were so close, it dwarfed the ships. A thousand kilometers from one side to the other, and beyond it, the weird nonplace of the slow zone, the other gates, and the ruins of a thirteen-hundred-world galactic empire that humanity aspired to salvage. Naomi was right. It didn't matter whether they were servants of some greater historical movement or individual, disconnected lives suffering the consequences of their own choices. It didn't change what they had to do.

The *Giambattista* reached a minimum in their vector curve and shut down their drive. A few seconds later, the *Roci* did the same, but by then, the sides of the giant ship were already sliding open. In the starlight, the thousands of tiny cheap boats looked like spores being thrown to the wind by a dark fungus, visible more by the starlight they blocked than by any actual color or shape of their own. This close, the ring gate dwarfed them. He couldn't keep from seeing it as a massive milky eye, staring blindly down at a sun that was hardly more than the brightest star among billions.

The connection request came to his monitor. Bobbie Draper. He accepted, and her face appeared on his screen. Her powered armor made her unhelmeted head seem small. Voices behind her spoke in Belter cant so fast that he couldn't make out the words.

"First wave's ready to go," she said. "Permission to deploy?"

"Granted," Holden said. "But, Bobbie? Really, really don't die out there."

"No one lives forever, sir," Bobbie said, "but as long as it doesn't compromise the mission, I'll try to live through it."

"Thanks."

One by one, and then in ragged groups, the small, weak chemical rockets began to ignite. All of them together didn't have the power of the *Roci*'s reactor, but they didn't need it. Their whole lives were the space from the ring gate to the station in the center of the slow zone. For most of them, less than that. And only one of them had Bobbie and Amos and their ground force. As Holden watched, the boats shifted like a flock of starlings, became a single, moving shape on an imaginary, tactical wind, and burned toward the gate.

And then through it.

Chapter Forty-Four: Roberts

She'd known it was coming. Even before they'd pried the specific information out of Jakulski, she'd known *something* was coming. It was a feeling that came up like a bad dream she couldn't shake. A premonition or just the kind of fear that seeped through anytime she had something important and too clear an imagination about how it would be to lose it. Knowing that the war was coming to Medina was almost a relief. At least she knew in broad strokes what to be afraid of.

The fear had made small changes feel large. When Jakulski brought them the news that their work schedule was shifting, Roberts couldn't keep from interpreting each change like tarot cards. Tracking down the signal drop on the interior of the drum was pushed off for a month, so maybe Captain Samuels thought it wasn't important for defense from the invasion. The retrofit of the water supply for lower g moved up, so maybe they wanted extra capacity ready in case the environmental systems were damaged. They spent a day installing redundant comm lasers so that they could always have a tightbeam line to Montemayor and the rest of Duarte's advisors and guards on the alien station. Everything that she could fit into the idea of fortifying against coming violence became more evidence that her fear was justified; the more evidence she had, the easier it became to see things as further proof.

It wasn't only her, either. The others in her workgroup were all suffering from the same dread. Jakulski was gone more often than not now, not supervising them except to tell them at the start what to do and ask at the end if they'd done it. And when he did come out after shift, he left early without giving any excuses beyond *Things need doing.* Salis was drinking more, showing up for shift hungover and angry and then not wanting to head back to his quarters when the day was done. Vandercaust…well, ever since the false alarm with the mole, Vandercaust had been a smaller man. Not in his body, but the way he moved through his life. Careful, amenable, tucking into himself like a snail. Once, just after they'd heard about the ice hauler burning out toward the Sol gate, they'd been in the bar when some young coya, drunk off her ass, had started off shouting about how the colony planets didn't deserve aid or attention. *They don't like being treated that way, they shouldn't have done it to us* and *They're just as bad as Mars only without the stones to back it* and *Come back five generations from now and maybe we'll be close to even.* Vandercaust had finished his drink fast and left without saying goodbye. Anything political got his back up now, even if it was something they all agreed with.

And still, Roberts found she needed the company. When the leaks and rumors got bad enough that Captain Samuels had to make an announcement—*Enemy ships associated with OPA factions outside the Free Navy are sending a large cargo ship and escort. We don't know their intentions. The Free Navy has dispatched fighters to back Medina up, but with the fighting so hot in the system, it is a minimum force.*—Roberts was almost relieved.

At least they could talk about it all openly now and not get Jakulski's balls in a vice.

When the enemy was on close approach to the far side of the ring, all the work on Medina ground to a halt. There were schedules and lists and work reports, but there were also enemies at the gate. Jakulski didn't show up to give them their daily orders, and even their freedom seemed ominous. They shifted to a bar where the wall screens were set to a local security newsfeed—the latest on the siege of Medina Station as it happened.

Diagrams of the positions of enemy ships and their Free Navy defenders. Analysis of who Aimee Ostman and Carlos Walker were and why they hadn't joined the Free Navy. Confirmation that the escort ship was James Holden's *Rocinante*. Beer. Dried tofu with wasabi powder. The camaraderie of the mob. It felt almost like gathering up to watch football, except their home was the pitch, and loss would mean the deaths of more than only people. The autonomy and freedom the Free Navy promised was balanced on the head of a pin.

"Did they get them?" Salis asked breathlessly. "Did we kill them?"

Roberts reached across the table, grabbing his hand and squeezing, waiting for the feed to update. For fresh information to come through. There wasn't any romance in the gesture. Not even a sexual invitation. There just wasn't a better way to express hope and fear and oh holy shit all at the same moment. Across the bar, three dozen people—maybe more—stared at the thick, confused images bleeding through the gate. If it hadn't been a live image, it could have gotten cleaned up almost to where the gate's weirdness didn't show at all. But jagged and bent right now was better than clear as nothing later on.

A flash of the *Rocinante*, blooming fire-bright. The whole room took in its breath. Waited. But when the glow faded, the enemy was still there. Salis spat out an obscenity and let her hand go. On the feed, the Free Navy attack ships were already gone, carried off into the black by their own rush to get to the *Giambattista* and

Rocinante before they'd reached the gate. For all the fucking good it had done.

"Es bien, es bien, yeah?" Vandercaust said. "Took a shot, bruised them. Make them rush is the thing. Keep them from going slow, being careful."

"You don't know what they've got on that ship," Roberts said. "Could be anything."

Vandercaust nodded, took a bit of tofu between his finger and thumb and squeezed it until it cracked. "Whatever it is, we'll put rail gun rounds through it until it's dust." He held out his green-powdered thumb like he was demonstrating the idea of dust. She nodded so tight and fast it was more like rocking back and forth.

"Dui," she said, wanting to believe it. Needing to. On the feed, the looming mass of the ice hauler had come to a relative stop on the far side of the gate and just off to the side where the rail guns couldn't fire through at it. So they knew that the defenses were there and to keep their heads down. That was too bad.

"What are they doing?" Salis said, not expecting an answer. In the feed, a hundred faint new stars bloomed around the ice hauler, wavering and inconstant. Then a thousand. Then double that. Roberts felt some part of herself step back, shock pulling her away from herself.

"Mé scopar," she breathed. "Are those *drive plumes*?"

The dots of light surged, all moving at once. A swarm of bright wasps, swirling, curving, and passing through the ring gate and out into their space. Her space. Here and there, a light flickered and died, one of the thousands sputtering and dying, but most flowed around each other, flight systems taking in the situation—their position, the alien station, Medina, the rings.

There were safe spaces where the rail guns wouldn't fire. Not behind cover, because apart from Medina itself there was nothing in the slow zone to hide behind. But the rail gun rounds wouldn't stop once they passed through the tiny attacking ships. Any of the enemy that could put themselves between the end of a rail gun and the ring of a gate or Medina itself would be safe. At least until the PDC and torpedoes of Medina Station could reach it. Like slivers of iron showing a magnetic field, the swarm burned for the lines defined by geometry and tactics. Or, most of them, anyway. The few that had failed spun helplessly in the void, threatening no one. And others ...

"Those fast-movers aren't ships," Salis said. "Those are torpedoes."

Roberts' hand terminal alerted in the same moment as Vandercaust's and Salis'. She was the first to pull hers from her pocket. The screen was red-bannered. The battle alert. She acknowledged, reporting her position. The assignment put her in a floating damage-control team. Jakulski and the rest of the higher powers in technical were waiting to see where they were needed. Where the damage came. It was worse than a hard assignment because her blood was fizzing with the need to flee or fight, and there was nowhere to go. If she could have run to a post, she'd have been able to pretend that she was doing something. That she could affect the wave of destruction flying toward her.

"Ah!" Vandercaust said. "There we go!"

On the wall screen, the rail guns had opened up. At first, it was only motion, the emplaced barrels—her barrels, the ones she'd put in their housings—quivering. Then the newsfeed overlaid the paths of the rounds, bright lines that vanished as quickly as they appeared, and with each flicker one of the enemy died. Roberts felt her jaw starting to ache from clenching it, but she couldn't relax. Salis grunted, his expression dismayed.

"Que?" Roberts asked.

"Wish we weren't doing, that is all," he said.

"Doing what?"

He gestured to the wall screen with his chin. "Sending stuff out past the gates. To where it goes away."

She knew what he meant. The starless nothing—not even space—on the other side of the gates was eerie when you thought about it too much. Matter and energy could be converted into each other, but not destroyed. So when something that went out beyond the sphere of the slow zone seemed to vanish, it had to go somewhere or be changed into something. But no one knew what.

"No option," she said. "Esá coyos making us."

"Yeah, it's only..."

Long, terrible minutes stretched. Roberts fell into something half panic and half trance. The lines flashed on the feed. Another dead enemy. Another slug of tungsten accelerated out of reality and into the blackness stranger than space. Now that she saw it through Salis' eyes, it made her nervous too. It was so easy to forget the profound strangeness all around them. They lived there, it was their home, so of course they had to defend it. But it was also a mystery they lived inside.

The timelessness of her attention and focus broke as a shudder passed through the incoming swarm, and her heart doubled its beat. A swirling motion that went through the drive plumes even as they winked out. The muttering in the room got louder.

"How fast they *burning*?" Vandercaust said, awe in his voice. He switched his hand terminal from the alert screen to a tracking program, streaming the data into it. "Esá can't have crew on. Jelly and smash if they were, juice or no juice."

Medina shuddered. The vibration was small but unmistakable. The first of the enemy were inside effective range. On the feed, the flicker of the rail guns was joined by slower, sweeping arcs of PDC fire, the bright pinpoints of Medina's own torpedoes. Roberts found herself muttering curses like they were prayer, and didn't know how long she'd been doing it. The flickers of enemy drive plumes began to thicken and coalesce into a single bright shaft, drawing a line between the alien station and Medina.

"They're getting between us," she said. "They got to stop them, they're getting between us. They're going to get here. They're going to board us."

"No one on them to board us," Vandercaust said again. "No es ships, those. Fists with engines to push them is all. Rams."

"We're still picking them off," Salis said. "Look, rail guns still firing."

It was true. The shots were careful, dangerous. They slid past Medina's drum so close Roberts imagined she heard them hiss on the way past. But the enemy kept dying, exploding into scrap and vapor. The wave of enemy torpedoes was already gone, turned to debris and bad intentions. And the ships, closer and closer but fewer every minute.

"We're taking hits," Vandercaust said, glowering into his hand terminal.

Roberts pulled up her own terminal. Pressure loss on the outermost layers of the drum. Not everywhere, but scattered. A hall here, a warehouse there. A water reservoir was holed, throwing mist and ice out in a pinwheel as the drum spun it away. The Mormons had built the outer parts of the drum thick against the hard radiation of space. But no one was dying. Not yet.

"How are they hitting us?"

"Dead scraps," Salis said. "It's the debris from the torpedoes. It's nothing."

It might have been true that it was only debris, but it wasn't nothing. As she watched, another alert opened, was flagged, assigned out. Her team wasn't called yet. Wouldn't be, she thought, until the bombardment stopped or something important enough to be worth risking all three of their lives took a hit. Around them, the other people cheered, and she looked up to see a spreading sphere in among the fading swarm. They got a big one, and the detonation had been enough to knock out a few of its nearest neighbors.

The thousands of wasps were fewer now. Two, maybe three hundred, and fading by the moment. The ones there were diving hard for Medina, dodging arcs of PDC fire, fleeing from the torpedo strikes, slipping outside their corridor of safety and being ripped apart by the rail guns. As the glittering lights fell to black, Roberts felt something in her gut and her throat. The laughter came out as barely a chuckle, but warm and full as tears, and grew to something deep.

They had come to take Medina, and they were failing. Yes, the station was taking its hits. Yes, they would be bloodied. But they would not fall. Medina was Free Navy now, and it would be Free Navy forever. Salis was grinning too. All around them, cheers started to go up with every rail-gun strike that plucked away another invader. Of them all, only Vandercaust seemed uncertain.

"Que sa?" Roberts asked him. "Visé like you're trying to rub your asshole with your elbow."

Vandercaust shook his head. Another flicker from the rail guns, another light gone out.

"Keep drifting, them," Vandercaust said. "Visé. They're in the shadow, yeah? Station's far enough away the rail guns can cover them and us with the same thumbnail. But then they...drift. Get where the rail guns can pick them off. What for they *drifting*?"

"Who cares, as long as they all die?" Salis said around a mouthful of grinning.

"Maybe they want to get killed," Roberts said. Joking. She'd only been joking.

The words hung there, floating over the table like smoke pooling when the luck was about to turn. She shifted her attention back to the screen, her joy and relief gone like they'd never been there. Cold washed her lungs and heart, a totally different fear than the tenseness and anxiety of the run-up. Another ship that should have died under Medina's PDCs or torpedoes died to a rail gun instead.

"What am I looking at, Vandercaust?" Roberts said, her voice hard but trembling. Vandercaust didn't answer, but hunched over his hand terminal, working it furiously with his thick, workman's fingers.

Another ship. Another. Less than a hundred of the enemy left, and they were peeling away like a flower blooming. Not even trying to keep course for Medina. All around, the room erupted in shouts and celebration. Over the cacophony, she barely heard Vandercaust say *Shit*.

She asked the question with her hand, and he passed the hand terminal to her. Already, the start of the battle looked like something out of history. The thousands of drive plumes flooding through the ring gate. Most—almost all—falling hard toward Medina.

Almost all. But a few failed. Their drives stuttering. Maneuvering thrusters blinking, throwing them into rough, cartwheeling spins. She remembered seeing them, discounting them. The enemy was so many, so cobbled together, so among the thousands, there were a few malfunctions. It only meant a handful they didn't have to worry about.

Except Vandercaust had flagged one. It glowed blue on his display as the battle proceeded. The rail guns turned toward the torpedoes that threatened Medina. The rounds spitting out. The enemy dying. But not the little green malfunction. It drifted, tumbling and dead.

Until it didn't.

When its drive burst back into life, it wasn't flying for Medina or retreating back for the Sol gate. It darted toward the alien sphere. The blue, faintly glowing artifact at the center of the slow zone where all their guns were placed. Roberts was trembling so hard now that the green dot seemed to dance in her hand, leaving bright traces behind it. A jittering afterimage of how they'd been tricked. Thousands of boats and torpedoes arcing through the vacuum like a magician's gesture meant only to pull the eye. And God damn, but it had worked.

She handed back the hand terminal, plucked up her own, put in an emergency connection request to Jakulski. Every second he didn't answer felt like another clod of dirt landing on her coffin. When he did appear, he was in the administration offices, outside the drum and on the float. His sated grin told her that even Captain Samuels hadn't figured it out yet.

"Que hast, Roberts?" Jakulski said, and for a moment, she couldn't talk. The longing to be in the world Jakulski and all the others around here were in—the world where they'd won—was a lump in her throat. The words wouldn't fit past it.

And then they did.

"Get a tightbeam to Mondragon," she said.

"Who?"

"No. Shit. Montemayor. Whatever la coyo la's name is. Duarte's people. Warn him. Warn all of them."

Jakulski's brow furrowed. He leaned closer to the camera, though where he was there was no pull to lean into. "No savvy me," he said.

"Consolidated-fleet jodidas just landed on the *other* station. They were never after Medina. They were coming for the rail guns."

Chapter Forty-Five: Bobbie

Regret coming along?" Bobbie asked, shouting over the noise of the boat.

Amos, across from her, shrugged and shouted back. "Nah. It's all right if the cap and Peaches get a little time together. Helps 'em get used to each other. Besides, this is fun too."

"Only if we win."

"That is more fun than losing," he said, and she laughed.

The boat was crap.

Once, it had been a cargo container. Not a real one either, built to standards for a mech or an automated dock to handle along with thousands of others with the same dimensions and hand-holds and doors. This had been a custom job, cobbled together in the Belt out of equal parts scrap and ingenuity. The second hull was added later, the welds still bright at the corners. The crash couches weren't actual couches, just thick sheets of gel glued to the walls with straps like climbing harnesses to hold their bodies against it. Add to that the fact that they had no active sensors, that they were on the tumble, that the dozen men and women with them were indifferently trained, that probably more than half of them had been involved in conspiracies against Mars and Earth in the not so distant past, that their weapons were old and their armor a collection from half a dozen different sources. And, of course, that if the enemy rail guns took notice of them, the first warning they'd have was that they were all dead. Bobbie should have been in a panic.

She felt like she'd just lowered herself into a warm bath. The anxious gabble of the soldiers might be in the mishmash polyglot of the Belt. She might only be able to follow half of it. She knew what they were saying. Antinausea meds kept the complex spinning of the boat from turning even less pleasant, and their bitter aftertaste was like coming back to a house she'd lived in when she was young. One rich with good memories and familiar places. She liked the *Rocinante* as much as anyplace she'd ever been since Ganymede. They were good people, and even in a weird way they were her friends now. The soldiers all around her weren't and would never be that. They were her command, and even if it was only for a moment, she felt like she was exactly where she belonged.

Her suit speakers chirped. Communications were the one active thing she'd decided would be worth the risk. Now it was time to find out if that had been a good call. She accepted the connection with her chin.

A burst of static, followed by a weird fluting sound, like wind blowing across the mouth of a bottle, static again, and then Holden's anxious voice. "Bobbie? How's it going in there?"

"Five by five," she said, checking the exterior cameras to make sure that was true. The blue glow of the alien station rose up from the bottom of her visual field and curved off to the left. A glittering star field of rockets. A glimpse of Medina Station looking smaller than a beer can. The proximity readings had a dual countdown: one

for the moment they passed inside the arc of the rail gun, the other
for when they'd slam into the station itself. They were both spooling down quickly. "We'll be on the surface in…three minutes."

"Are the troops ready?"

Bobbie chuckled and added the group channel in. "Hey. You
assholes ready to do this?"

The cheer that came through maxed out the speaker. She slid
back to the connection to the *Rocinante*.

"Good answer," Holden said, but tightly. The fluting sound
again. Distortion from the ring. She hadn't felt anything moving
through it. No discontinuity or sense of vertigo. It did manage to
fuck with sensors and comms, though.

"The mission's on track, sir," she said. "We'll get control of the
guns and get you in here."

"Alex is saying the attack ships have vectored past zero. They're
heading back in our direction now."

"We'll do it quickly," Bobbie said.

"I know," Holden said. "Sorry. Good hunting."

"Thank you," Bobbie said, and the connection dropped, the
comm indicator going to red. She went back to the exterior cameras, switched to a corrected view. The image was steady this
way, the tumble of the boat only showing in three jagged blind
spots that sped through it like cartoon bats. There were fewer of
the decoy boats now, but not none. And they'd made it in close
enough that the station was blocking all but two of the rail guns.
As long as those two didn't decide they were as interesting as the
torpedoes and empty landing craft speeding toward Medina,
they'd be fine. Except …

She grabbed the image, enlarged it. There at the base of the
nearest rail gun emplacement, a dozen meters from the massive
sky-pointing gun, a low, gray structure. Round as a coin, and
sloped so that no matter what angle debris or outgassing struck it
from, it would be pressed more firmly in place. It was a design she
knew inside and out. She waited for the fear to come, but all that
showed up was a grim kind of determination.

"Amos," she shouted, sending him a copy of the image. "Take a look at this."

The big man looked at his hand terminal. "Huh," he said. "Well, that complicates things."

She popped the group channel open.

"New information. The intelligence we had that the rail guns weren't guarded may have been faulty. I'm looking at an MCRN-design troop bunker right now. If there's one, there may be others."

A chorus of alarm and regret. Bobbie switched the channel controls, killing all the mics but hers.

"No whining. We knew this was a possibility. If you don't want to participate, feel free to leave now. Otherwise, check your seals and weapons and be ready for a fight when we hit surface. Our job is to get control of those guns."

She enabled their mics in time to hear a ragged chorus of *yes sir*s and one woman's voice calling her a bitch. If there'd been time for a lesson in discipline, Bobbie might not have ignored it, but hey. It was a high-stress environment and the OPA soldiers weren't marines. She'd work with what she had.

Following her own advice, she ran a weapons check. Her arm-mounted Gatling gun read a full mag, two thousand rounds of mixed armor piercing and high explosive. A single-use rocket launcher was hooked to a hard point on her back, and slaved to her suit's targeting laser. Powered armor at full charge. She didn't doubt that she was the single most dangerous thing on their little landing craft. That meant she'd be taking point.

The boat informed her that they'd passed beneath the rail gun emplacement's range. The computer started the maneuvering thrusters on their correction burns to stop the tumble and lit the main drive. The braking burn pressed her hard into the gel. Her vision started to tunnel, and she had to remind herself to tense her legs and arms, force the blood out of her muscles and into her brain. They still called it the slow zone, but the only actual speed limit there now was not getting crushed to death by the energy of stopping.

The boat hit hard, bounced, and hit again. Before it had stopped sliding, Bobbie had pulled her straps off and hit the button that blew the door completely off the ship. They wouldn't be using it to leave, no matter how things turned out. The landscape outside was as surreal as something in a dream. A plain of blue purer than a Terran sky, featureless and glowing. It cast shadows up across the ship, across her soldiers. Everyone's legs and crotches bright, their faces and shoulders in darkness.

A thick band of metal-and-ceramic almost a meter high stretched out ahead of her like a low wall, disappearing over a much-too-close horizon. The rail gun, its base hidden by the station's curve, rose up toward an eerie starless sky. She could hear the throb of its firing as static on her radio, feel it like a change in the air pressure or a sickness just coming on.

Bobbie had seen video feeds from the slow zone. She hadn't been prepared for her own sheer animal rebellion at how uncanny it was. Even in the most designed architectural spaces she'd seen— Epping Cathedral on Mars, the UN building on Earth—there was a sense of nature. The station and the ring gates out beyond it weren't like that. They were like a ship, but unthinkably huge. It was that combination of size and artificiality that brought the hair up on the back of her neck.

There wasn't time for it now.

"We've got no cover," she barked. "Spread out. Make it hard for the bastards to get us all. Now! Go!"

They jetted forward in a broken line, their suit thrusters more than enough to defy the barely perceptible gravity of the eerie blue sphere. Good tactics, moving in a hard to predict ragged line like that, even if it came more from a lack of discipline than from a plan. Ahead of them, a dark line on the horizon. A second wall to match the first, converging at the rail gun. Just beyond it would be the low blister of the bunker. She could hope they hadn't noticed her make landfall. That she could get her engineers to the base of the rail gun and cut into the control systems before the enemy knew she was there ...

"Heads up," Amos called.

The first enemy fire came when they were still twenty meters from the corner where the walls converged. Enemy troops in what looked like Martian light armor crouched low to use the wall as cover, aiming down at them. Bobbie's heart sank. The enemy knew she was there, and were in position. Charging the walls, getting to the base of the rail gun. They'd be killed before they managed it.

"Fall back," she snapped, then squeezed off a few hundred rounds along the top of the wall. The faces peering over disappeared. Some dead, some ducking, no way to know how many of each yet. The OPA soldiers followed orders, though. No one tried to stay behind and play the hero. The only cover she could be sure of was the curve of the station itself. Bullets flew past her. Where they struck the station, the blue showed streaks of yellow, bright as sparks that faded slowly back to blue. The rail gun was still spitting.

Once the station's curve had hidden the far wall, she jetted to a stop near the boat they'd landed in, and floated up until just the very top of the wall was visible above the curve of the station. She zoomed in, setting the optics to a high-contrast false color that would make any movement stand out like neon. Soon enough a shape moved. Someone emboldened to poke their head up for a quick look. She fixed on it, fired. It disappeared. Dead or ducking? No way to tell, that damned wall of metal in the way. The curve of the station protected her, but it also protected them. The other Martians. The ones, she was certain, who'd betrayed their world and armed the Free Navy. Was it so much to ask that one of them would get careless and come close?

Amos followed her lead without being told, and the others came behind him, hauling themselves up well behind her where the enemy rounds didn't reach and then crawling forward. The steel curve the enemy had looped around the station was wider than it was thick—eight meters across at least—plenty of room to lie on. They could move forward, push the enemy back centimeter by centimeter. Unless they were themselves pushed back. Unless the traitorous Martians had a boat of their own that could skim overhead and lay them all to waste.

She gestured to keep their eyes forward and tried opening a connection to the *Rocinante*. The static seemed thicker now, ticking along in time with the rail gun fire. But then the weird fluting sound and Holden on the other side of it like she was seeing him through a veil.

"How's it going there, Bobbie?" he asked.

"It's shit," she said. "We're encountering well-armed resistance in a fortified position."

"All right. How long is it going to take you to get past them? I'm only asking because we're looking at those fast-attack ships getting back here in a little under two hours, and it would be really great if we weren't here when they did."

"That's going to be difficult, sir," Bobbie said. The flickers of muzzle flash told her that someone on the enemy side had tried taking a shot, but they were gone again by the time she looked. "In fact we could use a little air support."

"Don't know how we do that," Holden said.

Naomi broke in on the line. "We've lost essentially all of the decoy fleet. Anything still flying would be chewed to kibble before it got to you."

"All right," Bobbie said. "I'm open to suggestion at this point."

Amos waved at her and pointed forward, toward the shifting pillar of the rail gun. She switched to a private connection with him.

"What about the power source?" he said. "These rail guns take a lot of energy to drive them and more to cool them off. And they've been going nonstop since we came through the gate. They've got to have a fusion reactor somewhere supplying the power. Maybe something salvaged off a ship. Maybe a couple truck-backs."

"Where would I find it?" Bobbie asked.

"If it was me, I'd put it right under whichever one of those surrogate cocks they figured was least likely to get shot at. Or they could all have their own."

She switched back to the *Rocinante*.

"What's going on?" Holden said. "Is Amos okay?"

"We've got something. I'll report back," Bobbie said, and dropped the connection. She waved the soldiers forward, switched to the group channel. "Hold this ground. Keep their eyes and attention here."

"Sa sa," one of them said. She didn't know which. "How long we need to keep it?"

"Until I get back," she said. *Or for the rest of our lives*, she added silently as she burned back toward the fallen boat.

The door had been blown completely off, and the hull was dinged to shit where they'd slammed it into the station. But she didn't need it to be pretty. She just needed it to fly, and it could still do that, at least for a little while. When she lifted away from the surface of the station, a few of the enemy took shots at her. Pointless with normal arms. The hulls might be cheap-ass crap, but they were cheap-ass crap meant to live through micrometeor strikes. The roar of the engine was just a vibration in her suit. She was leaving her people behind, and it killed her a little bit to do it. But it was the right call. There wasn't time to hesitate.

The station curve was so tight, she had to work to stay tucked in close to it. The rail guns knew about her now. If she poked her head up, they'd chop it off. She thumbed on the full sensor array as she sped, touring the station as quickly as she could. They'd circled the station like three belts around a basketball, a rail gun placed wherever the steel bands intersected. It wasn't hard to find them. Each of them was radiating heat as quickly as it could, maxing out the IR sensors in a way she'd never seen. But one—the one opposite the Sol gate—looked a bit hotter. If there was a single main reactor, that was her best bet. She set the little boat's course, overrode the proximity shutoff, and as soon as she felt it duck down in its final kamikaze burst, she undid her straps and jumped for the airlock.

If it had been a real drive, the plume would have killed her. Instead, every temperature alarm on her armor went off at once.

Her faceplate went opaque. A seal in her arm popped, sucking the skin around her elbow painfully until the secondary inflated and pressed down. For one terrifying second, she drifted above the station, blind and vulnerable. When vision returned, she could see the white bubble of the enemy bunker, and the twinkle of their muzzles as they fired. Bobbie painted the bunker with her targeting laser and launched the rocket on her back while at the same time firing her suit's thrusters toward the surface as fast as they'd take her. She hit the surface of the station harder than she'd meant to, jarring her teeth hard enough she tasted blood. There was one bright flash as the rocket detonated, but it was quickly overwhelmed by the second flash of their landing boat slamming into the rail gun's reactor.

Her faceplate went opaque again, but instead of the midnight black she'd suffered in the fire of the drive plume, it glowed a mottled brown. The radiation monitor flashed a red trefoil alert at her. But what fed her raw, animal panic was the wind. A thin, fast whistle of gas rushed past her, pushed her off from the surface.

When, seconds later, the faceplate cleared, a glowing cloud was expanding out from just beyond the horizon, a nebula slowly going dark. The surface of the station wasn't blue, but an angry acid green.

Oh, Bobbie thought as the station began to strobe green to white to black to green again. *This might have been a really, really bad idea.*

To her left and right, the steel bands around the station were wrong. At first, she wasn't sure how, but then she made out the gap between the steel and the surface, like a ring a size too large for the finger it was on. She switched to magnetic and IR, but they'd both burned out in the backsplash from the reactor failure. The station shifted slowly back toward blue. She had the irrational sense that it was aware of her. That she'd annoyed it, and had its attention. She used the suit's thruster and the thin microgravity drift to pull herself back down to the surface, half expecting it to grab her and haul her inside to be punished, but it didn't.

Her radio was hardened enough to work. "This is Sergeant Draper," she said. "Is the rail gun still firing?"

"THE FUCK DID YOU DO?" a man's voice screamed, high and frightened. She cut off all their mics.

"That's what I'm asking, soldier," she said, then switched over to private. "Amos?"

"Don't know what you did, Babs, but it fucked things up in all the best ways. Rail gun looks powered down, the few remaining assholes are pulling back toward assholeville, and I think these metal bands that everything's stuck to are moving a little."

"Yeah, I may have popped those loose."

"Impressive," Amos said. "Hey, look, I got to go shoot somebody."

"No problem," she said, and opened the channel to the *Rocinante*. "Okay. You guys still out there?"

"Bad guys are getting really, really close," Holden said. "Tell me you have good news."

"I have good news," Bobbie said. "You can come through the ring. In fact, if you could get over here and get us some air support, it would be much appreciated."

There was a general whooping, made strange and uneasy by the interference of the ring. Was it her imagination that it was louder now?

"You got them?" Holden said, and she could hear the grin on his face. "You took the rail guns? We control them?"

Her suit sensors showed the wall of steel nearest her was starting to shift. Just a few centimeters, but there was definitely movement. It was broken. It was all broken. The rail guns weren't going to defend anyone anytime soon.

"We don't," she said. "But at least no one does."

Chapter Forty-Six: Holden

Y ou know what I'd like?" Alex yelled down from the cockpit.

"If we could get out of here?" Holden yelled back.

"If we could get out of here. At this rate we're going to be sitting here with our jumpsuits around our ankles when the bad guys get back," Alex said. "There's a reason they don't call those things *slow*-attack ships."

Even though Naomi was strapped into the couch beside Holden's, she answered over the headsets so she at least wasn't shouting about it. "The *Giambattista*'s a big ship, Alex. You're just spoiled because you haven't had to drive a cow like that in years."

"Shit," Alex said. "I could have spun the *Canterbury* around in half the time this is taking."

Naomi's sigh was as close as she was going to get to agreeing with them. "Well, you were good at your job."

On the screen, the *Giambattista* slid slowly sideways toward the ring gate. The damage from the attack ships' first run had done something to unbalance the maneuvering thrusters, so a lot of the piloting involved rotating the ship and then waiting until the working thrusters spun into the right position to fire. The plumes of the returning attack ships were already visible. It wouldn't be long before the torpedo barrage would kick in again, unless the Free Navy was going for a wait-till-you-see-the-whites-of-their-eyes approach. The enemy had split, curving back toward them in an almost hundred-degree spread. It wasn't quite as bad as it could have been. If they'd taken the time to bring their attacks from opposite directions, defending the *Giambattista* with the *Roci* would have been almost impossible. But it would also have taken enough time to play the vectors and get in position that the *Giambattista* would have cleared the ring gate before they arrived. It was like they were all being forced to find a min/max point in a complex curve of inertia, acceleration, and a lot of dead people.

The *Giambattista*'s main drive fired, the plume dwarfing the ship, and Alex crowed in celebration.

"About time," Naomi said. "I'm matching course. We'll be through in twenty minutes."

Holden opened a connection to Bobbie. The seconds stretched out long enough that he started to feel his gut tighten. The connection came through, dropped, then reestablished just as Naomi said, "One of them's burning to pass through the gate with us." He'd get right back to that.

"We're looking at twenty minutes to get through the gate. Where do you stand?"

The weird interference of the gates made her reply thick and creepy. She was breathing hard, and until there were words with it, he was picturing her gut-shot and on the float. Or drifting down onto the surface of the alien station. He was reaching to switch over to Amos when she spoke.

"Amos's holding position against the enemy," she said. "I'm almost back to them. Suit ran out of propellant mass, so I'm hoofing it with the mag boots."

"You're running back to the fight?"

"Well, call it a fast shuffle," Bobbie said between breaths, "but it's fine. They put in. A big metal road. Goes right to 'em."

"Okay. We'll get some backup to you as soon as we can. Just don't get killed before we get there."

"No promises, sir," Bobbie said, and he would have sworn from her voice she was smiling when she said it. A blast of static, and the connection dropped.

"Okay," Holden said. "What have we got?"

"They're both shooting at us," Naomi said.

"You sound calm about that."

She looked over at him. Her smile was sudden and bright and made his heart ache a little bit. "It's all Hail Mary bullshit. It's not even an attack so much as an opportunity to let us screw up."

"Okay. So, not worried about that. What are we worried about?"

Naomi flipped the drive analysis of their pursuers over to his monitor. The nearer of the ships had altered its path, and the projected curve put them through the ring and into the slow zone five minutes after the *Roci* and *Giambattista* made the transit. They weren't breaking off. That was too bad.

"Do we have a plan for dealing with that?"

Alex answered over the ship comm. "I'd vote for shooting them." And a moment later, Clarissa, "Seconded."

Holden nodded to himself. It still felt weird hearing her. Maybe it always would.

"Okay, let's lay in a targeting solution."

"Did it while you were talking to Bobbie," Naomi said.

The PDCs chattered for a moment, then went silent. Cleaning up the Hail Mary attacks. Holden rubbed his hands on his thighs. Tapped his fingers together. Pulled up the tactical to see the ring and the alien station, Medina and the fast-attack ships.

"We'll have enough to defend everything even if both ships follow us in, right?"

"Hush," Naomi said.

Looking through the exterior cameras, the ring seemed to wipe away the stars as they passed through it. Alex did a short, hard braking burn, turning their nose toward the gate and the narrowing circle of stars beyond it. The *Giambattista* twisted and burned and twisted again, its remaining hatches opening. Pinpoint drive plumes streaked out from it, less than fireflies compared with the wide, glowing burst of the hauler's Epstein drive. Holden watched as a handful, and then a dozen, and then a hundred poured down toward Medina. The OPA coming to finish the job. The remaining landing boats spread out, a wide, diffuse target. At this distance, Medina's PDCs were useless, and the *Roci* could probably take out any torpedoes. But even if they did fire, they'd only take out a handful of soldiers and leave an army still behind.

He tried opening a tightbeam to the incoming attack ship, but the interference from the ring was too thick, so he switched to broadcast. "Attention incoming attack ship," he said. Naomi looked over at him, a question in her eyes. Not concern or worry, though. She trusted him. "This is James Holden of the *Rocinante*. Please break off your approach. We don't have to do it this way."

He waited. The tactical display was thinner than it had been. All they knew of what was happening in the solar system was what leaked through the gate. The Free Navy's attack ship didn't answer, but dove toward them.

"He ain't thinking this through, Hoss," Alex shouted down. "What do you want me to do?"

"Give them a chance," Holden said.

"And if they don't take it?"

"Then they don't," Holden said.

The ring grew smaller as they fell away from it, like looking up at the circle of a well from down in the water. The attack ship was braking hard toward the ring. Just as the first of the *Giambattista*'s second-wave ships were about to reach Medina and the alien station, the attack ship passed through the ring, launched a half dozen torpedoes, and exploded in a star-bright failure of their drive's magnetic bottle when Alex fired the *Roci*'s rail gun through it. Holden watched in silence as the expanding cloud of gas that had been a ship full of men and women spread out and began to fade.

He tried to feel some sense of victory in it, but mostly it just seemed absurd. The slow zone, the gates, even the merely human ships that had carried them out so far. They were miracles. The universe was filled with mysteries and beauty and awe, and all that they could manage to do with it was this. Chase each other down and see who was the faster draw.

Everything in the slow zone—the *Giambattista*, its cloud of attack boats, Medina Station, the *Rocinante*—seemed to pause for a moment. A connection request from Bobbie interrupted him, and he accepted it.

"We're secure down here," Bobbie said. She was still breathing hard. "Enemy has surrendered."

"We took them alive?"

"Some of them," Amos said.

"They put up a hell of a fight, even after it was hopeless," Bobbie said. "We lost some too."

"I'm sorry," Holden said, and was a little surprised to notice how much that was true. Not just something you said at times like this. "I wish there'd been another way."

"Yes, sir," Bobbie said. "I'm going to oversee putting the prisoners in a transport. But there's something you should know."

"Yes?"

"These aren't Free Navy down here. The people defending the rail gun network were Martian."

Holden let that sink in. "The ones from the coup? Duarte's people?"

"They're not saying anything, but that's my assumption. This could be important."

"See they're kept safe and treated well," Holden said.

"Already on it," Bobbie said and dropped the connection.

Holden shifted his monitor to the exterior cameras and shifted the view until he could see the *Giambattista*, the alien station, and—far enough away that it hardly seemed like more than a shaving of metal, invisible without the *Roci* enhancing it—Medina Station. He folded a hand over his mouth, turned on identification markers for all the landing skiffs and jerry-rigged boats, watched the display vanish under the cloud of pale green text, turned them off again and stared into the blackness. His eyes felt gritty. It was like all the anxiety and tension that he'd built up during the burn out to the ring had collapsed. Turned into something else.

"You all right?" Naomi asked.

"I was thinking about Fred," he said. "This? It's what he did. Lead armies. Take stations. This is what his life was like."

"This is what he retired from," Naomi said. "When he decided to start trying to get people to talk things out instead of shooting people, this is what he left behind."

"Well, let's see how that works," he said. He set up the camera, considered himself on his screen, and ran his fingers through his hair until he looked a little better. Still worn-out. Still tired. But better. He set the system to broadcast.

"Medina Station. This is James Holden of the *Rocinante*. We're here to take administration of the station and the slow zone and the gates back from the Free Navy. If you really want, we can spend a while shooting your PDCs and torpedo arrays until they don't work and then land all these boats. We've got a lot of people with guns. I figure you do too. We could all kill a bunch more of each other, but I'd really prefer that we do this without losing anyone else. Surrender, lay down arms, and I promise humane treatment for the Free Navy's command structure and any other prisoners."

He tried to think of something else. Something more. A sweeping speech about how they were all one species after all, and that they could shrug off the weight of history if they chose to. They could all come together and make something new, and all it would really take was doing it. But all the words he could think of sounded false and unconvincing in his mind, so he cut the feed instead and waited to see what happened.

Naomi slipped out of her crash couch, floated to the lift and down. She came back a few minutes later with a bulb of tea. Slipped back into her couch. Waited. If it went on much longer, Holden knew he'd have to launch the attack. The boats weren't built for much more than scooting from one ship to another. They'd start running out of air and fuel before long. But maybe a few minutes more...

The response came. Clear, unencrypted radio signal, as open as his demand for surrender had been. The woman in the Free Navy uniform was on the float in a very familiar room. The religious images on the wall behind her were like symbols from a recurring dream about violence and blood and loss.

Only maybe this time would be different.

"Captain Holden. I am Captain Christina Huang Samuels of the Free Navy. I will accept the terms of your surrender on the condition that you guarantee the safety and humane treatment of my people. We reserve the right to record and broadcast your boarding action to assure that all of humanity will bear witness to your behavior. I do this out of necessity and loyalty to my people. The Free Navy is the military arm of the people of the Belt, and I will not sacrifice the lives of my people or the unaffiliated civilians of Medina Station when there is no profit to be had from it. But I myself will stand now and forever against the tyranny of the inner planets and their exploitation and slow genocide of my people."

She saluted the camera and the message ended. Holden sighed, started up his broadcast again.

"Sounds good," he said. "We'll be right over." He killed the broadcast.

"Seriously?" Alex called from above. "'Sounds good, we'll be right over'?"

"I may kind of suck at this job," Holden called back.

The voice over the ship's comm was Clarissa's: "I thought it was sweet."

The fall of Medina Station took twenty hours from the first OPA ships docking to the last Free Navy operative being locked in a cell. Medina's brig wasn't anywhere near big enough, so it was reserved for the higher officials—the command staff, the department heads, the security officers and agents. The others—mostly technicians and maintenance—were confined to their quarters with the doors locked by the station system. Which meant, in the end, by Holden. He couldn't help feeling like he'd just sent a thousand people to their rooms to really *think* about what they'd done.

He set up his command post in the central security office in the drum. The spin gravity wasn't so high it would bother Naomi, and there was something restful about being able to collapse into his chair while they watched the newsfeeds from Earth. Bobbie Draper, now the acting head of security for Medina, sprawled at her desk, legs up, hands behind her head, looking as relaxed as he'd seen her since she and Amos had come on board the *Roci* again. One sleeve was rolled up, and a bright, blistered burn ringed her elbow in the shape of a vac suit's seal. She rubbed it gently. Caressed it. There was something unnervingly postcoital about her response to violence. Alex and Amos were in the next room where Naomi was combing through the station logs with an OPA engineer named Costas, arguing about something that involved yogurt and black beans. Only Clarissa hadn't come on the station, and Holden hadn't asked why. His memories of the *Behemoth* were bad enough. He couldn't imagine hers.

On the newsfeed, The Hague looked like a battered, sepia-soaked version of itself. The sky above the UN building was white with haze, but it wasn't dark. And Avasarala stood without a podium. Her bright-orange sari looked like a victory banner.

"The liberation of Medina means more than freeing one station from violent tyranny," she said, reaching the crescendo of the half-hour-long speech. "It means the reopening of the path to all the colonies and all the worlds that the Free Navy tried to lock away. It means the reconnection to the motive force of history, and *proof* that the spirit of humanity will never bow to fear and cruelty. And yes, since you've all behaved so nicely, I'll take some questions. Takeshi?"

A thin reporter in a gray suit stood up, a reed among the ranks of his professional fraternity.

"Shit," Alex said from the doorway. "Are there reporters anywhere else, or does she have all of them?"

"Shh," Bobbie said.

"Madam Secretary-General, you said that the attack on Earth was not an act of war but the lashing out of a criminal conspiracy. Now that you have captured prisoners, how will they be handled?"

"The conspirators will be brought to Luna and introduced to their lawyers," Avasarala said. "Next quest—"

"Just the ones from Medina? Or Pallas and Europa too? Won't that create a burden on the court system?" the gray man pressed.

Avasarala's smile was sweet. "Oh, that guy's fucked," Bobbie said.

"Oh yeah," Holden agreed.

"It will take some time to process everyone," Avasarala said. "But I have to put some blame for the delay on the Free Navy itself. If they wanted a faster trial, they shouldn't have leveled so many courthouses. Next question. Lindsey?"

"She shouldn't be milking this so much," Bobbie said while a blond woman stood in the gray man's place and asked something about reconstruction and the role of the OPA. "It's going to bite her."

"It's the biggest unambiguous victory we've had against Inaros," Holden said. "Everything else, he stripped to the studs and walked away from. Or left for us to crawl over, disarming his booby traps. Even the thing at Titan looks like it cost us as much as it got back. Earth needs a win. Hell, Mars needs a win. I'm just glad it's one that had Belters fighting on our side too."

"But if she builds it up too much, it's just going to be worse when we lose Medina again."

Holden looked over. "Why do you think we're going to lose it?"

"Because I had to kill the rail guns," Bobbie said. "Holding on to this place assumed we could *take over* the defenses. We didn't. We broke them. If we can get a dozen ships in here with guns like the *Roci* or maybe a pair of *Donnager*-class battleships, we can hold it. But that means getting them here, and we have to assume Inaros is throwing every spare grenade and bullet into whatever ships he has to burn here and kick our asses. And that's if his patron out past the Laconia gate isn't already sending the MCRN ships *he* stole to clear us out."

The knot in Holden's gut that had loosened a couple notches since he'd stepped onto Medina tightened back up. "Oh," he said. "So. Do we have a plan to address that?"

"Fight like hell and hope the bad guys spend so much time killing us they can't finish rebuilding before whoever Avasarala and Richards send next gets here."

"Ah."

"We've been screwed since the minute I blew up that reactor. Doesn't take away from the essential dignity of the situation. And this is a fine hill."

"A what?"

Bobbie looked over, surprised he hadn't followed the idiom. "Fine hill to die on."

Chapter Forty-Seven: Filip

What was it like?" Filip asked, trying to sound casual.

Her name was Marta. She had a wide face with a scattering of moles along her jawline like she'd been splatted by something. Her hair was lighter than her skin. Of all the people in the club, she was the one who seemed to have the most patience with the new guy. When the karaoke was going, she'd offered him the mic, even though he hadn't taken it. When the club had gotten crowded, she'd let him sit at the end of her table. Not with her, but not *not* with her either. She'd grown up in Callisto, born here. Worked for one of the warehouses doing compliance checks. She was about a year older than him. She'd been sixteen when it happened.

She narrowed her eyes and tilted her head. "What was the attack like? For for?"

"Wondered," he said with a shrug. The club was dark enough

she probably wouldn't see him blushing. "Heard about it since I came."

Marta shook her head, looked away. Someone jostled against Filip's back on their way toward the bar. He was about to apologize—was finding the words for it—when she spoke.

"Was eine day, yeah? Woke up in the morning, same same. Got ready for school. Mom made hash and coffee for breakfast. Just eine day, same like otra. Was talking with some friends in the common room and everything shakes, yeah? Just once. Just a little bit, but everyone feels it. We all ask each other, and everyone feels it. Then the teacher come in all rapiutamine and says we have to get to the hard shelters. Something going on over à los Martian yards. Figured a reactor blew. Knew it was bad though. We're hardly in when the next one comes, and it's worse. Lot worse."

"All the hits were on the Martian yard, though," Filip said.

"Same rock," Marta said with a shrug and a laugh. "Not like you can kick half a ball. Anyway, alarms are going off y everyone's crying. And then when they let us back out, it's just gone. Martian yard's delenda, and half of ours too. It was just...no sé. It was just everything before and then everything after."

"But you were okay," Filip said.

Marta shook her head, just a little. "My mom died," she said with a fake lightness. "Shelter she was in cracked."

Filip felt the words in his sternum. "Sorry."

"They said it was fast. She wouldn't have known even."

"Yeah," Filip said. His hand terminal chimed for the fourth time in the hour.

"You sure you don't want to answer those?" Marta said. "Your girlfriend's wanting you pretty solid."

"No. It's all right," he said. And then, "I don't have a mother either."

"What happened to yours?"

"Broke up with my dad when I was a baby. Dad always said he hid me away because she was crazy. But I don't know. I met her first time a few months ago, but she's gone again."

"Did she seem crazy to you?"

"Yeah," Filip said. Then, "No. Seemed like she didn't want to be there."

"Harsh."

"She told me that the only right you have with anyone in life is the right to walk away."

Marta coughed out a disbelieving laugh. "Kind of bitch says that to her kid?"

The doors to the club were built like an airlock with inner and outer doors either side of a short hall, but to keep the brightness of the common corridor out. A bright streak and a few silhouetted bodies showed both sets of doors opened at once. Filip wondered whether he should tell the girl more. *I thought I watched her kill herself, only it turns out she didn't die. She was only leaving again.* It was true, but it wouldn't seem like it. Some things you couldn't talk about except with people who'd been there. His hand terminal chimed again.

Someone shoved him, hard. Filip's stool tilted, and he grabbed the table to stop his fall. Marta yelped and stood up, shouting as she did. "Berman! Que sa?"

Filip turned slowly. The man who'd shoved him was his own age plus maybe a year or two. Deep-green jumpsuit with the logo of a shipping company on the sleeve. His chin jutted. His chest was pushed forward, his arms pulled back. Everything about him said he was looking for violence except that he wasn't hitting Filip.

"Que nammen?" the new man demanded.

"Filip," he answered. He was aware of the mass of the gun in his pocket like it was calling to him. Calmly, slowly, he put a hand against the grip of the pistol. Marta shoved her way between them, her arms wide. She was yelling about how Berman—who had to be the guy with the chin—was out of his mind. How he was stupid. How she was just talking with coyo and Berman was out-of-his-head jealous and fucked up too. Berman kept shifting his head to stare at Filip around her. Filip felt his own rage boiling up, like fumes off a fire. Draw the gun, level it just long enough for the coyo to know what was coming, then bang and the kick in his wrist. He was Filip Inaros, and he'd killed billions. He'd killed Marta's mother.

"It's okay," Filip said as he stood. "Misunderstanding. No harm, sa sa?"

"Pinché asshole *better* run," Berman shouted at Filip's back, and then Marta shouting some more and Berman shouting at her, and Filip was in the fake airlock and pushing through to the common corridor beyond. It was bright there. The smell of liquor and old smoke stayed around him for a few seconds before the gentle breeze from the recyclers pulled it away. He was shaking. Trembling. His hands ached with the need to hit something or someone. He started walking without any idea where he was walking to, just needing something to let him move. Let whatever beast was running through his bloodstream work itself out a little.

Callisto passed him as he went. Pale corridors wider than most of the stations and ships he'd been on, with a honeycomb pattern on the curved walls that made him think of a football. Banks of heaters made irregular tapping sounds as they glowed down from the ceilings, radiating at the top of his head the way that the cold of the moon's body crept up from the floors. People walked or rode bicycles or carts. He wondered how many of them had lost family in the attack on Callisto. In the story he'd told himself about the attack, it had all been Dusters that died. Soldiers whose work was to keep the Belt's head underwater until it drowned. And in his story, his father was the leader to unite the Belt, to lead it against everything that was bent on destroying their futures and erasing their pasts.

And he still thought that. Even while he doubted, he believed. It was like everything in his private world had doubled. One Callisto that had been the target of his raid. His critical victory that led to the bombardment of Earth and the freedom of the Belt. Another Callisto that he walked through now, where normal people had lost their mothers and children, husbands and friends in a disaster. The two places were so different, they didn't relate. Like two ships with the same name but different layouts and jobs.

And he had two fathers now. The one who led the fight against the inners and who Filip loved like plants love light, and the one who twisted out of everything that went wrong and blamed anyone but himself. The Free Navy that was the first real hope the Belt had ever had, and the Free Navy that was falling apart. Swapping out generals and leaders faster than air filters. They couldn't both exist, and he couldn't let either version go.

His hand terminal chimed again. He plucked it out of his pocket. The connection request came from Karal and the *Pella*. It was the twelfth he'd made. Filip accepted.

"Filipito!" Karal said. "Hell have you been, coyo?" He was on the command deck and wearing his uniform. Even had the collar done, which he usually didn't. It didn't make him look like he was military, though. He looked like himself, but in costume.

"Around."

"Around," Karal said, shaking his head. "You got to get back to the ship. You got to come *now*."

"For for?"

Karal leaned in close to the screen like he was going to whisper a secret. "Battle analysis leaked out à Medina, yeah? The rail guns are down. Medina has one ship guarding it. *One*, and it's—"

"*Rocinante*," Filip said.

"Sí no? Every ship with more than half a hull, Marco's putting them together. Retaking Medina like we're putting out a fire, us."

"Yeah," Filip said.

"Getting fresh juice. Topping up the reaction mass. And then we're gone. Meeting up with the rest of the navy on the way, but your father? I've never seen him like—"

A voice came from the hand terminal, snapping Karal's attention away from him. "*You found him?*"

"Que no?" Karal said, but not to him.

The image jumped, cutting from one camera to another. An empty crash couch with a vague shadow along one edge. The shadow fell back, gained resolution, became his father. Filip braced for abuse, for contempt. For all the condescension he'd been suffering. *Say it like a man. Say I fucked up.* His stomach was tight.

Marco beamed at him, eyes bright.

"Did you hear? Did Karal tell you?"

"About Medina, and the ship there." For some reason he couldn't explain he didn't want to say the name *Rocinante* out loud. He felt it would be like bad luck.

"This is our moment, Filipito. It has all come together perfectly. We bit them and bit them and bit them and faded into the dark until they went mad with it. They've pushed out past their defenses, and now we can come down on them like a *hammer*."

Them. He didn't mean Earth and Mars. He didn't mean the governments of the inner planets. Whether he knew it or not, Filip was certain—as certain as he'd been of anything—that James Holden and Naomi Nagata were *them*.

"That's good, then," he said.

"Good?" his father hooted. "This is it. This is the opportunity we've been waiting for. This is how we break them. All the half-loyal cunts in the OPA who trotted wherever Fred Johnson led them? Pa and Ostman and Walker—all of them. They all fell in with Holden, and we will take him away from them just the way we killed Johnson. We will punish them for their disloyalty."

Filip felt a little thrill of excitement. The idea of victory—resounding, triumphant, and final—was intoxicating. His father's joy bore him up, promised to wash away all his anger and his doubts. But there was another Filip, a smaller and less emotional one, who watched the swelling enthusiasm with disgust.

Luring Naomi and her lover out to Medina to be killed was the plan now. But more than that, it had always been the plan. They'd killed Fred Johnson as part of it. They'd abandoned Ceres too. The consolidated fleet's massive and coordinated attacks had been them falling for his father's brilliant strategy to lure them out.

And if it failed, if something went wrong, that would always have been the plan too. His father's new generals would change, getting better with every purge. And when it got so foul there was no way to pretend it into victory, it would be someone else who had failed. Maybe Filip.

"Highest burn we've ever done, but it will be worth it," Marco was saying. "It will carry rewards greater than anything before it. Only there isn't time to waste. We're launching inside the hour. All hands. All ships, *everyone*. We'll melt the fucking ring with our braking burn and char Holden to ash."

Marco clapped his hands, delighting in the prospect. Filip smiled and nodded.

"As soon as we're supplied," Marco said, growing a degree more sober, "we're gone. Be back to the ship in half an hour, yeah?"

"All right," Filip said.

Marco looked out of the screen and into his eyes. There was a softness in his expression. A kind of sensual pleasure almost indistinguishable from love. "This will be glorious," his father said. "They will remember this forever."

And then, like an actor having delivered his final line, Marco dropped the connection.

Looking up from his hand terminal felt like coming out of a dream. He'd just been someplace else, with someone. And now he was here again, in this corridor. If he turned around, he could go back to the club he'd been in. It seemed strange in a way he couldn't quite explain that his father's glorious battle plan and a common corridor of Callisto yards should exist in the same universe. Maybe because, in a way, they didn't.

The docks weren't far. There was a tube station that could have gotten him there in five minutes, but half an hour was more than he'd need to walk the distance. He put his hand terminal back in his pocket where it clicked against his pistol, a nearly inaudible tick with every step.

Moving from the residential corridors to the docks had a thousand little signals. There were none of the teenage girls here, and more of the people drifting through the intersections were wearing jumpsuits and tool belts. The air smelled different. Even if they used the same filters, the docks would always smell of welding and synthetic oil and cold. He still had twenty minutes.

The concourse between the military and civilian yards was shaped like a massive Y. Where the paths met, someone in the station had decided it would be a good idea to put a statue of something that looked like a wide, abstract Minotaur fashioned out of brushed steel. Directly above the weird art, a screen listed the berths and the ships in each of them. On the military side, there were seven Free Navy ships, an Earth transport they'd captured when they took the station, and three empty berths. He looked at the word PELLA for a couple breaths as if it were as much a piece of art as the uncomfortable man-bull beneath it. On the civilian side, almost a dozen ships. Prospectors, miners, transport. An emergency medical relief ship. He imagined there would have been more if there wasn't a war on.

Against the wall, another screen showed the exchange rates for fifty or sixty kinds of scrip—corporate, governmental, cooperative, commodity-based. A small gray rat scampered along the floor underneath the screen and squeezed itself into a hole Filip hadn't even noticed was there like it was falling into shadow. His hand terminal chimed, but he ignored it. The docks were right there.

Just down the corridor to the civilian docks, there was a waiting area with six rows of uncomfortable ceramic chairs facing each other and a bright orange recycler at the end of every other row. An old man in a fake leather coat and grimy pants stared blankly in Filip's direction, seeing him but not seeing him. A row of grimy kiosks dug into one wall. A noodle stall. A public terminal. Two union offices. Employment and housing brokers. Filip looked at them all with the same detachment he'd felt looking at the berth displays.

His hand terminal chimed again. He took it out without looking at it, switched it to his off-hand, and drew out the gun. The old man's stare was less blank now. He watched as Filip walked toward the chairs and fed first the gun and then the hand terminal into the recycler. Filip nodded to the old man, and after a long moment, the old man nodded back.

The employment broker's kiosk had bright marks of wear at the edge of the counter, worn into the metal by millions of tired elbows. The bulletproof glass had pits in it, tiny as stars. The woman behind the glass wore her gray hair in a buzz cut. The place smelled vaguely of piss. Filip walked to the counter and rested his elbows on the edge.

"I need work," he said like someone else was saying it.

The gray woman flicked her eyes up at him, then back down. "What can you do?"

"Environmental maintenance. Machining."

"Both or either?"

"Anything. I just need work."

The counter lit up. A virtual keyboard and a form. He looked at it, his heart sinking.

"Put in your employment ID," the gray woman said.

"I don't have an employment ID."

The flicker of her eyes was longer this time. "Union waiver?"

"I'm not in a union."

"No ID, no waiver. You're fucked, kid."

There was still time. He could run. He could catch the *Pella* before she left. His father would wait for him. They would burn out to Medina. They would take back the Belt for Belters, and it would be glorious. His heart started racing, but he put his hands on the edge of the counter. Squeezed like he was holding himself in place.

"Please. I just need work."

"I run a clean shop, kid."

"Please."

She didn't look up. He didn't move. The right corner of her mouth quirked up like it was somehow independent of the rest of her face. The counter blinked, and a shorter form appeared. PRÉ-NOM. NOM DE FAMILIE. RÉSIDENCE. ÂGE. COORDONNÉES.

"I'll see what I can do," she said, not looking up.

He put his finger on COORDONNÉES. "I don't have a hand terminal."

"You can come back tomorrow," she said like it was a common enough problem.

PRÉNOM: FILIP

NOM DE FAMILIE:

"You okay, kid?" The hard eyes on him. He nodded.

NOM DE FAMILIE: NAGATA

Chapter Forty-Eight: Pa

The light of the sun was strong enough to turn the tangerine-colored haze to its midday twilight. A bright patch showed its place. Saturn hung on the far side of Titan's atmosphere somewhere, along with the debris that had been a hundred or more ships. Michio remembered a moment in the chaos of the battle seeing Saturn on her screen. It had seemed so close, she could make out the complexity of the rings. She remembered it, but it might not have happened. Her memory of the violence was spotty.

The resort was astounding. The dome rose up fifty meters above the ground, a swirl of titanium and reinforced glass with ivy dripping down like hanging gardens. Terraces rose in curves, designed to create breathtaking views out of a featureless, hazy sky. Finches darted here and there, flickers of color, as artificial and foreign to the moon's environment as she was. As any of them were. From where she sat, Michio could look down on swimming pools and courtyards of fake brick and ferns. Bright foil emergency shelters were propped up next to luxurious wet bars. The wounded slept on chaise longues and deck chairs because the hospital beds were full.

The dome resorts had been built decades ago for the wealthy of Earth and Mars. A place for the captains of finance and industry to rest while they worked on building up the settlements on Saturn's moons and hauling ice from its rings. An exotic site for tourists to come and pretend they'd experienced life in the outer planets without ever having to experience it.

They had done a good trade ever since, and not only among the inners. For Belters, the resorts were as close to experiencing life on Earth as they would ever reach. Open air. A real, free-flowing atmosphere to look at if not to breathe. Food and liquor imported from Earth and Mars. And so it had become a kind of halfway point—a haven for Earthers in the outer planets and a version of Earth that Belters could enjoy. She wondered whether an Earther would find it as unlike Earth as she found it unlike the Belt. Maybe what they really had to share was its lack of authenticity.

She had never been here before, and if she had her way, she would never come back.

Footsteps sounded on the terrace behind her. She turned, winced, and then kept turning despite the pain. The burns on her back only itched now if she kept still. She was afraid, despite all the doctors had said, that she'd scar up and lose her ability to move if she didn't keep stretching the wounds.

Nadia's smile was weary, but real. She carried fresh bandages and a white tube of cream in one hand and a hand terminal in the other. Michio grimaced, then laughed ruefully.

"Is it that time again?" she asked.

"Such," Nadia said, "such are the joys. I brought you something to take your mind off it, though."

"Something good?"

"No," Nadia said, taking a seat behind her. "The Earther woman wants to talk to you again."

Michio shrugged off the paper robe from the hospital and leaned forward. Nadia passed the hand terminal to her and began examining the edges of the false skin that covered her wounds. The nerves that let her experience light touch were smothered by living bandage. The ones that reported pain were terribly sensitive. It was like being numb and skinned alive at the same time. Michio gritted her teeth. Waited. When she had made the full circuit—across Michio's back and down her left side and arm—Nadia sighed.

"It looks good?" Michio said.

"It looks terrible, but it's healing well. Basal growth all the way around."

"Well," Michio said. "Thank God for small favors."

Nadia made a small sound in the back of her throat, neither agreement nor dissent. Michio heard the soft crack as Nadia opened the tube of medicated lotion. Michio scooped up the hand terminal, opened her message queue. The new message from Earth was waiting for her, flagged as critical. Chrisjen Avasarala. The leader of Earth, and the greatest enemy Michio Pa had ever had. And yet here they were.

"We did this wrong," she said.

"What?" Nadia asked.

Michio lifted the hand terminal for Nadia to see. "We're working with the people we used to be fighting against."

"We'll fight them again later," Nadia said, like she was promising a sweet to a child, but only after she ate her real food. "Are you ready?"

Michio nodded, and Nadia smeared on the first finger-load of ointment. The pain was bright, like she was burning again. She started the message, tried to focus on it.

The old woman appeared, sitting at a desk. It wasn't the first time Michio had gotten a message directly from her or from the new prime minister of Mars, but more often she'd heard from generals or functionaries. They only seemed to include Michio when they were asking for something big. It very much gave her the sense of being the least important person at their table.

"Captain Pa," Avasarala said, and if there was an undertone of contempt in the words, it was only to be expected. Nadia moved lower on her back, new pain blooming just as the first swath began to fade. "The situation on Medina has gone pear-shaped. Holden and the OPA forces have succeeded in taking the station, but saw fit to annihilate the rail gun defenses. Which leaves them undefended. The Free Navy has deployed what appears to be every functioning ship they have left—fifteen in all—burning hard for the gate. The good news is that Inaros has essentially retreated from every other port and base in the system. The bad news, of course, is that he'll get Medina back, his supply lines to Laconia reestablished, and in a defensible position. Unless, of course, we find a way to stop him."

Avasarala took a deep breath, looked down, and when she looked up again, something had changed in her face. She looked wearier? Older? More determined?

"I am very, very sorry for the loss you suffered. It strikes close to home. I lost a spouse to this war as well. I can't imagine how devastating it must be to lose two. I would not ask this if it were not critical, but if you have any ships or influence with any factions that can help us to stop or slow Inaros before he reaches the gate, we need your help now.

"Nothing I can offer you will address the sacrifice you have already made, but I hope you will walk this last kilometer with me. And that we can end this together. Please let me know as soon as you can. The Free Navy is already burning."

The message ended, and the terminal dropped back to her queue. Nadia moved on to her side, and Michio flinched.

"Almost done," Nadia said.

"This is the second time one of our enemies has called me to pull them out of a fire."

"*Can* we do it again?"

"All we did last time was burn ourselves trying."

She'd known going in that there might be a price for leaving the *Panshin* behind. Titan was the largest of Saturn's moons. The Free Navy had its strongest presence outside the Jovian system there, projecting threat toward Enceladus, Rhea, Iapetus, Tethys. The ice buckers in the rings. Controlling the space without occupying it.

The *Connaught* and the *Serrio Mal* burned in spinward, looping up out of the ecliptic to come down on the Free Navy's ships from an unexpected angle. The burn hadn't been as hard as Michio had hoped. There hadn't been a chance to add reaction mass, and she'd had the sick fear that they'd end up losing the fight at Titan and not be able to retreat. Fifteen Free Navy ships had been stationed there. For most of her life, that wouldn't have been a very large number, but after so much war and so many people taking their ships out through the rings to new systems, it was respectable. It was more than the nine that the consolidated fleet threw at it. But then the point of all the attacks wasn't to win. It was to keep Marco's eye off the two ships skinning off toward Medina.

The Martian Congressional Republic Navy had taken point in the battle, engaging early and trying to pull the Free Navy's ships out of position in hopes that her own attack from the side would come unexpectedly. She remembered Oksana getting the tactical display. Fifteen of the enemy, nine friendlies. Oksana made a joke about how every ship in the battle had probably been built in the same shipyard. Evans had laughed, then sobered and said they were getting painted.

After that, Michio's memory became less reliable. She'd gone over the logs. Things hadn't turned on her that early, but the strike, when it came, was like a shotgun blast in her life. It took out a massive hole, but stray pellets had traveled forward and back in time, made smaller holes in her experience. She remembered giving the order to retreat, and Josep saying they'd lost core, but she didn't remember the hit that had made her decide to run. She remembered the smell of her clothing and hair burning. But the long, terrible moments between identifying the torpedo that cracked the *Connaught*'s back and the actual impact were gone.

What she knew from the logs was that the *Serrio Mal* and the *Connaught* had fired down into the heart of the Free Navy formation, drawing the enemy fire and scattering their position to open up corridors and blinds where the enemy PDCs weren't reinforcing each other. The Martian ships, being closer, had fired a massive barrage of torpedoes that managed to disable two Free Navy ships. She didn't know if the round that took out her drive was from the Free Navy or from a stray from the MCRN, but an enemy torpedo had managed to thread its way through their defenses and blow hours out of Michio's consciousness.

She had the strong impression of a broad-shouldered man with a shaved head and dark skin telling her he was going to make the pain stop but she had to put down the knife. She couldn't place when that had happened. She vividly recalled waking in a hospital room, and then waking there again without any sense of having fallen asleep in between the two.

The beginning of what she thought of as "after" was when she came to and found Bertold sitting at the edge of her bed, massaging her feet and singing a low dirge under his breath. She'd asked about Laura first, which in retrospect made her think she'd known something was wrong with her.

Bertold said Laura had been hurt. Was in a medical coma. They'd need to regrow part of her liver and one of her kidneys, but Laura was the wife of the pirate queen, and the doctors promised she'd be fine, given time.

Then he'd told her about Evans and Oksana, and they'd cried together until she slept.

The quarters they'd assigned this new, smaller version of her family were beautiful. Three bedrooms with wide, soft beds enough like crash couches that they were comfortable and different enough to seem like luxury. A food station with a narrower range of options than they'd had on the *Connaught* and brighter chrome. What the resort called a "conversation pit" that looked like a long, curved couch that had burrowed into the floor. Skylights opened to the dome, boasting natural light. A soaking bath big enough for two. Bertold, Nadia, and Josep the only ones to share it with her. Everything about it seemed too large and too small at the same time.

She waited until the ointment had soaked deep into her new, artificial skin, then put on what she called her "captain's uniform." Nothing really more than a formal shirt and a jacket with a vaguely military cut. She pulled on pants and boots, even though they wouldn't show in the message she sent back. Her mind was still fuzzy from the pain medications, and she didn't understand quite why being formal about the message felt so important to her until she sat down, framed herself, and began her recording.

It felt important because it was a surrender.

"Madam Secretary-General, I am very sorry to say that I don't have any aid to give. The ships I had to command are either dead or broken or scattered so far from the ring gate that they couldn't catch up to the *Pella* without killing everyone on board before they got to it."

The version of her on the screen looked tired. Bertold had cut her hair short so that the places where it had burned didn't stand out. She didn't like how it looked. A wave of grief washed over her, the way they often did now. The way they would on and off for the rest of her life.

"Thank you for your kind words about our casualties. They knew the risks when we took up this work. They were willing to die for the Belt. I wish they hadn't. I would like them here with me.

"I wish I could have done more."

There was nothing else to say, so she sent the message. Then, like prodding at an infected wound, she pulled up a tactical report. The whole system lay before her. The *Panshin* still lived and a handful of others. The nakliye at Eugenia. And there, vector-mapped from the Jovian system out toward the ring, the *Pella*. The remnants of the Free Navy. Two other smaller dots were on intersecting paths, but when she checked their estimated course, it was clear they were all on the same mission. Marco and his loyalists would pour through the gate together. An unstoppable force. If the rail gun defenses had still been in place, it still would have been a hell of a fight. Without them, it would be a slaughter.

Then, station by station, ship by ship, she scrolled through the system. It was the equivalent of the grease-pencil grid she'd drawn in some other lifetime, on a ship that was scrap and bad memories now. All of the things that people needed. Filters. Hydroponic supplies. Recycler teeth. Centrifuges for refining ore. Centrifuges for testing water. For working with blood.

She wondered if there were any colony ships still hiding out there in the emptiness, dark and watching in horror as humanity tore itself apart. She remembered the Doctrine of the One Ship. Remembered thinking of all the vessels in the Belt as being cells of a single being. She couldn't see it that way now. At best, they were all their own desperate bacteria floating on a vacuum sea that didn't care if they lived and didn't notice when they died.

And if Sanjrani was right, a worse collapse was only clearing its throat.

The door to the common corridor opened, and Josep slouched in. Nadia kissed him on her way to bed. Those were the shifts now. One to sit with Laura, one to sit with her, and one to sleep. A cycle of shared grief. Josep went to the food station, slid open a panel she hadn't noticed, and poured himself a glass of whiskey before he came to sit in the pit across from her.

"Skol," he said, raising his glass. The rim clinked against his teeth as he drank. For a moment, they sat there together in silence.

"Oops," she said.

Josep raised his eyebrows. "La magic word la."

"It was me," she said, wiping at her eyes with the cuff of her shirt. "I did what I always do, and I drove us straight to hell with it."

Josep's eyes were sunk back into his head. Exhaustion showed in his skin and the angle of his shoulders. "Don't follow your mind, me."

"I find someone, and I put my faith in them, and I go where they lead. And then all the gold turns to shit. Johnson and Ashford and Inaros. And now Holden. I don't know how I didn't see it coming, but I fell into it again with him. And now..."

"Now," Josep agreed.

"And the stupid thing," she said, her voice rising a little, growing thin and sharp as the drone of a violin, "is that I look at all this? I look at everything I was trying to do, and none of it happened. Wanted to make the Belt for Belters, and it won't be. I wanted to build a place where we could live and call our own, and there isn't one. Isn't a way to build one even. I don't even remember now why I thought I should be on Holden's side. To open the gates again? Get the flow of colony ships freed up? Make sure that none of the people I cared about would live?"

Josep nodded, his expression thoughtful and distant. "What would it mean if you'd dreamed it?" Josep asked.

"Dreamed what?" Michio said, shifting until her back hurt, and then shifting some more.

"This," he said. "That you'd fought for Inaros and then for Holden. That you'd lost people precious to you and ended in a place of luxury and healing?"

"It wouldn't mean shit."

Josep grunted. "Could be prophecy."

"Could be that the universe doesn't give a shit about us or anything we do and your mystic bullshit's just a way we try to pretend otherwise."

"Could be that too," he agreed with an equanimity that made her ashamed she'd said it. He took another drink of his whiskey, then put the glass on the floor and lay out full on the curving couch, his head coming to rest in her lap. His smile was warm and beautiful and filled with a humor and gentleness that made her heart ache.

"Didn't follow Holden, us. Standing against Marco put Holden beside you, yeah. But you were never his. We didn't fight Marco because of Holden. We fought because Marco said he was the champion the Belt needed, only turned out he wasn't."

"Yeah," she said, stroking his hair.

He closed his eyes in exhaustion. "Aber, God *damn* but we're still gonna need a champion."

Chapter Forty-Nine: Naomi

Medina's system logs were huge, larger than anything Naomi had expected. And, what was worse, not very well organized. It was an artifact of history in a way. The physical design had been intended for a generation ship cruising through the still-unknown ocean of interstellar space, but the logic systems came from Fred Johnson's military refit, which had then been repurposed when the ship went from battleship to permanent city in space. The old security systems hadn't all been cracked when the Free Navy took over, so there were partial records here and there, scattered by a variety of engineers trying to force their will on an already complex system.

Like cities back on Earth where era had built on era had built on the era before, the systems of Medina were shaped by long-forgotten forces. The thinking behind each decision was lost now in a tangle of database hierarchies and complex reference structures. Finding something interesting was easy. It was *all* interesting on some level. Finding some particular piece of information—and knowing whether it was the most recent or complete version of the data—was very, very difficult.

She used her office in the security station like it was a medieval monk's cell, only leaving it to go back to the *Rocinante* to sleep, then coming back to it when she woke. Instead of copying ancient texts with pen and ink, she spelunked the datasets, poked through file systems, asked Medina to find things, and then watched to see where it didn't search. Anything that seemed like it might be useful she copied or stripped out and then sent back. Work report logs from the days under the Free Navy's control, sent back to Earth and Mars. Landing papers outlining the supply flow in from and back out to Laconia. Accident reports from the medical systems. Traffic control comm logs from the ships that had come and gone. Anything might be useful, so she took everything and sent it back at the speed of light to Earth and Luna and Mars and Ceres.

It kept the fear at bay. Not perfectly, but nothing short of death was going to end fear perfectly. No matter how she distracted herself, there was a timer ticking down in the back of her mind. The days and hours until Marco and his ships arrived. There were other problems, other risks—the Free Navy loyalists still on the station, the strobing do-not-approach signal that was the only thing coming out of the Laconia gate—but none of them would matter once Marco arrived. All of it pushed her to get her work done quickly, efficiently. When the next thing came—and she didn't look what that would be straight in its eyes—she wanted to know that she'd gotten her work done.

And still, sometimes she paused. She found a personal journal tucked among the environmental reports like printed pornography tucked under a mattress. Entry after entry of a young man's private struggles with his longings and ambitions and feelings of betrayal. Another time, she was trying to recover what she could from a half-erased partition and came up with a short video of a girl—four years old at most—leaping off a bed somewhere on the station, landing on a pile of pillows, and dissolving into laughter. Reviewing the traffic-control logs, she listened to the voices of desperate men and women from the systems on the far sides of the ring gates demand and beg and plead for the supplies they felt they deserved, wanted, and sometimes needed to survive.

It was the first time she'd really understood the scale of the destruction Marco had brought. All the lives he'd traumatized and ended, all the plans he'd shattered. Most of the time, it was too big to wrap her mind around, but little glimpses like this made it all comprehensible. Terrible and sad and enraging, but comprehensible.

And it informed some of her decisions.

"Um," Jim said, sloping in through the door of his office. "So, sweetie? Did you mean to have the data feeds go out through all the rings? Because I'm noticing that you've started sending everything to everyone."

"I meant to," Naomi said, brushing the hair back from her eyes. It was almost the end of her second shift. Her back ached a little from sitting too long in the same position, and her eyes were dry and scratchy. "I don't know what's going to be useful, or who it's going to be useful to. And since it doesn't look like we'll be on Medina long enough to go through everything, I thought I'd send copies out everywhere. Give other people a chance to find whatever I'm missing."

"That's…ah."

"I know," she said. "I may have been spending too much time with you. I'm starting to think like you. Only, well. The way you used to, anyhow."

"I still think like that," Jim said, pulling a chair over behind hers and sitting. He rested his head on her shoulder. When he spoke, she could feel the vibration in his throat against her skin. "I worry more that it's going to do something unexpected and terrible and huge that I'll be responsible for, but I still think that way."

"An unshakable faith in humanity."

"It's true," he said, shaking his head. Or maybe nuzzling a little. "Against all evidence, I keep thinking the assholes are outliers."

She leaned her head against him, taking a little pleasure in his simple presence. He had a peculiar scent, low and complex and pleasant as potting soil. She didn't think she'd ever get tired of it. And he hadn't shaved recently. The stubble of ragged whiskers tickled her ear like a cat's tongue. On the monitor, the data broadcasts ticked over another tenth of a percent. Somewhere in the office, Bobbie was talking, her voice familiar and strong. The air recyclers clicked and hummed to themselves, the soft breeze smelling like plastic and dust.

She didn't want to ask the question, but she couldn't hold it in either.

"Any news from home?"

She felt him tighten. He sat back, and the part of her skin he'd been against felt cooler without him. She turned her chair so she could look at him. His face had the artificial mildness that meant he was trying to downplay something, as if by treating it casually he could diminish it. She'd seen all his expressions so many times, she knew what he meant, whatever he said.

"They're coming. Free Navy. There's still no sign of activity from Laconia at all, but Avasarala's tracking fifteen ships converging on the gate. Mostly from the Jovian moons."

"Any chance they'll come through one at a time so Alex and Bobbie can shoot them?" she asked with a feigned innocence. It worked the way she hoped. Jim laughed.

"I'm pretty sure they're all going to come through like a rugby team. If we could get a couple of the rail guns from the station working again, I think we'd have a chance. And some more rounds for them. Turns out shooting down a couple thousand targets can kind of burn through your supplies."

"Do we have a plan?"

"A couple," Jim said.

"Either of them good?"

"Oh, no. Not at all. Just different flavors of terrible."

The data feed chimed. The batch sent off, and waiting for Naomi to pick something else. More messages, more bottles. "All right. What are they?"

"The classics. Fight or flight. We've got the *Roci* and the boats that still work as boarding craft. One option is that we fill up the boats with troops, place them around the edge of the ring, and try to get people onto the Free Navy ships. It won't matter that they have ten times as many torpedoes as us if all the fighting's corridor to corridor. The *Roci* and Medina's defenses go after the ships we can't take control of. Massive slugfest, and hopefully we come out on top."

"And the chances that'll work?"

"Terrible, terrible chances. Very low. Dumb plan on every level. Much more likely that the boats will all get turned into metal shavings by Marco's PDCs before they even get close to boarding. And even if they do, those ships are going to have full crews to fight our people back."

"And flight?"

"Stock up the *Roci*, pick a gate, and get the hell out of Dodge before the bad guys show up in the first place."

"And leave Medina?"

"Medina. The *Giambattista*. Everything. Just turn tail and run like hell. Let the Free Navy hole back up in the slow zone and hope that the next wave the consolidated fleet sends can take it all back again and hold it next time."

"Where's the *Pella*?"

Jim sighed. "Oh, leading the howling pack."

Naomi turned back to her screen. "Then we're staying here."

"I haven't decided," Holden said.

"No, you haven't talked yourself into it yet," she said. "You know if we go, Marco's going to follow us. Maybe if we were a different ship or Marco was a different man, things wouldn't play out this way. We've got the choice of fighting here, with a few allies and insufficient supplies, or fighting on the far side of a ring gate with even less. That's the only distinction."

"I…well …" Jim took a deep breath, blew out. "Shit."

"How much of the debris from the wave of decoys can we police up?"

"Anything that hasn't drifted out past the rings," Holden said. "You're thinking put it all just inside the Sol ring and hope the Free Navy runs into it?"

"The gate's not that big," Naomi said.

"Three-quarters of a million square klicks," Holden said. "And fifteen ships coming through it. Even if we turned all our scrap metal into sand, the Free Navy's more likely to miss them and not even know they were there."

"I know," Naomi said. "But maybe one will get a lucky hit. And then there'll be one less. If we aren't playing the long shots, we're giving up. Long shots are all we've got left. And even if we lose—"

"I'm not looking at—"

"*Even if we lose*," Naomi said, "how we lose matters. You didn't set yourself to be a symbol of anything. I know that. It's just something that happened. But after it happened, you used it. All those video essays you put out, trying to show everyone that the people on Ceres were just people?"

"Those weren't about me," Jim said, but the guilt in his voice said he didn't believe it.

"They were you using the famous Captain James Holden to make people look at what you needed them to see. Don't be ashamed of that. It was the right thing to do. But everyone out there who saw them? Who made their own versions of them and added to the project of trying to remind each other that war isn't all ships and torpedoes and battle lines? If we're going to…" Her throat was tight now. The words stuck there. "If we're going to die, we should make it mean at least as much as your video pieces did."

"I don't know that those mattered," Jim said. "Did they do anything?"

"You don't get to know that," Naomi said. "They did or they

didn't. You didn't put them out so that someone would send you a message about how important and influential you are. You tried to change some minds. Inspire some actions. Even if it didn't work, it was a good thing to try. And maybe it did. Maybe those saved someone, and if they did, that's more important than making sure you get to know about it."

Jim sank down into himself. The mask of himself that he'd worn since Tycho slipped a little. She saw the despair under it.

"I shouldn't have come here," he said.

"You took this on because it was the risky job," she said. "You did it because it needed doing, and you don't ask people to take things on you wouldn't do yourself. Just like when you ran onto the *Agatha King*. You don't change, Jim. And I knew that coming in. We all did. We thought we'd make it, but we knew we might be wrong. We were wrong. Now we have to do this next part well too."

"Getting killed. This next part is getting killed."

"I know," she said.

They were silent, the two of them. Bobbie's voice, as far away as the stars, turned briefly to laughter.

"The videos were just stupid little art projects," Jim said. "Dying's not an art project."

"Maybe it should be."

He hung his head. She put her hand on it, feeling the individual strands of hair against her fingertips. The tears in her eyes didn't sting. They flowed gently, like a brook. There was no way to tell him all of it. The guilt she felt for bringing them all into Marco's orbit. The certainty in her heart that if she'd just seen what Marco Inaros was in time, none of them would have been in this position. If she said it, Jim would feel like he had to comfort her, to be strong for her. He'd close back up into himself. Or no. Not himself. Into James Holden. She liked Jim better. One long breath. Another. Another. The quiet intimacy of a perfect moment.

"Hey," Bobbie said, stepping into the room. "Do either of you—um. Sorry."

"No," Jim said, wiping his eyes with the back of his hand. "What's up?"

Bobbie lifted her hand terminal. "Do either of you know if we sent the incident reports on the missing ships to Luna? Avasarala said her science monkeys are really champing at the bit for those."

Naomi took a long, shuddering breath and then smiled. Perfect moment over. Back to work. "I'll get right on it."

"Okay," Bobbie said, stepping backward out of the room. "Sorry if I...you know."

"Have you eaten yet?" Jim said, standing up. "I don't think I've had anything since breakfast."

"I was going to after I was done here."

"Could you two bring me a bowl of something?" Naomi said, turning to her monitor again.

The BATCH COMPLETE message had given up on her and dropped back to her file-system prompt. She spooled through the traffic logs as Jim and Bobbie called back to the *Roci*. Their voices—Jim, Amos, Alex, Bobbie—mixed together. A little conversation about food and beer, who wanted to be together and who wanted to be apart. She had to force herself to concentrate. The log structure was a mess, one manager doing things one way, the next picking another.

It took the better part of an hour to be sure she'd gotten the data from all the times ships had gone missing. Some of them, she'd already seen back on Luna, but there were more that she hadn't. Almost two dozen ships had vanished, including, it seemed, one of the stolen Martian ships heading for Laconia. Ships from the colonies. One of the transport ships delivering for the Free Navy too. All sides had lost something.

Which was interesting.

She prepped the data package for Luna. This one, she encrypted. But as it sent, she reviewed her own copy again. The missing ships tended to be larger, but weren't always. They seemed to vanish most in high-traffic times...

Alex brought her a bowl of noodles and mushrooms and a

bottle of Medina-brewed beer. She was pretty sure eating it that she'd remembered to thank him. Not positive, though. There was a correlation if she plotted the high-traffic times to the incidents...No. This was wrong. She was looking at it the wrong way. They didn't just need to look at when things had happened. They needed to look at all the times Medina had seen similar conditions—high traffic, large-mass ships, mistuned reactors— and *nothing* had gone wrong. She scooped up the full flight data partition and started streaming it down toward Luna too, but she couldn't let it go.

Her back ached. Her eyes hurt. She didn't really notice. Here was a dataset built of high-traffic periods with and without mysterious disappearances. Here was one mapping the energy output and mass of the missing ships and trying to fit that curve against ships that had sailed through safely. The full encrypted dataset sent to Luna announced it was complete, which seemed awfully fast until she checked how long she'd been sitting there.

Five variables—preceding mass, preceding energy, mass of the ship, energy of the ship, and time. No single-point solution, but a range. A moving system of curves, rising with preceding mass and energy, falling with time, and, where the mass and energy curve of the other ships intersected it, disappearances. It was as if traffic passing through the gates created a wake, and when something large enough and energetic enough struck that wake, it vanished.

Her hands were trembling as she pulled her terminal out of her pocket. She didn't know if it was emotion or exhaustion or if the noodles and mushrooms had been so long ago she just needed to eat. Jim picked up the connection almost as soon as she requested it.

"Hey," he said. "Are you all right? You didn't come back to the ship last night."

"No," she said, meaning no she hadn't gone back to the ship, not no she wasn't all right. She waved the imprecision of the word away. "I think I have something interesting here. I need someone to look at it for me in case I'm just hallucinating from exhaustion."

"I'll be right there. Should I grab anyone else? What sort of 'interesting' are you looking at?"

"It's about the missing ships."

On the little screen, Jim's eyebrows rose. His eyes went a degree wider. "Do you know what's eating them?"

She blinked. On her monitor, two equations, five variables. Years of traffic logs to draw from. It was a perfect fit. Surely Luna would be able to confirm it.

But *Do you know what's eating them?*

"I don't," she said. "I know something better."

Chapter Fifty: Holden

It's not a huge dataset," Naomi said, turning as she reached the edge of the room and pacing back toward him. "I mean, it's the largest there is. There's not more out there we could get."

"Is that a problem?" Holden asked.

She stopped, stared at him, her hands wide and hard in a universal gesture of *Of course it's a problem*. "It may not scale. There may be other variables at work that just haven't come into play in these instances. If you wanted me to build an engine based around data like this, I wouldn't do it. Shit, an engine. I wouldn't trust a *ladder* based on this. Except that ..."

She started pacing again and chewing at the nail of one thumb. Whatever her exception was, she'd already moved on in her mind. Holden folded his arms, waited. He knew her well enough to recognize when she needed a little mental space. He looked down at the graphs on her screen. They reminded him of a heart monitor, but the shapes of the curves were very different. He was pretty sure that with an EKG, the initial spike went back down under the baseline. With this, there was a rapid rise, then a slow, sloping falling away.

No one else had come to the security station yet. Probably, they were all still on the *Rocinante*, eating breakfast in the galley. Or maybe stopping at one of the little kiosks in the docks where the locals still took their scrip.

Naomi stopped beside him, her gaze on the screen with his. Her lips twitched like she was talking to herself, having a heated conversation no one else was welcome to. Not even him. She shook her head, disagreeing with herself. She'd seemed calmer when she'd first called, but the more they talked about it, the more agitated she became. The more frightened, even.

It looked like she was starting to hope.

"So this thing. Is it a thing we can use?"

"I don't know what it is. The mechanism? I've got no idea. All we have is this pattern, but it looks so *consistent*."

He tried again. "Is this a consistent pattern we can use? And specifically, is there something here that maybe gives us a third alternative in that 'stay here and be slaughtered versus run away through one of the gates and be slaughtered' conversation?"

She took a long, deep breath and let it out slowly between her teeth. He'd kind of hoped she'd laugh, but she didn't. She sat at her workstation again, pulled up a complex equation that Holden couldn't follow.

"I think," she said, "we can simulate a high-traffic interval. Load the *Giambattista* with as much junk as we can weld on it. Overload the reactor a little so it's generating more energy. Then, when we run it through a gate"—she tapped the spike-and-decay curve—"we should get one of these. Not a big one, though. Even a massive ship is only one ship ..."

"And one of these is what?"

"It's an obstacle. It's something that the Free Navy ships may run into. If their ships have enough mass and enough energy that this line crosses the curve before it dies away...I think they just stop."

"Meaning they go where all the other eaten ships go?"

Naomi nodded. "We could put extra mass in the *Giambattista*. We've still got those attack boats. Some of them have fuel left in their drives. If we put them through at the same time, we could increase the curve a little. And Marco will almost certainly bring all his ships through at once, so that might help us. But I don't know the *mechanism*—"

"Hey," Holden said. "Do you know what Planck's constant is?"

"Six point six two six plus change times ten to the negative thirty-fourth meters squared kilos per second?"

"Sure, why not," Holden said, raising one finger. "But do you know why it's that and not six point seven whatever the rest of it was?"

Naomi shook her head.

"Neither does anyone else. They still call it science. Most of what we know isn't *why* things are what they are. We just figure out enough about how they work that we can predict the next thing that's going to happen. That's what you've got. Enough to predict. And if you think you're right, then I do too. So let's do this."

She shook her head, but not at him. "A massive *n* equals one study where our null hypothesis is that we all get killed."

"Not necessarily," Holden said. "They only have fifteen to our one. We might still take them. We have Bobbie and Amos."

This time she did laugh. He put his arm under hers, and she leaned against him. "If it doesn't work, we won't be any more fucked than we are now," she said.

"Probably not," Holden said. "I mean, weird, dead alien technology with effects we don't understand sweeping whole ships away without leaving a trace or explanation. That's probably safe to play with, right?"

The *Pella* and her fourteen warships—all that was left of the Free Navy—came closer to the ring, already past their halfway point and on their braking burn. Avasarala had sent a list of the tactics she was using to try to slow or stop the attack days before, and with a heaviness that said she knew it was all bullshit even before she got around to making it explicit. She'd ended with *I'll do whatever I can, but you might have to make do with being avenged. Sorry about that.* He wondered what she'd have thought about Naomi's discovery and their plan.

Holden felt every hour that passed, knowing Inaros and his soldiers were a little nearer. It was like someone pushing at his back, making him hurry. It would almost have been easier if it had been hours and days. At least it would have been over.

The captain of the *Giambattista* misunderstood at first, thinking that his ship would be lost to the whatever-it-was that the gates did. Naomi had to explain to him four different times that if it went well, the *Giambattista* would just sail into some other system, loaf around there for a few days, and then come back, unharmed. Once she convinced him that, even if it failed, it meant he and his crew would miss the battle, his objections evaporated.

Naomi coordinated it all—loading the boats back into their positions in the hold, retuning the reactor so that both the bottle and the reaction were working almost at the edge of their capacity. She took Amos and Clarissa with her to backload the *Giambattista*'s internal power grid so that everything was on the verge of overload without ever quite tripping. It reminded Holden of Father Tom telling him about bears when he was young. If a black bear wandered onto the ranch, the thing to do was to open your coat and raise your arms over your head, shout and make noise. If it was a grizzly, the only thing to do was very quietly to get as far away as you could. Only this felt like they were making noise at a grizzly in hopes that it would eat the other guy.

While Naomi made her preparations, he tried to make himself useful.

There were backlogs of communications from the colony worlds. Status reports and threats and begging. It was sobering to remember how many planets humanity had already spread to. How many seeds they'd planted in strange soils. With Naomi's flood of information just gone out, a lot of the colonies were only now beginning to understand why they'd been cut off. Only now hearing about what had happened to Earth and its solar system. The messages coming back flooded the comm buffers with rage and sorrow, threats of vengeance and offers of aid.

Those last were the hardest. New colonies still trying to force their way into local ecosystems so exotic that their bodies could hardly recognize them as life at all, isolated, exhausted, sometimes at the edge of their resources. And what they wanted was to send back help. He listened to their voices, saw the distress in their eyes. He couldn't help but love them a little bit.

Under the best conditions, disasters and plagues did that. It wasn't universally true. There would always be hoarders and price gouging, people who closed their doors to refugees and left them freezing and starving. But the impulse to help was there too. To carry a burden together, even if it meant having less for yourself. Humanity had come as far as it had in a haze of war, sickness, violence, and genocide. History was drenched in blood. But it also had cooperation and kindness, generosity, intermarriage. The one didn't come without the other, and Holden had to take comfort in that. The sense that however terrible humanity's failings were, there was still a little more in them worth admiring.

He did what he could to answer the most pressing messages, offer what hope he could. The voice, however briefly, of Medina Station. Coordinating supplies for all the colonies was more than he could manage. It would be full-time work for a staff of dozens at least, and he was only one man with a radio. Still, just seeing the need, dipping his toes into the oceanic task of being the physical hub of a thousand different solar systems, gave him a covert sense of hope for the future.

He'd been right. There was a niche here.

Providing the plan worked. Providing they didn't all die. Providing that any of a million things he hadn't even thought of yet didn't swing through and destroy everything he was still looking for and planning. There was always the forgotten arm. The thing you didn't see coming. Hopefully, the thing Marco Inaros wouldn't see coming either.

"So how long is this window or wake or whatever it is that we're shooting for?" Amos asked.

Time was almost out. The question now was just how fast Inaros wanted to be going when they came through the gate. If he cut the braking thrust and came through fast, it would throw off the timing. If the *Giambattista* went through the Arcadia gate too late, it would be the one to quickly, quietly vanish away. If it went through too early, Naomi's curve would already have decayed down to nothing and the Free Navy would pass into the slow zone in safety.

They'd gone back to the *Rocinante*. Alex and Bobbie in the cockpit, ready for battle if battle came. Holden and Naomi were strapped into the couches in the command deck. Amos, on float, had come up for the company as much as anything else. They weren't at battle stations yet. If it came to that, this was probably the last time he'd see Amos in the flesh. Holden tried not to think about it.

"It'll be maybe five minutes," Naomi said. "Part of that's going to depend on the mass and energy of the ships they bring through. If we're lucky, maybe as much as...ten?"

"That ain't much," Amos said with an amiable smile. He put a hand on the ladder up to the cockpit to keep himself from drifting. "You good up there?"

"Good as gold," Alex said.

"If this trick of Naomi's doesn't go, you think we can take 'em?" Amos said.

"All of them, probably not," Bobbie called down. "Some of them, for sure."

Clarissa rose up from the lift, a pale smile on her lips. She'd spent enough time on the float now to be natural with it. She moved from grip to grip along the wall like she'd been born a Belter. When she got to Holden, she held out a bulb from the galley.

"You said you hadn't been able to sleep," she said. "I thought you'd want some coffee."

Holden took it; her smile widened a degree. The bulb was warm against his palm. Probably it wasn't poisoned. She wasn't really likely to do that anymore. He steeled himself a little before he took a sip.

Medina Station was in the hands of the OPA fighters from the *Giambattista*, not that it would do much good. Its PDCs and torpedoes had, for the most part, been spent defending against Holden. What was left was a rounding error on what they'd have needed to hold back Inaros. The *Roci* was waiting almost behind the blue station at the center of the slow zone. If he'd trained the ship's cameras on it, he could have seen the ruins of the rail guns as clearly as if he'd been standing over them.

"Anything coming out of Laconia?" he asked.

"We don't have a repeater on the far side of that gate, but just peeping through the keyhole? Nothing," Naomi said. "No signal. No sign of approaching drives."

The *Roci* chirped out an alert. Holden pulled it up.

"Got something, Cap?" Amos asked.

"Incoming ships have changed their burn a little. They'll be coming in fast."

"And early," Naomi said. Her voice was like someone talking through pain. The *Roci*'s countdown timer adjusted itself, estimating that the enemy would come through the ring gate in twenty minutes. Holden washed the lump in his throat with Clarissa's coffee.

Clarissa pushed over to Naomi's couch, her sharp face bent by a frown. Naomi looked up at her and wiped her eyes. A droplet of a tear floated in the air, drifted toward the recycler intake.

"I'll be all right," Naomi said. "It's just that my son's on one of those ships."

Clarissa's eyes sheened over too and she put a hand on Naomi's arm. "I know," Clarissa said. "If you need me, you can find me."

"It's okay, Peaches," Amos said. "Me and the captain had a talk about it. We're good." He gave Holden a cheerful thumbs-up.

The timer ticked down. Holden took a long, slow breath and opened his channel to the *Giambattista*.

"Okay," he said. "This is Captain Holden of the *Rocinante*. Please begin your passage burn now. I need you to go through the gate in"—he checked the timer—"eighteen minutes."

"Tchuss, røvul!" the *Giambattista*'s captain said. "It has been, sí no?"

The connection dropped. On the screen, the *Giambattista* reported a hard burn starting. Holden shifted the display to show it. A single bright star in the blackness. A drive plume wider than the ice hauler that it was driving. He wanted to believe there was something off about the color of the light, as if the high-energy tuning Naomi had done with it was visible to him, but that was just his mind playing tricks. A new counter appeared on the display. The *Giambattista*'s expected passage through the Arcadia ring went from seventeen minutes to sixteen. The Free Navy's arrival—unless they altered course—through the Sol gate in nineteen. Eighteen.

Holden's gut was tight. His breath shuddered, and he drank another sip of coffee. He opened a second window, sensors trained at the Sol gate. From where they were, the Free Navy wouldn't be visible. Not yet. The angle was off just enough to hide them.

"Do we have the rail gun ready in case they get through?"

"Yes, sir," Bobbie answered smartly.

"Well," Amos said. "Me and Peaches better go strap in. You know. In case."

Clarissa touched Naomi's shoulder one last time, then turned and launched herself, following Amos down the lift toward engineering. Holden took a long, last drink and stowed the coffee bulb. He wanted it over. He wanted this moment to last forever in case it was the last one he had with Naomi. And Alex and Amos. Bobbie. Hell, even Clarissa. With the *Rocinante*. You couldn't be in a place like the *Roci* for as long as he had been and not be changed by it. Not have it be home.

When Naomi cleared her throat, he thought she was going to talk to him.

"*Giambattista*," she said. "This is the *Rocinante*. I'm not show-ing your internal power grid above normal."

"Perdona," a woman's voice came back. "Fixing that now."

"Thank you, *Giambattista*," Naomi said and dropped the con-nection. She smiled over at Holden. The horror of the situation was only a line at the corner of her mouth, but his heart ached to see it all the same. "Amateurs. You'd think they'd never done this before."

He laughed, and then she laughed with him. The timers ticked down. The *Giambattista*'s reached zero. The brightness of the drive plume blinked out, hidden by the curve of the Arcadia ring and the profound weirdness that was distance and space here. Where that timer had been, Naomi put up a display of a mathe-matical model she'd built. The spike of the *Giambattista*'s passage already starting to decay.

The line sloped down as, beside it, the timer for Marco's arrival turned to seconds. In the cockpit, Bobbie said something and Alex answered. He couldn't make out the words. Naomi's breath sounded fast and shallow. He wanted to reach over to her. To take her hand. It would have meant taking his eyes off the monitor, and so he couldn't.

The Sol gate flickered. Holden increased the magnification until the ring filled his screen. The weird, almost biological struc-tures of the ring itself seemed to shift and writhe. An illusion of light. The drive plumes of the Free Navy ships packed in together so tightly that it looked like one massive blaze of fire appeared on the edge of the ring, tracking in toward its center.

"You want me to take a potshot at them?" Bobbie asked. "Rail gun could probably reach them at this point."

"No," Naomi said before Holden could answer. "I don't know what sending mass through the gates right now would do."

A line appeared on the model, low on the scale. Moving toward the dying curve. The ring gate grew brighter with the braking burns of the enemy, until it looked like the negative image of an eye—black, star-specked sclera and intensely white, burning iris. The timer reached zero. The lights grew brighter.

Chapter Fifty-One: Marco

Marco's jaw ached. His chest hurt. The joints in his spine hovered at the edge of dislocation without ever passing through to it. The high-g burn scourged him, and he welcomed the pain. The pressure and the discomfort were the price his body paid. They were slowing on approach. The core of the Free Navy was going to reach Medina unopposed, and there was literally no one to stop it.

At a civilized thrust—an eighth, a tenth—and with some time coasting on the float to conserve mass, the journey out to the ring gate would have taken months. He didn't have months. Everything depended on reaching Medina before the scattered forces of the consolidated fleet could reach him. Yes, it meant driving the ships he had to the edge of their ability. Yes, it would mean putting some of the reserves from Medina under conscript to fuel his return to the system, and the people of Medina would have to make do with a little less until he could stabilize the situation enough to allow resupply.

This was wartime. The days for scrimping and saving and safety were gone. Peace was a time for efficiency. War was a time for power. If it meant he drove his fighters to the ragged edge of their ability, that was how victory came. Those who held back the most reserves for tomorrow were the ones least likely to see it. If the price was long days of unrelieved discomfort and pain, he'd pay that price and glory in it. Because at the end, there was rebirth. A shedding away of all his little missteps, a purification, and the seat of his final, permanent victory. And it was coming soon.

His error—he saw it now—was in thinking too small.

He had conceived the revolution that the Free Navy represented as a balancing of the scales. The inners had taken and taken and taken from the Belt, and when they didn't need it anymore, they'd dropped it and fled off to new, shinier toys. Marco had meant to put that right. Let the inners be the ones in need and the Belt find its independence and its strength. It was anger that had kept his view too small. Righteous anger. Appropriate anger. But blinding all the same.

Medina was the key, and always had been. But it was only now that he saw what it was the key to. He'd meant to close the gates and force the inner planets to address the consequences of generations of injustice. Looking at it now, it almost seemed like a gesture of nostalgia. A harkening back to previous generations. He'd made the classic mistake—he wasn't too proud to admit it—of trying to fight the last war on the next battleground. The power of Medina wasn't that it could stop the flow of money and material out to the new worlds. It was that it could *control* it.

The fate of the Belt wasn't around Jupiter and Saturn, or at least not those alone. In every one of the thirteen hundred systems that the gates led to, there were planets as vulnerable as Earth. The Belt itself would spread to all the systems, float like kings above all their subject worlds. If he had it all to do again, he'd have thrown three times as many rocks on Earth, destroyed Mars while he was at it, and taken his ships and his people to the colony worlds where there were no vestigial fleets to consolidate. With only Medina and the fifteen ships at his disposal, he could exert power over all the worlds there were. It was all about placement, audacity, and will.

He needed to find a way to talk Duarte into giving him a few more ships. But the promise to keep Laconia undisturbed had earned him everything he'd needed up to now. He didn't think another small request would be too much, especially given how much he'd sacrificed already. And if Duarte did object—

The *Pella* shuddered as the drive passed through some resonance frequency. Normally when that happened they weren't under high burn. It was strange how something that was hardly more than a chime at a third of a g could sound like the coming apocalypse at two and a third. He tapped out a message for Josie down in engineering: KEEP US IN ONE PIECE.

A few seconds later, Josie wrote back something obscene, and Marco chuckled through the pressure on his throat.

They'd taken their last respite before the battle four hours earlier, dropping the deceleration to only three-quarters of a g for fifteen minutes to let people eat and visit the head. A longer break would have meant burning harder now, and they were already running at the edge of their tolerances. But the advantages of an unexpected forced march were scattered through the great military strategists of history. Earth and Mars could only look on, eyes pressed to their telescopes, and wail. Earth and Mars and Medina too.

And on Medina, Naomi and her feckless Earther fuck buddy. James Holden, following in Fred Johnson's footsteps as condescending, patronizing hero of the poor, helpless Belt. When he died, the story of a Belt that had to be saved by self-congratulatory, faux-enlightened Earthers would bleed out with him, and good riddance. And Naomi ...

He didn't know yet what to do with Naomi. She was a conundrum. Strong where she should have been weak and weak where she should have been strong. It was like she'd been born inverted. But there was something about her. Even after all these years, there was something about her that begged to be tamed. She'd slipped away from him twice now. Whatever happened, there wouldn't be a third time. Once he had her in hand, Filip would return on his own. That wasn't worth worrying about.

When Filip had missed the launch from Callisto, Marco hadn't been surprised. The boy had been acting out for weeks. It was normal. Even late, really. Marco had tested Rokku's authority when he'd been much younger than Filip was now. Rokku had told him when to be there for launch, and Marco had intentionally come late to find the berth empty. He'd had to fend for himself on Pallas Station for seven months before Rokku's ship came back. The captain had met him on the dock and beaten him until he was bleeding from a dozen places, but Marco had been taken back in. If Filip needed the same experience, that would be fine.

Not that Marco would beat him. Better that he laugh a little and muss the boy's hair. Humiliation was always better than violence. To beat a man—even to beat a man to death—was at least proof that you took him seriously as a man. Though, looking back, Filip had really been starting to push as far back as when he'd shot the security coyo on Ceres. And God, Marco's jaw ached.

He shifted his fingers, pulled up the timer. The ring gate was only minutes away now. The *Pella* was shedding momentum with every second, making certain that when they passed through the gate, they wouldn't fly into a trap. Holden would be waiting. Watching the fire of their drive plumes. They weren't close enough yet for that to be a danger. Even if Holden fired his rail gun right now, the *Pella* would be able to react in time to dodge it. That wouldn't be true much longer. His compressed heart beat a little faster. His aching mouth twitched a little smile.

But discomfort was the home of the warrior, now as it had always been. He told himself that he embraced it. Welcomed it. And still, he was going to be glad when this part was done.

He typed in orders for the full force, gathering them in close enough that their drive plumes overlapped, using the vast, energetic cloud as cover to hide behind. Between that and the sensor interference of the ring, Holden would be firing as good as blind. Or at least that was the hope. The worst case was that Holden might take out two or three of his ships before they passed through the ring. But once they came close enough to target the *Rocinante*, crippling the ship would be nothing. Not destroying it, not unless they got unlucky. Trotting out James Holden's famed ship as part of the new Free Navy was too good an opportunity to miss. That was what Sanjrani and Dawes— all the others—missed. Leadership required a clear sense of appearance. Of *style*.

Fifteen minutes. Billions of people were watching him right now. As fast as the photons could travel back, the *Pella* and its fourteen fighting ships would be on every newsfeed, every hand terminal, every monitor in the system. He was fifteen minutes from the hinge point in history. Fourteen.

He checked their common vector. Coming into enemy territory, it was critical that they be neither so close together that a lucky hit by Holden could damage more than one ship nor staggered to give him time to take more shots. They looked good. They would be all right.

He wished now that he'd thought to make a recording to broadcast. It was the perfect moment. Even better than his initial call to arms. He thought of all the Belters in the system—those who'd stood by the Free Navy and those who'd been too cowardly or misguided and even the traitorous fragments of the OPA who'd taken arms with Pa against their own self-interest. He had to believe they all felt a sense of pride. Before him, they'd been slaves in all but name, and now they were a force equal to and stronger than the most powerful states humanity had ever conceived. How could they not feel awe at this? How could they not feel the joy in this?

The ring was close enough to see without magnification now. As wide as Ceres Station and still tiny in the vast darkness out here where even the sun wasn't more than a peculiarly bright star.

His ships would start evasive maneuvers as they drew close. Shifting places in their formation like shells on the table of a dockside hustler. He checked their vectors again, typed out an angry command to one of the ships that was drifting behind. The ring slowly grew larger. He increased the magnification and added false light. The material that made up the ring itself still defied the best minds in the human sphere. He wasn't really seeing it, of course. The image on his monitor was filtered through the brightness of their plumes. In truth, he was falling backward toward the ring, his face toward the faint and unimportant sun. His crash couch held him like he was resting in the palm of God.

A message appeared on his monitor from Karal: ALL SYSTEMS CHECK. BOA CAÇADA.

Marco typed back, not just to Karal, but to all of the *Pella*'s crew. GOOD HUNTING.

Five minutes until they passed through the gate and the battle for Medina began. The brief, decisive, ugly battle that would redefine what the Free Navy was. He willed them forward, pushing against brute physics with his mind. Smelling victory. Feeling it in his blood. Minutes slid by like hours, and also gone too fast. Two minutes. One.

Another message from Karal. WIR HAT POSSIBLE.

Beside it was deeper magnification of the ring filtered through the ship's system. A tiny blue dot that had to be the rail gun station, and there beside it, almost too subtle to see, a fleck of lighter darkness that could have been a ship on the float. The *Rocinante*.

Marco felt his whole consciousness narrow into that one tiny gray dot. Naomi. That dot was Naomi. She'd run out of the solar system to get away from him, and here he was. He could see her face in his mind. The empty expression she wore when she was trying not to feel. His grin hurt. His body hurt. But the little dot forgave it all. Except—

Something was wrong with his monitor. He thought at first that the image had gotten grainy, the resolution rougher, but that wasn't right. It was the same size, only he could see the parts

that made it up. He wasn't looking at the *Rocinante*. He was looking at photons streaming off a sheet of electrically excited plastic. The polymer chains glowed dark and light and dark. It was
like seeing a woman's body in painting across the room and then,
without warning, only the brushstrokes that made it up. Naomi
was nowhere in it.

He shouted, and could sense the pressure waves going out from
his throat. The clouds of molecules that made his fingers slapped
against the ones that were the control pad. He meant to type that
they should fire, that they should kill while the chance was still
with them, but he couldn't make out the letters in the splash of
photons that spilled off his screen. There was too much detail.

Where the air began and the crash couch ended was lost. The
boundary between his body and his environment blurred. He had
known since he was too young to remember learning that atoms
were made from more space than material, and that at the lowest
levels, the things that made atoms could bounce in and out of being.
He'd never seen it before. He'd never been so aware that he was a
vapor of energy. A vibration in a guitar string that didn't exist.

Something dark and sudden moved through the cloud toward him.

On the *Rocinante*, the ring gate grew brighter with the braking
burns of the enemy, until it looked like the negative image of an
eye—black, star-specked sclera and intensely white, burning iris.
The timer reached zero. The lights grew brighter. Then flickered
and went out.

Holden checked the sensors. Where fifteen warships on the
burn had been seconds before, there was just *nothing*.

"Huh," Amos said over the ship system. "That is super creepy."

Chapter Fifty-Two: Pa

Here we are. Back again," Michio said as she stepped onto the docks of Ceres Station.

"Hup," Josep, walking beside her, agreed.

When she'd left, she had been rebelling against a rebellion. Now she had come, whether anyone admitted it or not, to beg the powers of Earth and Mars for her freedom. She felt like the docks themselves should have changed too. Grown older and more worn the way her soul had. But the echoing music built from the clanking of mechs and power tools, the gabble of voices, was what it had been before. The smells of carbon lubricants and ozone was still as sharp.

A new coat of paint even left the old station looking brighter and younger and more full of hope than when she'd left. The signs had been replaced. The same corridors and lifts, but in bright, clean new fonts and half a dozen alphabets. She knew it was designed for the colonists and refugees fleeing Earth, but it seemed pointed that, of the languages listed, none was Belter Creole. Earth ran Ceres again, the way it had before Eros, and they were turning the station into a theme-park version of itself. The guard was for the most part ceremonial, but Michio was more than willing to bet their sidearms were loaded. It was awkward work, welcoming someone who was equal parts ally and enemy. She didn't envy them.

It had been six months now since the remarkable death of Marco Inaros and the great remnant of the Free Navy. Half a year just to bring the remaining players together to talk. She wondered how long it would take to actually do something that mattered. And what would happen when they all ran out of time. She felt like she had a tiny Nico Sanjrani in the back of her head counting down the hours until the Belt—no, until all humanity—needed the farms and medical centers and mines and processing facilities that they hadn't built because they'd been too busy fighting. Some nights it kept her awake. Some nights other things did.

She was half expecting them to take her to the same quarters Marco Inaros had assigned the last time she'd been here hammering out a plan for the Belt, but while it was in the same section of the station, the particular rooms were different. Their escort finished welcoming them, assured them that if they needed anything, someone from the hospitality service would be there to help. They bowed their way out the door, closing it as they left. Michio lowered herself to the couch in the suite's main room while Josep made his way through each of the rooms, taking stock and looking for surveillance equipment that was both certainly there and certainly too professionally installed to find.

Nadia, Bertold, and Laura were back on the new ship—a converted cargo hauler on loan from one of Bertold's cousins as long as they found ways to make the payments on it. After the sleekness and power of the *Connaught*, it felt cheap and flimsy. But her family was on it, so it was home in the same way that the couch her cheek rested against was raw-silk upholstery in a jail cell.

Josep's laugh was hard. He walked back into the room with a rectangle of something the color of cream and held it out to her. Not paper, but heavy card stock smooth as the couch. The writing on it was neat and precise.

Captain Pa—

Thank you for coming to the conference and for your courage in the struggles we have all endured together. With good faith and cooperation, we will forge the path still ahead.

It was signed Chrisjen Avasarala. Michio looked up at Josep, her brow knit.

"En serio? That doesn't even sound like her."

"I know," he said. "And come see! There's a fruit basket."

If.wars began with rage, they ended with exhaustion.

In the aftermath of the system-wide battle and its unsettling aftermath at the ring, the partisans of the Free Navy had felt an overwhelming sense of injustice. It was as if the disappearance of the *Pella* and its battle force had been a bad call in a football match, and they were trying to find a referee to shout down. Then, slowly, the understanding seemed to spread through all the stations—Pallas, Ganymede, Ceres, Tycho, and dozens more besides—that the war was ended. That they'd lost. A group on Pallas had issued a declaration that they were the New Free Navy and had set off a few bombs when the consolidated fleet arrived to take control of the station. The Jovian system—Callisto, Europa, Ganymede, and all the lesser bases there—had been the Free Navy's strongest ground and the one least touched by the fighting. A few patches of resistance there meant the violence would drag on for a few more weeks or months, but the outcome wasn't in doubt.

The specter of the Laconia gate and Winston Duarte hung over

Mars more than anyone else. Martian identity—proud cogs in the glorious terraforming machine—didn't square with military coups and mass defection. Mars wanted answers, and Laconia ignored them all magnificently. The only communication since the death of the Free Navy was a looped statement broadcast through the gate. A man's voice, inflected like a newsreader's, saying, *Laconia is under its own sovereign authority. This message serves as notice that any ships passing through the Laconia gate will be in violation of that authority and will be denied passage. Laconia is under its own sovereign authority ...*

The message had caused no end of debate in the Martian parliament while Earth drove two of its three remaining battleships out to the slow zone and parked them and their ancient but effective rail guns and nuclear torpedoes at the edges of the Laconia gate, ready to reduce anything that came out to gas and scrap. Avasarala called it a containment policy, and Michio supposed it was the sanest thing to do. Earth was in no condition to pick another fight.

By the time Rosenfeld Guoliang took the stand in The Hague, the first high-profile prosecution for the murder of billions on Earth, the vast and complex human zeitgeist was ready for it to be over. There would be other trials coming. Anderson Dawes had been captured. Nico Sanjrani turned himself in at Tycho. Of Inaros' original inner circle, Michio Pa was the only one not in a cell or dead. And she was at a cocktail party.

The meeting center in the governor's palace was built on three levels with stairways between them and a lot of plants. People in uniform and formal dress stood in pairs or small groups or alone with their hand terminals while servants carried trays of hors d'oeuvres and drinks. If anything specific was wanted—food or drink or a fresh pair of shoes, probably—they had only to ask. The lap of luxury. The highest circles of power and influence.

This was the real thing, something that Marco Inaros had only been able to play at. The stone walks were polished and the pillars were made of striped sedimentary rock pulled all the way from

Earth as a kind of boast. *We're so rich, we don't even use our own stone.* She'd never noticed it before, and she didn't know whether it left her amused or angry or sad.

"Michio," a woman's voice said. "Here you are. How is Laura?"

The old lady in the orange sari took Michio's elbow and led her along almost three full steps before she realized it was Avasarala. The old Earther looked different in person. Smaller, her skin a deeper brown, her pale hair taking up more of her face.

"Much better," Michio said. "Back on the ship."

"With Nadia and Bertold? And Josep stayed back in your rooms? Just so long as they know they're welcome. God damn, this is an ugly piece of architecture, isn't it?" Avasarala said. "I saw you looking at the pillars."

"I was," Michio said.

Avasarala leaned in close, her eyes bright as a schoolgirl's. "They're fake. The rock? Made it with a centrifuge and colored sand. I knew the builder. He was a fake too. Pretty, though. God save us all from good-looking men."

Michio surprised herself by laughing. The old woman was charming. Michio knew that this show of hospitality was just that. A show. And yet it worked; she felt more at ease. The time was going to come, and soon, when Michio was going to have to come to this woman and ask for amnesty. Ask this Earther to let her and her family go free for Marco's crimes. This moment made it seem like maybe the answer would be yes. Hope was a terrible thing. She didn't want to feel, and yet there it was.

She didn't know she was going to speak until she said it. "I'm sorry." What she meant was *I'm sorry I didn't stop the attack that killed your husband* and *I'm sorry I didn't see Inaros for what he was sooner* and *I would do it all differently if I could live my life backward and try again.*

Avasarala paused, looked deeply into Michio's eyes, and it was like seeing someone through a mask. The deepness there startled her. When she spoke, it was as if she'd heard every nuance.

"Politics is the art of the possible, Captain Pa. When you play at our level, grudges cost lives."

Across a narrow courtyard, James Holden turned and then came trotting over. He, at least, was the same height she remembered. He looked a little older than when they'd fought against Ashford on the *Behemoth*. Back in the God-who-could-have-known-they-were-the-good-old-days. She saw the surprise and pleasure as he recognized her.

"Captain Holden," she said. "Still weird to see you."

"Right?" he said with a boyish smile that seemed totally unaffected. He turned to Avasarala. "Can I pull you away for a minute? There's a thing."

Avasarala squeezed Michio's arm, then let it go. "Forgive me," she said. "Holden can't find his cock with both hands unless there's someone there to point him at it."

They walked away together, heads bent in conference. Behind a spray of ivy, Michio saw a tall, dark-skinned woman bent a degree forward as she laughed with the Martian prime minister. Naomi Nagata. She looked...normal? Unremarkable. Michio knew her from before, and still might not have known her if they'd passed in a common corridor or shared a tube ride. But this was the woman Marco had abducted before his attack on Earth, just so he could watch her look upon his power. The woman who'd turned away from him when they'd both been little more than children themselves. Michio would never know how much of the decision to take the last remnant of the Free Navy to Medina had been for cold tactical reasons and how much was because Naomi Nagata had been there. It was so petty and so small, and she had no trouble believing it. *When you play at our level, grudges cost lives.*

Carlos Walker strolled through an archway, caught her eye, and smiled. She'd known him mostly by reputation back when she'd been part of Fred fucking Johnson's OPA. Carlos Walker, with his playboy's manners and the weird religious streak, the sincerity of which no one seemed able to determine. He plucked two fresh flutes of champagne from a passing tray and made his way toward her.

"You look thoughtful, Captain Pa."

"Do I?" she said, taking the glass. "Well, then I suppose it must be true. And you? How does it feel being the unelected representative of the Belt?"

Walker smiled. "I could ask you the same."

She laughed. "I'm not representing anyone but myself."

"Really? Then what are you doing here?"

Michio blinked, but didn't know how to respond.

A little less than an hour later, a soft chiming and a discrete rush of personal assistants and aides announced the actual meeting. Pa let herself be carried along with a growing sense of displacement. The meeting room was smaller than she'd expected, and arranged in a rough triangle. Avasarala, a thin-faced man in a formal jacket, and two men in military uniforms sat at one corner. The Martian prime minister—Emily Richards—sat at another with half a dozen people in suits fluttering around her like they were moths and she was an open flame. And at the third, Carlos Walker, Naomi Nagata, James Holden, and Michio herself.

A second rank of chairs held dozens of people whose roles Michio didn't know. Senators. Businessmen. Bankers. Soldiers. It occurred to her that if she'd had a bomb, she could probably have crippled what was left of humanity's major governments by taking out this one room.

"Well," Avasarala said, her voice clear as a Klaxon, "I'd like to start by thanking all of you again for being here. I'm not fond of this shit, but the optics are good. And we do have some things to discuss. I have a proposal …" She paused to tap a command into her hand terminal, and Michio's chimed in response, as did everyone else's in the room. "…a proposal about the architecture by which we try to unfuck ourselves. It's preliminary, but we have to start somewhere."

Michio opened the document. It was over a thousand pages long, with the first ten a tightly written table of contents with

notations and subsections for every chapter. She felt a little wave
of vertigo.

"The overview looks like this," Avasarala said. "We have a list
of problems as long as our arms, but Captain Holden here thinks
he's come up with a way to use some of them to solve the others.
Captain?"

Holden, beside her, stood up, seemed to realize no one else was
going to stand up to talk, and then shrugged and bulled forward
with it. "The thing is the Free Navy wasn't wrong. With all the
new systems opened up, the economic niche that Belters have
filled *is* going to go away. There are so many reserves on these
planets that don't require we bring our own air or generate our
own gravity that the Belt is going to be outcompeted. And, no
offense, the plan up to now has been versions of 'sucks to be you.'

"There's a significant population of the Belt that's not going
to be able to move down a gravity well. They're just going to be
forgotten. Left to die off. And since that's not all that different
from how Belters got treated before, it was easy for Inaros to find
political backing."

"I wouldn't say that was the only thing that got him there,"
Prime Minister Richards drawled. "Having a bunch of my ships
helped him out."

The room chuckled.

"But the thing is," Holden said, "we've been going out there
wrong. There's a traffic problem we didn't know about. Under the
wrong conditions, it's not safe to go through the gates. Which we
found out because a bunch of ships went missing. And if the plan
is that just anyone who wants to go through the gates does so anytime they want to, more will go missing. There has to be someone
regulating that. And, thanks to Naomi Nagata, we now know the
load limit of the gate network."

He paused and looked around, almost as if he was expecting
applause before he went on.

"So that's two problems. No niche for the Belt. The need for
traffic control through the gates. Now add to that the fact that

Earth, Mars—all of us really—have taken enough damage in the last few years that our infrastructure won't carry us. We have maybe a year or two to really find ways to generate the food and clean water and clean air that we're *all* going to need. And we probably can't do that in our solar system unless just a lot more people die. We need a fast, efficient way to trade with the colony worlds for raw materials. So that's why I'm proposing an independent union with the sole and specific task of coordinating shipments through the gates. Most people who want to live on planets will just do that. But the Belt has a huge population of people who are specifically suited to life outside a gravity well. Moving supplies and people safely between solar systems is a new niche. And it's one we need filled quickly and efficiently. In the proposal, I called it the spacing guild, but I'm not married to that name."

A gray-haired man sitting two rows behind Emily Richards cleared his throat and spoke. "You're proposing to turn the entire population of the Belt into a single transport company?"

"Yes, into a network of ships, support stations, and other services necessary to move people and cargo between the gates," Holden said. "Keep in mind, they've got thirteen hundred and seventy-three solar systems to manage. There's going to be work. Well, thirteen hundred and seventy-two, really. Because of Laconia."

"And what do you propose to do about Laconia?" a woman behind Avasarala asked.

"I don't know," Holden said. "I was just starting with this."

Avasarala waved him to sit down, and reluctantly he did. Naomi shifted, murmured something in his ear, and Holden nodded.

"The proposed structure of the union," Avasarala said, "is fairly standard. Limited sovereignty in exchange for regulatory input from the major governing bodies, meaning Emily and whoever they elect once I'm out of this."

"*Limited* sovereignty?" Carlos Walker said.

"Limited," Avasarala said. "Don't ask me to put out on the first date, Walker. I'm not that kind of girl. The union will, of course, need to have support from the Belt. The first union president will be taking on a huge job, but I think we can all agree that we have a unique opportunity for that. Someone well-known both among Belters and on the inner planets."

Holden nodded. Michio looked over at him. His bright eyes and firm chin.

"Someone," Avasarala continued, "above—or at least apart from—factions and politics. Trustworthy, well-tested moral compass, and with a long résumé of doing the right thing even when it's unpopular."

Holden smiled, nodded to himself. He looked so pleased. Michio hadn't come to a meeting. This was an anointing. She was suddenly profoundly disheartened. It would probably improve her chances for getting amnesty, but—

"That is why," Avasarala said, "we need to draft James Holden."

Holden yelped like he'd been bitten. "What? Wait. No, that's all wrong. It's a terrible idea."

Avasarala frowned. "Then—"

"Look," Holden said, standing up again. "This is exactly the problem. This is what we keep doing. Forcing rules and leadership on the Belters rather than letting them pick for themselves."

A grumble passed through the room, but Holden just kept talking.

"If I can use this moment to nominate someone else instead. Someone with all the qualities Madam Secretary Avasarala just listed, and more. Someone with honor and integrity and leadership, and with the added bonus of actually belonging to the community they'd be leading."

And somehow—Michio wasn't sure how this had happened—Holden was pointing at her.

"Then I would nominate Michio Pa."

Chapter Fifty-Three: Naomi

The Blue Frog was closed for renovations, so after the meetings were over, she drove the cart to a pub two levels higher and a little to spinward. The sign beside the door was cheap steel set into the wall with the words COOPERATIVE FOURTEEN hand-welded into it. Naomi didn't know if the name had a history behind it, or if that was just the new style in naming clubs. On the other side of the door, the decor took on a much less industrial feel. The tables glowed in bright primary colors, and the walls were covered in strands of woven wire, looped and tied to look like old pictures of waterfalls. A low stage with a karaoke setup hummed and danced with itself, waiting for someone to break the ice. There was room for as many as a hundred people in the space, and counting herself and Jim, there were probably fewer than twenty. But it was also off-hours, so that made it hard to judge.

The crew were already there and, to judge from the empty bottles the waiter was clearing away, had been there for some time. As they walked across to them, Jim relaxed. The four of them gave a little cheer and made space for two new chairs at the table.

"What happened?" Bobbie said. "You were supposed to be here hours ago."

"Avasarala jumped me," Jim said, and Amos' empty, amiable smile got a degree wider. Jim laughed and shook his head. "No, I mean she tried to get me named as the head of the spacing guild."

"You know that name's not going to stick, right?" Alex said.

"Wait, she did *what*?" Bobbie said.

Jim held out his hands, a gesture of helplessness. "She gave out the proposal, and I gave my little speech about it, and then boom. Right at the front, she said I should be the one to help put it together. First union president. It probably took the first two hours just convincing her I wouldn't do it."

"Why didn't you take the position?" Clarissa asked. She seemed genuinely confused.

"Because then I'd have to do it," Jim said, waving to call the waiter back.

"Makes sense she'd want someone she could control calling the shots, though," Alex said.

"Avasarala doesn't think she can control Holden," Bobbie said. "But she also doesn't think anyone else can. She might just want someone from Earth in charge, at least as a figurehead. Makes the union *feel* like it's in her circle of influence. Fred Johnson was OPA to the marrow, but he was from Earth. He never totally got away from that."

The waiter trotted over and took Jim's order. Naomi leaned in around him so she could see Bobbie as she spoke.

"That was our point," she said. "If it's going to work, the Belt needs to know it's their own and not another set of scraps that the inners are tossing out." The waiter reached out, his fingers stopping just short of touching her shoulder. "Whatever your best stout is," she said, and he vanished with a nod. She turned back. "Anyway, we threw Michio Pa under the bus."

"She's perfect," Holden said. "She knows all the players in the Belt. She's not afraid to work with Earth and Mars. She's literally the former commander of Medina Station. Granted back before it was a station, but she's got a real familiarity with the ship. And look what she's been doing since she broke with Inaros. Coordination and distribution. *Exactly* the job we're looking at."

"Well," Alex said, "except with less piracy this time. I mean, assuming."

"Did she take the job?" Bobbie asked.

"She's coming around," Naomi said. "It was a long meeting."

"What about us?" Clarissa asked. Her voice had dread in it. A hollowness. "What do we do now?"

"We join the union," Jim said. "I mean, we'll need to vote on it here in the family, but it seems weird to push for a new architecture for the colonies and then not be part of it. And there'll be a lot of work for a good ship. We have a good ship."

Clarissa's gaze flickered up to Naomi, then, with an almost invisible smile, away. Jim hadn't understood what she'd really been asking. *Now that the war's over, do I still have a place here?* And he didn't know that he'd answered yes. He had a genius for assuming things that let Clarissa trust him. Naomi handed the girl a napkin so she wouldn't have to dab her eyes with a cuff.

"Seems to me," Alex said, "we should look at escorting colony ships. And making sure the ore or whatever the colony has to trade gets where it's going."

"Lot of trade in-system too," Amos said. "Don't *have* to go out past the gates."

"Yeah," Alex agreed. "But there's more planets out there than I'm going to be able to see in my lifetime. I'd like to get to a few of them."

The waiter returned with Jim's gin and tonic and her own stout. When she tried to pay, the transaction was already zeroed out. The waiter smiled at her, shook his head, and said, "On the house." Naomi nodded her thanks. Jim was already drinking.

Bobbie was the only one who seemed quiet, her hand wrapped

around a glass. Alex and Amos told Clarissa stories about New Terra and going through to the new worlds. Jim drank and chimed in on occasion, the political meeting starting to fade and his shoulders slipping a little lower as he relaxed. But Bobbie kept her own council until Naomi finished her second drink, took the Martian's hand, and tugged her away.

"Are you all right?" Naomi asked.

"Yes," Bobbie said in a voice that meant *no*. "It's just…this is really the end of the terraforming project, isn't it? I mean, I knew that, but…I don't know. Trying to get us all to here helped distract me. But this agreement they're hammering out. It's the shape things are going to have from now on."

"Yeah," Naomi said. "And it's going to be different."

"All my life, changing Mars. Making it a viable ecosystem…it's just always been a thing. Hearing about rules and laws and systems for how that's never coming back…I don't know. It's kind of hitting me that it's really gone."

"Probably, yeah," Naomi said, but Bobbie went on as if she hadn't heard her. As if she was saying something out loud for the first time. Discovering her thoughts by hearing them expressed in her own voice.

"Because Inaros and all the Free Navy people, they weren't fighting for Belter rights or political recognition. They were fighting to have the past back. To have things be what they've always been. Sure, with them on top maybe, but…Earth's not going to be humanity's home anymore. Mars isn't going to be Mars, not like I knew it. Belters aren't even going to be Belters now. They're going to be…what? Shipping magnates? I don't even know."

"No one does," Naomi said, leading Bobbie forward. The big Martian didn't seem aware that they were walking. "But we're going to find out."

"I don't know who I am in that world."

"I don't either. None of us does. But I know that I have my ship. And my little family with it."

"Yeah. That sounds like a plan."

"Good," Naomi said, and put a microphone in Bobbie's hand. "Let's pick a song."

The pub filled up more at shift change, but for once no one seemed to take much notice of Jim or any of the rest of them. Even when Naomi got a standing ovation for what in retrospect must have been a deeply flawed version of Devi Anderson's "Apart Together," nobody seemed to recognize the crew of the *Rocinante* as being anything but the people at table six. It felt good knowing that could still happen sometimes. By the end of the night, even Clarissa had a turn on stage. It turned out she had a good singing voice, and after she got down, a local boy with Loca Griega tattoos tried to hit on her until Bobbie gently made it clear nothing was going to happen.

They took the tube back to the dock, filling up almost half of a car just themselves, still a little tipsy, still talking too loud, laughing at nothing really. Alex's Mariner Valley drawl got thicker, and Bobbie mimicked it, egging him on until they sounded like parodies of themselves. Jim, least involved with the hilarity and still somehow central to it, sat back against the rattling wall of the car, his hands behind his head and his eyes half-closed. She didn't really understand what she and Jim and all the others were reacting to until they were at the ship. Seeing the *Rocinante* locked in the docking clamps was like falling into a familiar pair of arms. They were giddy because Jim was giddy. And Jim was giddy because, for once, he'd just avoided being responsible for the future of the whole human race.

It seemed like a fair thing to celebrate.

Back on board, the group moved together to the galley, not ready yet for the day to be over. Clarissa made herself some tea, but there wasn't any more alcohol. Just the six of them, lounging in a galley designed to serve many more. Alex, sitting with his back against one wall, told a story about when he'd been in training on Olympus Mons and the mother of one of the other recruits had arrived to complain that the drill sergeant was being too rough on her son. That led into Bobbie talking about a time when she and her squad had all gotten food poisoning at the same meal, but bullied each other into training the next day regardless, then spent the day puking into their helmets. They were all laughing together, sharing parts of the lives they'd had before they came here. Before the *Rocinante* was their home.

Eventually, without the flow of conversation abating, Alex made enough chicken with peanut sauce for everyone and passed bowls out while Clarissa told a surprisingly funny story about being in a prison writing workshop. Naomi ate the chicken with a fork, leaning against Jim as she did. The sauce wasn't like Belters made it, but it was good enough.

She felt Jim getting near the end of his endurance. He didn't say anything, but she knew from the sound of his breath and the way he unconsciously tapped his leg like a child trying to stay awake. She felt the exhaustion herself. It had been a long day, and the stakes had been high. The pleasant buzz left over from the pub was starting to fade, and deep, muzzy tiredness was slipping into her joints. But she didn't want the moment to end either, any of the moments with these people in this place, even though eventually they had to. No, not *even though. Because.*

Because eventually they had to. Nothing lasted forever. Not peace. Not war. Nothing.

She stood first, taking her bowl and Jim's and Bobbie's, since she was done with it, and feeding them into the recycler. She stretched, yawned, held her hand out to Jim. He took his cue. Alex, who was talking about a music performance he'd seen on Titan back when he'd still been in the service, nodded his good night. Naomi led Jim to the lift, then to their cabin with the occasional sound of laughter filtering through to them, fainter the farther they went, but not absent. Not yet.

Jim fell onto the crash couch like a marionette with his strings cut, threw one arm across his eyes, and groaned. In the light, he looked young again. The stubble on his neck and along the side of one cheek was thin and patchy, as if it were growing in for the first time. She could remember when the prospect of Jim and his body had been as powerful as a drug to her. Powerful enough that she'd been driven to take the risk of being with him. He hadn't known then how much of a leap it had been for her. He probably still didn't know now. Some things were secret even after you told them. He moaned again, shifted his arm, looked up at her. His smile was equal parts exhaustion and delight. Exhaustion from what they'd been through. Delight because it was done. And because they were both there.

"Do you think Pa will take the job?" he asked. He sounded almost wistful.

"Yes, eventually," Naomi said. And then, a moment later, "How long have you been planning that?"

"The idea of the union, or Pa in particular?"

"Pa."

Jim shrugged. "It was pretty clear early on that having an Earther be the head of it wasn't going to work. I thought Fred would be able to find someone. So I guess I started looking at her for it right around then. Consciously, anyway. She was kind of perfect, though. She broke with the Free Navy in order to help the Belt. No one else did that, or at least not as openly. And she won every fight she led her people into. I think the ones who need to take her seriously, will."

Naomi sat on the edge of the crash couch. It shifted with the change in the center of their combined weight, moving Jim a few centimeters closer to her. He stretched out an arm as invitation, and she settled back into it. "Do you think she'll enjoy it?"

"I don't know. I'd hate it, but maybe she's different enough from me she'll find something to redeem the process. The important thing is I think she'll be good at it. Plays to her strengths. At least I don't know anyone who's likely to do better."

"I hope you're right," she said. "You really think you couldn't have done it?"

"I was never an option. There's too much history. Maybe an Earther can do it in a generation or three when things have been different for a while."

Naomi laughed, moved her head to rest beside his. "By then something else will have happened."

"Yeah," Holden said. "That's true. But in the short term, I really do think she's the best one for the job. I'm just glad she was here. My second choice for the job would have been you."

She sat up, looking into his eyes to see whether he was joking. A long way away, Amos laughed just loud enough for the echoes to reach her. Jim's expression was somewhere between chagrin and amusement.

God, he'd been serious.

"You could have done it," Holden said. "You're smart. You're a Belter. Your opposition to the Free Navy's as good or better than Pa's. You have a track record that Earth and Mars would have been comfortable with, and enough connection to the Belt to make you plausible to them."

"You know I wouldn't have done it, right?"

"No," Jim said, and there was something almost like sorrow in his voice. "I know you wouldn't have wanted to. I know you would have hated it. But you would have, if you had to. If there wasn't someone else. Too many people would have needed you for you to turn them all away."

She lay back down, considered the idea, and shuddered.

"I know, right?" Jim said. "And how are you doing?"

She took the hand of the arm she was lying across in hers, drew it gently around her like he was a blanket. He had asked her that every few days since the war ended. How was she doing? It sounded like an innocuous question, but it carried more than its own weight. She'd killed her old lover, her old friends. She wished with a longing as powerful as thirst that there had been a way to save her son. Jim wasn't asking if she was all right so much as how bad was it. There was no good answer for that. *I will carry this guilt and sadness for the rest of my life* was just as true as *I lost my son years ago*. Her comfort was that she was still alive. That Jim was. And Amos and Alex. Bobbie and Clarissa.

She was as much a monster as Clarissa or Amos had ever been.

She was someone who'd found a way to save her little chosen family when everything seemed lost. The two didn't balance, but they existed together. Pain and relief. Sorrow and contentment. The evil and the redeeming could sit together in her heart, live together, and neither one take the edge off the other.

And Jim knew that. He didn't ask because he needed an answer. He asked because he needed her to know the answer mattered to him. That was all.

"I'm all right," she said. The way she always did. Jim reached out his other hand and dimmed the lights. Naomi closed her eyes. They felt very comfortable that way. She could hear from Jim's breath that he wasn't asleep. That he was thinking about something.

She kept herself awake, just a little. Waited for him. Little flickers of dream danced in at the edge of her mind, and she lost track of her body every now and again.

"Do you think we should go out to the colonies?" he said. "It seems like maybe we ought to. I mean, we've been to Ilus. And if we can sort of blaze the trail? Make it normal? Maybe it'll be easier for Pa to get more Belt ships to take the risk."

"Maybe," she said.

"Because the other thing we could do is stay here. There's just a lot of work that's going to need to happen here. Rebuilding. Beefing up Medina for when Duarte comes back. Because you know whatever he's doing is going to be a problem eventually. I don't know where we should go next."

Naomi nodded. Jim rolled in closer to her. The warmth of his body and the smell of his skin were consoling.

"Let's just stay here for a minute," she said.

Epilogue: Anna

*A*s with astronomy the difficulty of recognizing the motion of
the earth lay in abandoning the immediate sensation of the
earth's fixity and of the motion of the planets, so in history the
difficulty of recognizing the subjection of personality to the laws
of space, time, and cause lies in renouncing the direct feeling of the
independence of one's own personality. But as in astronomy the
new view said: "It is true that we do not feel the movement of
the earth, but by admitting its immobility we arrive at absurdity,
while by admitting its motion (which we do not feel) we arrive at
laws," so also in history the new view says: "It is true that we are
not conscious of our dependence, but by admitting our free will
we arrive at absurdity, while by admitting our dependence on the
external world, on time, and on cause, we arrive at laws."*

*In the first case it was necessary to renounce the consciousness
of an unreal immobility in space and to recognize a motion we*

did not feel; in the present case it is similarly necessary to renounce a freedom that does not exist, and to recognize a dependence of which we are not conscious.

Anna savored the moment, then closed the text window and made the same, small sound that she always did when she finished the book. Anna loved the Bible and felt comforted and lifted up by what she found in it, but Tolstoy was uncontested for second place.

The accepted etymology of the word *religion* was that it came from *religere*, meaning "to bind together," but Cicero had said its true root was *relegere*, "to reread." The truth was, she liked both answers. What brought people together in a sense of love and community and the impulse to go back to beloved books weren't that different for her. Both of them left her feeling calmer and renewed. Nono said it meant she was an introvert and an extrovert at the same time. Anna couldn't really argue against that.

Officially the ship was the *Abdel Rahman Badawi* operated by Trachtman Corporation out of Luna, but everyone on board called her the *Abbey*. The complex history of the ship was written in her bones. The hallways were different shapes, depending on the style when they'd been added in or what salvaged ship they'd been taken from. The air always smelled like new plastic from the recyclers. The thrust gravity was kept at a thin tenth of a g to conserve reaction mass. The cargo decks far below Anna now were cathedral-high and piled with all the things that the new colony on Eudoxia—shelters, food recyclers, two small fusion reactors, and a wealth of biological and agricultural materials—would need. There were already two other settlements on Eudoxia. It was one of the most populous of the colony worlds with almost a thousand people on it.

When the *Abbey* arrived, that population would triple, and Anna and Nono and Nami would be part of it. Would live out the rest of their lives, chances were, finding ways to raise food they could eat, learning about their new, broad, and problematic Eden. And hopefully, building the spaces and institutions that would shape humanity's presence on that world forever. The first university, the first hospital, the first cathedral. All the things perched just outside reality, waiting for Anna and her fellow colonists to bring them into being.

It wasn't the retirement Anna had expected or hoped for. Some nights she dreaded it. Not for herself so much as for her daughter. She'd always thought of Nami growing up in Abuja with her cousins, going off to university in Saint Petersburg or Moscow. She felt wistful now, knowing that Nami would likely never have the experience of living in a huge, sprawling urban environment. That she and Nono wouldn't grow old together in the little house near Zuma Rock. That her own ashes, when she passed, would be scattered on unfamiliar water. But Abuja also had a few thousand less mouths to feed. Out of the remaining billions on Earth, it was nothing, except that enough nothings together might add up to something after all.

Her cabin was smaller than the house with two tiny bedrooms, a little sitting area with a scruffy wall screen, and just enough storage for their personal items. There were twenty like it in their hall, with a shared lavatory at one end and a cafeteria at the other. Four halls like hers on the deck. Ten decks on the ship. Right now, Nono was at the galley on deck three singing with a bluegrass quartet. The youngest of the musicians—a rail-thin, red-haired man named Jacques Harbinger—had used almost his whole personal space allotment on a real hammer dulcimer. Nami would be coming back from school on deck eight, where Kerr Ackerman was using the ship tutorials to teach the two hundred or so children about biology and survival techniques tailored for Eudoxia. After they both came home and they'd all had dinner in their own galley, Anna was going to the Humanist Society meeting on deck two, where she'd already won the role of the loyal opposition to George and Tanja Li, the young atheist couple who ran it. She didn't fool herself into believing anyone would change anyone else's mind. But the trip was long, and a good philosophical discussion passed the hours pleasantly. Then home to work on her sermon for next week.

She remembered something she'd read, she didn't know where, about the life of ancient Greece. The private space had been thin there too, most of people's hours spent in the streets and court-yards of Athens and Corinth and Thebes. A world where every-one's home was not their castle but their dorm room. It was exhausting, but exhilarating too. She could already see the early shapes of the community they would eventually become. And the efforts she made now would have an effect on what happened when they reached their new home planet. The decisions they made in building their township would be the seed crystal for the city that might one day rise up from it. A few hundred years, and the work Anna did now to make this group a kind, thoughtful, centered one might be able to shape a whole world.

And wasn't that worth a little extra effort?

She heard Nami's voice before the door opened, serious and per-cussive the way she got when she was focused on something. She didn't talk to herself often, so Anna assumed she had someone from school with her. When the door opened, she was proven right.

Nami walked into the little common room, practically drag-ging a sullen Arab boy behind her. He started a little when he saw Anna. She smiled without showing her teeth, didn't quite make eye contact, didn't move. She'd learned more about how to be with traumatized people in the last year than she'd ever hoped to know, and much of what she came to understand was that humans were domestic animals like dogs and cats. They responded poorly to threats and well to a gentle building of trust. Not rocket sci-ence, but easy to forget.

"This is Saladin," Nami said. "We have a group project."

"Good to meet you, Saladin," Anna said. "I'm glad you could be here."

The boy nodded once, looked away. Anna had to resist the urge to try to draw him out, ask him where he lived, who his parents were, how he liked his classes. She was always impatient to help people, even when they weren't ready to be helped. Maybe espe-cially then.

Nami, nattering about the great-man theory and technological ratchets and railroading time as if to fill the conversation for both of them, went to her bedroom and came out with her school tablet. Anna hoisted an eyebrow. "That's been here all day?"

"I forgot it," Nami said lightly. Then, "Bye, Mom," as she marched out the door.

Saladin hesitated like he was surprised to have been left alone with a grown-up. Anna looked close to him, but not straight on. He nodded and ducked out the door after her daughter. She waited for one breath, and then another, and then—knowing it was a bad idea—crept to the closed door and peeked out. Nami and Saladin were walking down the narrow ship corridor, squeezing close to be side by side. His right hand was in her left, and as far as Anna could see, Nami was still talking animatedly about whatever she was talking about while Saladin, rapt, listened.

"So what's your group project?" Anna asked.

Dinner that night was spiced beans and rice that very nearly mimicked the real thing. Nono was tired after her rehearsal, and Anna was expecting the Humanist meeting to be intense and a little taxing, so they'd taken the food back to their rooms instead of staying in the galley. Nami sat cross-legged with her back against the door while Anna and Nono took two of the chairs that folded down out of the wall. The walls were close enough that even though they were on opposite sides of the room, their knees almost touched. It would be almost a year living in the *Abbey*. By the time they reached Eudoxia, they might not remember what open space felt like anymore.

"History," Nami said.

"Big subject," Anna said. "Any particular part of history?"

Nono looked up at her from under her eyebrows, so maybe Anna wasn't being quite as casual and nonchalant as she thought. Nami didn't seem to notice anything, though.

"No. All of it. We're not talking about what happened in history, we're talking about what history is. So, you know"—she gestured in a circle with her spoon—"is the important thing about history the people who actually did things, or if they hadn't been alive, would the same basic things have happened, just with other people doing them? Like with math."

"Math?" Anna said.

"Sure," Nami said. "Two different people came up with calculus right at the same time. So maybe everything's like that. Maybe it doesn't matter who leads a war because the things that made the war happen weren't leaders. They were how much money people had or how good their land was for making food or something. That's the section I'm writing. Saladin's writing about the great-man theory, but it's old because they only talk about men."

"Ah," Anna said, cringing at how obvious she felt. "Saladin's doing that?"

"It's about the idea that without Caesar, there wouldn't have been a Roman Empire. Or without a Jesus, there wouldn't have been Christianity."

"Hard to argue against that," Nono said.

"It's a history class. We're not talking about the religious part. And then Liliana's doing the section on the technological ratchet, where the thing that changes is how well we understand how to make things like medicines and nuclear bombs and Epstein drives, and that everything else about history is cyclic. The same things happen over and over again, but it just seems different because we have different tools." Nami frowned. "I don't understand that one yet. But it's not my section."

"And what do you think?" Anna asked.

Nami shook her head and scooped up a last spoonful of almost-beans. "It's dumb to break it up like that," she said around her food. "Like it's one thing or it's something else. That's not how it ever is. It's always that there's somebody who does whatever it is. You know, conquers Europe or decides that it's a great idea to line aqueducts with lead or figures out how to coordinate radio frequencies. You never have one without the other. It's like nature versus nurture. When do you ever see one without the other?"

"That's a good point," Anna said. "So how does the project work?"

Nami rolled her eyes. Oh God, they were in eye-rolling ages now. It seemed so recent that her little girl had been free of contempt. "It isn't like that."

"What isn't like what?"

"Mother. Saladin isn't my boyfriend. His parents died in Cairo, and he's here with his aunt and uncle. He really needs friends, and anyway Liliana likes him, so even if I did, I wouldn't. We have to be careful. We're spending our whole lives together, so we need to be really gentle. If we mess it up, it's not like we can just change schools."

"Oh," Anna said. "Is that something you talk about at school?"

The eye-roll again. Two eye-rolls in one night. "That was you, Mom. You're always saying that."

"I guess I am," Anna agreed.

After they were done, Nami took their bowls and spoons and drinking bulbs back to the galley for them, an echo of the way she used to clean up after dinner back at home. When that had been home. Then she was off to study with Liliana and, for all Anna knew, Saladin as well. Nono took her turn being alone in the room. Anna made her way toward the lift and deck two for the Humanist Society, her hands touching the walls at either side of the corridor as if to steady her. *It is necessary to renounce a freedom that does not exist*, she thought, *and to recognize a dependence of which we are not conscious.* And it was true, as far as it went.

But it was also a mistake to lose sight of all the individual lives and choices and flashes of pure dumb luck that brought humanity as far as they'd come. History, she thought, was perhaps better considered as a great improvisation. A thinking-through of some immense, generations-long thought. Or daydream.

The problem, of course, with the idea of nature versus nurture was that it posed a choice between determinisms. That was something Nami seemed to grasp almost instinctively, but Anna had to remind herself of it. Maybe history was the same way. Theories of how things had to have happened the way they did only because, looking back, they'd happened that way.

Tomás Myers, a short, thick-set man in a formal white shirt, held the lift for her, and she trotted to it so as not to seem ungrateful. It lurched a little as it rose.

"Going to the Humanist meeting?" he said.

"Once more into the breach." She smiled back.

As they rose, she felt the first inklings of the week's sermon starting to fall into place. It revolved, she thought, around Tolstoy's idea of an invisible dependence and the choice they'd all made to come to the *Abbey*, and Nami saying, *We're spending our whole lives together, so we need to be really gentle.*

Because that was always true. The *Abbey* and Eudoxia were small enough it became impossible to ignore it, but even among the teeming billions of Earth, they were spending their lives together. They needed to be gentle. And understanding. And careful. It had been true in the depths of history, and at the height of Earth's power, and it would still be true now that they were scattering to the more than a thousand new suns.

Maybe, if they could find a way to be gentle, the stars would be better off with them.

The story continues in...

PERSEPOLIS RISING

Book SEVEN of the Expanse

Keep reading for a sneak peek!

Acknowledgments

While the creation of any book is less a solitary act than it seems, the past few years have seen a huge increase in the people involved with The Expanse in all its incarnations, including this one. This book would not exist without the hard work and dedication of Danny and Heather Baror, Will Hinton, Tim Holman, Anne Clarke, Ellen Wright, Alex Lencicki, and the whole brilliant crew at Orbit. Special thanks are also due Carrie Vaughn for her services as a beta reader, the gang from Sakeriver: Tom, Sake Mike, Non-Sake Mike, Jim-me, Porter, Scott, Raja, Jeff, Mark, Dan, Joe, and Erik Slaine, who got the ball rolling.

The support team for The Expanse has also grown to include the staff at Alcon Entertainment and Syfy, and the cast and crew of The Expanse. Our thanks and gratitude go especially to Hallie Lambert, Matt Rasmussen, and Kenn Fisher.

Special thanks also go to Leo Tolstoy, translators Louise and Aylmer Maude, and Project Gutenberg for Pastor Anna's comfort reading.

And, as always, none of this would have happened without the support and company of Jayné, Kat, and Scarlet.

extras

orbit

meet the author

JAMES S. A. Corey is the pen name of authors Daniel Abraham and Ty Franck. They both live in Albuquerque, New Mexico.

if you enjoyed
BABYLON'S ASHES
look out for

NEW YORK 2140

by

Kim Stanley Robinson

As the sea levels rose, every street became a canal. Every skyscraper an island. For the residents of one apartment building in Madison Square, however, New York in the year 2140 is far from a drowned city.

There is the market trader, who finds opportunities where others find trouble. There is the detective, whose work will never disappear— along with the lawyers, of course.

There is the internet star, beloved by millions for her airship adventures, and the building's manager, quietly respected for his attention to detail. Then there are two boys who don't live there, but have no other home—and who are more important to its future than anyone might imagine.

Lastly there are the coders, temporary residents on the roof, whose disappearance triggers a sequence of events that threatens the existence of all—and even the long-hidden foundations on which the city rests.

a) Mutt and Jeff

"Whoever writes the code creates the value."

"That isn't even close to true."

"Yes it is. Value resides in life, and life is coded, like with DNA."

"So bacteria have values?"

"Sure. All life wants things and goes after them. Viruses, bacteria, all the way up to us."

"Which by the way it's your turn to clean the toilet."

"I know. Life means death."

"So, today?"

"Some today. Back to my point. We write code. And without our code, there's no computers, no finance, no banks, no money, no exchange value, no value."

"All but that last, I see what you mean. But so what?"

"Did you read the news today?"

"Of course not."

"You should. It's bad. We're getting eaten."

"That's always true. It's like what you said, life means death."

"But more than ever. It's getting too much. They're down to the bone."

"This I know. It's why we live in a tent on a roof."

"Right, and now people are even worried about food."

"As they should. That's the real value, food in your belly. Because you can't eat money."

"That's what I'm saying!"

"I thought you said the real value was code. Something a coder would say, may I point out."

"Mutt, hang with me. Follow what I'm saying. We live in a world where people pretend money can buy you anything, so money becomes the point, so we all work for money. Money is thought of as value."

"Okay, I get that. We're broke and I get that."

"So good, keep hanging with me. We live by buying things with money, in a market that sets all the prices."

"The invisible hand."

"Right. Sellers offer stuff, buyers buy it, and in the flux of supply and demand the price gets determined. It's crowdsourced, it's democratic, it's capitalism, it's the market."

"It's the way of the world."

"Right. And it's always, always wrong."

"What do you mean wrong?"

"The prices are always too low, and so the world is fucked. We're in a mass extinction event, sea level rise, climate change, food panics, everything you're not reading in the news."

"All because of the market."

"Exactly! It's not just that there are market failures. It's that the market is a failure."

"How so?"

"Things are sold for less than it costs to make them."

"That sounds like the road to bankruptcy."

"Yes, and lots of businesses do go bankrupt. But the ones that don't haven't actually sold their thing for more than it cost to make. They've just ignored some of their costs. They're under huge pressure to sell as low as they can, because every buyer buys the cheapest version of whatever it is. So they shove some of their production costs off their books."

"Can't they just pay their labor less?"

"They already did that! That was easy. That's why we're all broke except the plutocrats."

"I always see the Disney dog when you say that."

"They've squeezed us till we're bleeding from the eyes. I can't stand it anymore."

"Blood from a stone. Sir Plutocrat, chewing on a bone."

"Chewing on my head! But now we're chewed up. We're squoze dry. We've been paying a fraction of what things really cost to make, but meanwhile the planet, and the workers who made the stuff, take the unpaid costs right in the teeth."

"But they got a cheap TV out of it."

"Right, so they can watch something interesting as they sit there broke."

"Except there's nothing interesting on."

"Well, but this is the least of their problems! I mean actually you can usually find something interesting."

"Please, I beg to differ. We've seen everything a million times."

"Everyone has. I'm just saying the boredom of bad TV is not the biggest of our worries. Mass extinction, hunger, wrecking kids' lives, these are bigger worries. And it just keeps getting worse. People are suffering more and more. My head is going to explode the way things are going, I swear to God."

"You're just upset because we got evicted and are living in a tent on a roof."

"That's just part of it! A little part of a big thing."

"Okay, granted. So what?"

"So look, the problem is capitalism. We've got good tech, we've got a nice planet, we're fucking it up by way of stupid laws. That's what capitalism is, a set of stupid laws."

"Say I grant that too, which maybe I do. So what can we do?"

"It's a set of laws! And it's global! It extends all over the Earth, there's no escaping it, we're all in it, and no matter what you do, the system rules!"

"I'm not seeing the what-we-can-do part."

"Think about it! The laws are *codes*! And they exist in computers and in the cloud. There are sixteen laws running the whole world!"

"To me that seems too few. Too few or too many."

"No. They're articulated, of course, but it comes down to sixteen basic laws. I've done the analysis."

"As always. But it's still too many. You never hear about sixteen of anything. There are the eight noble truths, the two evil stepsisters. Maybe twelve at most, like recovery steps, or apostles, but usually it's single digits."

"Quit that. It's sixteen laws, distributed between the World Trade Organization and the G20. Financial transactions, currency exchange, trade law, corporate law, tax law. Everywhere the same."

"I'm still thinking that sixteen is either too few or too many."

"Sixteen I'm telling you, and they're encoded, and each can be changed by changing the codes. Look what I'm saying: you change those sixteen, you're like turning a key in a big lock. The key turns, and the system goes from bad to good. It helps people, it requires the cleanest techs, it restores landscapes, the extinctions stop. It's global, so defectors can't get outside it. Bad money gets turned to dust, bad actions likewise. No one could cheat. It would *make* people be good."

"Please Jeff? You're sounding scary."

"I'm just saying! Besides, what's scarier than right now?"

"Change? I don't know."

"Why should change be scary? You can't even read the news, right? Because it's too fucking scary?"

"Well, and I don't have the time."

Jeff laughs till he puts his forehead on the table. Mutt laughs too, to see his friend so amused. But the mirth is very localized. They are partners, they amuse each other, they work long hours writing code for high-frequency trading computers uptown. Now some reversals have them on this night living in a hotello on the open-walled farm floor of the old Met Life tower, from which vantage point lower Manhattan lies flooded below them like a super-Venice, majestic, watery, superb. Their town.

Jeff says, "So look, we know how to get into these systems, we know how to write code, we are the best coders in the world."

"Or at least in this building."

"No come on, the world! And I've already gotten us in to where we need to go."

"Say what?"

"Check it out. I built us some covert channels during that gig we did for my cousin. We're in there, and I've got the replacement codes ready. Sixteen revisions to those financial laws, plus a kicker for my cousin's ass. Let the SEC know what he's up to, and also fund the SEC to investigate that shit. I've got a subliminal shunt set up that will tap some alpha and move it right to the SEC's account."

"Now you really are scaring me."

"Well sure, but look, check it out. See what you think."

Mutt moves his lips when he reads. He's not saying the words silently to himself, he's doing a kind of Nero Wolfe stimulation of his brain. It's his favorite neurobics exercise, of which he has many. Now he begins to massage his lips with his fingers as he reads, indicating deep worry.

"Well, yeah," he says after about ten minutes of reading. "I see what you've got here. I like it, I guess. Most of it. That old Ken Thompson Trojan horse always works, doesn't it. Like a law of logic. So, could be fun. Almost sure to be amusing."

Jeff nods. He taps the return key. His new set of codes goes out into the world.

They leave their hotello and stand at the railing of their building's farm, looking south over the drowned city, taking in the whitmanwonder of it. O Mannahatta! Lights squiggle off the black water everywhere below them. Downtown a few lit skyscrapers illuminate darker towers, giving them a geological sheen. It's weird, beautiful, spooky.

There's a ping from inside their hotello, and they push through the flap into the big square tent. Jeff reads his computer screen.

"Ah shit," he says. "They spotted us."

They regard the screen.

"Shit indeed," Mutt says. "How could they have?"

"I don't know, but it means I was right!"

"Is that good?"

"It might even have worked!"

"You think?"

"No." Jeff frowns. "I don't know."

"They can always recode what you did, that's the thing. Once they see it."

"So do you think we should run for it?"

"To where?"

"I don't know."

"It's like you said before," Mutt points out. "It's a global system."

"Yeah but this is a big city! Lots of nooks and crannies, lots of dark pools, the underwater economy and all. We could dive in and disappear."

"Really?"

"I don't know. We could try."

Then the farm floor's big service elevator door opens. Mutt and Jeff regard each other. Jeff thumbs toward the staircases. Mutt nods. They slip out under the tent wall.

To be brief about it—
proposed Henry James

b) Inspector Gen

Inspector Gen Octaviasdottir sat in her office, late again, slumped in her chair, trying to muster the energy to get up and go home. Light fingernail drumming on her door announced her assistant, Sergeant Olmstead. "Sean, quit it and come in."

Her mild-mannered young bulldog ushered in a woman of about fifty. Vaguely familiar-looking. Five seven, a bit heavy, thick black hair with some white strands. City business suit, big shoulder bag. Wide-set intelligent eyes, now observing Gen sharply; expressive mouth. No makeup. A serious person. Attractive. But she looked as tired as Gen felt. And a little uncertain about something, maybe this meeting.

"Hi, I'm Charlotte Armstrong," the woman said. "We live in the same building, I think. The old Met Life tower, on Madison Square?"

"I thought you looked familiar," Gen said. "What brings you here?"

"It has to do with our building, so I asked to see you. Two residents have gone missing. You know those two guys who were living on the farm floor?"

"No."

"They might have been nervous to talk to you. Although they had permission to stay."

The Met tower was a co-op, owned by its residents. Inspector Gen had recently inherited her apartment from her mother, and she paid little attention to how the building was run. Often it felt like she was only there to sleep. "So what happened?"

"No one knows. They were there one day, gone the next."

"Someone's checked the security cameras?"

"Yes. That's why I came to see you. The cameras went out for two hours on the last night they were seen."

"Went out?"

"We checked the data files, and they all have a two-hour gap."

"Like a power outage?"

"But there wasn't a power outage. And they have battery backup."

"That's weird."

"That's what we thought. That's why I came to see you. Vlade, the building super, would have reported it, but I was coming here anyway to represent a client, so I filed the report and then asked to speak to you."

"Are you going back to the Met now?" Gen asked.

"Yes, I was."

"Why don't we go together, then. I was just leaving." Gen turned to Olmstead. "Sean, can you find the report on this and see what you can learn about these two men?"

The sergeant nodded, gazing at the floor, trying not to look like he'd just been given a bone. He would tear into it when they were gone.

Armstrong headed toward the elevators and looked surprised when Inspector Gen suggested they walk instead.

"I didn't think there were skybridges between here and there."

"Nothing direct," Gen explained, "but you can take the one from here to Bellevue, and then go downstairs and cross diagonally and then head west on the Twenty-third Skyline. It takes about thirty-four minutes. The vapo would take twenty if we got lucky, thirty if we didn't. So I walk it a lot. I can use the stretch, and it will give us a chance to talk."

Armstrong nodded without actually agreeing, then hauled her shoulder bag closer to her neck. She favored her right hip. Gen tried to remember anything from the Met's frequent bulletins. No luck. But she was pretty sure this woman had been the chairperson of the co-op's executive board since Gen had moved in to take care of her mom, which suggested three or four terms in office, not something most people would volunteer for. She thanked Armstrong for this service, then asked her about it. "Why so long?"

"It's because I'm crazy, as you seem to be suggesting."

"Not me."

"Well, you'd be right if you did. It's just that I'm better working on things than not. I experience less stress."

"Stress about how our building runs?"

"Yes. It's very complicated. Lots can go wrong."

"You mean like flooding?"

"No, that's mostly under control, or else we'd be screwed. It takes attention, but Vlade and his people do that."

"He seems good."

"He's great. The building is the easy part."

"So, the people."

"As always, right?"

"Sure is in my line of work."

"Mine too. In fact the building itself is kind of a relief. Something you can actually fix."

"You do what kind of law?"

"Immigration and intertidal."

"You work for the city?"

"Yes. Well, I did. The immigrant and refugee office got semi-privatized last year, and I went with it. Now we're called the House-holders' Union. Supposedly a public-private agency, but that just means both sides ignore us."

"Have you always done that kind of thing?"

"I worked at ACLU a long time ago, but yeah. Mostly for the city."

"So you defend immigrants?"

"We advocate for immigrants and displaced persons, and really anyone who asks for help."

"That must keep you busy."

Armstrong shrugged. Gen led her to the elevator in Bellevue's northwest annex that would take them down to the skybridge that ran west from building to building on the north side of Twenty-third. Most skybridges still ran either north-south or east-west, forcing what Gen called knight moves. Recently some new higher sky-bridges made bishop moves, which pleased Gen, as she played the find-the-shortest-route game when getting around the city, played it with a gamer's passion. Shortcutting, some players called it. What she wanted was to move through the city like a queen in chess, straight to her destination every time. That would never be possible in Man-hattan, just as it wasn't on a chessboard; grid logic ruled both. Even so, she would visualize the destination in her head and walk the straightest line she could think of toward it—design improvements—measure success on her wrist. All simple compared to the rest of her work, where she had to navigate much vaguer and nastier problems.

Armstrong stumped along beside her. Gen began to regret sug-gesting the walk. At this pace it was going to take close to an hour. She asked questions about their building to keep the lawyer distracted from her discomfort. There were about two thousand people living in it now, Armstrong answered. About seven hundred units, from single-person closets to big group apartments. Conversion to residen-tial had occurred after the Second Pulse, in the wet equity years.

Gen nodded as Charlotte sketched this history. Her father and grandmother had both served on the force through the flood years, she told Armstrong. Keeping order had not been easy.

Finally they came to the Met's east side. The skybridge from the roof of the old post office entered the Met at its fifteenth floor. As they pushed through the triple doors Gen nodded to the guard on duty, Manuel, who was chatting to his wrist and looked startled to see them. Gen looked back out the glass doors; down at canal level the bathtub ring exposed by low tide was blackish green. Above it the nearby buildings' walls were greenish limestone, or granite, or brownstone. Seaweed stuck to the stone below the high tide line, mold and lichen above. Windows just above the water were barred with black grilles; higher they were unbarred, and many open to the air. A balmy night in September, neither stifling nor steamy. A moment in the city's scandalous weather to bask in, to enjoy.

"So these missing guys lived on the farm floor?" Gen asked.

"Yes. Come on up and take a look, if you don't mind."

if you enjoyed
BABYLON'S ASHES

look out for

PROVENANCE

by

Ann Leckie

*A power-driven young woman has just one chance to secure
the status she craves and regain priceless lost artifacts prized
by her people: She must free a thief from a prison planet from
which no one has ever returned.*

*Ingray and her charge will return to her homeworld
to find their planet in political turmoil at the heart of an
escalating interstellar conflict. Together they must make a
new plan to salvage Ingray's future, her family, and her world,
before they are lost for good.*

1

"There were unexpected difficulties," said the dark gray blur. That blur sat in a pale blue cushioned chair, no more than a meter away from where Ingray herself sat, facing, in an identical chair.

Or apparently so, anyway. Ingray knew that if she reached much more than a meter past her knees, she would touch smooth, solid wall. The same to her left, where apparently the Facilitator sat, bony frame draped in brown, gold, and purple silk, hair braided sleekly back, dark eyes expressionless, watching the conversation. Listening. Only the beige walls behind and to the right of Ingray were really as they appeared. The table beside Ingray's chair with the gilded decanter of serbat and the delicate glass tray of tiny rose-petaled cakes was certainly real—the Facilitator had invited her to try them. She had been too nervous to even consider eating one.

"Unexpected difficulties," continued the dark gray blur, "that led to unanticipated expenses. We will require a larger payment than previously agreed."

That other anonymous party could not see Ingray where she sat—saw her as the same sort of dark gray blur she herself faced. Sat in an identical small room, somewhere else on this station. Could not see Ingray's expression, if she let her dismay and despair show itself on her face. But the Facilitator could see them both. E wouldn't betray having seen even Ingray's smallest reaction, she was sure. Still. "Unexpected difficulties are not my concern," she said, calmly and smoothly as she could manage. "The price was agreed beforehand." The price was everything she owned, not counting the clothes she wore, or passage home—already paid.

"The unexpected expenses were considerable, and must be met

somehow," said the dark gray blur. "The package will not be delivered unless the payment is increased."

"Then do not deliver it," replied Ingray, trying to sound careless. Holding her hands very still in her lap. She wanted to clutch the green and blue silk of her full skirts, to have some feeling that she could hold on to something solid and safe, a childish habit she thought she'd lost years ago. "You will not receive any payment at all, as a result. Certainly your expenses must be met regardless, but that is no concern of mine."

She waited. The Facilitator said nothing. Ingray reminded herself that the gray blur had more to lose than she did if this deal didn't happen. She could take what was left of the payment she'd brought, after the Facilitator's commission—payable no matter what happened, at this stage. She could go home, back to Hwae. She'd have a good deal less than she'd started with, true, and maybe she would have to settle for that, invest what she had left. If she lost her job she could probably use what connections remained to her to find another one. She imagined her foster-mother's cold disappointment; Netano Aughskold did not waste time or energy on unambitious or unsuccessful children.

And Ingray imagined her foster-brother Danach's smug triumph. Even if all Ingray's plans succeeded, she would never replace Danach as Netano's favorite, but she could walk away from the Aughskolds knowing she'd humiliated her arrogant brother, and made all of them, Netano included, take notice. And plenty of other people with power and influence would take notice as well. If this deal didn't go through, she wouldn't have that, wouldn't have even the smallest of victories over her brother.

Silence still from the gray blur, from the Facilitator. The spicy smell of the serbat from the decanter turned her stomach. It wasn't going to happen.

And maybe that would be all right. What was she trying to do anyway? This plan was ridiculous. It was impossible. The chances of her succeeding, even if this trade went ahead, were next to nothing. What was she even doing here? For an instant she felt as though she had stepped off the edge of a precipice, and this was that barest moment before she plunged downward.

Ingray could end it now. Announce that the deal was off, give the Facilitator eir fee, and go home with what she had left.

The blur across from Ingray gave a dissatisfied sigh. "Very well, then. The deal goes forward. But now we know what to think of the much-vaunted impartiality and equitable practice of the Tyr."

"The terms were plain from the start," said the Facilitator in an even tone. "The payment was accurately described to you, and if you did not consider it adequate, you had only to demand more at the time of the offer, or refuse the sale outright. This is our inflexible rule in order to prevent misunderstandings and acrimony at just this stage of the proceedings. I explained this to you at the time. Had you not expressed your understanding of and agreement to that policy, I would not have allowed the exchange to go forward. To do otherwise would damage our reputation for impartiality and fair dealing." The gray blur did not reply. "I have examined the payment and the merchandise," said the Facilitator, still calm and even. "They are both as promised."

Now was Ingray's chance. She should escape this while she still could. She opened her mouth. "Very well," she said.

Oh, almighty powers, what had she just done?

The assigned pickup location was a small room walled in orchids growing on what looked like a maze of tree roots. A woman in a brown-and-purple jacket and sarong stood beside a scuffed gray shipping crate two meters long and one high, jarringly out of place in such carefully tended, soft-colored luxury. "There is some misunderstanding, excellency," Ingray suggested. "This is supposed to be a person." Looking at the size and the shape of the crate, it occurred to her that it might hold a body.

Utter failure. The dread Ingray had felt since the gray blur had demanded extra payment intensified.

Not moving from her place at the far end of the crate, not looking at it, not even blinking, the woman said, primly, "We do not involve ourselves in kidnappings or in slave trading, excellency."

Ingray blinked. Took a breath, unsure of how to continue. "May I open the crate?" she asked, finally.

"It is yours," said the woman. "You may do whatever you wish with it." She did not otherwise move.

It took Ingray a few moments to find all the latches on the crate lid. Each came apart with a dull snap, and she carefully shoved over one end of the heavy lid, wary of sending it crashing over the back of the crate. Light glinted off something smooth and dark inside. A suspension pod. She pushed the lid a few centimeters farther over. Reached in to pull back the cover over the pod's indicator panel. Blue and green lights on the panel told her the pod was in operation, and its occupant alive. She could not help a very small exhalation of relief.

And maybe it was better this way. She could delay any awkward explanations, could bring this person to the ship she'd booked passage on without anyone knowing what she was doing. She pushed and tugged the crate lid back into place, relatched it.

"Your pardon," she said to the woman in the brown-and-purple sarong. "I didn't anticipate that . . . my purchase would arrive packaged this way. I don't think I can move this on my own. Is there a cart I can borrow?" How she would get it onto a cart by herself, she didn't know. And if they charged for the cart's use, well, she had nothing left to pay for that. She might have to open that pod, right here and now, and hope its occupant was willing and able to walk. "Or can it be delivered to my ship?"

With no change of expression, the woman touched the side of the crate, and there was a click and it shifted toward Ingray, just a bit. "Once you have claimed your purchase," the woman said, "it is no longer in our custody and we will not take any responsibility for it. This may occasionally seem inconvenient, but we find it prevents misunderstandings. You should be able to move this on your own. When you are clear of our premises and have reenabled your communications you'll be shown the most efficient passable route for objects of this size."

extras

There must have been some kind of assist on the crate, because although it had to be quite heavy it slid easily, though it swung wildly until Ingray got the trick of moving it forward without also sending it sideways. And she almost lost control of it entirely when, coming out of a nondescript doorway into a broad, brightly lit black-and-red-tiled corridor, she blinked her communications back on and a long list of alerts and news items suddenly appeared in her vision. A surprising lot of news items, when Ingray had set her feed to winnow out local news, all but the most urgent. Though the largest and brightest of them—large enough that she couldn't help reading it even as she desperately swung the shipping crate away from crashing into a wall—was definitely of more than local interest. GECK DIPLOMATIC MISSION ARRIVES IN TYR, it read, and smaller, beneath that, TYR SIILAS COUNCIL APPROVES REQUEST FOR PROVISIONS, FUEL, AND REPAIRS. Well, of course they had approved it. The Geck were signatories to the treaty with the dangerous and enigmatic Presger, and whatever anyone felt about who had made that treaty and how, no one was fool enough to want to break it.

Her attention to the headline brought up a cloud of more detailed information, and opinion pieces. CONCLAVE A BLATANT RADCHAAI POWER GRAB shouted one, and CONSCIOUS AI MAKES ITS MOVE AT LAST—IS THIS THE BEGINNING OF THE END FOR HUMANITY? asked another. A quiet voice whispered in her ear that a noodle shop she'd eaten at six times since she'd arrived here was open and nearby, with a relatively short queue—a personal alert Ingray had set days ago and forgotten to turn off. She hadn't eaten breakfast, or the cakes the Facilitator had offered her. But suddenly noodles sounded very good.

There wasn't time. The ship she'd bought passage on departed in three hours, which meant she had to be aboard in less time than that. And even if she'd had time—and any money at all—she could hardly queue for noodles with this body-size crate in tow that she could barely steer. She thought away every message except the route to her ship, and kept going. She could eat on board.

The route she'd been given kept her mostly out of the station's busiest areas, though on Tyr Siilas "less busy" was still quite crowded. At first she was self-conscious, afraid she'd attract unwelcome curiosity pushing a suspension-pod-size crate through the station's thoroughfares, but the crowds split and streamed around her without contact or comment. And she was hardly the only person pushing an awkward load. She had to swerve carefully around a stack of crates full of onions, apparently trundling along under its own power, and then found herself stuck for a few frustrating seconds behind what at first she took to be a puzzlingly tall mech, but when it finally moved she realized it was actually a human in an environmental support suit, someone from a low-gravity habitat, to judge from their height and need to wear the suit.

At one point she had to wait a half hour for a freight lift, and then spent the ride pinned against the lift's grimy back wall. She regretted wearing her stiff, formal sandals and the silk jacket and long, full skirts that she'd kept when she'd sold the rest of her clothes, with the intention of looking as seriously businesslike as possible. Very probably pointless—the Facilitator likely didn't care so long as her money was good, and whoever was on the other side of the deal she'd made couldn't see her anyway.

As soon as she was off the lift she girded up her skirts, and took off her sandals and set them on the crate along with the small bag that held everything else she owned now—her identity tabula and a few small toiletries—and then set out on the long stop-and-start trek through the docks, swerving around inattentive travelers when she could, the time display in her vision reassuring her, at least, that she still had plenty of time to reach her ship, which was, predictably, in the section of the docks farthest from where she'd entered.

She arrived at the bay tired, frustrated, and anxious. The bay was much smaller than she'd expected, but then she had only ever taken the big passenger liners between systems. Had taken one here, but she could not afford even the cheapest available return fare home on such a ship. She'd known this ship was small, a cargo ship with a few extra berths for passengers, known that her trip home would be cramped and unluxurious, but she hadn't stopped to consider what that would mean now that she was bringing this crate with her. If this had been a passenger liner, there would have been someone here she could turn the crate over to, who would make sure it got to Ingray's berth, or to cargo. But the bay was empty. And she didn't think she could get both herself and the crate into the airlock.

While she stood thinking, a man came out of the airlock. Short and solid-bodied, and there was something undefinably odd about his squarish face—something off about the shape of his nose, or the size of his mouth. His hair was pulled back behind his head, to hang behind him in dozens of tiny braids. He wore a gray-and-green-striped lungi and a dark gray jacket, and he was barefoot—less formal than what nearly everyone here wore for business dealings or important meetings, but still perfectly respectable. "You are Ingray Aughskold?"

"You must be Captain Uisine." Ingray had booked this berth through the Tyr Siilas dock office, days ago, before this ship had arrived here. "Or is it Captain Tic?" Somewhere like this, where you met people from all over, it was difficult to know what order anyone's name was in, or which one they preferred to be addressed by.

"Either one," said Captain Uisine. "You didn't say anything about oversize luggage, excellency."

"No," Ingray said. "I didn't. I wasn't expecting it myself."

Captain Uisine was silent a moment. Waiting, Ingray supposed. Then, "It's too large for the passenger compartments, excellency. It will need to be loaded into cargo. That's accessed on the lower level. But it's sealed up at the moment. And I'm not opening it before I see a duly registered Statement of Contents."

She didn't even know there was such a thing, or that she might need it. Then again, she'd never expected to have to deal with cargo at all. "I can't..." She really ought to have eaten something that morning. "I can't leave it behind. Is there time to open the cargo access?" She thought she was standing quite still, but she must have moved the hand that rested on the crate, because now it slid forward. She grabbed for it.

Captain Uisine laid a hand on it to stop and steady it. "Plenty

564

of time. Departure's delayed. Have you not checked your notifications? We're here another two days."

"Two days!" It didn't seem possible. She summoned her notifications to her vision, and saw what she would have seen immediately if she'd checked her personal messages—a brief, bare note about the delay, from Captain Tic Uisine. *Unavoidable delay*, the note called it, *due to current events.*

Current events. Of course. Ingray pulled up the news, looked closer at the information about the Geck diplomatic mission. Which mentioned, quite clearly but further in than she'd bothered to look, that arrivals and departures were being rearranged to fit the Geck in as quickly and safely as possible.

There was no arguing with that, no recourse. Even if Ingray had been traveling with Netano Aughskold, who had herself not infrequently demanded (and received) such priority, it wouldn't have done any good, and not just because this wasn't Netano's home system. The Geck were aliens, not human. They almost never left their homeworld, or so Ingray understood, and had done so now only to attend to urgent matters regarding the treaty with the alien Presger. Before the treaty, the Presger would tear apart human ships and stations—and their passengers and residents—seemingly at a whim. Nothing could stop them, nothing except the treaty, which the Radchaai ruler Anaander Mianaai had signed in the name of all humanity; the Presger apparently did not understand or care about whether there might be different sorts of humans, with different authorities. But no matter how anyone felt about the Radchaai taking on that authority, no one wanted the Presger to start killing people again.

Eventually the Geck had also become signatories, and much more recently the Rrrrrr. And now there was a potential third new nonhuman signatory to the treaty, and a conclave, called by the Presger, to decide the issue. Probably everyone anywhere in the unthinkably vast reaches of human-inhabited space was aware of it, had opinions, wanted to know more, wanted to know how this conclave would affect their futures.

Ingray couldn't bring herself to care just now. "I can't wait two days," she said. Captain Uisine said nothing, didn't make the obvious comment—there was no avoiding the wait, and he had no control over it. Didn't take his hand off the end of the crate. Probably wise—Ingray didn't know how to turn off the assist. "I just can't."

"Why not?" he asked. Serious, but not, it seemed, terribly invested in Ingray's particular problems.

Ingray closed her eyes. She would not cry. Opened her eyes again, took a breath, and said, "I spent everything I had settling up at my lodgings this morning."

"You're broke." Captain Uisine's eyes flicked to Ingray's bag and jacket and sandals still perched on top of the crate.

"I can't not eat for two days." She should have had breakfast that morning. She should have eaten some cakes, when she was dealing with the Facilitator.

"Well, you can," said Captain Uisine. "As long as you have water. But what about your friend?"

Ingray frowned. "My friend?"

"The person you're traveling with. Can they help you out?"

"Um."

Captain Uisine waited, still noncommittal. It occurred to Ingray that even if Captain Uisine charged for carrying the crate in cargo, it would likely be less than a passenger fare. Maybe she'd have enough to at least buy a meal or two between now and when the ship finally left. "And while you're thinking about that," the captain added before Ingray could speak, "you can show me the Statement of Contents for the crate."

For a panicked moment, Ingray tried to think of some way to argue that she shouldn't have to show one. Then she remembered that so far the Facilitator seemed to have anticipated what she would need to bring the crate away with her. She pulled her personal messages into her vision again, and there it was. "I've just sent it to you," she said.

Captain Uisine blinked, and gazed off into the distance. "Miscellaneous biologicals," he said after a few moments, focusing again on Ingray. "In a crate this size and shape? I'm sorry, excellency, but I didn't hatch this morning. I'll be exercising my right to examine the contents myself, as outlined in the fare agreement. Otherwise that crate is not coming aboard."

Damn. "So," said Ingray, "the person I'm traveling with is in here."

"In the crate?" He seemed entirely unsurprised.

"In a suspension pod in the crate, yes," Ingray replied. "I didn't expect em to come this way, I thought I would just, you know, meet em and bring em here, and..." She trailed off, at a loss how to explain any further.

"Do you have authorizations permitting you to remove this person from Tyr Siilas? And before you mention it, I am aware that such authorizations aren't always legally necessary here. I, however, do always require them."

"An authorization to take someone on your ship?" Ingray frowned, bewildered. "You didn't need one for me. You didn't ask me for one, for... my friend."

Still not changing expression, Captain Uisine said, "I don't transport anyone against their will. I say that specifically in the fare agreement." Which Ingray had read, of course; she was no fool. But obviously she hadn't remembered that. Hadn't thought, at that point, that it would be an issue. "I can ask you right now, do you want to leave Tyr Siilas and go to Hwae..."

"I do!" Ingray interjected.

"...and you can tell me that." His voice was still serious and even. "This person cannot tell me if e wants to go where you are taking em. I don't doubt there's some very compelling reason you are bringing em aboard in a suspension pod. I would like to be sure that compelling reason is eirs, and not just yours."

"But..." But he'd already said that this wasn't a matter of Tyr Siilas law. And if he refunded her money, she might be able to find another ship for the same fare, but if she went through the dock office again she'd have to pay another fee, which she didn't have. She might be able to find passage on her own, but that would take time. Maybe a lot of time. She sighed. "I don't know why e's in a suspension pod." Well, actually, she had some idea. But that wasn't going to help her cause with Captain Uisine, plainly. "I went to pick em up, and this is how I found em."

"Is there some medical reason this person is traveling in a suspension pod?"

"Not that I know of," she said, quite honestly.

"E didn't leave you any message, or any instruction?"

"No."

"Well, excellency," said Captain Uisine after a few moments, "I suggest we open the pod and ask em.